A Quarter of Magic

ZOË TYSON

ISBN: 1477508791
ISBN-13: 978-1477508794

Contents

Chapter 1

An Unfortunate Discovery

There were three things that Miloney Merren wished for on a daily basis.

One, was that he wished he lived somewhere else.

Two, he wished he could swap his sister for a nicer one.

And three, he wished the horrible creature that stood in the corner of his classroom would die.

Today was no exception. Milo still fervently wished for all these things. But unfortunately, none of these wishes were possible, because one, he wasn't allowed to live anywhere else - ever.

Two, no amount of magic could turn his sister into someone else.

And three, the horrible creature that stood in the corner of his classroom was immortal.

He gazed gloomily out of the classroom window, thinking he should start wishing for something more realistic.

There was a light tap on the classroom door and the teacher, Miss Dianda, went to open it.

The students sighed and slouched back in their chairs, glad for a small reprieve from the boring lecture on magical sources.

Despite the disapproving glare of the creature in the corner, the students muttered quietly amongst themselves but then the classroom door slammed shut and all mutterings abruptly stopped.

Miss Dianda was regarding the creature with a wretched look on her face.

She pushed her honey coloured hair back from her face and smoothed down her plum coloured suit that she always wore, and slowly she turned to face the students.

Milo (he hated being called Miloney) felt his heart begin to race because he knew what was coming. Miss Dianda didn't have to say anything. It was obvious by her face.

Someone had been 'discovered'.

He could feel his palms grow sweaty. Was today finally the day he had been dreading for years?

"Who is it?" someone asked.

Please don't be me, please don't be me. Milo shut his eyes trying to keep his breathing steady and then a boy called Walter asked,

"Is it Milo?"

Walter Pymus who was sat behind Milo jeered nastily and gave Milo a hard thump on the back for good measure when Miss Dianda wasn't looking. If there was anybody that Milo hated most in this world, it was this pudgy boy sat behind him.

Milo felt himself growing red. There were a few snickers in the classroom and he tried hard to ignore them but it was too late. He was wound up. His emotions were too highly charged.

He felt a familiar tingling sensation down his arms and gasped as he realised he was starting to lose control.

He dug his nails into the palms of his hands as hard as he possibly could and concentrated purely on the purple welts that were forming.

It was working. The tingling was subsiding just a little.

"That's enough Walter," Miss Dianda's voice was harsh. "No it's not Miloney, its Chaney Hilt who's been discovered."

And just like that the tingling sensations stopped completely, transforming into relief.

Milo wiped the small beads of sweat that had formed on his forehead and tried to concentrate on what Miss Dianda was saying.

"Chaney has been discovered to have a very small gift. Barely any magic at all really." The teacher shot an angry glare at the creature in the corner. "So if everyone could please make their way outside in an orderly fashion to the courtyard where we are required to watch Chaney's.....Chaney's exile."

Miss Dianda's voice caught in her throat and she turned away quickly from them. Milo felt a wave of guilt mixed with nausea. He had been so relieved to hear that he had not been the one who had been 'discovered' that he had barely given a thought to poor Chaney.

Reluctantly, Milo followed the other students out of the classroom in a single file behind the creature from the corner of the room.

This particular creature was called Lowish and like all the others of its species, it was revolting. Its brown leathery face was pockmarked and its eyes were black as coal.

Most of the creatures were totally bald but Lowish was easily recognisable by the patches of black hair that sprouted from his temples and partially hid the pointedness of his long ears. His nose was also long and pointed and like the others of his kind, he towered over humans and wore a coat of armour made of a stunning silver metal.

In one corner of the armour an 'L' for Lowish had been engraved, just in case, God forbid, the humans had trouble identifying him.

Milo stared at the back of Lowish's slightly flattened head feeling nothing but revulsion. There really was nothing good about the creatures. They had a unique magic which as far as Milo could tell, consisted of teleporting, branding anything that enraged them - most often humans - and the ability to kill you with just a point of their finger.

Not great qualities!

The students exited a door in the school building and entered a large courtyard which was situated in the centre of the school's circular arrangement of buildings. The courtyard functioned as a number of things – a sports ground, a lunch area (when the weather was nice) and on days like today, a place for exiles to take place.

The courtyard was already full of students and teachers who were quietly and resolutely gathering together in little clusters.

In the middle of the courtyard was a magnificent looking healing tree which was renowned for its healing properties and like most of the trees on the Water Quarter, its bark was twisted and glistened with rivulets of water that ran up through its twisted grooves and out of the tips of its lush green leaves.

On a day like today when the sun was shining, the effect was beautiful. To Milo, this only seemed to make a mockery of the poor girl stood under its beauty, with its leaves shimmering above her head like a halo.

A wooden table that was normally used for lunchtimes had been placed under the tree and stood on top of it looking pale and as though she might pass out at any minute was Chaney Hilt.

Milo felt an elbow in his ribs and jumped as though being hit by a bolt of lightning.

He turned to see a thin wiry boy with a face full of adolescent acne.

"What do you reckon she can do?" the boy asked him.

It was Tanner. Milo's 'sort of' friend. And he was staring at Chaney with more relish than should have been acceptable under such circumstances.

Milo shrugged. "Does it matter?"

"Aren't you at least curious?" Tanner leaned in closer to Milo. "Maybe she can like mould rocks with her hands or something," he said in a whisper. "Or fly, or make things disappear, or..."

Tanner went on and on but Milo didn't hear him. He could only hear his own heart frantically beating against the magic that was bounding around inside him like a pea in a drum.

What the hell was wrong with him?

"Milo are you listening?" Tanner elbowed him again.

"Uh huh" He stared at Chaney, trying to shut Tanner out.

Chaney was wearing a pale blue skirt made of a light billowy material and every time a small breeze came she fought against keeping it from blowing up around her waist. Her hand must have slipped because the fabric flew up around her, revealing pink knickers.

She made a little screeching noise and clutched the fabric tight in her hands, pulling it back down, her pale face now the colour of her underwear.

Milo lowered his eyes. As if the poor girl wasn't already embarrassed enough.

"Ha! Did you see that?" Tanner practically doubled over laughing. "Good one Chaney!" he called out. A few people turned and stared at Tanner in horror.

"Show some respect," someone said.

"Whatever," Tanner mumbled. "Can't they take a joke" he said to Milo.

"Just shut up!" Milo said more harshly than he intended. More people turned to stare. He put his hands over his ears. "Just shut up," he said more quietly.

"Woah!" Tanner held up his hands. "Chill out freak. I was just having a laugh. I don't want to see this either you know. Just thought Chaney might have liked a bit of banter at her send off."

Then he shook his head. "To think I fought your corner last week when Walt was going to take you down. What a waste of time. I should have let him." He stormed off and Milo stared after him.

Let him go. It was best.

He mentally crossed Tanner off a list of quickly diminishing friends. It was fine. It wasn't like he had been a true friend anyway. Milo didn't need him. What he needed was to be alone right now.

Alone to deal with the demon inside him.

He stared up at Chaney. Was this how she had felt. Had she been alone? Had she had no friends that she could share her secret with?

"Attention please!" a familiar gruff voice rang through the courtyard, breaking into his thoughts and all eyes turned to a creature who looked nearly identical to Lowish.

This creature was called Droges who was Council Leader on the Water Quarter. That meant Leader to the creatures and Leader to the humans.

Besides the fact that Droges had the initials C.L. engraved on his armour to signify his position, he was also easy to identify because he had a battle scar running from the tip of his ear to an unsightly cleft in the middle of his chin. And unlike the other creatures, his suit of armour consisted of a two piece in an ugly shade of grey.

Milo felt a surge of anger as he watched the smug satisfied expression on Droges's evil twisted face and tried to control the tingling sensations that had returned.

"You all know why Chaney is here," Droges was saying, his gruff voice more of a growl. "Chaney has been discovered to have a gift of magic." The word 'magic' came out as a hiss between his brown pointed teeth.

"But what Chaney is able to do is of no matter. What does matter is that she has a gift of magic at all. As you are well aware, our town of Syanna, or indeed any town on the Water Quarter, will not tolerate mortals who have these kinds of gifts."

Milo bit down on his lip. What he really meant to say was 'Terramangs' will not tolerate mortals who have these kinds of gifts'.

The towns' people couldn't care less. It was the Terramangs - the creatures of evil - that were insanely jealous of anyone having magic other than themselves.

Milo glanced at Chaney again. She was the second person on Syanna to be exiled in the space of half a year. Normally someone was 'discovered' maybe once a year. But this year...things seemed more intense...

...this year...his own magic had taken on a mind of its own.

"Magic in humans is unnatural," Droges was saying and drawing Milo's attention back. "And so it is with regret that Chaney must be exiled for her own safety as well as yours."

Waves of rancid burning, which were so horribly associated with the creatures, were coming from Droges thick and fast. He turned to Chaney.

"Do you have anything you wish to say before you are exiled Chaney?"

The whole crowd was deadly silent as all eyes rested upon Chaney who was trembling uncontrollably but still clutching tight to her skirt. To the girl's credit, she managed to speak but her voice was so shaky it was difficult to understand her.

"I didn't mean to....hardly any magic....barely any...the desk was already broken, I.."

"Enough!" Droges barked, cutting her off. He pointed his long boney finger at her and Milo had to resist the urge to gag as his rancid odour filled the courtyard.

Milo sucked in his breath, glimpsing one last look at Chaney's white face and then her scream of terror filled the courtyard.

Milo was blinded by a bright white light and when he rubbed his eyes Chaney was gone.

Thick black mist was swirling around the place she stood, as was always the way after an exile.

The sign of doom itself.

"Let that be a reminder to you," Droges said to the silent crowd. "Now go back to classes."

Then in another flash of light, Droges disappeared.

Milo silently watched the black mist that was lingering around the spot Chaney had stood. He always morbidly thought of the remaining black mist as the exiled person's ashes- and felt a strange detachment as it spread its thin wisps around the sombre courtyard.

For about the thousandth time in his young fourteen years, he wondered where the place of exile was.

He wondered if someone as fragile as Chaney would survive it.

There were a few minutes of subdued silence followed by a few muffled sounds of crying from Chaney's classmates and teachers and then as was always the way after an exile, everyone began to file back out of the courtyard to resume their normal activities and try and pretend as though nothing had happened.

Miss Dianda gathered her students closely around her and hoarsely cleared her throat. When she spoke her voice was a whisper but it was urgent and thick with emotion.

"Chaney's exile has been a harsh reminder to us all that we must be extra vigilant in hiding any magical gifts we think we may have."

The students glanced self-consciously at each other. Each one of them thinking the same thing - how many of them were secretly hiding a gift of magic?

Milo avoided their eyes. For as long as he could remember he had been able to move objects with his mind using the magic that he had been gifted with from birth. But each day it was getting harder and harder to control.

Each day was a ticking time bomb.

As Lowish approached their small circle Miss Dianda quickly straightened up and said in a loud, cheerful voice that sounded forced.

"And before you go back to class I have an exciting announcement to make." She looked across to Lowish who nodded once to signal his permission for her to continue.

"Droges has agreed to let us hold an end of year dance." Miss Dianda smiled encouragingly and immediately there was a ripple of excited chatter among the classmates, all memory of Chaney's exile already forgotten.

'Just great!' thought Milo. He hated dances of course. He couldn't dance and he never had a date to go with so this was just great!

Many of the students glanced curiously at Lowish, hoping for further clarification on this sudden generosity but he remained silent. His face as expressionless as ever.

Milo subconsciously rubbed at his wrist where a Terramang had branded him years ago for doing something which he could no longer remember it had been so insignificant, and he wondered if the dance was a hidden agenda.

He had no time to dwell on it however because at that moment a fist was jammed hard into his back. Resisting the urge to cry out in pain, Milo forced himself to stare straight ahead, willing himself not to rub his back where the muscles were in spasm from the punch.

"So who you taking to the dance Miloney? Er would that be no one?" the boy behind him laughed maliciously and Milo did not need to turn around to know that it was Walter Pymus who had spoken, the pudgy boy who Milo hated most in the world.

Then his arm was being twisted up painfully behind his back whilst Walt as he was more commonly known, taunted him over and over again.

Who you taking to the dance? Who you taking to the dance?' until a strong smell hit their nostrils and Walt released Milo's arm.

It was the smell of burning.

Rancid, sharp and it made Milo want to vomit.

Lowish was giving them a warning look.

Milo felt himself redden as his classmates' chattering turned to sniggering as their curious faces turned to his direction, waiting to hear who he, Miloney Merren, the boy who never had any real friends, might be taking to the dance.

Milo turned around silently to glare at the overweight boy with freckles behind him, where flecks of spit pooled at the corner of his podgy mouth. He felt the tingling sensations start up his aching arm as anger bubbled up inside him and he wanted nothing more than to send the wooden desk that Chaney had been stood on flying into the ugly boy's head.

"Miloney did you hear me?"

Milo jumped as he realised Miss Dianda was speaking to him. "Sorry what?"

"Miloney. Droges wants to see you." The teacher regarded him closely, an odd expression on her face.

Milo's mouth went dry. "Why?"

"I don't know," she said. She put a hand gently on his shoulder but in his anxiety he felt a rush of magic surge through him that was so strong it took his breath away.

"I'll go now," he said quickly shrugging her off, frightened that somehow she might be able to feel the magic surging through him. In his haste he dropped his backpack.

His classmates sniggered as they sidestepped the contents that spilled out of the bag. Milo ignored them and concentrated on stemming his magic.

The tingling sensations had returned with full force.

He could feel all eyes on him as he piled his books and pens, with fumbling hands, into his bag. A small trickle of sweat made its way down his forehead but as he put the last book into his bag, heart hammering, he realised with dismay that he couldn't stop the magic.

He quickly scoured the courtyard trying desperately to focus on anything that wasn't lightweight - like the desk and his classmates. Carefully avoiding Lowish who was rounding up the remainder of the students, Milo's eyes landed on the healing tree.

There was a loud cracking noise as the magic transferred itself from Milo to the tree. One half of the tree began to creak and sway as it began to separate itself from the other half.

Milo paled. It was literally splitting itself in two.

Seconds later there was a rip roaring splintering sound as the branches tore themselves from the trunk and crashed down to the ground.

There were shocks and gasps among the students that still lingered in the courtyard and those who were already inside the school dashed back out again to see what had happened.

Milo frantically wiped away the small beads of sweat that were trickling down his clammy neck and tried to appear confused and shocked like the rest of his classmates. This was incredibly hard to do when he was breathing too fast and his stomach was in knots.

He stared in shock at the amount of damage he had done to the tree. He hadn't even been trying to move it; he'd just been trying to displace the magic.

Milo gagged as a strong rancid odour hit the back of his throat. Lowish was staring at the tree with a strange expression on his face.

"Everyone inside. Quickly," he growled. "It's just a tree. It's about time the water destroyed the thing."

Milo almost laughed out loud. The stupid creature thought the water had destroyed the tree! But then he felt a firm hand on his shoulder and he turned to see Miss Dianda staring down at him wide eyed.

"Go!" she said. Her voice was barely a whisper but the urgency in her voice startled him. "I'll do what I can to cover for you. Just go!"

***

Milo ran down the school corridors faster than he had ever run in his life.

Right now he was pretty sure he was running for survival.

Miss Dianda had discovered what he was. And if she had seen him use magic, then how many more had? The thought made him feel sick.

He was still in a panic when he exited the school and smacked into Lowish. The impact was hard enough to rattle the hinges on Lowish's armour. Feeling slightly stunned, Milo took a step back, seeing his own scared reflection looking back at him in the polished silver.

"Where do you think you're going?" Lowish stared at him, his face expressionless.

"Home," Milo stuttered.

"Not so fast. Droges wants to see you. I'm to escort you to him. You were supposed to wait for me just now." Lowish gave him a disapproving look.

"Sorry. I didn't know." Milo mumbled. His conversation with Miss Dianda hadn't gotten very far!

ZOË TYSON

"Why does Droges want to see me?" Milo's voice did not sound like his own. It sounded like he was listening to someone else from far away.

"He has a request for your father."

"Oh." Milo relaxed a little. Then this was immediately replaced by a wary suspicion. Milo's father was a potion maker and a highly respected one. Most of the residents on the Water Quarter had paid him a visit at some point or other to request a potion from him. Most of the potions were for healing purposes though and Milo could not imagine why Droges, an immortal creature, would want a healing potion.

And more worryingly, why couldn't Droges go and ask his father himself?

"Come on," growled Lowish. "Droges doesn't like to be kept waiting."

Reluctantly Milo fell into step next to the Terramang.

***

Lowish didn't speak as he escorted Milo to the Drome, which was home to Droges and all the other Terramangs. The only sound that could be heard was the small clinking of his armour as he walked.

"Is the Drome in Syanna today?" Milo asked Lowish. The Terramang grunted a 'yes' and Milo sighed with relief.

The Drome was enchanted and was not always in the same place.

It was always in the water and mostly in the same place which was on Syanna, in the valley, midway between the school and the forest, but occasionally its location would change and it would appear somewhere else on the Water Quarter. When that happened, it could take a couple of hours by boat to reach it.

It was the Terramangs' way of protecting it, although Milo doubted anyone would even dare to damage it.

Rumour had it that the Drome had huge legs hidden beneath the water which moved it to a new location when all the humans were asleep.

Milo wasn't sure he believed this. Or maybe he didn't want to believe it because there was something creepy about a huge building walking about on huge legs.

"Why don't you ever teleport me to the Drome Lowish?" You know...when it moves out of Syanna?"

The words escaped Milo before he'd had chance to think about them. He bit down on his lip, suddenly afraid that Lowish would teleport him. But it was something that he had wondered about a lot lately. He had often heard students from other classes say that their Terramangs teleported them to the Drome whenever it moved location. They rarely took a boat.

But Lowish never teleported his students.

Lowish gave him a strange look. "Is that what you want?"

Milo thought about it. Did he? He supposed he was mildly curious as to how it felt to be suddenly transported somewhere else but then again he was always glad to sail on the water and clear his head.

"No," he answered. "Boating is good."

Lowish nodded, looking a little perplexed. "Fine. But don't know why we're having this discussion. We don't need a boat today. Like I said, the Drome's in the usual place. Come on hurry it up."

Lowish increased his pace and Milo regarded him thoughtfully. Lowish was something of an oddity, even for a Terramang.

He shrugged off his thoughts.

No Terramang was ever easy to work out.

The first time Milo heard about the Terramangs' obsession for 'discovering' was in the middle of a bedtime story his mother told him when he was eight.

Some bedtime story!

Milo remembered the story clearly. One moment his mother had been telling him a great story about a boy with magical powers who could move things with just his mind, and the next she had confused him by saying that he was just like the boy in the story, only he must keep his powers a secret or else the Terramangs would send him away to a far off land.

That night Milo had had worrisome dreams about searching for a faraway land because even though it frightened him, he couldn't help but be a little curious. He dreamed that it was in the clouds on the Air Quarter or underneath the volcano of the Fire Quarter or across one of the beautiful streams that ran through his own Quarter.

"Come on! Keep up!" Lowish growled, bringing Milo out of his reverie. They turned a corner and Milo drew in a breath.

The Drome, the Terramangs' base, loomed ahead, dark and foreboding and Milo was instantly plunged into its cool long shadows.

It was situated on its own little island with a huge drawbridge leading to the entrance. From this location Milo could just make out his house further up the hillside.

He swallowed with longing, imagining the smell of his mother's freshly baked butter biscuits and sweet scented herbs. Keeping those images locked in his mind, Milo followed Lowish across the drawbridge, the wooden floorboards creaking underfoot.

He hated this place but he never failed to be awed by the sight of it.

The Drome was a huge castle like structure, made of black marble and had a mishmash of turrets, clumped together in a haphazard manner which was both chaotic and artistic. Water trickled up and down through the grooves of the black marble stone, giving it a shiny, glass like appearance. It was both terrifying and beautiful.

'A dark structure to inhabit darkness itself' Milo thought grimly.

Digging his nails hard into the palm of his hand Milo followed Lowish through a huge arch shaped doorway and entered a long corridor. The smell as always was so overwhelming that Milo fought the urge to be sick. The stench of burning flesh and something else he couldn't identify followed him down the dark corridor that was lit only by dim candelabras that hung on the cold drab walls. The building was less impressive inside. There was no décor, no warmth.

Just a coldness that ran right into Milo's bones.

They entered a glass elevator which Milo knew was also a way of transport to the other Quarters and he looked longingly at the button which said 'Fire Quarter'. But Lowish pressed the button marked 'Droges' and the elevator plunged downwards with a speed that made Milo's head spin.

Moments later the glass doors opened and Milo followed Lowish down another corridor similar to the one above. A man shuffled past them in a dark navy prisoner's uniform. His face was sunken and had a grey pallor that matched Droges's armour.

Milo shuddered. The man was a prisoner.

Lowish knocked once on Droges's door and then entered.

The C.L was sat behind a long table flanked by two Terramangs on either side of him. Droges eyed Milo with interest and then a strong smell of burning filled the room.

"Sit down Miloney."

Milo did as he asked and sat in a chair on the opposite side of the table. Droges wasted no time in telling Milo exactly what he wanted.

"I want your father to create a potion for me and it must be done in absolute secret. No one else is to know about it. Understand?"

Milo nodded. "What kind of potion?"

"I have it written on this piece of paper." Droges passed him a small folded slip of paper.

Milo opened it and felt a sharp burning sensation in his eyes. They stung so much that he couldn't see anything past the tears. He dropped the piece of paper and immediately the sensation disappeared. The only trace that anything had happened was the wetness of the tear tracks still on his cheeks.

"The paper is enchanted," Droges told him. "No one can read it except your father. I thought I just made that clear."

Milo held his tongue, feeling humiliated as he wiped at his wet cheeks. "Can I go now?" he said.

Droges picked up the piece of paper he had dropped and stared intently at Milo for a moment before folding the paper and passing it back to him. "Yes. Go and give your father the paper and then return here in two hours for your exile."

Milo's heart nearly stopped. "What?"

"You heard me."

Milo swallowed hard. "My exile?"

Droges regarded him coolly and puffed more rancid air into the room. "I know that the healing tree at the school has been destroyed," he growled. "And I know that it was destroyed by magic." The corners of his mouth curved up into a slow smile.

"And I know that it was you."

Chapter 2

Humps, Bumps and Exile

Milo felt sick. "I...I.." he tried to splutter some excuse but Droges held his hand up, silencing him.

The Terramang on Droges's left who Milo knew to be called Wylaffaton and was Droges's second in command leaned over to whisper to him and Milo took this opportunity to bide for time.

He glanced around the room, his eyes falling on the back wall which was made entirely of glass and for a second Milo was calmed by the ripples of clear water that sloshed gently against the glass. The water was full of natural magic and at this lower level, Milo could feel its intensity.

It was both calming and overwhelming.

"Wylaffaton believes your exile should take place right here, right now. But I disagree," said Droges. "People like you need to be made an example of."

Milo opened his mouth to protest but Droge waved his hand casually. "You shall be exiled in two hours' time when I have gathered a sufficient number of people to witness your departure. Apart from lame excuses is there anything you wish to say?"

Milo dug his nails hard into his hands and forced himself to hold Droges's gaze. Before he could reply, Lowish cleared his throat and shocked everyone by saying,

"I have something to say."

A strong wave of burning filled the room and Droges's face was contorted with unhidden fury. "Well?..What is it?" he demanded.

"Miloney was in the courtyard with me when the tree collapsed," said Lowish. "He was collecting his stuff together when it happened. It wasn't him. The gifted one is still out there."

The three Terramangs looked at Lowish in amazement. Milo was equally stunned. Had a Terramang just stuck up for him?

And more to the point - why?

Droges seemed to tremble with anger. He slowly rose from his seat and Milo held his breath. But Wylaffaton quickly leaned into Droges, whispered something in his ear, and after a minute's intense silence Droges sat back down.

Lowish shifted his feet nervously. Milo almost felt sorry for him.

Almost.

"Thank you Lowish but you are mistaken," Droges said calmly.

Too calmly.

"Lucky for me I have a more reliable source than you." At this Droges turned to address Milo.

"Word travels fast Miloney. Your friend Walter Pymus was most adamant that you destroyed that tree." Droges's voice was level but his eyes glowed with satisfaction.

Milo felt a surge of anger and dug his nails into his palm so hard he drew blood.

Walt had grassed him up? He couldn't believe it. Walt was a bully. Everyone knew that. But Milo never had him down as being a traitor. Grassing up someone to a Terramang was the worst kind of betrayal.

It was despicable.

"He's no friend of mine and he's lying. It wasn't me." Milo swallowed down the bitter taste in his mouth as he struggled to understand how one of his own could side with a Terramang. He stole a glance at Lowish but he was staring straight ahead, light reflecting off his armour as he swayed slightly.

Droges looked at Milo with an almost bemused expression. "Here's what I'm going to do Miloney. If you can give me the name of the person who did destroy that tree then I will exile that person instead. I think that is a fair proposition. You have two hours." Droges turned away from him then and Wylaffaton waved a hand dismissively in the air.

"That marks the end of this session. Miloney, Lowish will escort you back here in two hours."

Lowish obediently grabbed Milo's elbow and started to lead him from the room.

"Wait!" Droges bellowed and Milo's heart leaped with hope. "Lowish, you will remain here. I am not finished with you yet."

Lowish dropped Milo's elbow but not before Milo saw the flash of fear in his eyes. Milo had barely shut the door behind him when he felt the floor shudder followed by the unmistakable sound of a Terramang screaming.

For the second time that day, Milo almost felt sorry for Lowish.

Almost.

***

Milo had barely gotten outside the Drome's entrance when he was yanked roughly to the side. He turned around to see his older sister Penelope and his heart sank. She was one of the last people he wanted to see right now. It was fair to say that he didn't have the best relationship with his sister. She was his complete opposite.

In every way.

Not only did she have dark brown eyes and long dark hair as opposed to Milo's green eyes and short blonde hair but also she had dozens of friends as opposed to his 'could count on one hand' number of friends and who in fairness were pretty lame friends too.

Penelope was confident and popular and the most self-involved person that Milo knew. If Penelope could marry her own reflection, she would.

Oh and she was also annoyingly psychic.

"It's taken me ages to find you! I've been in and out of the Drome twice already." Penelope complained. She looked agitated and wiped a hand across her flushed forehead. She flicked back her long black hair, regarding him with curiosity.

"I have just had a vision," she said bluntly. "Is it true that that fat boy Walt has just grassed you up?...Did you destroy the healing tree? Have you been discovered?" She reeled off her questions in quick succession.

Milo nodded, afraid to look her in the eyes, unsure of how his sister, the temperamental, unsympathetic, and sometimes hormonal sixteen year old, would take this news. But in typical Penelope fashion she smirked and said. "I knew it. What the hell were you thinking?"

"I wasn't thinking, I was busy trying not to blast apart the entire school," he snapped at her. "In case you hadn't noticed, my stupid magic has had a mind of its own the last few months."

Penelope sighed and rubbed at her temples. She couldn't say much to that because she had been suffering the same fate. She had been having vision after vision, so much so that she had been suffering around ten headaches a day. "When are you to be exiled?"

"In about two hours, unless I can give Droges a name of someone else who used the magic."

Penelope's eyebrows rose in surprise. "Ok, well that could be interesting.."

Milo could see his sister's mind ticking away furiously. She narrowed her eyes at him. "And apart from the Terramangs, who else knows you've been discovered?"

"No one."

"Good. Well let's leave it that way until we've thought of a way to get you out of this."

"And just how are we going to do that?"

"Think of someone to blame of course." Penelope rolled her eyes and tapped him hard on his forehead. "Droges has given you the perfect get out you idiot." She shook her head in an 'I can't believe you're my brother' kind of way and then began walking at a fast pace towards the forest.

Milo quickly caught her up. "We can't blame it on anyone else," he said. "I was the one who used magic. I was the one who destroyed the tree. I can't send some innocent person into exile Pen."

Penelope glanced back at him over her shoulder with a smirk. "Not even Walter Pymus?"

Milo hesitated. That thought was so tempting....but no, he couldn't. Walt was a bully and a grass but Milo wasn't sure he had the guts to blame him for something he didn't do. Although he really wished he did.

He was about to tell Penelope this when he noticed something strange..

"Pen look at the water! Have you seen this...Penelope look!"

Penelope turned to him impatiently and looked to where Milo was pointing.

Syanna was usually a beautiful town. The warm balmy air always made everything look a little hazy but it gave the water that flowed through the town a mystical feel. Where the currents ran up through the hillside, waterfalls cascaded down into the valley and every building was surrounded by water. Water so clear it looked like glass. On a normal day the dusky red and yellow brick buildings were reflected so clearly in the water that it looked as though there was a second city beneath its depths.

But today something had gone horribly wrong.

Today what could only be described as weird 'humps and bumps' had appeared in the water that surrounded the Drome and the valley.

Milo stared in awe as the humps rose up and under the water creating huge waves so that the buildings reflected in the water looked elongated and warped.

"What's going on Pen?"

Penelope shrugged and casually smoothed down the green satin dress she was wearing. "Who knows. It's probably nothing. Don't worry about it Milesey we've got more important things to think about..like your exile." She looked pointedly at him.

Milo sighed and reluctantly he followed her into the forest, glancing back several times to look at the weird water humps around him. Through a gap in the trees he could just make out the houses up the hillside and the stream of water that was flowing up it. He frowned as it splashed uncharacteristically onto the lush mountainside.

"Where are we going Pen? You do realise I have only two hours, actually less than that now until I'm exiled. Sent away for good.." Milo emphasised for good measure. "I should go and tell Mum and Dad."

"You don't have to if we figure out someone else to blame." Penelope finally stopped walking and sat on a bench near the edge of the trees. "This'll do, no one will hear us talking here."

Milo sat down next to her wondering miserably how his day had come to this - sat on a bench with his annoying sister trying to think of a scapegoat for his exile.

Penelope offered him a butter biscuit, which he took but instead of eating it he absently began rolling the crumbs between his fingers and flicking them onto the ground where instantly little bubbles of water appeared to try and wash the crumbs away.

"Isn't today Tuesday?" Milo frowned at Penelope.

"Yeah so? And you're worried about that why?"

"I'm not worried," said Milo. "I'm just wondering why you're not at the Plaza. You always go." The Parish Plaza was a small town on the Water Quarter about half an hour away by boat that held a shopping sale every Tuesday evening. Since Penelope had turned sixteen a couple of months ago, and had a raise in her allowance, she had not missed a single Tuesday.

Until now.

"School must have finished by now," he said, trying to work out what time it must be. As if in answer his stomach growled and he took a bite of butter biscuit.

Penelope gave him a frustrated look. "Obviously I would love to be at the Plaza right now but it's not everyday you find out your only brother has been discovered."

She shook her head. "Idiot," she muttered under her breath. But her expression was not angry. She looked more like she was trying to work out a complicated maths equation in her head.

"Right," she said after creasing up her face for a few seconds. "Enough distractions..." She took the biscuit from Milo and threw it away. "Who do you want to blame for the tree thing? Shall we make a list of potentials?"

Milo shrugged. "No point. I'm not going to blame anyone."

"Ok so Walt is the obvious one to blame," Penelope said choosing to ignore him. "But is there anyone else that you know of who has a gift they are hiding? And don't you dare say me."

Milo's lips stretched into an involuntary smile but it didn't last long. "No," he said. "I don't know anyone except us. And Aunt Dor obviously."

"Neither do I for definite but I'm pretty sure Lucas Tyborne is hiding something. He is freakishly strong. He works at the restaurant and you should see how many crates he can carry and..."

"Penelope I can't blame Lucas, he's an ok guy. Not him."

"Ok then we're back to Walt. He's the one who grassed you up in the first place Milesey, you can't let that fat boy get away with this." Penelope's face was determined but Milo shook his head.

"No."

Penelope threw her hands up in frustration. "You can not let that fat boy get away with this!" she repeated. Her face had taken on an aggressive look but then it relaxed as another thought occurred to her.

"Or...how about that skinny girl Peg that Walt knocks around with. That girl seriously shouldn't be allowed out with a face as ugly as that."

Milo sighed. "I don't know Pen. It's not right."

"And neither is exiling my brother."

For the first time, Milo noticed a catch in his sister's voice and suddenly he did not want to be having this conversation any more. A pale blue leaf fell from a branch above him and landed on his lap.

It was a luck leaf.

Milo very carefully picked it up and placed it in the palm of his hand where it wriggled.

His eyes widened. He had never managed to catch a luck leaf before. He wondered if they really did bring the finder good luck. Well if there was ever a time he needed luck, now was that time.

He made a silent wish and then gently blew the leaf where it hovered a few seconds in mid air before floating off to the place where wishes were granted.

Milo fervently hoped that place wasn't the Drome.

"You do know that luck leaves are just a myth right?" Penelope was eyeing him with a bemused expression.

"Look I'll make you a deal," he said standing up and not looking her in the eye. "I have about an hour and a half left until Droges needs an answer. In that time I'll think about blaming Walt, if you'll just get off my case for the next hour whilst I go home and see Mum and Dad."

"I promise I'll think about Walt," he told her as she started to protest.

Penelope sighed. "Fine." She cleared her throat and then quickly dabbed at her eyes whilst she thought Milo wasn't looking. Then quite suddenly she gasped and clutched at her head making a horrible wailing noise.

Milo knew immediately that she was having another vision and his heart beat a little faster. When Penelope had a vision, it was always about something connected directly to her.

And that meant it could involve him or his parents.

He wanted to do something to comfort her but he knew from experience that there was nothing he could do. So he stood by her side awkwardly until it had finished.

It lasted about ten seconds and then Penelope looked up at him with bloodshot eyes. "Well that wasn't a big one, but it was a good one." She managed a slight smile.

Milo shot her a surprised look. "How do you mean?"

"Your worries could be over little bro" said Penelope as she rubbed at her eyes.

"Ooh..kaay.." Milo narrowed his eyes in suspicion. "But why?" Although this should be good news, he was getting a decidedly uneasy feeling in his stomach.

"Because it looks like Mum and Dad have found out about your exile and Aunt Dor is already on the case," explained Penelope. "She's at our house right now and she's already planning on taking you away somewhere. Maybe you won't have to blame Walt after all, more's the pity." Penelope looked genuinely crestfallen about this.

"Come on," she said. "Let's go home before my friends see that I'm hanging out with my loser brother."

Penelope's face was two shades paler after having her vision and there was a light sheen of sweat on her forehead, but as she began to make her way through a gap in the trees at the edge of the woodland there was a definite spring in her step and Milo hurried after her feeling slightly lighter too inside.

Of course Aunt Dor would have known about his exile.

His Aunt had an unusual gift.

She was not psychic in the same way Penelope was but she had a gift of knowing things. Milo likened it to an intense type of instinct. And if anyone could get him out of this mess it was Aunt Dor.

They headed for the transport boat that would take them up the hillside to their house.

"If we hurry maybe I can make the sales after we've spoken to Aunt Dor," Penelope mumbled as they wound down a path that led to an edge of water where transport boats were docked.

"If I get there too late then all the good stuff will have gone. And if that happens, that fat boy is seriously going to get..." she stopped speaking as they reached the dock.

"Oh just great!" Penelope waved her hands up in frustration.

There was a sign saying that the boats were out of action due to the 'turbulent water'.

"Well I might as well forget it now." She began to walk at an angry pace towards the watery hillside. Milo had to practically run to catch up to her.

"I'm sorry," he muttered, knowing that she had missed her shopping for him.

Penelope grunted something inaudible and her bad mood only worsened as they began the tedious climb up the hillside in the direction of their house. But Milo was grateful that she was going fast. The quicker they got home the better. Milo was painfully aware of the time ticking away.

He had an hour left at most until he was possibly exiled.

He could only hope that Aunt Dor could get him out of it.

***

"Your Aunt Dor is here," Mrs Merren shouted cheerfully as soon as Milo and Penelope walked into the house.

Milo and Penelope exchanged confused glances.

Their mother did not sound like someone who had just found out her only son was to be exiled. They peered into the small kitchen where she was busying herself with herbs and other cooking ingredients.

Lovely smells tickled their taste buds.

"How was school?" she enquired. Her mouth was stretched into a genuine smile with no evidence of a single tear track on her face. "Are you heading to the sales tonight Penelope?"

Penelope scowled. "No, the damn boats are out of action."

"Ok well don't swear about it," Mrs Merren chastised her and then held out a tray of freshly baked butter biscuits in Milo's direction.

Milo frowned, refusing the biscuit. His mother shouldn't be acting so normal surely? Not after hearing about his exile. Something wasn't right about Penelope's vision.

"Where's Aunt Dor?" Penelope asked her, shrugging off the offer of more butter biscuits. "I just had a vision. Is she here?"

Mrs Merren frowned. "Yes she's here. Everything ok Penelope?" Mrs Merren put down the tray of biscuits and gave her daughter a worried look.

"I don't know. I need to speak to Aunt Dor."

Mrs Merren sighed. She was used to her daughter's guardedness when it came to her visions and had long since found it was easier to let her deal with them in her own way. "Well I think she's in the study with your father."

Leaving their mother to continue chopping herbs and spices whilst humming happily to herself, Milo and Penelope hurried down the narrow hall that led to the study to hear their Aunt Dor and their father speaking in hushed tones. The door was slightly ajar and their urgent voices filtered into the hallway.

The twisted feeling in Milo's stomach was back again. Something was going on and he knew instinctively that he wasn't going to like it. Simple common sense told him that Aunt Dor couldn't save him at all.

How could she?

Where ever she tried to hide him, Droges would find him.

Guilt washed over Milo as he realised that saying goodbye to his Aunt would be harder than saying goodbye to his own parents. Milo's parents weren't gifted and although they had been great with the whole support stuff, they couldn't understand completely what it was like for him and Penelope. They couldn't imagine what it was like to have magic running through your blood that was always going out of control.

They didn't understand what it was like living on a knife edge.

But Aunt Dor did.

Aunt Dor had promised to take him to the Fire Quarter for a visit in three years' time when he turned seventeen, the legal age for limited travel.

Subconsciously Milo began to conjure up the pictures of the Fire Quarter from his school text books. The Fire Quarter, the capital of the Quarters. The Fire Quarter, the richest Quarter. The Fire Quarter, where there were rumoured to be dragons,

and volcanoes and purple skies and no illegal magic and dragons...

and no Terramangs and...dragons...and...

Penelope interrupted his thoughts by tugging on his arm and putting a finger to her lips. Then she pulled him up against the wall next to the door so they could listen.

"This is going to affect Penelope too," their father was saying.

"Yes but you know as well as I do that Milo is going to be the one who is in danger."

Milo tensed at hearing his name. Aunt Dor sounded calm but there was an edge to her voice that Milo hadn't heard before.

He couldn't see her from his hiding position behind the door but he could just imagine her stood there wearing something like a neat grey suit with her silver hair twisted up into a neat bun that was probably swaying slightly as she voiced her opinions to Milo's father with her usual quiet determination.

"We have to get him away from here," she was saying in her calm, controlled way. Milo's heart leapt at her words.

She did have a plan after all.

Penelope glanced silently at him in an "I told you so" kind of way.

There was an audible sigh from their father and what sounded like a fist slamming down onto something.

Milo and Penelope flinched slightly.

They had never known their father to raise his voice before. Ever. Never mind slam something.

"And how are we supposed to take him somewhere without the Terramangs finding out. It's impossible. The only thing to do is to fix the imbalance."

Milo exchanged another look with Penelope. "Imbalance?" he mouthed to her. But Penelope shushed him and leaned against the door frame to listen.

"Well that's not going to happen is it," Aunt Dor tried to reason. "And so the only option is to try and move him somewhere. If we don't, then Milo will be killed or there's a good chance that he will kill someone."

Milo's breath caught in his chest.

Kill someone....what was she talking about?

He hadn't realised he had been gripping Penelope's arm until she grimaced and began unclenching his fingers.

There was a moment's silence on the other side of the wall in which Milo could hear nothing except the rapid beating of his own heart and then his father said in a voice so quiet they had to strain to hear him,

"I know."

Those two words were so full of resignation that Milo felt as though he had just been given a death sentence without knowing why.

There was another silence beyond the wall and then Aunt Dor's voice projected loud and clearly.

"I know you're there children. You might as well come in."

Chapter 3

A Rozey Situation

Penelope gave an exasperated sigh at being caught out but Milo was having trouble making any noise come out of his mouth. When he finally found his voice, the words came out cracked and strained.

"What are you talking about? Are you talking about my exile?"

Aunt Dor paled whilst Mr Merren tightly gripped the sides of the study table. "You've been discovered?" he said.

"We thought you knew. I've just had a vision about Aunt Dor planning to take Milo away," Penelope said in a rush. "Milo used his magic to destroy a tree at school and Droges found out."

Milo gritted his teeth, glaring at Penelope as Aunt Dor and his father looked at him wide eyed.

"I didn't deliberately destroy the tree," he said feeling his face grow red.

"But don't panic," Penelope told them. "He doesn't have to be exiled if he tells Droges it was someone else who used magic and then Droges will exile that person instead."

Mr Merren's eyes widened further as he quickly tried to process this sudden shock of information and then they narrowed in disapproval. "Penelope I don't think blaming someone else is the answer."

"Why didn't I know this had happened. I should have sensed it." Aunt Dor mumbled to no one in particular. "I should have known what had happened to Milo."

She sagged heavily against the study desk looking flustered and agitated. "This imbalance must be messing up my magic."

ZOË TYSON

"What imbalance? Would one of you just explain what's going on?" Milo was starting to feel the tingling sensations again and he had to bite down hard on his lip to stem them.

Aunt Dor sighed heavily and looking as though she had the weight of the world on her shoulders, began to explain.

"The Terramangs have been stealing magic from the other Quarters," she said in a resigned voice. "And it's completely messed up the balance of our magic here on the Water Quarter. You probably noticed the strange behaviour of the water outside."

Milo's brain immediately conjured up images of the weird water humps and overflowing streams. "I told you something wasn't right," he mumbled at Penelope who ignored him. Instead she was looking suspiciously at their Aunt.

"Why would they steal magic? They have more power than any human." she said bitterly.

"I know. I don't know why Penelope. I don't even know how they've done it. I didn't even know something like that was possible. I just know that they have and now it's too late to even return it."

"So what are you saying?" Penelope's voice was shrill.

"The balance of the Quarters has been upset and unless it's rectified then...." Aunt Dor's voice trailed off as her gaze flicked towards Milo.

"Then what Aunt Dor?..." The lingering taste of butter biscuit in Milo's mouth was quickly turning to bile.

"Then the other Quarters will be seriously depleted of magic and as we all know, we can't live without magic," she paused to breathe in deeply. "And as for the magic in our own Quarter...well...it will become so intense that the water will destroy our homes and land and those people who have physical gifts....like yourself Milo... will find that their magic intensifies so much that...."

"That they will end up dead or end up killing someone." Milo finished for her, finally understanding what she had been talking about before.

Aunt Dor nodded.

"Do you know how absurd that sounds?" Milo's voice grew stronger as anger began to override his anxiety.

"The two things completely contradict themselves. Which is it.. am I in danger of my life or am I about to kill Penelope in her sleep?"

Penelope gave him a disdainful look but Milo kept his concentration on his father and Aunt.

Aunt Dor put a gentle hand on his shoulder, her silver bun swaying slightly as she did so.

"Both could be possible Milo. You see...unfortunately your gift is so physical that you could severely underestimate your strength. You could do harm to yourself and others."

Milo thought of the way he had blasted the healing tree apart barely focusing any energy and knew that she was right.

"And what about Pen?" he looked at Penelope who was hovering awkwardly in the doorway absently fingering a diamond shaped stone that hung on a delicate twisted gold chain around her neck.

"More and more visions," Aunt Dor said with a sad smile at her niece.

"Great," mumbled Penelope. "More damn headaches."

"Well actually it would be more than that dear, it would..."

"I know! I get it Aunt Dor." Penelope snapped at her. "Basically what you're trying to tell me is that my life will be one big long vision with a headache so bad that I'll barely be able to get out of bed."

Aunt Dor said nothing.

"Wow I am psychic," Penelope remarked coolly.

"Well there must be a way we can re-balance the magic." Milo insisted, refusing to register the growing panic inside of him. He wasn't sure which was worse - choosing exile or staying on the Water Quarter being ruled by his own magic.

"Well in ancient times this used to happen a lot," said Aunt Dor. "Not because someone was stealing the magic but because the magic itself was not as balanced as it is now," she clarified.

"And yes, there was a way to balance it. It was quite simple really. Someone who is multi-gifted must make a circle.."

"Actually it's someone who is multi-gifted from each Quarter, must make the circle," Penelope corrected her.

She was sat on the corner of the study desk holding a heavy book in her lap. Milo recognised it immediately.

It was their father's encyclopaedia.

Where as most kids had nice bed time stories when they were little, Milo and Penelope had been read stories from the encyclopaedia.

Milo could still memorise the most interesting parts.

As the Terramangs only authorised magical theory and not practice to be taught at school, Mr Merren had decided to give his kids a wider background. It wasn't the same as practising magic first hand, but at least they hadn't grown up completely clueless. Like some children had.

Penelope cleared her throat. "In situations of a magical imbalance, it says here that someone who is multi-gifted - or in other words has many gifts - must join together to create a powerful circle to balance the magic. But they alone are not enough. They must use a water charm."

Penelope stopped speaking and looked up at them. "A water charm? Like the one I have around my neck?" She fingered the gold chain around her neck to look down at the diamond shaped stone that hung from it.

Water charms were extremely rare but Penelope had been lucky enough to have been given one by Aunt Dor as a present years ago in the hope that it might control her headaches.

Aunt Dor nodded. "Yes. Just like that one." But then she shook her head. "But at present it's of no use."

"Why not?" Penelope shut the book hard, creating a cloud of dust and gave Aunt Dor an impatient look.

Mr Merren took the book from her and placed it back on the shelf she had taken it from.

"Because there is no one from our Quarter who is multi-gifted," he said. "Therefore the circle can not be made."

"How can you possibly know we don't have a multi-gifted when people hide their gifts?" Penelope counteracted.

It was a fair question.

Aunt Dor exchanged a look with Mr Merren and shrugged. "My own intuition for one. And also because we talk to other people on the other Quarters sometimes. Apparently other multi-gifted can always sense if there is another one around. But there is no one on our Quarter. They've checked."

"The last known multi-gifted on our Quarter was a woman named Alanya Roze," said Mr Merren, "but she was exiled years ago."

The taste of bile in Milo's throat intensified as he processed this. "So that solves my exile problem then," he said drily. "If I'm exiled then I can give that charm to Alanya Roze."

"No, that's not what I meant." Aunt Dor's voice rose in her anxiety. "I'm just saying that the only person who can help to restore the imbalance is in exile."

"Yes and now I've got the opportunity to go and find her," Milo insisted and then wondered why he was even suggesting this.

It seemed ludicrous. Perhaps this imbalance was messing up his brain as well as his magic.

Penelope began shaking her head. "And then what Milesey? Say you do find this Alanya Roze and tell her about the imbalance, then what? If she's multi-gifted and she's never returned from exile then what chance will she have now? None is my guess. Don't you think she would have come back by now if she could."

"But Alanya most likely doesn't have a water charm with her," Mr Merren said, looking deep in thought. "I wouldn't like to guess the extent of that woman's powers combined with a water charm. She is quite possibly the most powerful person that our Quarter has ever known. If anyone can find a way back from exile then its Alanya Roze."

Penelope shot him an angry glare. "Are you saying that Milo should be exiled?"

Mr Merren began to pace the study. "I don't know. I don't know what I'm saying," he ran a hand through his short blonde hair that curled up at the back of his neck just like Milo's did, and then sat down wearily on the edge of the desk.

"I just don't know."

"Look.." said Milo, "what you're saying is that if this imbalance isn't fixed then we're all probably going to die?"

His father nodded.

"And the only people who can help to save it are the multi-gifted from each Quarter?"

Again his father nodded.

"So are the multi-gifted on the other Quarter's still alive?"

"Yes. As far as we know."

"And the only multi-gifted from our Quarter has been exiled?"

Another sombre nod.

Milo was beginning to feel uncomfortable. How could he avoid being exiled now when he had a chance to find the person who could fix the imbalance. He wanted to shout childishly that life wasn't fair and that he didn't deserve to be exiled.

But seriously what was the use?

"No.." said Penelope reading his mind, "you're not going."

"Look Pen...if I don't find Alanya Roze then you're going to have the biggest headache of your life."

Penelope just stared at him, not in the least bit amused.

"Well a thank you might be nice," Milo said in his most annoying 'little brother voice'.

But for once there was no smirk on Penelope's face.

She jumped down off the desk and looked him in the eye. "Even if Alanya does come back and fix things, you won't be able to come back. Droges would kill you."

Milo said nothing. That was probably true so there was nothing he could say to make her feel better.

Penelope's jaw clenched and then she leaned against the desk, her face crumpled in pain. Her eyes rolled back slightly.

She was having a vision.

When she was finished her eyes were all red and blurry and Milo wasn't entirely sure whether it was due to her vision or from crying. She looked directly at Milo but didn't say anything.

But she didn't have to. It was obvious.

"You saw me in exile didn't you?"

Still she said nothing.

"Penelope!" he shouted at her and she stood up straight.

"Fine! Yes I saw you and I saw her, Alanya Roze. You gave her my charm. But that doesn't mean..."

"Look.." Mr Merren held up his hand. "Wait outside for a minute kids. I want to discuss this with your Aunt."

"But it's my exile," Milo objected, not caring that he sounded petulant.

"Just wait outside. Please.."

Reluctantly Milo and Penelope stepped out of the office and leaned against the closed door, trying to listen in again. But this time they couldn't hear anything.

Milo and Penelope said nothing to each other. They stood like that for about five minutes, wallowing in anger and frustration, and then they both caught a smell of rancid burning wafting underneath the study door. Milo exchanged a look with Penelope and then burst into the study.

Penelope right behind him.

Droges smiled in satisfaction as he saw Milo's look of dismay.

"Ah there you are Miloney."

Milo's father and Aunt Dor were standing tall with their heads held high but they looked pale in the face. Droges was stood between them, a hand resting on each of their shoulders.

Milo glanced at the time dial on his father's desk. "It's not been two hours yet," he said feeling a rising panic.

Droges smiled his evil grin again. "I decided to shorten it. I got bored. So...who destroyed the healing tree?" He pressed down threateningly on Aunt Dor's shoulder, making her wince.

Milo swallowed. "Me. It was me."

A fresh wave of stench filled the study. Droges's grin stretched nearly to his ugly pointed ears.

"Go outside. Lowish is waiting to escort you to the Drome. Your exile will take place near the drawbridge."

"No! You can't do this," Penelope went to stand protectively in front of Milo.

Droges pushed her roughly and she fell to the floor.

"Be thankful I didn't brand you." Droges looked at her with disgust and then turned to Milo.

"Now go outside Miloney."

"Wait!" Penelope addressed Droges and then glanced at Milo. "I want my brother to help me up first. If that's allowed? I've bruised my ankle," Penelope shot a look of loathing back at Droges.

Droges grunted and Milo took that as a 'yes'.

He leaned over Penelope to help her up and as he did so she pulled him closer so that she was completely obscured from Droges.

She grabbed the diamond stone that hung around her neck and yanked it hard so that the chain broke. The stone was the size of his finger nail and she thrust it into his hand.

It felt cool in his sweaty palm.

She looked up at him wide eyed, silently conveying to him to do the only thing left to do.

Find Alanya Roze.

***

Five minutes later Milo was being escorted to an awaiting crowd by Lowish with the same four words going around and around in his head.

Must find Alanya Roze, must find Alanya Roze.

Lowish ushered him through the crowds that had formed on the Drome's drawbridge and Milo swallowed down the lump in his throat as he saw a large wooden podium, partially obscured by the crowd that had been set up for his benefit.

He had not managed to persuade his mother to stay at home and he spotted her in the crowd, her face wet with her tears. Beside her stood Penelope, Aunt Dor and his father.

Milo had only just remembered to give his father the piece of paper that Droges had given him. Milo still didn't know what was on it but his father's expression had immediately changed to one of concern when he had opened it. Milo thought he even looked distressed as he had continued to mull over the piece of paper whilst Milo had been saying his goodbyes. Right now though Milo couldn't worry about that. Right now he only had one concern.

Must find Alanya Roze.

He avoided the sympathetic gazes from the crowd as he sloshed through the water that was now seeping onto the drawbridge. In the last few hours the imbalance had gotten worse and water was starting to come into peoples' houses. Milo could literally feel the tension and magic in the air.

It hummed in his every nerve ending.

He stepped onto the podium with shaky legs and was surprised to see that he wasn't alone. There was another girl already up there and he realised this was going to be a double exile. Somehow that made him feel slightly better.

He didn't want to be alone.

The girl gave him a small smile as he went to stand beside her and he started when he saw who she was. He didn't know her well, but he knew of her. Everyone knew who she was.

She was Vylett Roze, daughter of multi-gifted Alanya Roze.

Must find Alanya Roze.

Was it a coincidence she was here too? Did she know her mother was the key to re-balancing the Quarters? Unfortunately Milo couldn't ask her any of this because he had hidden Penelope's water charm under his tongue and he couldn't speak without spitting it out.

He had contemplated swallowing it but that would mean having to wait for it to come out the other end and....gross! Luckily, when Lowish had briefly searched him he had taken his silence for nervousness.

"Hey," Vylett greeted him and Milo managed a watery smile back. Her huge blue eyes echoed his own relief at having an ally during this most humiliating of events.

Milo had never had much interest in girls before but he couldn't help noticing what an attractive blue her eyes were. She was however wearing some very strange clothes. Her pale blue trousers matched with a pink t-shirt made an eye catching combination, and not in a good way. Even her blonde pigtails were tied with bright colours.

She looked younger than fourteen.

She looked fresh and smelled nice though and Milo was suddenly conscious that he hadn't changed since he had been 'discovered'. His clothes were sweaty and dirty. All evidence of his horrible day and he knew without doubt that his white blond hair was stuck up at all angles.

He felt his face warm. Vylett didn't appear to notice. He tried to focus on what she was saying amongst the dim hum of the surrounding crowd.

"It's Miloney isn't it?"

He nodded, oddly embarrassed that she knew his name.

"Well looks like we've attracted quite a crowd." She gestured to their audience and laughed light heartedly but the shakiness in her voice gave away her anxiety. Again Milo could only nod.

Then as Droges began silencing the crowd with his loud booming voice, Vylett grabbed his arm and pulled him close to her and whispered ever so softly.

"Why are you anxious about my mother? Please tell me what you know."

Milo was startled. Could this girl read his mind? If so that was the coolest gift - and the most unnerving he decided as an after thought.

He was saved from having to answer because Droges and his second in command Wylaffaton were suddenly by his side, surrounding him in a stench filled haze.

Droges made his usual speech about the gifted being unworthy, blah blah blah and then he raised his finger at himself and Vylett.

Milo's stomach turned. This was it then! He wondered if it would hurt. He felt Vylett grasp his fingers. Her hand was clammy and he gave it a reassuring squeeze.

He found Aunt Dor's face in the crowd and tried to give her a smile but he felt like something was breaking inside of him.

He glanced one last time at the surrounding hillside of Syanna and nostalgia tugged at his heart. He saw this view every day of his life and every day he wished it was the fiery depths of the Fire Quarter he was looking at. He had dreamed of visiting the Fire Quarter ever since he could remember but right now he would have given anything for things to go back to how they were.

He closed his eyes and opened them again when he heard an unmistakable laugh ringing out clearly from the silent on looking crowd.

Walt's fat face was positively glowing.

"See you Miloney! Or actually, I won't be seeing you. Ever again!"

Although Milo couldn't say anything back to him, for fear of revealing the water charm, he forced himself to grin at Walt in a way that he hoped conveyed something like 'whatever'.

Droges's lips twisted into a sneer, his eyes black ice and Milo couldn't stop his heart racing. He didn't think he had ever been so scared.

Vylett was smiling at a man in the crowd Milo recognised as her father. He was crying openly and Vylett was trying to tell him it was ok.

Milo was feeling increasingly lightheaded. So much heartache.

He heard Penelope shout his name, her anguished voice carrying loud and clear through the now silent crowd and Milo felt a lump in his throat. He turned away, hiding his face. He did not want his family to see him cry.

"Say goodbye," Droges said and Vylett clutched Milo's hand tighter. Through the roaring in his ears Milo heard his mother's scream like a knife through his heart...

...and then he was spinning in a whirl of black mist.

***

Milo's vision was a blur and he felt disorientated from the spinning sensation that had suddenly hit him like a thunderbolt. He had no idea if he still had hold of Vylett's hand, he couldn't even see her through the black mist.

His stomach did a double flip and he reached his arms out wildly to grab hold of something...

...and felt nothing but air.

He felt a pulling sensation behind his navel and began to panic but seconds later the spinning sensation stopped as suddenly as it had started and then he was lying on solid ground, feeling stunned and confused.

He spit out the water charm wondering how he hadn't choked on it and shouted "Vylett!"

Her hand found his in an instant. "I'm here."

The mist slowly cleared and they quietly observed their new surroundings.

They were standing on a completely flat stretch of land. Spinning around, Milo could see they were in an enclosure of sorts, surrounded by mountains with some woodland in the centre. Aside from the woodland it felt like they were stood in a huge arena.

Milo felt a jolt of something unfamiliar course through his body. He stared at Vylett. "Do you feel that? The magic feels different here. I wonder where we are?"

But Vylett was staring past him. "I don't know" she mumbled, "but I do know that we're in trouble. Look!"

Milo whirled around to see two very large and very scary looking creatures standing beside them.

And they did not look happy.

Chapter 4

Orlost

Milo swallowed loudly wondering if they should make a run for it but one of the creatures grabbed his wrist whilst the other took hold of Vylett.

Milo had no idea what they were.

They weren't Terramangs but they definitely weren't human either.

They were as tall as Terramangs but they were a lot beefier and although their limbs looked like a human's, their faces were twice as big and weirdly flattened as though something even scarier than them had squished them.

Milo instantly hated the watery redness of their eyes and the grotesque whiteness of their skin which seemed to turn translucent the closer they got to you.

The one grabbing him bent down and sniffed him.

Milo's initial reaction was to use his magic to blast the creature away from him but there was something powerful about it that kept him rooted to the spot - besides which, the creature's iron grip hold on his arm made it difficult to do anything else.

"Urrgh..I think they want to eat us." Vylett cringed in disgust as the creature holding her sniffed at her face with its practically non-existent nose. "What do we do?"

Milo summoned up his courage to draw on his magic but the creature let go of him.

"They're legal," it said to its partner. Milo looked at Vylett in confusion. What was that supposed to mean?

"Legal for what?" Vylett bravely challenged him. She barely came up to the creature's waist but those huge blue eyes of hers dared them to answer her.

The creature who had been holding her glanced down at her un-phased. "You're legal to be here. The Terramangs sent you. You are expected to go towards those trees over there to wait further instruction." It pointed to the patch of woodland Milo had noticed in the middle of the wide arena.

Milo didn't need telling twice. The sooner he was away from these freaks the better.

"Who are you?" he asked as he cautiously backed away from them.

"We're cross-patchers," said the creature. Its voice was deep and gruff but not as threatening as Milo would have expected. "We protect the portals."

"Portals?" asked Vylett.

The creature gave a weary sigh. "Portals to other Worlds."

It rolled its eyes at their blank expressions and gave another heavy sigh as though it were having to explain something quite simple to a tiresome two year old.

"You have just entered a portal," it explained impatiently. "And it's our job to make sure you entered legally. We don't just let everyone through, or else it would be crowded. Places of magic need balance."

"Yeah so I've been told" Milo mumbled, his mind conjuring up images of the Water Quarter with the water sloshing everywhere it wasn't supposed to.

Vylett waved them a hasty goodbye and began to lead them towards the woodland.

"Well they were pleasant," Milo said once his heartbeat had slowed to a more normal speed.

"So.. we're in a whole other World," Vylett mused. "Well if its entrance is protected by those things then no wonder no one ever escapes. They probably won't ever let you leave without the Terramangs' permission."

"I wonder where everyone is," Milo wondered aloud as they walked.

There was no one to be seen and Milo wondered what time zone they were in because by rights it should be early evening now. His tired body was certainly telling him it was evening but this place was still light.

Except it wasn't a light that he was accustomed to seeing.

It didn't look like early dusk, or early sunrise or even midday. There was just an eery dim light that had a pinkish haze to it.

As the trees came closer into focus, Milo and Vylett became more acutely aware of how silent it was. There were no birds or nature sounds. There was no wind or cloud.

It was as if someone had frozen time.

"It was your sister who was calling your name back there in the crowd wasn't it?" Vylett asked Milo after a few moments of silence.

Milo nodded feeling a little embarrassed. "Yeah. I really didn't think she cared that much."

Vylett smiled and shook her head looking a little bewildered. "She's your sister. Of course she cares." Then she paused and gave him a small sideways glance. "Plus I know that for a fact because I could read her emotions."

Milo looked at her surprised. "Emotions?"

Vylett smiled again. "Yeah. Emotions."

He nodded slowly, quietly digesting her admission. Then he narrowed his eyes at her. "Does that mean you can't read minds?"

Vylett laughed. "Don't worry Miloney, I can't read minds. Just emotions. I just get a sense of what someone's feeling really. It's no big deal. Sounds more impressive than it actually is, believe me."

Milo relaxed, feeling relieved that she couldn't read his actual thoughts. "That's cool."

Vylett gave a short laugh. "Except the Terramangs. I can't read any of their emotions. Probably because they're not human. My powers obviously don't extend to immortal creatures." She smiled and rolled her eyes pretending that this was a hardship, but then she turned serious, giving him an inquisitive look.

"Can I just say that the way you demolished that healing tree was incredible. I didn't see it myself but I saw the aftermath. Incredible" she repeated.

Milo felt his face flush bright red. "It was an accident," he said. "I didn't mean to release my magic. I just couldn't control it."

"Yeah well I know how that feels. That's the reason I ended up here too. Everyone's emotions kept getting tangled up in my head until I just didn't know what was real anymore."

Vylett's shoulders sagged, releasing the tension that had obviously been weighing her down. She seemed relieved to finally be telling someone her story.

"And then today Wylaffaton sussed it out and my time was up."

Milo grimaced, feeling angry as he imagined a smug look on the face of Droges's second in command.

He felt a tingling rush down his arms but it was mild in comparison to how he had felt on the Water Quarter. Now that he wasn't around the imbalance anymore, he already felt more in control of his magic.

"It was because of the imbalance thing that's going on. It's messing everything up.." Vylett explained and then paused, giving him a questioning look. "I take it you did realise there was an imbalance?"

"Yeah of course I realised. Those ten foot waves kind of gave it away." His words came out in an embarrassing splutter.

Blimey had he been the only one who hadn't figured it out?

They walked in silent for a few moments and then Vylett blurted out, "so what do you know about my mother?" Those big blue eyes interrogated him with mild curiosity.

"I thought you said you couldn't read my mind!" Milo shot her an accusing look.

"I can't but I really wish I could," Vylett said, "because then it would have been easy to work out what you know about her. So shoot, tell me what you know."

Milo sighed. "Not much really. The reason I was thinking of her was because my family think she might be able to help fix the imbalance."

Vylett stopped walking and stared at him wide eyed.

Milo pulled out the water charm which he had safely stowed in his jeans pocket and quickly filled her in on what Aunt Dor had told him.

"Basically, my Aunt, and my father's encyclopaedia.." he added, "believe that your mother is the only one who can fix the imbalance. Apparently, if a multi-gifted from each Quarter join together and make a circle, using a water charm, then the magic can be re-balanced again."

"Oh that's right," Vylett said taking the charm from him and inspecting it with appreciation. "Circles were used a lot in the olden days to re-balance magic. But only the multi-gifted were powerful enough to do it. And it's true that my mother is the only multi-gifted that the Water Quarter has..well had.." she amended.

"But...." she gave him back the charm and her face became grave. "But if my mother has never been able to return all these years then I don't see how she can now."

"Me neither," Milo admitted. "But my sister's psychic and she had a vision in which she saw me finding your mother. My father thinks that your mother's powers combined with this water charm can give her a really good chance of returning to Syanna. Anyway.. I promised them I'd try to find her and help her."

Vylett nodded, clearly deep in thought.

Milo cleared his throat, unsure of how to word his next question. "Vylett, don't take this the wrong way but what if the lady my sister saw in her vision was not your mother?

Vylett frowned at him. "What do you mean?"

"Well she was exiled years ago after all and who knows what's happened to her in that time. Who knows what goes on in this place." Milo glanced warily around the deserted arena and felt a little stupid.

Apparently not much.

"What if she's..? You know.."

Vylett raised her eyebrows. "Dead?"

Then to Milo's surprise, Vylett smiled, subconsciously fiddling with her pigtails. "She's not dead Miloney because I only have one gift. If she was dead I would have inherited all her gifts. I'm her only child."

"Oh."

There was not a lot Milo could say to this. He should have known that. Penelope was always telling him to use his brain more. It was a known fact after all that when a parent who was gifted died; their gifts were passed on to their first born child.

When Milo was little he had been delighted to discover that his parents had no gifts that could be passed down to Penelope.

They carried on walking, taking in the vast landscape of mountains that surrounded them.

They were dark and imposing and impossibly tall. The eery pink glow made them look shiny and tinted. Despite the huge expanse of land, Milo felt claustrophobic, as though the huge mountains were closing in on him. He tore his eyes away from them.

"Do you think it's a coincidence that you've been exiled the same time I find out that your mother can help the Quarters?" he asked Vylett.

"I don't know." Vylett's brow furrowed up in concentration. "Maybe. Maybe not. Although I think I am swayed to maybe not. I think its coincidence."

She paused, suddenly seeming shy.

"You see...it was you I was thinking about when Wylaffaton sussed me." she admitted.

Milo's eyes widened. "Me? Why?"

Vylett gave him a sideways glance. "Well everyone was thinking about your discovery and the healing tree. It was hard to shut out all those emotions. It kind of sent me over the edge. I was speaking to my friends as though I had been included in their conversations, when I hadn't. Their emotions had just got tangled up with reality."

"So your friends grassed you up?" Milo was shocked. But then hadn't the same thing happened to him?

Vylett shrugged. "I guess they were too shocked to disguise their feelings. Wylaffaton just happened to be close by. I don't blame them."

She smiled then. "All the school kids think you're a hero Miloney."

Milo gave a short laugh, feeling a little embarrassed. "It was just a tree." The idea of him being a hero seemed genuinely funny. One day he had no friends, the next he was a hero.

He shook his head in disbelief still feeling as though he were in a dream.

His day has started off so normally.

"Well I got grassed up too," he said. "Only it wasn't a friend. More of an enemy. Walter Pymus told Droges I blasted that healing tree."

"I know," Vylett said and there was genuine sympathy in her eyes. "That was really low."

They plunged into silence then and Milo felt small in the huge expanse of the arena they were in. Feeling stuck for something to say he said, "please call me Milo. I hate Miloney."

Vylett nodded and then sucked in a breath as they reached the edge of the woodland. There were voices.

Several of them and they could see people moving about through the trees.

"Is it wrong that I feel excited about seeing my mother again when the Water Quarter is in so much danger?" Vylett said. "My father is still there and I know I should be worrying about him."

Vylett's father, Aubreus Roze was one of the most prestigious businessmen on the Water Quarter but he was a nice man and right now he must be hurting to have just lost his only child.

"Of course not." Milo told her. "You haven't seen her since...well how old were you when she was exiled?"

"Three."

"So how can that be wrong? Er will you recognise her though?" Milo didn't think he could remember anything from when he was three years old, except perhaps for an old toy ball set that he used to like.

"Definitely. My father is a great artist and he gave me a drawing of her when I was young. She's beautiful."

Vyett's eyes looked glazed as she became lost in her memories. And then snapping out of it she said. "Come on let's go and find her."

She grabbed Milo's hand and excitedly started pulling him into the woodland.

There were about twenty or so people, talking quietly in small groups. Immediately Milo and Vylett began to scan the crowd for Alanya. Although in truth Milo couldn't really look for Alanya because he didn't know what she looked like.

"I don't see her," Vylett sighed. But Milo was too busy noticing what the people were wearing to offer any sympathy at that moment. Apart from a couple of kids their age who were wearing normal clothes, the others were all wearing the same thing - navy tunics which looked horribly familiar.

"Look at what they're wearing," Milo said to Vylett. "It's the same uniform the Drome prisoners wear."

Vylett made a face. "Uurgh the Terramangs really have made this place a prison."

And then as though the creatures had sensed their name being mentioned, Milo could smell them.

His heart sank.

He didn't know why he was so surprised. Had he really expected them to leave them alone once they were exiled?

The crowd of people grew silent in anticipation. The first Terramang that came into view, Milo didn't recognise. He was shocked however to see that the second one was Lowish. Then his heart plummeted even further as Wylaffaton emerged from the trees and then finally Droges.

So even in the place of exile there was no escape from those two.

The Terramangs homed in on everyone, forming a circle around them. North, south, east and west. Milo felt Vylett twitch nervously beside him and he squeezed her hand. It was the longest moment of silence that Milo had ever known.

Everyone was waiting.

At then at long last, Droges finally spoke, or rather shouted, at the crowd.

"Welcome new ones!"

The CL's deep gravelly voice sounded strange is this desolate place but it took Milo only a moment to realise why.

There was no echo.

Despite being surrounded by mountains, there was no reverberation of sound.

"If you are not a newcomer then return to your base at once," growled Wlaffaton.

Milo watched the uniformed crowd slowly move out of the circle, and through the woodland leaving only him, Vylett and three other non-uniformed people. A few of the uniformed ones glanced back at them and for the first time Milo really noticed their eyes.

They looked strangely vacant.

...Except for one. A girl. And for some reason she hadn't followed the others. She was standing to the side watching them with a vague interest at the edges of the trees.

Milo stole a quick glance at the three other newcomers. They definitely looked of similar age.

Milo guessed they were around fourteen, possibly fifteen.

There were a boy and girl who looked so alike they must be brother and sister. They both had jet black hair, very pale skin and features so sharp they could have been carved out of wood. The boy had the most prominent cheek bones that Milo had ever seen and the girl had a long sleek ponytail.

And like her brother she was wearing tight fitting clothes.

All in black.

But she wore a strange looking wide belt around her waist which had little pockets on it that looked like they might be used to store stuff. Although what kind of stuff Milo couldn't imagine.

He found he couldn't stop staring at them both.

They were unusual looking but stunning at the same time. Milo suddenly felt self-conscious of his scruffy appearance and wild hair that was starting to curl at the nape of his neck because he desperately needed a haircut.

He felt better when he glanced at the other newcomer who looked even more casual than he did.

This boy looked amazingly laid back considering the circumstances and weirdly cheerful. His skin was tanned and he had a mass of shoulder length blonde curly hair that kept falling into his eyes. At a distance, Milo might have mistaken him for a girl.

When Droges began addressing them, his welcome speech was short and to the point but very final.

"Welcome to Orlost," he said.

So that's what this place was called. Milo was a little disappointed.

It was decidedly uninteresting.

"I know some of you already," said Droges as he stared unnervingly at Milo and Vylett. "The others I shall get to know."

Droges then launched into details about who he was and why they were all on Orlost, which Milo and Vylett thought strange until they realised that the three other newcomers were not from the Water Quarter.

Indeed they were from different Worlds altogether.

Milo was completely horrified to discover the Terramangs had been using portals to hunt for new prey. Evidently ruling the Water Quarter was not enough for them. They had scoured other Worlds instead. Wasn't it enough that they were stealing magic from the Quarters?

They were going power mad!

"You will follow my rules here, understood?" Droges looked at each of them in turn.

Everyone nodded apart from the chiselled girl with the weird belt who jumped up from where she had been sitting, or rather sprang, several feet into the air to land agilely onto her feet.

She called Droges a name that Milo assumed was some kind of swear word and then glared at him with her hands on her hips.

Milo held his breath.

There was no denying the girl's bravery but this was a stupid thing to do.

As Milo predicted, Droges pointed his finger at her and branded her arm. The girl cried out in pain but was wise enough to keep her mouth shut and sit back down.

"So what are the rules?" asked the cheery blonde haired boy whose grin had now disappeared.

Droges smiled unpleasantly. "The rules are simple. You try to leave and you die." Then he clapped his hands together. "So...now we understand each other, Abigail here will escort you through the woods and to your base which will be your new home. Enjoy humans!"

Droges smiled another evil smile and then the four Terramangs disappeared in a flash of bright white light.

***

The girl called Abigail was the uniformed girl who had been standing off to the side.

She approached them with an air of cockiness.

Her hair was a mass of shoulder length coppery red curls. Milo thought she would have looked quite pretty had she not been scowling.

"Hey," she said by way of introduction. "I'm Abigail Bookman. Come with me." she said without further ado.

A few minutes later the five of them were following Abigail through an overgrown path in the woodland. The leaves were brown and sparse and there were no flowers or pleasant bird sounds. Apart from the pink hazy glow in the atmosphere Milo couldn't see anything special about this place what so ever and he couldn't help but compare it to the forest on Syanna where the leaves on the trees were plush green with the odd blue luck leaf mingled in, which like just a few hours ago, occasionally floated down to a lucky finder.

He thought of the wild exotic species of plants that were so colourful they took your breath away and felt a pang of homesickness. Then chastising himself for being pathetic he pushed away the memories and tried to think positive.

Must find Alanya Roze

He turned to Vylett who was walking behind him and said quietly, "maybe your mother is at the base."

Abigail whirled around to face them. "Look...if you lot want dinner tonight you need to talk less and walk more. The warden is very strict about meal times. But if you do want to talk let's get the introductions over with."

She pointed at the cheerful looking blonde haired boy. "You! What's your name and why are you here?"

Milo decided he did not like Abigail.

The blonde haired boy on the other hand did not seem to mind.

"Thought you'd never ask Abs," he flashed his gleaming white teeth at her in a huge grin.

"My name is Abigail." Abigail said between gritted teeth.

The boy shrugged and said, "Ok.. well I'm Helico Balatton. I'm from a place called the Towerlands, and here's what I can do." As Helico stood ready to demonstrate his gift Milo could imagine a drum roll going off in the boy's head and then without any warning Helico was gone.

He had literally disappeared.

"Where is he?" Abigail said trying and failing to look unimpressed.

"I'm here," came Helico's voice from directly behind Abigail.

Ah so that was his gift, Milo mused. Invisibility.

Abigail screamed loudly, her pale cheeks erupting in bright red blotches in a mixture of fear and embarrassment. Milo and the others stifled giggles as Abigail's face got redder and redder.

"Very impressive I'm sure," she said heatedly.

The black clad brother and sister were actually twins. Their names were Eli and Iza Equarte and came from a place called Tyarett City.

Apart from Abigail, who Milo thought was too bossy and too arrogant, they all seemed like a good bunch.

Eli was definitely the quieter one out of them all but he seemed pleasant enough and to be fair appeared to have his hands full keeping his energetic sister in control.

Iza was frequently springing into the air much to Abigail's frustration.

Milo exchanged an amused glance with Vylett. Iza's energetic nature may be just what they needed to help stay positive in this place.

Must find Alanya Roze.

Unfortunately they never got to find out what gift Eli had, or Abigail for that matter because soon they had arrived at their base.

Their new home was in the form of a large shabby looking building. It was very long, built on one level and made of wooden slats. Judging by the many sections of varying shades of wood, Milo guessed it had been extended several times. It looked in serious danger of falling down at any moment and Milo was glad there appeared to be no wind in this place.

"So this is going to be home," said Iza dismally. "It's a bit military looking."

"Hey at least we've got cover over our heads. Be thankful we're not sleeping in those woods," Eli said resting an arm around her shoulders.

"And as long as they've got food in there, I don't care what it looks like," said Helico as he followed Abigail up some steps which led to a door.

They walked through the door into what appeared to be a common room. There were a few people, all of different ages, sitting around on battered old sofas and uncomfortable looking armchairs. All of them looked up with an interest that seemed to light up their vacant eyes when they saw Milo's group enter.

Milo took in the rest of the room. It was square shaped and as well as the sofas and armchairs, there were several large cushions scattered about on the floor which looked surprisingly comfy.

Like the walls, the floor consisted of wooden slats and looked cold and bare except for a small lime green rug which added some much needed colour to the room.

Through an open door to his right, Milo got a glimpse of a kitchen. There was a waft of something cooking which smelt surprisingly good and he turned to grin at Helico who rubbed his stomach eagerly.

Then Milo felt shivers down his spine.

He recognised a few people in the room.

Some had been exiled just a few years ago but there was something wrong with them. All of them had strange vacant eyes, their mouths slightly open. Some had small spots of dribble pooling at the corners of their mouths. Milo was suddenly reminded of the zombies from his story books that he used to read when he was younger.

Helico nudged Milo lightly in the ribs. "Hey do you think we're going to end up looking like these lot soon?"

Milo swallowed. "I hope not."

But then in a corner of the room, slouched in a chair looking nearly twice her age, was Chaney Hilt. The girl whose exile Milo had witnessed just earlier today in the school courtyard.

Taking one look at her Milo knew they were doomed.

Chapter 5

Real or Not Real?

"Milo...what if my mother is like these people?" Vylett's huge blue eyes searched Milo's as she surveyed the strange looking vacant people in the common room. Her eyes had teared up when she had spotted Chaney.

Chaney had the same vacant eyes. She didn't even know who they were. She wouldn't speak or appear to be listening. She wasn't doing anything. Just sitting there, lost in her own world. But weirdly still clutching that pale blue skirt of hers, as though her hands had seized up after her exile.

Milo met Vylett's eyes but he had no answer.

Thankfully at that moment a woman entered the common room and introduced herself.

"My name is Miss Coldridge and I am the warden here on Orlost," she said in a brisk tone. She was middle aged, skeletal thin and her greying hair hung lank and dull about her gaunt face.

A smile would have been nice, thought Milo.

He noticed she wasn't wearing the drab navy uniform. She had a brown fabric fitted skirt with a white blouse that was made of a crinkled material. A large green pendant hung around her neck and despite her lanky hair, her face was perfectly made up.

"Unfortunately you have missed dinner so I will show you straight to your dorms." she announced.

Helico groaned and Milo's already aching stomach protested loudly. He was starving. They all were.

Was a small snack really too much to hope for?

"Well you did insist on showing off and wasting time," Abigail volunteered.

Iza looked ready to swing for her and might have too if Miss Coldridge hadn't gestured them to follow her.

She led them down a dark corridor lit by a few gas lamps and stopped outside a door.

"This is the activity room where you will be served all your meals," she said brusquely. Milo tried to ignore the wonderful smells that were coming from under the door.

"What are the activities?" asked Iza,

"Excuse me?" Miss Coldridge gave her a confused look.

"The activities? You said meal times are held in the activities room. So what activities are you talking about?"

Was is Milo's imagination or did Miss Coldridge seem particularly agitated by this question?

"Miss Equarte…" the warden said slowly,

Milo thought it was unnerving how she knew their names.

"Orlost is not an entertainment programme. The activities are for the Terramangs' use only and need not concern you for the time being. Now if that is all…" Then as though she had to be somewhere else she quickly pointed out the girls' dorm and the boys' dorm and bade them goodnight.

But before she left them she said. "And understand this...there is no way out of this place, so don't even try looking. Many before you have tried and failed, and unless you suddenly develop a magic like that of the Terramangs then I'm afraid you are stuck here like the rest of us. The sooner you get used to that, the better."

"Oh.. and I wouldn't bother trying to climb those mountains either," she added. "There is a force field up there that will kill you." Her face softened slightly at their startled expressions and for just a few seconds her voice lost that briskness.

"Trust me, the sooner you learn to accept your fate here, the easier it will be to adapt and get on with your life."

As she turned to leave, Vylett said. "Miss Coldridge? I believe my mother is here too. Her name is Alanya Roze. Where might I find her?"

Miss Coldridge paused in her step and turned to face Vylett with a startled expression on her face but then she composed herself so quickly that Milo almost thought he'd imagined it.

"No, I'm afraid there is no one of that name here. You must have been mistaken." Then she turned on her heel and left.

Abigail quickly followed her but not before Milo saw the confused expression on her face.

Abigail knew exactly who Alanya Roze was.

***

The dorm, Milo found, was pretty much as he expected. Very basic and very drab with just a couple of windows.

There were several long rows of beds, each with a bedside table and a small locker. The boys found some empty beds and began rummaging through their lockers. There were several sets of the horrible navy uniforms, but surprisingly also a toothbrush, hairbrush and other small essentials.

There was also a list of rules of 'what not to do' on Orlost. Milo scanned down the list;

Do not enter the activity room outside of meal times

Do not wander the corridors after bed time

Do not use magic

Do not disrespect warden or Terramangs - and this includes face pulling and back stabbing

And then written afterwards in heavy ink - Acts of treason will not be taken lightly

Then there was a list of meal times and an extra note saying that uniforms must be worn at all times.

Milo grunted in disgust. He felt a rush of tingling down his arms and screwed up the list into a tight ball. He flung it to the back of his locker and then reluctantly changed into the uniform. Remembering Penelope's water charm in his jeans pocket he transferred it to the pocket of his new pants for safe keeping.

As he climbed wearily into bed he only had one thought. Where the hell was Alanya Roze?

After it became apparent that Orlost was never going to get dark, Milo began to get frustrated at the pink light in the room.

He couldn't sleep.

He could hear the soft gentle snores of people around him and Helico's heavy breathing in the next bed and sighed.

It wasn't just the pink light. His stomach hurt because it was so empty and the bed sheets were too thin and scratchy against his skin and then of course he was wondering about Alanya's whereabouts.

He swallowed back tears and realised how dry his throat was. He hadn't even had a drink tonight, or cleaned his teeth for that matter. He decided he would go to the washrooms, get a drink, freshen up and then go to sleep.

A few minutes later Milo was tiptoeing down the corridor with his toothbrush to the washrooms.

It was not one of his better ideas.

All the gas lamps had gone out, he could barely see his own hands in the darkness of the passageway and he realised he couldn't remember the way properly.

Did he need to turn left or right when he came out of the dorm?

Too late now, he had turned right and so that was where he was going.

He felt his way along the wall until he came to a corner. He was debating to turn left or right again when he saw a glimpse of light coming from under a door. Thinking it was probably the washrooms he headed straight for it.

He moved quickly. It was creepy in the corridor and he had the eery feeling that he was being watched. His nerves were completely on edge but his dry throat spurred him on.

When he reached the door he realised with a sinking feeling that it wasn't the washrooms at all, but the activity room.

But at least he knew where he was now. The washrooms were just further down the corridor.

And then he saw the shadows that were moving in the light under the door. There was someone in there...

...and then he heard a scream.

A scream that held such terror that Milo was sure it would stick with him for a very long time. It had sounded like a girl's scream but he couldn't be sure.

Startled, he put his ear to the door. There was an unusual clunking sound, like the chugging and turning of machinery. At the sound of what he was sure was a girl whimpering, he quickly pulled back from the door.

Milo's heart beat wildly as he contemplated what to do. Should he go in there? If the girl was in trouble then he should go in there.

He reached for the doorknob but couldn't bring himself to open it. Milo listened as the terrible whimpering noises got louder and louder until he could stand it no more. He put his hands over his ears to drown them out and then feeling like a terrible coward, pulled them away again.

Silence.

He put his hand to the doorknob, willing himself to turn it.

"What are you doing?"

The voice from behind him startled Milo so much he thought his heart would burst out of his chest. He let go of the handle and turned slowly to see Miss Coldridge glaring at him. Her face looked menacing in the glow of the candle she was holding.

Milo put a hand to his chest trying to slow his racing heart. "You startled me!"

"I demand to know what you are doing out here? Why aren't you in bed?" Miss Coldridge's face was harsh and dragon like in the semi darkness.

"I...I couldn't sleep," Milo stammered. "It was so light and I was so thirsty. I needed a drink and so I was just going to the washrooms...only..."

"Only what?

"Only I heard something. Coming from behind this door.."

Miss Coldridge looked at him suspiciously, the candlelight distorting her features as it trembled slightly in her hand.

"What did you hear?"

"A scream," he said feeling his heart quicken as he remembered the scream of terror coming from behind the very door that they were stood next to.

"I was going to go in and see if anyone was hurt....that's all," he finished. He suddenly felt stupid and Miss Coldridge was looking at him with a strange expression on her face.

"You must never enter this room unsupervised, do you understand? If you think someone is hurt then you come and get me. I have my own room next to the Kitchen. But as it is Mr Merren, there is no one in the activity room tonight. You were mistaken."

She started to usher him away from the door. "You have had a long day and need to get some sleep."

"But.. the light.. under the door.." Milo started to say.

"What light?"

"There!" he pointed to the floor and stopped.

There was no light.

Only the dim, fading light of Miss Coldridge's candle.

"I don't understand," he muttered.

"You are tired Mr Merren," Miss Coldridge said wearily. "And seeing as though it's your first night here, I'll let you off any punishment for wandering about at this late hour. You may continue to the washrooms but in future, make sure you go before bed."

"Yes Miss Coldridge," Milo's stomach made an embarrassing grumbling noise as he reluctantly walked away from the activity room.

"Oh and Mr Merren?"

"Yes?"

Miss Coldridge hesitated and then said, "if you happen to get a little lost on your way back and end up in the kitchen instead.." She paused. "Well…I hear that cook often forgets to clean up the leftovers from dinner. Perhaps tonight is one of those nights."

Milo could have sworn that she winked at him, or was it just the flickering of the candlelight playing tricks? Then she turned and walked away from him, wrapping her dressing gown (a warden's luxury no doubt) more tightly around her. Then Milo was plunged into darkness once again.

He smiled. Perhaps Coldridge wasn't so bad after all.

Ten minutes later Milo was back in bed, his stomach much less hollow after devouring some left over bread and ham that he had found in the fridge. Much to his surprise the food had tasted astonishingly good. The ham had been tender and juicy and the bread had a sweet nutty taste that made him want more.

It was almost, but not quite, as good as his mother made.

By the time he finally fell asleep, Milo had convinced himself that the scream he had heard had been nothing more than his delusional brain working overtime from lack of sleep and food.

***

Vylett had just fallen asleep when she was woken up by a creaking noise. For a moment she was so disorientated that she thought it was the sound of the water on Syanna digesting the garbage.

Then there was another creaking noise and Vylett realised with a start that the door to the dorm was opening, creaking noisily on its hinges. She glanced at the bed to her left where Iza lay but she was fast asleep.

A figure loomed closer in the darkness and Vylett felt her heart beat faster. There were cloths hung at the windows so it was quite dark in the room but it was clear to see that the figure was heading her way.

Heart in her mouth she lay absolutely still.

Then the figure stopped and through her half open eyes, Vylett was shocked to see a girl throw herself onto the empty bed to her right and crawl under the bed covers.

Vylett breathed a sigh of relief. This girl belonged in their dorm.

But where had she been all night?

The girl sniffed loudly and Vylett snuck a peek at her, startled to see she was shaking and crying. Then Vylett spotted the wild red hair and realised it was Abigail, the stroppy girl who had shown them to their base.

...and who knew who her mother was.

Vylett wanted to ask her about why Miss Coldridge had lied but then she felt Abigail's emotions hit her like a tidal wave.

She gasped.

Abigail's emotions were so strong that for a few seconds they completely overpowered Vylett's own senses so that all she felt was Abigail's distress.

The girl was in silent torment.

Vylett turned her head away and tried to block the other girl's emotions out. After what seemed a lifetime, Vylett felt the emotions subside as Abigail finally drifted off to sleep.

Vylett swallowed down the sick feeling she was getting. There was no doubting that Abigail had been in trouble tonight.

She closed her eyes to try and sleep but it didn't come. She was still trying to make sense of Abigail's turbulent emotions. And then there was the worry of her mother too. Miss Coldridge had obviously lied about knowing her and Abigail had realised this. But right now Vylett couldn't ask Abigail about it because Abigail was far too distressed.

And then there was her father. Back on the Water Quarter, alone and grieving.

Vylett rubbed at her eyes with her fists, wanting to get rid of the images. In the end it was all too much for her exhausted brain to deal with and she fell asleep.

Some time later when Vylett had passed the first stages of sleep, she had a vision and it was the first vision she had ever had. Afterwards she might have wondered if it was a dream had she not been absolutely convinced that it wasn't.

The vision was of her mother who appeared before her, a floaty dreamy figure, dressed in white. Her father's drawing did not do her justice. Her mother's face was beautiful and Vylett wanted to reach out and touch her and ask her where she was but it was like she was paralysed. Her mother was reaching her by possessing all of her senses and Vylett could only watch.

Then her mother was showed her an image.

...water.

But this was not water from the Water Quarter. This water was so very black you could see nothing beneath it except your own reflection.

Then the image disappeared.

Vylett wasn't sure exactly what it meant but she did get a sense that she had to cross the water to be able to find her mother.

Once the images had gone, Vylett could move again and she was surprised to feel her face was wet with tears. She let out a big breath - all she had to do was find the black water to find her mother.

But where was the water?

She had only seen woodlands and mountains on Orlost. Vylett wrapped the duvet around her more tightly and then smiled. Of course there was water. Her mother was multi-gifted.

She wouldn't be wrong.

Chapter 6

Red Heads know Best

When Milo entered the activity room for breakfast the next morning, he half expected to see a dead body or some other ghastly sight. But as delicious smells of frying bacon and eggs and other mouth watering smells hit his nostrils it was hard to imagine that he had heard any screams at all in this room last night.

Perhaps Miss Coldridge had been right. Maybe he had just been over tired.

The food smelled so good he felt light headed.

The room was quite large, with big wooden tables scattered about and a long table right in the middle which was loaded with all kinds of food. Cereal, bread, muffins, eggs, salads, meats.

It was a breakfast banquet.

"Wow this looks delicious," said Eli as they began to pile up their plates.

Milo was wondering who the cook was when his plate was knocked from his hands. He watched in dismay as the plate smashed and his food splattered the clean wooden floor.

But the noise of his smashing plate was drowned out by the sound of high pitched screeching that was coming from the two girls who had ploughed into him and were now locked in a struggle near the banquet table.

Milo quickly moved away as they knocked into the bowls and plates and was startled to recognise the long sleek black pony tail and the fiery red hair amidst the chaos of broken cutlery and the futile attempts of Miss Coldridge who was trying to separate them.

It was Iza and Abigail.

What the hell were they doing?......

Milo had seen fights before. He had had several of them with his sister Penelope. Although those had been rare because she was too afraid of breaking a nail but as far as girl fights went, this one was up there with the best of them.

He had never seen anything like it.

The hair pulling and nail scratching were familiar but Iza's gift and weird looking belt had definitely given her a different type of fighting strategy. Whatever gift Abigail had, she either didn't want to use it or had decided it was useless in the fight.

Milo watched in amazement as Iza leapt agilely around Abigail, confusing her and then taking her by surprise and grabbing her in a head lock. Then expertly she whipped a lethal looking knife from out of her belt.

For a horrible moment Milo thought she meant to kill Abigail with it but then she grabbed a handful of Abigail's hair and held the knife to it.

"Talk!" she screeched at her. "Talk, or I'll cut it off."

Miss Coldridge was beside herself with anger and seemed utterly helpless to correct the situation.

Milo was relieved that no Terramangs were around.

"We have to do something," Vylett had appeared by Milo's side looking anxious.

Milo looked at the two girls and knew without a doubt that if he got involved he would come off the worst. These girls looked vicious and were probably embarrassingly stronger than he was.

Helico on the other hand....with his muscly physique, could probably prize them apart no problem. That is if he could pry himself away from the masses of food first. He had plonked himself down at a nearby table and was stuffing food into his mouth whilst watching the spectacle with great interest. It wasn't until Eli jumped in to break the girls up that he stood up to help.

"Helico help Abigail," Eli shouted to him as he managed to drag Iza off Abigail.

"I'm fine," Abigail snapped, shrugging Helico off her. She tried smoothing down her wild curls to no avail, checking them carefully to see if Iza had managed to chop off any of them.

Two minutes later a furious Miss Coldridge was marching Iza and Abigail out of the activity room where she declared that she would separate them for the rest of the day and they would go without meals until they could learn to be civil again.

Once the mess had been cleaned up and some sort of normality had been resumed in the activity room, Milo ate his breakfast half heartedly. It had not been a good start to his first morning on Orlost.

"I don't know what got into her," Eli said miserably as he pushed a barely eaten muffin around on his plate.

"I do," said Vylett. She put down her fork and began to explain. "Do you remember last night when Coldridge so obviously lied to me about knowing my mother?

The others nodded. Everyone had realised.

"Well I felt Abigail's emotions and I could feel that she knows who my mother is and that she was confused as to why Coldridge lied to me. Anyway to cut a long story short I told Iza about it this morning. And as you've just witnessed, she wasn't happy about it. She was dead set on getting the truth out of Abigail."

"Figures," Eli mumbled. "My sister just can't leave things alone."

Helico chuckled whilst still shoving food into his mouth. "So what did that pretty redhead say to make Iza so mad?"

"Well that's just it. Abigail wouldn't say anything," said Vylett. "She just clammed up."

"But I still can't imagine why Iza would get so worked up about that," said Eli.

"Well that wasn't the only thing Abigail wouldn't talk about." Vylett took a deep breath and looked at each of them in turn. "I had a vision last night and Iza thought Abigail could help with it."

As Vylett proceeded to tell them about her mother and the black water, Milo began to feel a small spark of hope. Even Helico stopped eating.

"Are you saying that if we find your mother then we might find a way out of this place?" he said raising just one eyebrow in a way that made Milo jealous. He had always wanted to be able to do that.

Vylett shrugged. "Maybe. I don't know. But me and Milo have to try, if for just for the sake of the people from our World." She proceeded to tell Eli and Helico about the imbalance on the Water Quarter and Penelope's vision.

"Iza knew that finding my mother was important to me and she was trying to get Abigail to tell us what she knew about the water from my vision last night. But Abigail just refused to tell us anything," Vylett sighed. "And then Iza just lost it and went for her."

"And do you think Abigail did actually know something about the water from your vision Vylett?" Milo could no longer concentrate on eating.

"Yeah she knew something."

"So how do we make her tell us?" Milo raised his voice in his agitation and then shut his mouth as Miss Coldridge came back into the room. She gave him a hard glare, her hawk like eyes watching for any more misconduct.

"Well we can't torture Abigail into telling us but I think I might be able to talk to her," said Vylett in a low voice and then she bit her lip as a rounded lady with rosy pink cheeks put down a tray of drinks on their table.

Milo glanced up in surprise and the lady laughed. "Don't be startled boy. I don't bite but I do cook some of the best dishes you'll ever taste and as long as I'm the chef in this place that will always be the case."

Her eyes were slightly glazed as she cleared away empty bowls. "I couldn't help overhearing you just now," she said to Vylett. "If you want to talk to Abigail she's helping me in the kitchen. That's her punishment for fighting." The cook glanced quickly at Miss Coldridge and then turning back to Vylett she said, "you can talk to her now if you like whilst Miss Coldridge is busy in here. But make it quick."

"My name's Bea by the way and you'll be seeing me most days. Oh and welcome to Orlost" she added with a wry smile.

***

They had decided it was best if Vylett spoke to Abigail alone as she was the only one who could read Abigail's emotions and therefore had more of a chance of finding out the truth.

After witnessing the fight, Vylett approached the kitchen fully expecting to be met with a hurl of abuse so she was totally surprised to see Abigail crouched on the floor and crying. Vylett immediately wanted to zone into the girl's emotions but refrained from doing so not just because it was an invasion of someone's privacy but because she wanted Abigail to trust her.

"Can I talk to you Abigail?" Vylett crouched down beside her without waiting for an answer. To her relief, Abigail did not attack her or try to push her away.

"As long as you don't keep listening to my 'feelings'," Abigail sniffed and made air quotes with her fingers.

"I promise," Vylett said and then she looked around at the tiny kitchen wondering how Bea managed to cook so much food in this tiny space. "Where's Iza?" she prompted when Abigail continued to sniff and say nothing.

"I don't know and I don't care," Abigail's words came out in a growl. "But I hope whatever Miss Coldridge has in store for her is something horrible and demonic that will fit her personality."

Vylett couldn't quite shut out the wave of bitterness that flooded into her from Abigail.

"I think Iza was only trying to help me," Vylett offered. "Although I totally agree that she could have done it differently," she added quickly on seeing Abigail's fierce expression.

"What do you want Vylett? I have work to do thanks to your friend Lara Croft."

"Who?"

Abigail stood up and brushed down her uniform. She gave Vylett a hint of a smile as she began loading dishes into the sink.

"No one. It doesn't matter. She looks like someone from a computer game from my World, that's all." Abigail's smile quickly vanished again and Vylett noticed the heavy dark circles under her eyes.

Helping Abigail to pile up some of the dishes, she said. "Look Abigail.. I saw you coming back into the dorm last night and I saw how upset you were. I didn't mean to invade your feelings but sometimes I can't help it when the feelings are strong. I think I know what happened to you last night and what's been happening to you for a while."

"Oh?" Abigail paused in her work to give Vylett a questioning look. "So what's your theory Miss mind reader?"

Vylett ignored Abigail's sarcastic reference to her gift and tried hard not to zone into her feelings. "Ok well here's what I think. I think the Terramangs are stealing peoples' gifts and they've stolen yours. That's why you didn't fight back this morning when Iza attacked you. You couldn't."

Abigail pretended to look impressed. "Well congratulations! You get full marks Vylett Roze."

"And I know Coldridge has had her gift taken too."

That got Abigail's attention.

Her eyebrows rose in genuine surprise and a wry smile crossed her lips. "Is there anything you don't know?"

"Yes plenty actually. I can tell that lots of people around here have had their gifts taken but unlike you and Coldridge most of them do not seem to be..." Vylett struggled for the words. She was picturing Chaney and the other weird people with the unseeing eyes.

The people she had now come to think of as 'the vacants'.

"Sane?" Abigail volunteered. She was scrubbing the same plate over and over until Vylett took it out of her hands and made her look at her.

"Exactly. And I think that's clean. I can see my reflection in it. Tell me what's going on Abigail."

Abigail grabbed the plate back off her and continued scrubbing.

"Abigail..?.. Just tell me."

Abigail sighed and finally put down the plate. "Fine." She dried her hands on a cloth and threw it back to Vylett.

"Well Miss mind reader it's like this. Although I am gifted - or was gifted - I've no magic in my blood."

Vylett was confused. "What do you mean?"

"I mean that in my World there is no magic. I just happen to be able to do something that seems like magic. I don't know why I can do it. I just can. But for you...and those other losers you've made friends with...you come from a World where there is true magic and so you have true magic in your blood too." She paused and narrowed her eyes at Vylett. "Do you see where I'm going with this?"

Vylett shook her head. "Not really. Tell me." But now she had asked the question, she wasn't sure if she wanted to know the answer.

"Well Coldridge says that when the Terramangs take away your gift, they end up taking some of the magic from your blood too. I guess it's like taking away a part of your soul. And that's when you become like the weird ones." Abigail picked up another plate and began scrubbing. "Poor old sods. They haven't a clue who they are, what they are or where they are. They are just a shell."

"Shell.." Vylett mumbled, feeling numb inside. "But how are the Terramangs taking away gifts? How is that even possible?"

"Oh believe me if the Terramangs want something badly enough, they will make it possible."

Wasn't that the truth! Hadn't they already succeeded in stealing magic from the Quarters!

Vylett struggled to ignore the intense waves of bitterness that were radiating from Abigail and said, "Ok...so why are they still trying to take your gift if they've already taken it?"

Abigail shrugged. "Who knows...because I'm still sane and they think I must have more magic in me to take? They're seriously stupid. But be prepared Vylett, they might be stupid but they will try and get what they want. Soon it'll be your turn."

Vylett felt a cold chill run down her spine. If she was about to become shell she had to find her mother and soon!

"Ok one more question. Why wouldn't you tell Iza about my mother? I know that you know who she is."

Abigail put down the plate so hard it cracked.

"Damn! She sucked at her finger where she cut it on the sharp edge of the plate. It wasn't a deep cut but Abigail was looking very pale faced. Vylett wished she had a potion to heal it.

Instead she quickly rummaged through the drawers and found some clean cloth. It was a poor substitute but she ripped a piece off and handed it to Abigail. "Here it might help stem the bleeding."

"Thanks." Abigail wrapped the cloth around her finger and sighed deeply, all the strength seemed to be sapped out of her. She looked resolute as she spoke her next words, not quite meeting Vyett's eyes.

"I didn't tell Iza anything because it was none of her business. Alanya is your mother and so you should be the one to hear the truth."

Vylett's heart began to beast faster. "Which is?"

Abigail finally met her eyes. "She's dead Vylett."

***

For a few seconds Vylett completely lost her resolve and she was bombarded by Abigail's emotions. She was further stunned to realise that Abigail had been very fond of Alanya and truly believed she was dead. It took only a few more moments for Vylett to remember this wasn't true and that Abigail was mistaken.

"She's not dead Abigail. She sent me a vision last night and also if she were dead then I would have inherited her gifts."

"What do you mean?" Abigail looked utterly perplexed.

"If my mother were dead I would have all her gifts by now," Vylett explained. "That's how it works in my World."

Abigail seemed to consider this. "Well maybe I'm wrong then. Ask Coldridge, she's the one who told us she was dead, although I don't know why she didn't tell you that herself. It beats me why she lied to you."

"Well how did she tell you she died?"

Abigail scraped back her wild red hair with a hair tie and screwed up her face like she was trying to remember.

85

"It was something along the lines of Alanya had been trying to fight Droges but she couldn't defeat him and he killed her. I've only been here for about six months and Droges took my magic easily but your mother....she was different to all the others. She came from a World with magic and yet she didn't lose her sanity. She never became like the other weird ones.

For some reason Droges could never seem to steal her magic. I don't know how she did it." Abigail shook her head in admiration. "It must have made him crazy. Anyway I guess in the end he gave up and killed her. I imagine she put up a good fight but I guess even someone as super talented as your mother didn't stand a chance against an immortal."

"But that can't be what happened. My mother didn't die Abigail," Vylett bit on her bottom lip thoughtfully. "And I can't get a proper sense on Coldridge's emotions. It's like she knows how to block me out. But if I could find the water my mother showed me in the vision I had last night then maybe I can find her and find out what's going on."

Abigail raised her eyebrows. "You can't get a read on Coldridge? Interesting.." She picked at the piece of cloth on her finger, looking thoughtful. "She must be using magic."

It was Vylett's turn to raise her eyebrows. "She still has magic?"

"Strangely yes. Coldridge was a bit like your mother in the sense that the Terramangs couldn't seem to steal her magic."

"So why haven't they killed her?"

"Oh I think they intended to," said Abigail. "But Coldridge convinced them to make her a warden and basically do their bidding. She promised to do as they said and would keep all us kids in line."

Abigail gestured around her. Have you noticed it's nearly all kids in this place?" she said. "Don't you think that's strange?"

Vylett shrugged. "Not really. Where I come from, magic becomes more pronounced in teenagers. Maybe its hormone related. Who knows. But teenagers find it harder to control magic."

Abigail seemed satisfied with this. "So..this water you talk about..the one from your vision..?"

"Yes, it's very dark water," Vylett began to explain, "and..."

"I know about it," Abigail cut her off. She threw the remains of the broken plate into a waste bin and wiped her hands. "Iza told me about the water. Shouted it at me actually. Look.. I'm not positive about this but I think the water you're talking about is in here. Come on I'll show you, not that it's going to lead you anywhere though."

"The water is here, in the kitchen?" Vylett glanced around in bewilderment as she followed Abigail through a back door in the kitchen.

"There's a storage room back here," Abigail explained as she led them into a dimly lit area which was crammed with crockery and food supplies. The walls were lined with cupboards and chillers and Vylett was greeted with a smell of garlic and other strong herbs.

"Bea really takes her work seriously," Vylett mused as she followed Abigail through yet another door.

They entered what looked like some kind of boiler room. It was small and laced with a network of pipes and turning cogs that made a continuous whirring noise. Abigail began pushing on a large round grate on the floor and Vylett quickly bent down to help her.

"You know you look a lot like her. Your mother I mean," Abigail said as they worked together to push aside the heavy metal grate.

Vylett didn't answer. She was too filled with emotion.

It was the nicest compliment anyone had ever given her.

Seconds later they were stood staring at a hole in the ground with the sound of sloshing water coming from it.

...sloshing black water.

Chapter 7

Strange Activities

Milo was outside near the base, dwindling away the time with Eli and Helico when Vylett found them. Milo could immediately tell by the urgency in her step and the slight flush in her cheeks that her talk with Abigail had been productive. Making sure no Terramangs were patrolling the area, Vylett quickly filled them in on her findings.

"But we can't search the water until tomorrow morning," she explained. "Bea has to keep a close eye on Abigail today in the kitchens. Abigail says the best time to explore will be tomorrow morning whilst Bea is busy serving breakfast." Vylett ran a hand through her matted blonde hair.

There had been no time for showers last night.

"I don't think Abigail was convinced the water led anywhere but she's as desperate as the rest of us to get out of this place. When I left her just now she seemed quite excited. I know she comes across as arrogant and cocky but she's been through a tough time here and I think she'll help us find my mother."

Milo nodded hoping Vylett was right. The alternative was too horrible to think about.

He thought the whole thing about Coldridge lying about Alanya's death was strange but in the end the evidence spoke for itself. Vylett had not inherited her mother's gifts, therefore her mother must still be alive.

"I can't believe the Terramangs are stealing peoples' magic. Is it not enough that they've been stealing magic from the Quarters," Milo said angrily as they headed back inside the base. After hearing about Vylett's conversation with Abigail, he knew now that the scream he had heard last night in the activity room must have been Abigail.

The Terramangs had been trying to steal her gift.

The word 'activity room' had now taken on a whole new meaning and filled him with a certain dread. Milo found himself feeling sorry for the red headed girl with the stroppy attitude.

"Apparently those creatures can never have enough power," Eli's chiselled cheekbones looked more prominent than ever as he spat the words out between gritted teeth.

"And if we don't get out of here soon we are going to become shell," Vylett said dismally.

They entered the base with heavy hearts. "By the way what punishment did Iza get?" she asked as they wandered amongst the creepy looking vacants in the common room.

"Coldridge took away her belt," said Eli. "She's going to be crazy mad about that. She loves that belt."

Helico chuckled, "And she got toilet duty."

***

Later that evening Vylett had just fallen asleep only to be woken again by someone shaking her.

Startled she opened her eyes and found Miss Coldridge staring back at her. The warden put a finger to her lips and whispered, "you need to come with me."

Vylett glanced sleepily around the room. Drapes were still hung at the window. Everyone was still asleep. "But it's the middle of the night. Where are we going?"

"Just come with me," Miss Coldridge impatiently pulled her bed covers aside and practically dragged her out of bed. She wanted to at least put some shoes on her bare feet but Miss Coldridge was already pulling her by the elbow.

She saw Abigail looking at her wide eyed from under her covers as she passed her bed and then Vylett knew.

She knew.

The place where Abigail had gone last night was where Miss Coldridge was taking her now.

She felt a wave of nausea - the Terramangs were going to take her gift. That couldn't happen. She hadn't found her mother yet.

She felt her blood run cold and she tried to resist but Miss Coldridge was gripping her elbow hard.

"Let me go. Where are we going?" Vylett demanded as they left the dorm and entered the hall.

"The activity room." Miss Coldridge did not meet Vylett's eyes.

The activity room? "But why there?"

As they reached the activity room, Miss Coldridge turned to look at her with an expression Vylett found hard to read.

"Because it's your turn."

That's what Abigail had said to her. "It'll be your turn next."

Miss Coldridge opened the door to the activity room and gently pushed her through the door way.

"Go on Miss Roze, they're waiting for you. Oh and Miss Roze?"

"Yes," Vylett turned to look at her.

"Don't fight them. It will be easier," and then the warden closed the door leaving Vylett in the eagerly waiting hands of Droges and Wylaffaton.

***

Milo had been having a dream about sewage water that was filled with horrible flesh eating creatures when someone shook him awake. He was surprised to see Abigail looking down at him. At least he thought it was Abigail, he was disturbed by the fact that his dream was mingling in with reality and Abigail's face looked a lot like the flesh eating monsters.

"What are you doing in here?" he said sleepily and rubbed his eyes as her face appeared to sprout horns through that mass of wild red hair.

She nudged him roughly. "Will you wake up! The Terramangs are about to take Vylett's gift. We have to try and save her."

At this, Milo was wide awake and Abigail had resumed her normal pale features. Her red hair had a fiery glow to it by the hazy pink light of the window. Eli and Helico were also awake and alert.

"What's the plan Abs?" Helico gave her a sleepy grin but his eyes were full of concern.

Abigail glared at him. "My name is Abigail and the plan is for you all to shut up and listen to me if we want to save Vylett and get out of this place."

***

Abigail's plan was crazy crazy crazy. It was the only word that kept popping into Milo's head as he followed Abigail outside into the pink hazy world of Orlost that evidently never got dark.

Crazy crazy crazy!

"I'm sure there must be a better plan than this," he complained as the four of them ran through the woodland trying to keep up with Abigail who could easily run faster than any of them.

"Well if you can think of one then tell us now because we have about ten minutes until those scumbags take Vylett's gift and then her sanity." Abigail shouted back to him over her shoulder.

Milo decided to shut up.

Ten minutes until Vylett ended up like the rest of the vacants. It was too horrible to even contemplate. He shivered even though he was sweating from exertion and concentrated on their crazy plan as they exited the woodland and headed for the place where he and Vylett had first entered Orlost after their exile.

"So what now... do we just wait? We don't have time," Eli said.

"Oh they'll be in here," said Abigail. "My guess is in about 5 seconds....4....3....2...1.."

Right on cue the two beefy cross-patchers with the flattened faces who had admitted Milo and Vylett onto Orlost materialised before them.

And they looked no happier than the last time.

They did seem surprised however. Milo guessed they didn't get visitors very often.

"We can't let you leave. Terramangs orders," one of the ugly brutes growled at them.

"I know we can't leave," Abigail held her head high. "Well not through this way anyway. But we have found another way out and it's one that you don't have any control over. But I want to know if there will be any other cross-patchers at the other side waiting for us and if there are will they admit us? We want to know what we're up against before we leave."

The cross-patchers looked first at Abigail and then at each other in confusion. Their mean eyes narrowed in suspicion and Milo found he was holding his breath. He didn't see how they were ever going to fall for this.

"There are no other portals out of here. If there were we would know about it. You lie." The cross-patcher raised his arm to strike Abigail but Helico jumped in front of her.

"Wait! She's not lying," he said quickly. "We can show you. It's very well hidden."

The cross-patcher who had raised his arm dropped it again and turned to his ugly mate.

"You stay here whilst I check this out." Then he grabbed Abigail roughly by her arm and pushed her forward. "Start walking and you'd better not be lying. Where is it?"

"The activity room," Abigail lied, following the crazy plan.

Milo followed them feeling only slightly more hopeful. Phase I successful. But he knew that it would only take one simple mistake for them to end up dead.

***

Vylett stared past Droges and Wylaffaton at the strange assortment of equipment that had replaced the dinner tables and knew she was in trouble. 'Torture' equipment was the first word that came to her mind.

"What is this stuff?" she murmured.

Droges gave her a small smile which turned her stomach and gestured to a piece of equipment nearest to her that consisted of a solid metal table with a weird looking suction device suspended above it.

"Come lie on here please. If you co-operate with us then you will be back in your bed before you know it. If you don't co-operate then this will be an unpleasant experience for both of us. Mainly for you I might add but as I have things to do outside of Orlost that are of more importance than you then I shall find the delay unpleasant to say the least. So do we understand each other?"

'No!' Vylett wanted to scream at him.

She looked frantically around the room wondering what she might be able to use as a weapon but she knew it would be fruitless. She could never overpower a Terramang.

Feeling resigned, she sat on the edge of the table and gripped the sides tightly. Maybe Milo would manage to find her mother before his own gift was taken.

Wylaffaton grabbed the weird suction device from above her which had numerous wires and leads attached to it - all with sharp points - and then he pushed her back so she was lying flat.

She tried not to flinch as he grabbed her forearm and roughly pierced her skin with one of the leads.

She cried out as a sharp stabbing pain shot through her arm.

Her next reaction was to try and move but Wylaffaton held her in place with his impossible strength.

She looked down to see the tip of the lead weaving its way under her skin and screamed as it tore through the flesh and muscle. She thought she might lose consciousness and then the pain eased.

"Now this will only take a few seconds," Wylaffaton said as he reached for a large red button on the device. Then Wylaffaton paused as he heard movement outside the door. He glanced at Droges.

"What's going on out there?"

Droges stomped to the door, furious at the interruption. When he opened it Vylett was not the only one surprised to see one of the ugly cross-patchers that had intimidated her and Milo standing in the doorway. It looked so threatening with its huge body filling the entire doorway and its huge nearly translucent head peering in that even Droges took a step backwards.

"What is the meaning of this?" Droges demanded as the cross-patcher pushed him aside and appeared to sniff around the room. The creature ignored him and took absolutely no notice of Vylett strapped to the table as he took it upon himself to walk around the room sniffing it out.

Vylett watched with trepidation as Droges and Wylaffaton flanked the creature demanding to know why it had entered their base. Before she could even think through what she was doing, she used their distraction to pull the leads out of her skin, ignoring the pain as the needles tore at her flesh.

She jumped off the table.

If she could just sneak past them whilst they were pre-occupied.....

And then Droges whirled on her. "Don't you move. Stay where you are."

The burning stench in the room stepped up a notch and then Vylett was thrown backwards with the force of Droges's brand.

She winced as the burn stung her shoulder.

She lay on the floor wondering why it didn't hurt more and realised she was probably in some kind of shock.

She watched Droges and Wylaffaton trying to brand the cross-patcher - unsuccessfully - and felt as though she were observing from inside a giant bubble.

Their voices sounded muffled and distant.

Then as Droges and Wylaffaton began to physically remove the cross-patcher from the room, the bubble burst as Vylett felt strong arms lift her from the floor. She gasped in surprise and looked around to see who it was but there was no one there.

She was just floating in an invisible pair of arms.

She felt a hand clamp across her mouth and then Helico's voice soft in her ear. "Just stay quiet."

Vylett slumped against him in relief feeling shaky on her legs. It was just Helico. But what was he doing? He was going to get himself killed.

But before she could whisper for him to go, he put her back on the ground and she felt him leave her side. She stood stock still as Droges and Wylaffaton managed to drag the enraged cross-patcher to the door.

It was shouting over and over, "Where is it? Where is it? I know it's in here." And then just as the three horrible creatures reached the threshold, looking as though they were moulded into one, a large piece of equipment in the corner of the room flipped over.

It was tall and metallic and it hit the floor with a crash.

Droges turned on Vylett in a flash. "What did you do?"

"Nothing," she backed away from him, reeling from his fowl breath and then to her left another piece of equipment crashed to the ground, then another and another.

Helico was wrecking the place.

"It's that boy from the Towerlands," roared Wylaffaton. "Get him."

Both the Terramangs started firing brands into thin air in the hope of hitting Helico, but the equipment kept on flying around the room.

Vylett had to duck several times to prevent herself being decapitated. Then Droges pushed her roughly through the open doorway. "Go back to your dorm," he growled at her. "I'll deal with you in the morning."

Vylett found herself shut out in the corridor with the realisation that Helico was trapped inside the activity room. Feeling helpless she wandered down the corridor wondering what to do when more hands grasped her wrists. This time her saviour was in the visible form of Abigail who told her to be quiet and pulled her down the corridor with an urgency that was starting to make Vylett's heart race.

What was going on?

It soon became clear however when Abigail dragged her to the grate in Bea's kitchen where Milo, Eli and Iza were all waiting nervously.

"About time," Iza looked a little manic. "I was imagining all sorts of horrible things. I thought that cross-patcher may have been too late or ...."

"Did you plan all this...with the cross-patcher.. and Helico coming for me?" Vylett looked at them all incredulously.

"Of course we did," said Abigail. "I'll tell you about it later but right now we need to get going before the Terramangs start looking for us."

"But we can't go now, Helico's still in the activity room. He's trapped in there with Droges."

"No I'm not, I'm here," Helico's voice sounded from somewhere behind them and then he materialised, looking extremely out of breath but otherwise unharmed. "Now come on we haven't got much time. Let's go."

They dropped down into the hole which was a greater drop than Vylett had anticipated and heard a noise above them. They were about to make a run for it when Abigail said, "it's just Bea. She's going to close the grate for us."

Bea's beet red face peered down at them and even in the darkness of the hole they could see the fear in her eyes. "Be careful kids."

"We will and thanks Bea, I'll never forget this."   Abigail shouted to her.

"Good. Because if you find a way out I'm expecting you to come back for me first. Oh and Abigail I thought you might want this.." Bea held up a rag doll which had bright pink cheeks and stringy yellow hair and then threw the doll down the hole to her.

Then the cook wished them luck and closed the grate on them.

Chapter 8

The Black River

The second they had entered the hole Eli had taken charge and no one had complained. Eli was sensible and intelligent and a very leadership kind of guy. Once the grate had closed they were plunged into darkness and then to Milo's relief Eli produced a flashlight.

Whilst they had been waiting for Vylett and Helico, Eli had packed a rucksack with a few essentials and also some food from Bea's kitchen.

Once they had established by the dim light of Eli's torch that they were in some sort of passageway and it only went in one direction, Eli lead the way and they quickly began trudging through shallow stinky sewage water, having to walk in single file because the passageway was so narrow.

Milo wrinkled up his nose at the smell. "Does this look like the water in your vision?" he asked Vylett.

Milo's initial joy at Vylett's successful escape had been replaced with a feeling of revulsion at the treatment she had endured in the activity room. She had a gaping hole in the shoulder of her uniform where a nasty brand was clearly visible and both her arms were covered in streaks of blood. She had insisted she was fine but Milo still felt sickened none the less.

"Maybe," she said. "The water seemed to be dark."

"Well it's definitely dark down here," Iza's voice echoed loudly. "Does anyone else feel things crunching under their feet?" There was a definite tremble in her voice.

"Do you ever stop complaining?" Abigail retorted back.

Had Iza been walking next to Abigail Milo felt sure another fight would have broken out between them but luckily Iza was behind Eli whilst Abigail was at the back of their formation. Iza it turned out though was more interested in interrogating Abigail than fighting with her.

"So why make such an effort to save Vylett Abigail? I can't imagine that you've done that for any of the other poor suckers on Orlost. But I'm curious Abigail, was it because Vylett knew how to get us out of here? No offense Vylett."

"None taken," Vylett mumbled.

Abigail answered Iza by calling her a name that Milo assumed was some kind of swear word from her World and refused to say anything else to her. Milo guessed that Iza had hit the mark with Abigail but to be fair to Abigail she had risked her neck tonight and he didn't think any of them would ever forget that.

"How long before you think the Terramangs will find us?" Milo said after they had been sludging through the water for a while.

"Well hopefully they're too stupid to think of this place," said Abigail. "This place is just a sewer drain so hopefully they won't look here for a while. Thank God Bea agreed to put the grate back for us or else the chances of them finding us would be greater."

"And also for now they'll just be looking for Helico. They won't be counting on all of us going walk about. They probably think we're all tucked up in bed. With any luck they won't discover we're gone until morning."

Helico who was walking behind Milo made a snorting noise. "Yeah well things didn't exactly go according to plan back there. I'd planned on running out with Vylett whist the Terramangs were distracted with that cross-patcher, but the Terramangs had practically pushed it out of the room before I'd had chance to save Vylett. That's when I just started destroying stuff to distract them."

Helico began making 'boom' noises in the darkness, which echoed off the slimy concrete walls.

"I didn't plan on being trapped inside with them but hey it all worked out in the end."

Because Droges had guarded the door to stop Helico escaping, Helico had resorted to smashing the window and making a run for it. He had then run straight back into the base whilst the Terramangs were looking for him outside.

Abigail pointed out that this probably worked out better than the original plan which was to grab Vylett and make a run for it whilst the cross-patcher distracted Droges by looking for a portal.

Milo sincerely hoped that Alanya was somewhere at the end of this passageway. He didn't like the sensation of things crunching beneath his feet and his ankles were starting to feel numb from the cold. Eli's torch made eery flickering images on the walls, lighting up the greenish looking water that trickled down it and he was starting to feel decidedly claustrophobic.

"So what's your doll about Abs?" Helico asked Abigail after a while.

For once Abigail didn't shout at Helico for shortening her name and instead readily launched into the story behind her doll.

"It's my something old, something new doll,' she explained. There was a childish excitement in her voice as she described the doll that she had tucked into the waistband of her uniform.

"Your what?" said Iza making a snorting noise.

"It's my good luck doll and I especially don't expect you to understand Iza," Abigail's voice was tight but after encouragement from Helico she continued. "Where I come from when someone gets married it's a tradition that the bride is given something old, something new, something borrowed and something blue. They're supposed to bring her luck. Anyway when I was really small, I was given a doll by my Gran." In the darkness the others could hear her patting the waistband of her trousers.

"She said it wasn't the usual tradition but she was never really the traditional type my Gran. Anyway she gave it to me so that when I get married some day I can dress the doll in something old, something new, something borrowed and something blue." Abigail's voice sounded melancholy in the darkness.

No one knew quite what to say. To talk about marriage at fourteen seemed alien.

"Oh I know I'm too young to get married," Abigail brushed them off, sensing their discomfort in the darkness. "I'm not saying I want to get married now you bunch of idiots. But I like to keep it on me for good luck. I call her Victoria Sparkle."

"In our traditions, the bride is given some kind of present which contains the water from our Quarter, along with blue luck leaves," Vylett told her.

"Ok now don't bite my head off Abigail but that doll didn't exactly bring you luck if you got sent to this place did it?" said Iza and in the darkness you could hear the mild amusement in her voice.

Abigail gave a sharp laugh that sounded hollow in the tight passageway. "Hey don't underestimate Victoria Sparkle Iza, I have faith in her. I fully believe that everything happens for a reason and that I've been brought here to Orlost for a purpose."

Abigail faltered. "I'm just not sure what that purpose is yet."

"So you could meet me of course Abs!" Helico called out. Everyone laughed, including Abigail and for a moment the intenseness of the sewers was lessened and then Milo smacked hard into Vylett's back.

"Sorry," he mumbled. "Eli why have you stopped walking. I almost broke my nose."

"There's a dead end here," said Eli and he shone his torch to show them the blank wall he had encountered.

"Oh just great," said Iza. "We've come all this way just to hit a dead end."

"No. There must be a way out," Vylett's voice was an octave higher. "Try pushing it Eli. This must be the way. It has to be."

Eli pushed but it was solid brick.

"Wait I have an idea, let me through," said Milo. The others flattened themselves against the passage wall and Milo trudged through the sludge to the wall. "I reckon I could move these bricks and blast them apart. But you'd best all stand back. My aim's not always so great."

They moved back and Milo concentrated, letting the tingling sensations come. He willed the bricks to move, staring intently at the wall and then released his magic. There was a loud crashing noise as the bricks collapsed and then a burst of natural light filtered through that was blinding after being in the darkness of the passageway.

The others cheered appreciatively and then one by one they clambered through the rubble.

They found themselves at the edge of a narrow river with the blackest water Milo had ever seen.

It was surrounded by woodland.

When they turned to look behind them there was just a hazy mist where the passageway had been, along with a weird orange rock that was carved into the shape of a strange looking head with long hair as black as the river.

"This can't be Orlost," said Vylett. "It feels too different."

"It feels like there's a different magic here," Helico agreed, dipping his hand into the black water.

Helico was right, it was hard to pinpoint exactly why it had magic but it was somehow perfectly obvious to all of them that it had. Just as they had known Orlost's magic was different. It was as if their brains had been programmed to recognise magic.

"This is it! This is the water from my vision," there was excitement in Vylett's voice. "I recognise it now."

"This place is beautiful," Iza mused, running a hand through her long ponytail which was as black and shiny as the water. It may have been beautiful but Milo had the eery sense that those woods were not as quiet as they seemed.

There was something very unnatural about this natural looking place.

There was a small wooden rowing boat which was conveniently docked by the side of the river as if it had been expecting them.

Another eery thought!

"What do we do now?" Milo said eyeing the boat warily. He looked around desperately hoping to see sight of Alanya but this place looked huge, she could be anywhere.

"I think we need to board the boat," said Vylett and then before any of them could stop her, she stepped onto it.

***

As soon as Vylett's foot touched the boat she had another vision. Actually she had two but the first one was strangely blurred and jumbled.

She had a sense of watching someone falling and not being able to stop them. That someone landed with a thud and lying next to them was another face. At least she thought it was a face - the vision was so blurry.

Then she saw cheeks that were painted red and eyes which were unnaturally large and she realised she was looking at a doll.

Then the vision changed and she was lost in the new images that her mother was showing her. There was a quick image of a cave which was lavishly decorated with chandeliers and cream carpets and then she was looking at an elevator.

She saw herself walk into the elevator and press a button.

And she knew without a doubt that that elevator would take her to her mother.

Then the images disappeared and Vylett woke up.

She was drenched in sweat and surprised to see that she was lying on the floor of the boat. She felt weak and shaky and then taken aback to see five pairs of eyes looking down at her with concern.

"I'm ok," she reassured her friends. "I just had a vision. I'm ok" she repeated. She felt like she had to keep saying it because she needed to believe it.

Finding her mother was going to be much harder than she'd thought.

***

Apparently they didn't need oars to steer the boat. It seemed to know where it was going and took them at a steady speed, in a steady direction.

The black river was about twenty feet wide and twisted and turned around many bends. Every so often the six of them would get covered in tiny leaves that fell on them from the many trees whose lush green leaves hung over the river like sweet smelling feathery curtains.

It was a place of undeniable beauty.

An array of flowers and plants in a multitude of vibrant colours bordered the edges of the river.

Every so often though the hairs on the back of Milo's arms and neck would prickle and a chill spread through him. He was certain it stemmed from the woods, although he wasn't sure why. Perhaps it was the strange way that from to time the leaves seemed to part themselves even though there was no breeze.

The six of them were slightly subdued after hearing Vylett's vision.

If her vision was correct then after the water they had to find some caves and an elevator before they found Alanya. Milo was glad Eli had brought along some food because it was going to be a long journey. They could only hope that the boat knew where it was going.

They snacked on the fruit and cherry tarts that Eli had brought and savoured a few bacon and cheese rolls before reluctantly deciding to save the rest of the food.

Abigail was particularly subdued after hearing about the doll in Vylett's vision but refused to believe that Victoria Sparkle could bring anything but good luck.

"I didn't know you'd cut yourself," she suddenly said to Helico. To Helico's surprise and obvious delight Abigail grabbed his hand and inspected the piece of cloth which until now none of them had noticed wrapped around Helico's hand. There were a few specks of red on the material where blood had seeped through and Milo now noticed Helico's ripped sleeve in his uniform where he had torn off a piece to use as a bandage.

Helico shrugged. "It's only a small cut from breaking that window. It's no big deal." He waved off their concern but Milo suspected he would have shrugged off an amputated hand in order to impress Abigail.

The boat continued to take them down the black river and Milo was just starting to feel sleepy when Eli said, "the river's getting narrower."

Milo thought 'narrow' was an understatement. Up ahead the river appeared to flow into a stretch so narrow that Milo wasn't sure if their boat would fit.

He was about to voice his concern to the others when the boat was jolted from beneath them. Abigail who was sitting in front of him fell backwards off her seat. Her legs swung upwards and her shoe flew off in the process.

Milo grabbed it before it fell in the water.

He knew he should have been concentrating on what had jolted the boat but right then he was fascinated by Abigail's strange looking shoe. They had large heels but no backs to them and the pointed toes were covered in a brown fur which now smelled a bit like sewer water.

They looked oddly out of place with her blue Orlost uniform.

"How can you walk in these?" he asked in wonder.

Abigail stared at him in disbelief. "Something beneath that creepy black water has just tried to tip us from our boat and all you can think about is my shoes!"

"Er yeah what was that anyway?" Milo peered over the side of the boat. "I don't see anything…"

And then he did see something.

No sooner had he said the words, bubbles appeared on the surface and there was a deep rumbling sound below the water, deep within the pit of its belly. Not unlike the sound the water made back on the Water Quarter when it was digesting rubbish.

Milo only hoped that whatever was making that rumbling noise, it didn't think humans were rubbish.

Unfortunately it looked like he was very wrong.

A large perfectly round slippery head that was a murky white colour and the size of a huge rock boulder, slowly rose out of the black waters.

The creature's nose, or rather the place where its nose should be – because it didn't appear to have one – was level with Milo's.

"Woah!" Milo jumped back, just as the creature's mouth opened so wide that Milo could have swam down into the tunnel of shiny liquids that was its oesophagus.

"Man that thing is uglier than the Terramangs," Helico jumped up and the boat rocked dangerously. The good thing was that this resulted in the creature's head disappearing back under the water.

The bad thing was that the rest of it decided to make an appearance.

The boat jolted and something that looked like a large tentacle slapped over the side of the boat.

Helico kicked out at it but it didn't move.

"God it's some kind of giant squid!" shouted Abigail.

Milo wasn't sure exactly what a squid was but he didn't like the look of it and the horror on Abigail's face told him it wasn't something she was used to either.

"How many legs do these things have?" he asked her as he jumped out of the way to avoid another tentacle.

"About eight I think."

Oh great!

"If Coldridge hadn't taken my belt I could have stabbed it with my knife or used my pellet gun." Iza said angrily.

Milo shot her a wary look, "you scare me sometimes Iza."

As a fifth tentacle narrowly missed Milo's head he realised he was still holding Abigail's shoe. He considered its lethal looking heel.

It seemed a lame idea but worth a try.

He lunged the heel into a tentacle with all the force he could muster, only vaguely aware of Abigail's wait of protest.

It worked!

The squid creature made a howling noise and retracted its injured leg. But as it did so it dragged the boat downwards and the next thing Milo knew they were all in the water.

The water was nothing like the water on Syanna.

It was freezing cold for one thing.

Milo's limbs nearly seized up as he plunged beneath its black surface and then once he resurfaced and started treading water he realised that it had a heaviness to it that he wasn't used to. He was a good swimmer but he felt as though the water was pulling him down.

The others were also struggling but the boat had not waited for them. It was sailing away from them and none of them could swim fast enough to catch it.

Milo felt like he was having one of those bad dreams where someone was chasing him only he couldn't run because his legs felt like lead.

Only in his dreams that someone was not usually a giant squid!

The squid's tentacles were reappearing out of the water in an effort to grab them and Eli began yelling out orders.

"Swim towards that narrow part! It won't fit through there."

They swam as fast as they could through a water that felt like sinking sand and Milo cursed when he saw their boat steer itself into the narrow stretch of river. It was a snug fit but it did fit and it continued its journey, now free of passengers.

Why couldn't they have just kept their balance and they would be free by now.

"Oh god!" Iza cried as the squid's head appeared next to her. "We're not going to make it."

Milo watched in horror as Iza grabbed hold of its head and sprang up onto it. He had to admire her courage but her impact was like a raindrop on its head. Milo considered using his own gift to blast the squid away from them but he couldn't do that without risking all of their lives.

His aim just wasn't that great.

He had moved those bricks without too much problem but no one had been attached to them then. And the damage he had done to the healing tree was still permanently fixed in his mind!

It wasn't worth the risk. There was no way he was going to risk hurting his friends.

"Iza, jump down and I'll try to move it," Milo yelled to her but Iza was already yelling to her brother.

"Eli try and stun it!"

As Milo struggled to keep his head above the surface he realised that he still had no idea what Eli's gift was but he hoped that whatever it was it was enough to sink this awful creature into oblivion.

Eli hesitated and Iza shouted down to him, "Just do it! They'll understand."

"Fine."

Milo wasn't quite sure what there was to understand but there was no time for questions. He just kept on swimming with the others, their arms aching with exhaustion and then Milo's nostrils filled with an all too familiar scent.

Burning.

Confused and heart beginning to race, he glanced back...

...and recoiled in horror.

Eli was branding the squid just like the Terramangs branded humans.

In his shock Milo forgot to tread water and sank beneath the black water. He resurfaced with a mouth full of salty tasting water and feeling as though his legs were filled with lead. His arms ached with the effort of keeping afloat. He forced himself to keep swimming, to catch up with the others, all the while his tired brain processing what he had just seen.

Eli's gift was burning!

No wonder Eli had kept it a secret. He'd been embarrassed. He'd thought Milo and Vylett would judge him. Understandable really given that they lived in a World ruled by Terramangs.

Milo heard, rather than saw, the squid make a horrible squealing noise. In the next instant Iza was swimming beside him whilst Milo caught a glimpse of the squid sinking beneath the water.

Its burnt tentacles made a horrible hissing noise as they made contact with the water.

Much to everyone's relief it didn't resurface and a few minutes later the six of them had safely reached the narrow part of the river where the water was more buoyant and they could swim relatively easy.

"I think there's a current up ahead," shouted Abigail who was in the lead and apparently as strong a swimmer as she was a runner.

And then she screamed and it was too was too late for any of them to do something.

They had hit a strong current and even Abigail was not strong enough to turn back around.

They fought wildly against the torrents of water that were sucking them along at an alarming speed. Their panic increased as up ahead the current appeared to propel them straight towards...

...Nothing!

They were heading straight for a waterfall.

Frantically, they tried to swim in the other direction but it was impossible. The current was too strong.

Vylett floated by Milo, shouting his name and he just managed to grab hold of her hand as they went over the edge.

Chapter 9

Cave Hunting

Was it possible to have a heart attack whilst falling?

Milo thought it was.

The pounding of his heart and the deafening roaring noise of the waterfall merged into one sound as he free fell down the cascades of water. As he lost hold of Vylett's hand, he had only one thought,

'Please don't let her die'

He tried to shout her name but he could barely breathe under all the water.

Then he felt a strange pulling sensation behind his navel followed by a jolt in his stomach as his limbs stopped flailing and his body slowed down until he was hovering in mid air.

And then it was as though he were suddenly a puppet whose strings were being pulled against his will. He felt himself being manoeuvred out of the water fall and propelled across it so that he could see a ravine far beneath them. Far below he could make out their long wooden boat gliding effortlessly down the waterfall and realised the boat would have gotten them down it safely had the squid not appeared.

He looked across from him relieved to see Vylett and the others were all gliding across the ravine too, several paces apart.

He continued to glide until he reached the edge of a bank surrounded by caves where he hovered ever so slightly before his invisible strings were cut and he fell in a heap onto the grassy bank.

Everyone lay exhausted, letting the relief sink in of still being alive.

Milo crawled next to Vylett.

Before coming to Orlost, apart from his sister, he had barely spoken to girls, let alone hugged one but that's exactly what he did now.

It was instinctive.

Perhaps it was because they'd been through so much already in such a short space of time. You couldn't share an exile with someone and not feel some sort of connection.

It had given them a bond that would never break.

"I didn't mean to let go," he said, holding her gently like he was afraid she might break.

"I know you didn't. It wasn't your fault," she said hugging him back.

The next thing Milo did was check that the water charm was still in his pocket.

To his relief, it was.

Without the water charm it was almost pointless to go on searching for Alanya Roze because even if with the remote possibility that they found her and found a way back to the Water Quarter, their efforts would be fruitless without the water charm.

Without the charm Alanya couldn't make the circle and couldn't save the Quarters.

"Hey Abs what's wrong? Speak to me, tell me you're ok."

They turned to see Helico attending to an extremely shaky looking Abigail.

"It's ok Abigail, you're safe. Something saved us," Milo told her.

Abigail ran a hand wearily through her wet matted hair which was plastered to her forehead.

"Milo it wasn't a something that saved us you idiot. It was me."

***

It turned out that levitating things was Abigail's gift.

She could make things float and had rediscovered her magic whilst plummeting down the waterfall. The only explanation they could think of was that the mouthfuls of black water she had swallowed did indeed contain magic and had somehow re-booted her gift back into action.

She was now exhausted and weakened from the effort of using her gift on all of them but Milo had never seen her so happy.

She was smiling and laughing in a way that made her look prettier and there was a hope in her eyes that hadn't been there before.

Much to all their amusement she even began playfully untangling a strand of Helico's wavy blonde hair. Her enthusiasm was so contagious the others laughed too, caught up in the giddy moment of still being alive.

Even Iza took time out of their feud to pay her a compliment.

"I should probably say thank you for saving the day Abigail. So..thank you."

Abigail gave her a tiny smile, which bordered slightly on the smug side. "You're welcome Iza."

Both their tones were awkward and frosty, but it was progress.

"Actually I think we should thank Eli too for getting rid of that squid thing," Abigail said and turned to Eli with a curious look. "What exactly did you do to it Eli, what is your gift?"

As everyone looked to Eli expectantly, Milo realised that he had been the only one who had seen it.

Eli exchanged a look with Iza before glancing awkwardly at Milo.

So they knew that he had seen.

"Er, I'll tell you later," Eli avoided their eyes. "It's hardly worth talking about right now."

Milo thought that the others would understand. Eli was hardly like the Terramangs. But he wasn't about to say anything if Eli didn't want to discuss it.

"Right now we need to concentrate on those!" Eli pointed to the cluster of caves that Milo had seen when Abigail had been saving them from falling to their deaths. "Are these the caves you saw in your vision Vylett?"

Until now Milo had been too preoccupied to notice them. Now though as he stared at the strange cluster of caves he felt his previously good mood sink somewhere into his toes.

This place was no where near as enchanting as the black river.

There was nothing to see for miles along the banks of the ravine except an ominous assortment of caves.

There were hundreds of them.

All different shapes and sizes.

Some were piled on top of each other and some appeared to lead underground.

There was the same creepiness to them that Milo had felt from the woods near the black river and the sheer number of them made his head hurt.

"I think they must be," Vylett said quietly.

She rubbed sub-consciously at the brand on her shoulder and Milo put an arm around her.

"Come on then let's go and have a look. We can't be far from your mother now. You said that in your vision there was an elevator we had to find too. Well.. perhaps the elevator is somewhere inside one of these."

He scanned the enormous collection of caves and wondered how long they would have to search. He also wondered why the hell an elevator would be needed in this sort of place but he kept his mouth shut for now.

Abigail seemed less enthusiastic about going in the caves. "Well if we're searching caves you're all going to have to take turns carrying me," she said.

"Excuse me?" Iza made one of her snorting noises.

"Well I only have one shoe thanks to Milo," Abigail gave him a pointed look.

Milo had forgotten about Abigail's shoe and felt himself grow red. He had this powerful gift to move things and yet there he had been, whacking the squid with a girl's shoe, which was now somewhere deep under the black water with the squid.

"I've not had a lot of practice moving stuff with my mind you know," he tried to justify. "I couldn't exactly practice back home where it was illegal and I didn't want to risk blasting that thing away without knowing what would happen. It could have squashed you or...."

Abigail who had been sat on the grass, wearily stood up and threw off her remaining shoe.

"It's fine Milo. It's not going to kill me walking barefoot. But if it gets painful then I expect you to be the first to offer to carry me."

Milo mumbled something in assent and then Eli took charge again and led them to the nearest cluster of caves.

"What exactly are we looking for?" said Iza as they entered the first cave which was cold, bare and uneventful.

"Well in my vision there was a cave which was nicely decorated as though someone lived there and also there was an elevator which I assume we need to take or else just look for someone who might be able to help," said Vylett. "Although I don't think there is anyone nearby because I can't feel any other emotions except all of ours."

As they randomly searched the caves, Milo noticed that they were all freezing inside, even though the outside air was stiflingly warm.

The icy cold temperature of the caves made him feel as though he were being watched.

"It could take days to search these," complained Abigail after they had again found nothing in what must have been about the twentieth cave they had searched. So far all the caves they had been in had been cold, bare and had nothing in them that remotely resembled an elevator.

Milo knew Abigail was right. There had to be a quicker way.

"Do you sense anyone yet Vylett?"

Vylett shook her head. "No. But I am sensing Iza's brain ticking away furiously right now. What are you thinking Iza?"

Iza exited the cave they were in and stared at the masses of caves around them, determination etched into her sharp features.

"All of these caves have all been the same so far right? They're all dark and freezing and creepy. But Vylett said that the cave she saw in her vision was all lovely and beautiful. Well... I reckon I could leap all over these caves in no time and hopefully be able to spot something."

She paused thoughtfully. "Unless the cave's underground and then we're stuffed."

"I suppose that might work," said Eli slowly. "But ..I don't know Iza...I don't like the idea of you going off by yourself."

"Relax bro, I'll come straight back."

"But what if the cave is miles from here?" said Abigail wearily. "How do the rest of us get there? I don't fancy cave climbing in bare feet."

Iza rolled her eyes at her. "And you accuse me of whining. Abigail use your brain would you! That's where you come in. You can levitate us."

"Oh I'm glad you have such confidence in me," Abigail slumped down onto a boulder outside the cave. "Because I don't. I don't think I can levitate you all again. I'm too tired still."

"Well you'd best get some rest then Abigail because there's no such thing as can't."

And then before Eli could change her mind, Iza kissed him on the cheek, waved at the others and leapt fifty foot into the air. She landed on one of the higher level caves and then bounded quickly out of sight.

"God damn it Iza," Eli mumbled under his breath.

"She'll be ok," Milo assured him. But an hour later when Iza still hadn't returned, he felt less sure. He kept telling Eli that there were a lot of caves to be searched but he knew he didn't sound very convincing.

There was really nothing to do but wait.

Abigail - who rapidly appeared to be having a change of heart to Helico's charms ever since he had injured himself saving Vylett from the activity room - spent the time resting with her head on his shoulder whilst Milo and Vylett taught Eli a game using pebbles called 'Quarter Luck' that was popular on Syanna.

Although it was a relatively easy game, Eli found it difficult to grasp.

His mind was too much on Iza's absence to concentrate.

"Where is she?" he asked for the hundredth time. "I'm going to look for her." He stood up knocking aside the pebbles.

"Just give her a bit more time," said Vylett. "There really are an awful lot of caves to look through. Here have a snack." She raided his rucksack and passed him a bacon roll. Eli munched on it half heartedly all the while scanning the wide expanse of caves for his twin sister.

Milo wondered if he would have been so concerned if it was Penelope who had run off cave hunting.

He didn't think so.

He was pretty sure he would be wishing she'd taken up permanent residence inside of one of them with one of her many male admirers that she so frequently liked to toy with.

Then Milo was filled with a pang of guilt, tinged with sadness. Right now he would welcome the sight of his sister.

He gave Eli's shoulder a reassuring squeeze whilst checking for the water charm in his pocket with his other hand.

Its warmth was comforting.

Must find Alanya Roze

"Do you think they'll find us?" Helico asked absently as he wrapped a piece of Abigail's hair around his finger.

No one needed to ask who he was talking about. He meant the Terramangs.

"Yes." said Vylett. And her immediate response, her complete lack of hesitation, startled Milo. She sounded as though she had never been so sure of anything in her life.

"They might not," Abigail interjected. "This place is huge. They would have to know where to look first."

"Don't underestimate them," said Vylett. "Trust me. We know.." She exchanged a glance with Milo.

Milo agreed with her. One hundred percent. But all the same...something had been niggling him. But until now, he hadn't had a chance to talk about it.

"Before I was exiled, Lowish stuck up for me," he told them now. "I don't know why, but it made me think. Maybe not all Terramangs are evil to the core. Maybe Droges just scares most of them into doing what he wants."

Vylett shook her head adamantly. "I'm sure Droges does scare them but don't be fooled by what Lowish did Milo. You know there's no good in any of them."

She put her arm gently on Milo's. "Lowish gets as much satisfaction from branding people as Droges does." She shook her head again. "No. If Lowish stuck up for you then there must have been an ulterior motive. He must have been thinking there was something in it for him."

Milo sighed knowing she was right. But just for a second he had hoped. But he knew that if Lowish caught them now he would take them back to Droges.

No doubt about it.

"Well I just hope they don't find us yet," said Eli. "Not whilst Iza is still missing."

"She's not missing," Abigail started to say but gave up when Eli began gazing off into the distance.

"What exactly did Iza used to carry in that belt of hers anyway?" Milo asked Eli after just a moment's hesitation of thinking this might be an intrusive question.

Truthfully he just wanted to distract him, into thinking of something other than Iza's fate.

Eli shrugged. "Just stuff."

"What kind of stuff?"

Eli shrugged again. "Stuff she needed to get by."

"Like weapons." said Abigail in a dead pan voice. "Because yeah pulling knives from your belt and threatening to cut off someone's hair is really what you need to get by."

Eli ignored her sarcasm but Milo thought she had a point.

Knives were not something normal kids usually carried around.

Well not on the Water Quarter anyway.

"Iza really needed weapons to get by?" Vylett's face mirrored Milo's own disbelief.

Eli laughed at her expression but it was lacking in warmth. "Our parents couldn't afford to send us to a good school," he said looking sombre. "We lived in a place called Tyarett City and you could say it wasn't exactly high up on the sophistication scale."

"The kids we associated with at our 'not so good school'" he air quoted these last words. "Well they weren't exactly nice kids. The teachers couldn't seem to keep them in line. They used magic whenever they wanted. They tried to compete with each other."

Eli sighed. "They were locked in some kind of power struggle. Me and Iza refused to be a part of it and so generally the rest of the kids hated us. That's why Iza had the belt, to protect herself."

"But using weapons against other kids seems a bit extreme," Abigail said.

Eli gave her a sharp look. "We had to be extreme Abigail. Our parents were next to useless. Hardly ever around. We had to look after ourselves."

"Besides," Eli shrugged. "Iza never actually used them. But she had them just in case. And there weren't just weapons in her belt," he added. He glanced away, looking awkward and began to grate a couple of stones together from their game.

"There were pills," he said quietly.

No one said anything.

Eli looked up at them a little sheepishly. "You know...pills to get her through the day."

"Oh great! So Iza is going to be even more unhinged now without her sanity medication," Abigail said bluntly.

"Abs you could sound a bit more sympathetic," Helico frowned at her.

"I'm sorry Helico, but I never grew up with parents either. My parents died when I was young and I was pretty much brought up by my gran. My life was tough sometimes too but I didn't need weapons. I didn't need pills.."

There was an awkward silence and Milo felt like telling her to grow some sensitivity. Although he was starting to think that

Abigail was actually ok, at times like this he wanted to tell her to shut her mouth.

Eli gave her a hard look. "Well some people do Abigail."

Milo nodded. He thought he understood Iza a little more now.

Another half hour passed and then another during which time Eli grew more and more agitated.

"Iza will be fine," Abigail told him. "We have my good luck doll remember," Abigail patted the waist band of her trousers where a rather wet and bedraggled Victoria Sparkle still sat snugly.

"She's brought us luck already by getting us this far. So don't worry Eli."

It wasn't exactly an apology for being insensitive about Iza but Eli nodded in appreciation, realising that from Abigail this was probably as close to an apology as he was ever going to get.

Vylett who had been fiddling with one of the stones chewed on her bottom lip. "Look don't get mad alright Abigail but I really do think we should be concerned about my vision of Victoria Sparkle. It looked like someone got hurt and as you're the one with the doll...then..." She let her words trail off as Abigail gave her an exasperated look.

"Perhaps your vision was just a warning for me to watch my step. So don't worry Vylett, I'll watch my step." Abigail clearly refused to be unperturbed.

"Ok but I know it meant something. That's all I'm saying. It worried me and maybe we should consider what it means."

Abigail took all of five seconds to consider it before she arrived at her conclusion. "Well we've just fallen down a waterfall," she said slowly. "Perhaps that was what you saw. And now we're all fine, thanks to me. So no need to worry, mystery solved," then she flashed Vylett a pointed look.

"I'm not leaving her behind Vylett."

"No of course not." Vylett exchanged a look with Milo but neither of them said anything.

Abigail was in a relatively good mood and it was better to keep it that way.

A moment later Eli jumped to his feet. "That's it! I can't bear it any longer. I'm going to look for her. It's getting dark. Something's wrong. I know Iza, she wouldn't leave me worrying like this. Something must have happened."

He turned to the rest of them. "You lot stay here in case she comes back."

"No way we're all this together. We're coming with you," said Helico. "We're not losing you too."

"Yeah besides my bum is going numb sat here," Abigail got up from the boulder she was sitting on and then stopped.

"What's this?" She crouched down, examining the far side of the boulder which was adjacent to a cluster of other rocks and gasped. "It's a woman's face."

"Let me see," Milo crouched down next to her and felt his heart quicken. "That's the same face that was carved into that orange rock where we entered the black river. Do you remember?"

"I wonder who she is?" said Helico peering over his shoulder.

"I don't know but let's hope we don't meet her," said Abigail, screwing up her face as she warily studied the strange orange faced rock. "She looks weird. She's orange!"

"I don't care if she's green and has blue spots. Maybe she's the key to finding my mother," there was clear excitement in Vylett's voice.

Milo was less excited.

There was something about the weird orange rock face that screamed only power and uncertainty.

"Look at this..." Helico pointed to an engraving in tiny writing on the top of the boulder.

It said, "please enter"

"Help me move this," Helico said after trying to push the boulder and finding it wouldn't budge.

"Here let me," said Milo. "These are the only times I feel useful." He focused his magic and willed the rock to move.

It toppled over easily.

In its place was a hole the size of the boulder but as they watched, it expanded to double its size, so that the group found themselves staring down into a large pit with a spiral staircase leading down into it.

"We can't go down there. Not without Iza," said Eli. Up until now, Eli had not contributed a word about their discovery.

Milo looked at him and saw true fear in the other boy's perfectly chiselled face.

He felt sorry for him.

"Of course not. We'll wait for Iza," he said.

And then the most beautiful voice that Milo had ever heard echoed from within the pit.

It ascended up the spiral staircase, melodious and sweet.

'You have twenty seconds to enter, then the way shall be closed to you.'

"What should we do?" Abigail turned to them frantically. "I think this must lead to the cave in Vylett's vision. I really do. This could be our only chance."

She was right.

Milo somehow knew that the voice was right too. Once that entrance closed it wouldn't re-open for them.

It was now or never.

According to Vylett's vision, they had to find a cave in order to find an elevator. He had a feeling that this was the cave they were supposed to enter. But Iza was still missing...

"We need to find our friend first," Milo found himself shouting down into the pit.

The lovely voice answered him instantly.

'What you seek is inside…twelve seconds left..'

"Did you hear that Eli? Iza must be inside," said Abigail.

Eli didn't look convinced, "I don't know…"

"She could mean my mother," Vylett reasoned. "We seek her too."

'Eight seconds'

"God!" Eli put his hands to his head then he shouted into the pit. "Is Iza inside?"

'What you seek is inside' the voice repeated. '5 seconds'

Everyone looked to Eli.

Milo guessed this was probably the hardest decision the boy had ever had to make.

Eli didn't answer but Vylett put a foot onto the spiral staircase. "Good lets go. Quick! she said.

As they scrambled clumsily onto the stairway, Eli said, "I didn't say yes."

"You didn't have to," said Vylett. "I sensed it. Sorry Eli, there wasn't time to spare."

"No worries," Eli mumbled.

As the hole above them closed with a loud grating noise, Milo couldn't help but think this was going to be worse than the black river.

Chapter 10

The Memory Ball

They were only in darkness for a few seconds before the staircase lit up with a thousand sparkling lights and started slowly to revolve taking them downwards into the surrounding dark pit.

As Milo gripped the handrail which was dotted with the small twinkling lights, he noticed that the previously concrete steps he had been standing on were now a shiny cream marble.

Now instead of worrying about what awaited them at the bottom of the staircase, he couldn't help but worry instead about leaving dirty shoe prints on the polished marble.

It was a bizarre thing to suddenly worry about and he wondered where it had come from.

"We're near the bottom. Look!" said Vylett.

There was nothing more frightening than being propelled into a darkened pit with who knew what at the bottom of it. So when Milo looked down and saw a large cave lit with chandeliers and whose walls glittered with silver pearls and pretty tapestries and not dark, gooey slime, he immediately relaxed.

"This is it," Vylett murmured. "This is the cave I saw in my image. We're on the right track. We're close to my mother."

As the luxurious looking cave came closer into view, Milo wished that the spiral staircase would turn faster.

The cave was so comforting somehow.

It made him wonder why he had ever been worried.

Then he heard Vylett's deep intake of breath and turned to see a woman whose face Milo recognised from the boulder.

Her rock statue did not do her justice.

She was breathtakingly beautiful.

Yes her face was orange, and the black twisted strands of her hair vaguely resembled the tails of sea creatures from the Water Quarter.

But those aside.. she was graceful and not in the least bit threatening.

Her eyes were a pearly silver colour like the pearls that decorated the cave walls and her flawless orange skin shimmered.

She oozed elegance and kindness that flowed into Milo's every pore.

She stood staring at them, a small smile played on her crimson lips.

When she spoke it was in that same beautiful melodious voice that they had heard when they entered the spiral staircase.

"Welcome," she said. Milo almost forgot the others were with him because it seemed to him that her welcome was for just him alone.

That is until Vylett nudged him uncharacteristically hard.

"Ouch! What the.."

"She's not human Milo," Vylett said as though this should make some difference. She was glaring at him and looked almost angry.

It seemed Abigail was also angry because Milo heard her tell Helico to 'close his mouth before his jaw dropped off.'

Milo turned back to stare at the beautiful woman.

He didn't think he ever wanted to stop looking at her.

Then the staircase jolted forward and they were thrust into the elegant cave which suddenly expanded to at least three times its size as soon as they stepped onto the lush cream carpeted floor.

"Please feel at home children. I am Audrina," the lady said to them.

ZOË TYSON

She walked up to Milo and he froze as she pressed her cheek against his. He could smell the sweet intoxicating smell of her perfume but he wasn't sure how this was possible when he was pretty sure he wasn't breathing right now.

Then Audrina did a weird thing.

She kind of rolled her cheek against his and then she stepped back.

Milo touched his cheek, feeling strangely elated.

Next to him Vylett recoiled as Audrina tried to do the same thing to her. Don't!" she said coldly.

"And don't touch me either you weirdo," Abigail said when Audrina approached her next.

"I mean no offense," said Audrina. "This is just our way of greeting."

"Well we don't want it," said Abigail.

"Hey speak for yourself Abs," said Helico not taking his eyes off Audrina. "I want one of those cheek roll things."

There was a slapping noise as Abigail's hand found Helico's cheek. "How's that for a cheek roll." Abigail's eyes were so wide she looked seriously deranged.

"I think I need to give you a different welcome," said Audrina with just the slightest frown on her face.

She clicked her fingers and the spiral staircase disappeared leaving a marble fountain surrounded by hundreds of twinkling lights in its place.

From the marble fountain sprang fragrant orange water.

Audrina smiled at them. "Would you care for a drink? I can assure you it tastes much nicer than the black water."

"Yeah that would be great," Milo moved towards the fountain but Helico and Eli got there first, each scrambling to put their mouths in the water.

"There's enough for everyone," Audrina laughed and the lights on the fountain twinkled in harmony with her voice.

The boys stopped fighting for a second so they could listen to her.

"Don't drink that," said Vylett as Milo went to dip his head under the fountain.

"Why what's wrong with it? What's wrong with you?" He felt irritated. Why was Vylett being so weird about Audrina?

"What's wrong with you?" Vylett shot back. "And you two?" she looked at Eli and Helico. "Eli don't you want to know where Iza is?"

"Iza….?" Eli murmured and he blinked a few times, remembering his sister. "Yeah I..of course..I.." and then he forgot what he was saying because Audrina spoke again.

"Oh the water won't kill you," she said. "I want my guests to come back again."

"Who are you?" Abigail asked rudely.

The orange lady who Milo was quickly coming to think of as the orange princess, laughed.

Oh that sweet melodious laugh.

"I told you. I am Audrina." She produced some glasses out of thin air and began filling them with the orange water from the fountain.

"You must be thirsty. The black river is not very thirst quenching from what I hear."

But Abigail just glared at her, looking as though she wanted to slap her across the face too.

"How do you know we came from the black river?"

Milo had no idea what was wrong with the girls. Audrina seemed perfectly nice and the water hadn't appeared to poison him.

In fact it had tasted delicious.

Although he couldn't have described it because he had never tasted anything like it.

Audrina however didn't seem offended by Vylett and Abigail's rudeness. She held out a glass to Abigail.

"Once someone comes into my caves I know everything about them." She held out another glass to Vylett. "Please drink Miss Vylett Roze from Syanna who can read emotions."

Vylett's jaw dropped open but Milo, Helico and Eli applauded enthusiastically.

"Impressive!" said Helico. "Hey Vylett, can you read Audrina's emotions?"

"No Helico. She's not human." Vylett's voice was a grimace and she didn't take her eyes off Audrina.

"Ok here's what's going to happen," said Audrina in an authoritative voice. "It's clear that the boys need some alone time and the girl's need some shopping time."

At the word shopping, Audrina immediately had the girls' attention.

"Shopping? Here in the caves?" Abigail sounded dubious but her tone was less frosty,

Audrina laughed her sparkly laugh. "Everything you need is here Abigail Bookman. Including shoes and coffee."

"I love shoes and coffee." Abigail's eyes lit up. "How did you know that? Can you take us now?"

And just like that Audrina was now her best friend.

Without giving the boys a backward glance, Vylett and Abigail started to follow Audrina out of the luxurious cave and into a narrow corridor that had appeared and was lit by more twinkling lights.

"What about us Audrina? What do we do with our alone time?" Milo knew he sounded petulant but he didn't want Audrina to leave.

Audrina looked back at him over her shoulder and smiled that ever so sweet smile that was only for him. "I have provided you a feast my dears."

Milo glanced back at the cave but there was no food.

Still, he trusted Audrina.

If she said she would provide a feast, she would provide a feast.

"I need to find my sister," Eli said. His voice sounded unsure.

Something like guilt stirred in Milo. "Yes," he said. "Perhaps we should eat later. We should find Iza."

"Everything you need is here," Audrina smiled at them. "I am holding a memory ball tonight. After you have eaten I will take you there. All of you. Iza will be there."

At this Eli relaxed and Audrina led Vylett and Abigail down the narrow twinkling corridor.

As soon as she was gone, the corridor sealed itself and the boys were left alone in the tapestry filled cave.

As Milo saw Vylett disappear, his senses appeared to awaken and he panicked for about two seconds until a huge display of food appeared before them.

It was more than a feast.

It was a banquet.

For the time being, tasting this delicious looking food was all that mattered.

Thoughts of Vylett and Iza disappeared from his mind as he took a large slice of luminescent orange cake.

***

Vylett had never had so much fun.

Audrina was turning out to be the perfect hostess.

The twinkling narrow corridor she had led them down contained hundreds of shops. It seemed that whatever clothing she fancied she found it.

She had never been a huge fan of clothes shopping before. There were only a few shops in Syanna that had decent clothes and she very rarely had any inclination to go to Parish Plaza where Milo's sister Penelope and loads of other girls liked to go.

But Abigail did love shopping. She told Vylett she was an expert on fashion and in no time at all she had Vylett kitted out in a lovely turquoise dress that matched her eyes. It had little pockets just below the hips that were lined with silver beading and a silver bejewelled belt that tied in a loose knot around her waist.

Abigail said it would be perfect for the memory ball.

Abigail herself found a sleek black dress with emerald green embroidery down the front which complimented her red hair. She had found some shoes, much to her delight, so she didn't have to walk around barefoot any more and she had also insisted on having a clutch bag so that she could still carry Victoria Sparkle.

She settled on a sequinned green satin bag to complete the look.

After buying several more outfits and little knick knacks, Vylett decided her pigtails were too childish for her new turquoise dress.

"I think a need a more elegant look for the memory ball tonight," she told Audrina.

"Then so be it Vylett," Audrina waved her hand and the next outlet they came to was a hair salon where an eccentric man with spiky black hair and an orange face like Audrina's was ready to greet them.

For at least an hour Vylett was completely pampered as the friendly man coloured her nails, applied make up to her face - for the first time in her life - and arranged her hair into elegant loose curls.

She felt like a princess.

They'd even been allowed the luxury of showering and washing their hair.

"Thank you Audrina," Vylett gushed as she admired her new look in the brightly lit mirrors of the salon.

Her stylist and Abigail showered her with compliments and Vylett felt lightheaded by the time they entered a quaint café where several orange coloured waitresses were waiting to serve them.

Whilst Abigail drank mugfuls of coffee and Vylett drank too much juice, Audrina talked with the waitresses about her memory ball.

"I wonder what it's in memory of," Vylett whispered to Abigail as she sipped her fifth glass of juice.

"Well why don't we go see," said Audrina, appearing by her side. "It's already started. Most of my guests will have arrived by now.'

"Which is not good," she added distantly. Her beautiful face clouded over. "A good hostess should never be late for her own party. Come children."

They followed Audrina out of the café and where as before there had been an endless corridor of shops, there was now a single black marble door.

Abigail's new shoes clinked loudly on the smooth stone floor as they followed Audrina to the door.

Vylett quickly smoothed down her dress. She had never been to a ball before and she felt excited.

Abigail giggled with nervous anticipation and grabbed her hand.

They were still giggling like silly children when Audrina opened the black marble door.

...And that's when they stopped giggling.

Abigail gasped and dropped Vylett's hand and rushed through the marble door.

Vylett could only stand in awe. Her legs felt rooted to the spot.

This was one ball she would definitely remember.

But she wasn't looking at the mass of chandeliers that hung from the ceiling in a thousand different colours.

She wasn't looking at the elegance of the huge ballroom with its large marble pillars and silver and orange decorated tables.

She wasn't even looking at the huge tiered cake that was at least twenty foot tall and each tier a different colour to match the chandeliers.

She was looking at the woman who was standing before her, ready to greet her. The woman from her visions who had been absent from her life for far too long.

She was looking at her mother.

***

It seemed to Milo that only two minutes had passed before Audrina came back to take himself, Helico and Eli to the memory ball.

He knew though by the lack of food left on the banquet table and the fullness of his belly that it had been much longer than that.

As Audrina led them through some impressive black marble doors, Milo felt an apprehensive excitement.

He had never been to a ball before.

How was he supposed to act? He hardly felt dressed for it in his navy Orlost uniform.

He kept his eyes on Audrina as they entered the ballroom, looking for her assurance and found himself, as always, entranced by her presence.

It wasn't until Eli shouted 'Iza!' that he forced himself to take his eyes off the orange princess.

Eli was running through a crowd of people that were stood near a giant multi-coloured cake.

The rest of the room was no less impressive however, with its chandeliers and lavish table decorations. A few orange waitresses were walking around with platters of food. There was a quirky song playing which Milo didn't recognise and the room was buzzing with conversation and laughter.

Everyone looked happy.

Milo noticed that lots of people were hugging and kissing and he wondered if this was a reunion party.

Maybe that's what Audrina meant by a memory ball.

Perhaps it was to reminisce with those who you hadn't seen for a long time.

Milo saw Eli disappear behind a large orange drinking fountain and was about to follow him when he felt someone tugging on his arm. He looked down to see a small girl of about six years of age staring up at him. Milo felt sure he didn't know the girl but he was getting a strange sense of de ja vu.

"Where's mummy?" asked the girl. She had dark hair and pretty eyes but her mouth was set in a sullen sneer and angry tears were pooling in her brown eyes.

"Where's mummy?" the girl repeated.

"I er..I don't know," said Milo feeling helpless and looking around for Audrina who seemed to have disappeared.

"Grrrr," the girl stubbornly stamped her foot and put her hands on her hips. "I've lost her. You need to find her."

The girl was irritating and clearly spoilt but somehow Milo felt compelled to help her. He glanced around for Audrina but he couldn't see her.

The ballroom was crowded, she could be anywhere.

Sighing he turned back to the little girl. "Ok so where did she…".

He stopped. The girl was gone.

Well never mind, she would find her mother sooner or later.

He turned around and got the shock of his life as a man walked straight through him. He looked solid and he looked as real as Milo but he had literally walked right through him.

What just happened?

Milo shivered as he realised it must have been a ghost. It wasn't that he was unaccustomed to seeing ghosts.

Quite the opposite.

They often popped up around Syanna. But the difference was they didn't look solid.

They were always hazy and transparent.

Feeling a hand on his arm, Milo turned around, expecting to see the little girl again and then froze. His breath caught in his throat.

Standing before him, looking as stroppy as ever was….

Penelope.

"Penelope! What….what are you doing here?" he said stupidly. And then his heart raced as he thought of the ghost that had just walked through him.

Tentatively, he reached out a finger to touch her. Relief flooded through him. She was solid.

She was alive.

Penelope smiled crookedly and then laughed. "Hey Milo! You look like you've just seen a ghost."

"I have. I had.." Milo swallowed. "For a second I thought you were dead. I can't believe you're here. What happened? Where you exiled? How did you find this place? Did you have a psychic vision?" His words came tumbling out, question after question.

"I'm not dead Milo," Penelope scoffed. "Although you smell like you are. You smell strange."

"What?" Milo absently sniffed at his uniform. It smelled of the black river.

Salty and stale.

Penelope was frequently telling him that he smelled strange but after the emotional trauma of his exile and the very public scene she had made, this was not one of the first things he had expected his sister to say to him at their reunion.

He ran a hand through his tussled hair. "Never mind about how I smell. What happened to you? How did you end up here?"

Penelope looked at him blankly and then she slowly rolled her eyes at him in typical Penelope fashion. But she said nothing.

"Penelope what happened?" Milo repeated. "Vylett said that Alanya showed her an elevator in a vision and we have to take that elevator to find her...have you had any more visions of Alanya?"

Penelope gave him a vacant look like she was struggling to remember and then slowly in an almost robotic fashion, she turned her head.

Milo followed her direction and saw two women engaged in conversation. One had another worldly beauty about her.

She was slim, with flowing blonde hair that reached her waist and she wore a long white dress made of layers of a floaty thin fabric that shimmered.

Her skin was pale and creamy and she had the kindest blue eyes that Milo had ever seen. They sparkled with joy as she engaged in deep conversation with a younger girl dressed in pale blue who was also pretty but more petite. She also had blonde hair and...Milo did a double take.

The girl was Vylett!

Had it not been for those unmistakable blue eyes he wouldn't have recognised her.

The dress, the new hair, the make up! She looked so different.

Gone were the girly colourful pigtails and the child like persona, and in her place was a young lady with a developing beauty.

Milo found he couldn't speak.

"What are you looking at? Such a loser," Penelope mumbled.

"Er…what? I can't believe that's Vylett..she looks…"

"Stupid?" Penelope offered.

Milo frowned at her and then looked again at the woman Vylett was talking too. She looked very much like Vylett.

"Penelope is that Alanya?" Milo looked at Vylett again and this time he could see tears running down her face whilst the other woman fondly stroked her hair.

"It must be," he mumbled. "But what happened to needing the elevator?"

Penelope wasn't listening to him though. "I have to go, Spencer's waiting for me."

She started to walk away but Milo grabbed her arm. "Wait! Where are you going? Spencer's not here." Spencer was Penelope's latest boyfriend. "What's with you Penelope? What the hell happened to you?"

Penelope threw her head back and laughed. "I'm going to get that fat boy for you Milo," she said and then she grabbed a hand mirror from her purse and began to examine her already flawless hair.

Milo frowned. "Walt? Yeah I know you are Pen but Walt's not here."

At least Milo fervently hoped he wasn't.

He scoured the room for Audrina. Perhaps she would know what was wrong with Penelope.

Then as Penelope smoothed down her long white satin dress Milo was hit with a moment of de ja vu.

Milo stared at her dress. Something was very wrong here.

"Hang on a minute Pen. That's the dress you wore for your prom last year. Why are you wearing that?"

Penelope rummaged through her purse ignoring him. She pulled out a gold coin and waved it in front of him.

"Look what Spencer gave me. I'm saving up coins to travel to another Quarter when I turn seventeen next year. Think I might go and visit the Fire Quarter. I hear the dragons there are amazing. What do you think?"

Milo stared at her. She was taunting him about the Fire Quarter because she knew how much he wanted to go there but she was speaking to him in an almost robotic fashion.

"You know what I think Pen. You know I can't wait to see the dragons. And you know that I'll be jealous as hell if you get to see them first. But right now I have other things to think about. Like finding Alanya Roze and giving her your water charm. So she can find a way back to the Water Quarter? And make a circle with the other multi-gifted. Remember?" Milo felt like he was talking to a small child.

Penelope gave him a crooked smile. "Aunt Dor is never wrong,"

Milo made a noise of frustration. "I think you need help Pen. Come on I'll take you to find Audrina. You'll like her. She helps everyone."

Milo turned to find Audrina, but felt an invisible force turn him back to face Penelope.

He felt a mixture of confusion.

Now he was looking at Penelope again he thought maybe he would take her to Audrina later.

Right now it was more important to have a reunion with his sister wasn't it?

Penelope laughed. "Are you looking for that skinny girl who that fat boy hangs around with? Shouldn't be allowed out with a face like that."

A memory stirred in Milo. Hadn't Penelope said something very similar to that about Walt's sidekick Peg yesterday before he was exiled?

Why did she keep sprouting stuff she had already said?

"Pen?..." Milo felt fear bubbling up in him. He started to look for Vylett. He should really go and speak to Alanya. Then Penelope grabbed his head and forcefully turned it so that he was staring in the other direction.

He gasped.

Standing right before him was his Aunt Dor.

Chapter 11

Tricks or Treats?

This couldn't be happening. It really couldn't. Yet his Aunt was here.

She was standing right before him.

Milo rushed to her and her arms wrapped around him in a big hug.

She felt solid. She felt real.

"Aunt Dor! You don't know how good it is to see you," Milo felt choked up. For now, questions and answers could wait. What did it matter if things were a little weird. He was with his family again.

Well some of them.

As if reading his mind, his mother and father appeared through a gap in the crowd. He clasped a hand over his mouth, turning to Penelope in confusion.

"How?.." words failed him. Perhaps Audrina had arranged this ball for him. Maybe it was a surprise party, the type where more and more people you know jump out and surprise you.

Normally he hated those things. But today he could make an exception.

Penelope flicked her hair back. "Oh Milo you are such a loser."

Something Penelope said nagged at Milo's brain. It was like he was missing something very obvious.

It wasn't just her disjointed conversation or the feeling of de ja vu.

It was something else.

And then as his mother wrapped her arms around him, it hit him. The obvious thing that he had been missing.

The excitement he had felt on seeing his family twisted into a tight knot that made him feel sick.

Penelope never called him Milo.

Never.

She always called him Milesey.

He could feel the room starting to spin as the realisation dawned on him. She wasn't real.

None of them were real.

Ok they were solid. They weren't ghosts. But they weren't real either.

The multi-coloured lights in the room seemed to dance before Milo's eyes so that he felt he were in the middle of a huge glitter ball that was rolling faster and faster.

Audrina's words came flooding back to him. 'I'm holding a memory ball tonight'.

Oh yes, this was a memory ball alright. It was a ball full of his memories.

That's why Penelope had been repeating things she had already said. That's why she was wearing her prom dress.

They were all memories.

Penelope was just a memory.

Ok so some of the things she had said were new but none of it was real. Penelope never called him Milo.

Audrina had messed up that part.

Milo stepped back from his family. "You're not real," he said.

When they continued to just stand and smile at him, he shouted with more emphasis, as loud as he could. "You're not real! Go away!"

He blinked as they evaporated before his eyes. Disappearing into little puffs of mist.

Panic engulfed him.

No, he didn't mean it. He wasn't ready to let them go.

"No! I don't care if you're just memories!" he screamed. "Come back." He was so worked up, he barely registered the tingling sensations shoot down his arms.

Before he could stop his magic, the top of the giant multi-coloured cake which was in his line of vision, exploded. There was a moment in which there was an impressive display of cake coloured fireworks and then the rest of the cake wobbled precariously before toppling over and creating a huge mound of cream and messy goo.

None of the guests batted an eyelid.

He thought he heard a wail. Possibly from Audrina. He was about to go find her but then immediately that thought lost him because Penelope, Aunt Dor and his parents had reappeared in front of him.

He found he was shaking with relief. They laughed and hugged him and kissed him.

Except Penelope of course who continued to flick back her hair and call him a loser.

"Come on," he said. "Let's eat that ruined cake." He started to lead them towards the multi-coloured cake mountain when a voice sounded in his head.

"Be strong. Syanna needs you."

Milo didn't recognise the voice but he paused. The Water Quarter was still in trouble. The real Penelope was still in trouble.

Aunt Dor laughed and tugged on his arm. "It's so good to see you Milo."

Her eyes twinkled and her silver hair bun swayed. A lump formed in Milo's throat. He didn't want to say goodbye. What if it was too late for the Water Quarter?

What if his family were already dead?

What if this was his only chance to keep seeing them? Memories were better than nothing weren't they?

"Milo! Be strong!" The voice sounded more persistent in Milo's head and then his surroundings changed as images of Syanna flashed before him.

He was viewing them as though through a misty window and Syanna as he knew it was in chaos.

Buildings were sinking.

People were screaming as they tried to salvage what was left of their belongings.

He saw his classmates bobbing up and down in the water and Milo glimpsed a sense of what they were feeling.

The water's magic had intensified so much that the people in the water were terrified of the feeling it gave them.

Some looked crazed.

The residents of the Water Quarter were consuming so much magic that sooner or later they would not be functional. They would be crazed animals, driven insane.

They would kill each other.

As if confirming his thoughts, images appeared of people that Milo knew, floating lifeless in the water. A timid girl from his class called Lianna Payne. A small boy called Luce who Milo didn't know very well and then his teacher, Miss Dianda floated by.

She was face down but there was no mistaking that wavy honey coloured hair and the plum coloured suit she always wore.

Milo was struggling to breathe.

"Stop it!" he cried. He shut his eyes but the images were still there. Then the image changed and Milo saw his mother.

She was by herself, huddled in a room in the upstairs of their house, clinging on to some possessions whilst she watched the lower level sink. Just as Milo was wondering where his father was, the image flashed to the Fire Quarter.

He knew it was the Fire Quarter because he could see a volcano and a few dragons outside of the window of the boardroom that his father and Aunt Dor were in.

They were sat at a table with Aubreus Roze, Vylett's father. All three of them were staring at nothing.

With a start Milo realised that they were becoming vacants.

The Fire Quarter's magic was dwindling away.

For some reason his father and Aunt Dor were visiting the Fire Quarter and now they were becoming shell.

Just when Milo thought he couldn't take any more, the images stopped. And he was staring at the memories of his family again, back in Audrina's ballroom.

He was short of breath and his face felt wet.

He must have been crying.

He cursed the voice in his head for showing him those images but he knew now what he had to do.

He stared at Penelope, Aunt Dor and his parents and took a deep breath.

"Go away you're not real," he shouted.

Penelope disappeared in a puff of mist, followed by Aunt Dor and his parents.

Milo felt a great sense of loss in his gut like never before but he forced himself to inspect the rest of the ballroom. He felt a pressure to look away from it but he resisted it.

He had seen the truth just now and that was more powerful than Audrina's stunts.

He saw Audrina walking towards him from the far corner of the room and he paused, feeling himself weaken as she smiled that irresistible smile that made him feel was just for him.

Then Vylett's laugh distracted him and Milo forced himself to concentrate on his friend.

She was holding hands with Alanya and they were giggling and dancing.

"Vylett!" Milo called to her and began to run towards them. He stopped as a little girl stood in front of him.

It was the little lost girl.

She scowled at him, screwing up those pretty features and Milo shook his head in disbelief. He couldn't believe he hadn't realised it before.

It was Penelope. As a little girl.

They had once played a game of hide and seek and Milo had convinced Penelope that their mother had disappeared completely.

At the time, Milo had been overjoyed to see Penelope on the receiving end of a joke for once.

He looked at the young Penelope remembering their childhood. He swallowed the lump in his throat.

"Go away," he told her. "You're not real." She scowled and disappeared in a puff of mist.

Milo ploughed on and reached Vylett just as Alanya spun her around out of his reach.

"Vylett, that's not your mother," Milo reached out to grab her but Alanya waltzed her out of reach from his grasp.

Vylett laughed and continued to twirl around in Alanya's embrace. Milo didn't even know if Vylett had acknowledged his presence.

"Vylett, she's just a memory. Don't you see it? You need to listen to me."

He reached for her again but Alanya whirled her around, blocking him.

"Stop doing that!" he angrily tried to brush Alanya aside but his hand went straight through her.

Shocked, he pulled his hand back.

He heard an amused giggle and turned to find Audrina standing next to him.

"You can't touch her Milo. She's not your memory to touch." Audrina's voice was still syrupy sweet but Milo could have sworn that her eyes had taken on an orange tint that matched her skin.

Milo processed what she had just said. So the man who had walked through him earlier...the man who he had thought was a ghost...he hadn't been a ghost.

He had been someone's memory.

Milo looked at Audrina as if seeing her properly for the first time. And took a step back from her.

"Don't be silly Milo. You don't need to be afraid of me. But you do need to relax and enjoy my ball. Were you not happy to see your family? That's what you wanted wasn't it?"

"But they're not real," he said. "You're twisted. I want to leave. Now. And I'm taking my friends with me."

Audrina's eyes hardened and the orange tint in them darkened. "Then leave. I can't stop you. The exit's over there."

The exit door which Audrina pointed out looked oddly out of place in the glamour of the ballroom.

"What! Just like that?" Milo said suspiciously. "I don't believe you. I don't believe you want us to leave."

"You're right, I don't."

"But you'd just let us walk out that door anyway. Why?"

Audrina smiled and for the first time Milo saw another façade behind that perfect smile.

Sadness.

"I can't physically stop you. Unfortunately. You're the one who has the physical power Miloney Merren," Audrina looked at him wistfully.

"So you re-created our memories instead to try and get us to stay," Milo said slowly as he struggled to understand Audrina's mind.

Audrina shrugged. "It's a lonely life in these caves. Besides, no one else has ever complained before," she gestured around at the crowds of people.

"Are these people all of your prisoners?!" Milo was both fascinated and sickened at the same time.

"I told you. They can leave if they want to," Audrina stared at him, her eyes glowing more orange by the second.

Milo stared back at her, forcing himself to meet those silvery pearl eyes and not be swayed by them.

"Very clever trick you play Audrina. But playtime is over. Me and my friends are leaving."

He turned back to Vylett but Alanya had whisked her off somewhere into the crowd. He took a step forward to look for her and stopped as his teacher Miss Dianda appeared before him.

Milo swallowed and tried not to think of the image he had just seen of her floating dead in the water back on Syanna.

With more confidence than he felt, he turned to face Audrina. "Now you're just desperate. I never liked school."

And then he sped off into the crowds.

A massive wailing noise filled the ballroom. Now Audrina was really angry.

Milo kept running.

Now and again he ran through peoples' memories which was a strange experience and something he never wanted to get used to.

He saw Abigail first.

She was holding hands with a man and a woman whom he presumed where her parents judging by their fiery copper coloured hair.

"Abigail!" Milo shouted at her and to his surprise she actually turned to him. Her eyes were bright and shiny.

"Oh Milo! These are my parents," she gushed. "They died when I was little but they're here now. Can you believe it?"

'No,' Milo thought miserably, he couldn't believe it. He felt like he was in the middle of some horrible nightmare from which he would never wake from. How could he possibly coax Abigail away from her dead parents?

Somewhere in the distance he heard Helico's unmistakable laugh.

He ran towards the sound and found Helico lifting a young girl of about seven or eight years of age above his shoulders. The girl giggled and cried "higher, higher Helico."

"Helico, Abigail needs you!" It was the only thing Milo could think of to say that might get Helico's attention.

It worked.

Helico turned to him and his grin faltered for a second. "Abs?... Where is she?"

And then the girl on Helico's shoulders pulled his hair to get his attention and Milo lost him again.

Damn!

"She's not real Helico. Please listen to me. Audrina's tricked us. This is all a cruel trick. That girl is just a memory. Look…"

Milo thrust his hand through the memory of the little girl.

Confusion flashed across Helico's face but then he grinned. "Good trick Milo," and then he pointed up to the girl on his shoulders. "Say Hi to my little sister. Her name's Neira,"

"You must be strong," the voice inside Milo's head urged.

There was only one way in which Milo ever felt strong - and that was when he was using his gift.

Hoping Helico would forgive him, Milo drew on his magic and directed it at Helico.

Helico flew across the room with more force than Milo had intended and smacked hard into the exit door.

Still.. it was the location Milo had intended and the knock Helico had taken had seemed to shaken him to his senses. Helico shook his head and glanced around him in confusion.

Milo was beside him in an instant. "Helico listen to me. Audrina has tricked us. She is using our memories to keep us here. We have to leave now. Don't look at this room. Keep your eyes shut or on the door whilst I go and get the others. Promise me you'll stay here."

Helico nodded, rubbing his shoulder and looking shell shocked.

Then Milo took off, racing through the crowd to find the others.

***

Each passing second seemed to last at least a minute.

Eventually after a few agonising moments, Milo heard a wail coming from Audrina. He followed the sound and a few seconds later he found Abigail pale faced and teary eyed.

Her parents had vanished.

"What the hell is happening Milo?"

"It's ok," he told her. "Go to the exit door and wait for me. Helico is already there."

Abigail nodded. She gave Audrina a hateful stare and went dutifully to the exit door.

"The game's over," Milo said to Audrina. And then forcing himself to look away from the orange princess he ran away into the crowd.

When he found Vyett she was still dancing with Alanya. She had not been as strong as Abigail in facing the truth.

Feeling both guilty and cruel, Milo drew on his magic and Vylett flew across the room.

She passed through peoples' memories until she landed in an ungainly heap by the exit door where Helico broke her fall. "Sorry Helico," Milo mumbled.

If they ever did find the real Alanya Roze, Milo was going to ask her to teach him how to use his magic properly.

He glanced restlessly round the ballroom. Now for Eli and Iza.

There was another wail from Audrina and Milo found her near Eli. Milo flinched when he saw her. Audrina's eyes had changed from pearly silver to fiery red.

She no longer looked beautiful, just frightening.

Next to Eli was....Iza?

"Iza is that you?" Milo went to touch her but his hand went straight through her.

His heart sank. She was just a memory. Iza wasn't here after all.

Audrina had lied.

"Eli that's not Iza! Come on we need to get out of here."

Eli looked dazed as he let Milo drag him through the crowd and to the exit door. To Milo's relief the others were still waiting for him.

He pulled the door knob to the exit door and was knocked roughly aside as Audrina tried to block him.

Milo shoved the orange princess with all his might but her body felt as solid as stone. He focused his magic and tried to blast her.

But just as he'd thought, she didn't even flinch.

"You can't stop us," he told her. "You know you can't."

"I need friends. Is that so bad?" said Audrina. She sounded whiney, like a child.

"You need sectioning," said Abigail.

Abigail had her eyes closed, blocking out any more memories that might appear but Audrina blew gently in her face and Abigail opened them looking startled. "Hey!" she protested.

"I really could be your friend if you'll let me," Audrina smiled at her.

"If you want friends so much then why don't you just leave this place and find some," said Vylett.

Audrina's beautiful face contorted in rage. "Don't you think I would if I could. But I was born here, so here I must stay."

Audrina gave a humourless laugh. "Do you know that I have the luxury of living forever but if I leave my caves I will die. I'll never get to see what is beyond this World. Can you imagine what it feels like to be confined to one place forever?"

Despite what she had done, Milo found himself actually feeling a little sorry for Audrina.

But only little bit.

Not enough to stay.

"We're leaving now," he said.

"I warn you, you do not want to be on the other side of this door. Once you go through that door you can't come back." Audrina's voice actually sounded shaky.

"That's definitely not a problem," Milo told her and he yanked open the exit door.

The others followed right behind him. As they filed out into the darkness that awaited them beyond the door, Audrina's wail of despair was so intense that Milo was sure he could feel his bones rattling.

They were all through the door except Eli, who had suddenly hesitated on the threshold.

Vylett must have got a sense of what he was feeling because she cried, "no Eli!"

Before anyone could stop him, Eli stepped back into the ballroom.

The last thing they saw was Iza's memory grabbing him and Audrina's satisfied smile as she slammed the door shut on them forever.

"Eli!" Milo went to pull the door handle but it disintegrated in his hands, followed by the door itself. There was nothing there anymore but stone.

Eli was gone.

Chapter 12

Everything's Peachy

"Let's just keep walking," said Milo once it became clear that their route back into Audrina's ballroom was well and truly blocked.

"But Eli…" Abigail's voice drifted off into the dark silence.

"Eli and Iza are gone. We can't help them now. We have to keep moving." Milo knew he sounded harsh but if he let himself think too much about what had just happened he might break down completely.

They had to find Alanya now. There would be time to worry about Eli and Iza later.

"We're dropping like flies," Abigail muttered as they fumbled their way down the darkened passageway. "Did anyone see Iza in there?"

"Not the real one," Milo said.

No one spoke for a while after that. The only sound was Abigail's heels clicking on the stone floor.

"I wish we had a torch or something," mumbled Helico. "Can't see a damn thing in here."

The cave they had entered seemed to be one endless dark long corridor.

"Eli was the one who had the torch," said Abigail and then she stopped walking. "Oh god Eli was the one who had the back pack. Now we don't have any food, or drink or..anything!"

Click, click, click. Her heels got louder as she quickly increased her pace.

"Abigail where did you get those shoes from? You could have picked some quieter ones!" Milo snapped at her.

He couldn't help it. They were starting to drive him insane. He couldn't hear himself think.

He heard Abigail make a huffing noise in the darkness. "Not so long ago you thought my shoes might save us against the squid."

Milo was about to apologise but Abigail wasn't finished. "If that devious orange hag Audrina hadn't distracted me with.." Abigail faltered, "with those..memory things..then I would have remembered to bring all the other shoes which I got in her caves. Maybe you would have liked some of those better Milo." Her voice was sarcastic. "And why are you staring at me like that Helico? You're creeping me out."

It was hard to tell in the darkness but Helico appeared to be staring intently at Abigail.

"I'm trying to see what you're wearing but it's hard to make out in the dark. You're definitely not wearing the Orlost uniform. Neither are you Vylett." Helico squinted at Vylett in the dark.

"Did Audrina give you those? You could have got me and Milo some. We still look like convicts. But you two...I know it's dark in here but I can tell you're wearing nice dresses. Have you seen them Milo?"

"Mmm yeah," Milo mumbled. He was glad that the cave was dark so that no one could see him blushing as he remembered how pretty he thought Vylett had looked.

"Well I suppose Audrina did have good taste in fashion," said Abigail begrudgingly. "Even if she was twisted and ugly."

"Do you mean ugly in her personality or ugly in her appearance?" asked Helico.

Uh oh! thought Milo, bad thing to say Helico.

The click clicking noise of Abigail's heels stopped. Milo's eyes had adjusted to the dark well enough to see that she was stood glaring at Helico with her hands on her hips, just like she had that very first day they had met her on Orlost.

"Well it was obvious to everyone who had eyes that you, Milo and Eli thought she was the most stunning thing you had ever seen. Isn't that right Vylett?"

"Er yes," Vylett sounded awkward and Milo could feel her eyes on him in the darkness.

"Oh don't be jealous Abs. You're just as beautiful. You have to admit though, there was something very different about her," Helico said.

Milo thought Helico's choice of words was still not great.

"You mean her ugly fish hair and ugly orange face. Yes that was very different Helico. It was u.g.l.y" she said the word slowly and deliberately. "She transfixed you boys to see her differently. Can't you see that?"

Helico made a noise of frustration. "Oh and I suppose she didn't transfix you girls to go shopping at all did she? Don't you think it was strange that one minute you hated the woman and then as soon as she offered to take you shopping she was your new best friend. Huh Abigail?"

There was a silence then. And then came the loud click click of Abigail's heels, which got faster and faster as she stormed off down the passageway.

Milo guessed it was Helico calling her Abigail and not 'Abs' that had really got her back up.

"Hey come on Abs you know I only like red heads," Helico called after her as he rushed to catch up to her.

Milo suddenly felt awkward now that he and Vylett were all alone for the time being.

"Audrina's face was very orange," he said sheepishly as he scraped a finger along the slimy surface of the cave wall. "I've never been a big fan of orange actually."

His eyes had become more accustomed to the darkness of the cave and he didn't think he imagined Vylett smiling at him.

"You forget that I can sense your thoughts Miloney Merren," she scolded lightly. "You do so like the colour orange. But that's sweet."

She was still smiling. Milo thought the depth of colour in his face right now was probably on a par with Audrina's.

Once again he was glad the cave was dark.

"I hope those two make up again soon," Milo said as the cave suddenly bended sharply to the left. "A happy Abigail is so much more pleasant than a grumpy Abigail."

Vylett laughed. "I agree. I think they'll be fine but.." she stopped speaking.

"What's up?"

"The walls feel different. Don't they?"

Milo ran his finger across the wall again. The sliminess had gone. Instead the walls felt smooth and spongy.

He could easily press his finger into it.

"That's strange," he said. "Why would cave walls be soft?"

Vylett didn't answer.

"Vylett?" Milo turned to face her and found her lying unconscious on the ground.

Before Milo had chance to panic about Vylett being unconscious, her eyes snapped open and she jumped to her feet.

"What just happened?" he said. "Are you ok?"

"I had a vision. Quick we need to get moving. The elevator's not far but something's going to try and stop us." She grabbed his arm and started to run down the passageway.

"Wait! What's going to stop us?" Milo cried after her.

Vylett stopped short and shakily pointed her finger down the passageway.

"That."

Standing several metres in front of them was the most unthreatening woman that Milo had ever seen. But the fact that Vylett had referred to the woman as 'that' and not 'her' suggested to him that the woman was not human.

He felt weary. He had barely gotten over the shock of the other non-human they had just met.

This woman before them was the total opposite to Audrina however.

She looked at least a hundred years old for a start and she didn't have an orange face. Although you could have been mistaken for thinking that she did because her face was covered in so much dirt.

She was small, with long white straggly hair that looked like it hadn't been washed or combed in years, and was dressed in what looked like an assortment of rags and cloths. Except for a long black cloak that was far too long for her.

It tied in a knot at her throat and gathered in folds around her feet.

She held a walking stick in her withered hand and was hunched so far over that Milo could barely see her face.

Her feet however were unfortunately all too clear to see. She was barefoot and had the ugliest feet that Milo had ever seen.

They turned his stomach.

The skin was flaky and peeling and there were copious amounts of dirt between the toenails which were long, yellow and crusted.

"We're supposed to be afraid of this woman?" Milo said as the woman continued to shuffle back and forth.

He found it hard to believe.

"Maybe she's going to try and kill us with those toenails," he joked. "They look pretty lethal."

Vylett nudged him with her elbow to silence him but the woman stopped shuffling and raised her head towards them so that they could finally see her face.

"Is that so?" she said and Milo felt a cold chill that made the hairs on the back of his neck prick up.

The feeling was mixed with danger and power and it was an eery feeling that gave him a strange sense of de ja vu. As though he had had that feeling before.

Then he remembered that he had.

It was the feeling he had gotten when he had looked at the woods on the black river.

He shuddered as he looked at Peaches's face. Her skin bore a striking resemblance to her feet - flaky, dirty and wrinkly with yellow crusty patches around her eyelids. Her eyes looked strangely timeless however.

When she had spoken, Milo noticed that half of her teeth were missing.

"Who are you?" Vylett edged towards her and Milo quickly joined her.

The woman eyed them and grinned a horrible toothless grin. "Peaches," she said in a voice that was gruffer than a Terramang's. "My name is Peaches."

"Peaches? Really?" Milo couldn't stop himself. He had to concentrate not to laugh. Peaches was a feminine name. A pretty name.

This woman was far from pretty.

"Something wrong with my name boy?" Peaches growled at him. "How about now?"

Her face suddenly changed to a much younger version of herself. Her eyes were the same but her skin was young, smooth and unblemished.

She was pretty but the overall effect was grotesque given the fact that her body and hands and feet were still the old Peaches.

It was unnerving and Milo's laugh died in his throat.

Peaches chuckled and reverted back to her old face. She scratched her hand with one of her long dirty fingernails and then plucked out several of her hairs.

She closely inspected them and then to Milo's horror she put them into her mouth and began eating them with a look on her face that suggested they tasted like yesterday's dinner.

"I need new hair," she grumbled and then her sharp eyes landed greedily on Vylett's clean shiny hair. "You have lots of it," she noted.

"Mmm yes, but it's not for eating," Vylett glanced nervously at Milo.

"Look we mean no harm," Milo told Peaches. "Can we just come past you and then we'll be gone. We just need to take the elevator. Is it near here?"

He thought about just barging past her. It couldn't be difficult. She looked as though she could be knocked down by a breeze. But then he remembered Vylett's vision and how Vylett seemed to think this woman was definitely a threat.

Unfortunately, Vylett's visions had so far been accurate.

Peaches glowered at Milo and stamped her foot. The whole passageway shook with a wrath that was more frightening than Audrina's, and Milo and Vylett slammed into the cave walls.

Had the walls not been spongy, Milo's shoulder would have been smashed to pieces.

"I am a cross-patcher," said Peaches once the passageway had stopped shaking. "The elevator is at the end of this passage but the passage is my patch. If you want to cross it you have to make me a deal."

Milo groaned. Peaches was a cross-patcher!

He hadn't imagined that they would come in all shapes and sizes.

He glanced around him sceptically. If Peaches was a cross-patcher then this must be some kind of portal they had found. But there didn't look to be anything special about the passageway.

"What kind of deal?" Vylett asked her.

Peaches laughed. "They type of deal where one of you stays and the rest can go. Those are the rules and they're not up for negotiation." Peaches eyed Vylett's hair again.

Vylett shivered. "We all need to leave together," she said.

"Not possible," said Peaches.

"But you must have already let our friends past you," Milo argued, wondering how Abigail and Helico had avoided her.

"You mean these two?" said Peaches and she raised her eyes to the ceiling.

Milo felt a nervous apprehension as he followed her eyes upwards.

There, stuck flat to the ceiling like a couple of bugs, were Helico and Abigail. They looked like they were desperately trying to speak but couldn't move their lips.

"What have you done to them?" Milo looked at Peaches in horror who merely grinned her toothless grin at them.

"Cut out their tongues and sewn up their lips."

Milo put a hand over his mouth, feeling so sick he couldn't speak properly. He felt like his own tongue had been cut out.

"The red headed one wouldn't make me a deal," said Peaches. "Gave me some lip she did." The old woman grinned up at a furious looking Abigail and absently plucked out a few more of her hairs. "So I sealed hers."

Milo tried not to gag as she chewed away on her own scanky hair.

"Let them down," Vylett demanded.

Peaches shrugged. "As you wish…."

Helico and Abigail fell to the floor.

Hard.

The floor wasn't spongy like the walls and they cried out in pain. To Milo it was a lovely sound. Relief washed over him.

Peaches hadn't really cut out their tongues.

He and Vylett gingerly helped them to their feet. Helico had to lean heavily on Milo as he couldn't put weight on his ankle properly.

"You evil, disgusting.." Abigail made a swipe for Peaches but the passageway shook again and all she succeeded in doing was throwing herself off balance.

The passageway shook harder and all of them slammed into the walls. The walls might have been spongy but they were dense. Milo's body felt beaten up. He felt sure he wouldn't be able to move properly tomorrow – that is, if he even made it to tomorrow.

At this rate, Peaches's passageway may well become his tomb.

Peaches's face flashed eerily between the young and old version again and then she dragged Vylett up from the floor by her hair.

Vylett grimaced in pain as Peaches twisted a clump of her blonde hair around her grimy fingers and started pulling. Vylett kicked out at her but Peaches easily side stepped the kick.

"Will you make the deal?" Peaches said in a steely voice.

"Yes," said Helico.

Milo looked at him in surprise. Helico returned his gaze and Milo realised he was just trying to buy for time.

"Very well," said Peaches, finally releasing Vylett. "Which one of you is staying here with me?"

No one answered.

How could they possibly choose to leave someone behind? They had already lost two of their friends.

"I see," said Peaches. "Perhaps you are divided in your decision. But know this..if you don't make me the deal then all of you die."

She grinned then and Milo felt those horrible chills on the back of his neck.

"Maybe you need a little help deciding."

She laughed and the ground beneath them began to creak loudly.

"I'll be seeing you," Peaches said and then the ground beneath their feet opened up.

***

No one knew quite how it happened but as the earth crumbled beneath their feet the four of them got separated.

They didn't realise it was happening until it was too late.

Huge cracks were appearing in the ground and they were too busy desperately trying to sidestep them to notice.

The cracks got bigger and bigger until they merged into one huge crater in the ground which was at least ten feet wide and getting wider by the second.

On one side of it were Vylett and Helico and on the other side, Milo and Abigail.

It didn't take a genius to work out what Peaches had done. Peaches had wanted to know if they had been divided in their decision and now she had acted on her words.

She had divided them.

Conveniently she had now disappeared.

Vylett frantically looked at the others. "What do we do?" she cried.

The crater was still getting wider and they were slowly being forced to back up against the sponge walls, whilst the ground they were standing on was becoming a ledge, getting narrower and narrower.

Helico stood next to Vylett flitting in and out of visibility in his anxiousness.

"If the floor disappears completely then cling on to the sponge in the walls," he suggested.

"But then what? We can't hold on forever," Abigail cried.

"You could levitate us," Milo told her as he grasped for a good hold on the sponge walls.

Abigail glared at him. "I can't do that forever Milo. Just how gifted do you think I am!" Her green satin clutch bag slipped from her shoulder and she flung it away impatiently. Victoria Sparkle fell out of the bag and landed on the other side of the crater.

Helico called out to Peaches in desperation. "Come on Peaches let's do a deal. We can work something out."

But still the crater continued to get wider. Any minute now they would be free falling down into it. The ledge was barely three foot wide now.

Then suddenly it stopped moving .

Milo looked at the others, each one of them looking just as relieved as he felt.

Vylett began to shuffle across to Victoria Sparkle.

"No leave it it's just a doll," Helico tried to grab her arm as she inched her way along the ledge but she shrugged out of his grasp.

"It's Abigail's good luck doll," she said absently. "And Abigail needs some luck right now."

"Ok Victoria Sparkle," she murmured as she grabbed the doll. "Now's the time to show us if you really do bring good luck." Then the ledge suddenly jolted and Vylett lost her footing.

Another crack appeared and Vylett fell through.

***

Vylett barely had time to panic. She saw Helico rush towards her as she wildly reached out towards the sponge walls to steady herself but it was no good.

In what felt like slow motion, she slipped off the ledge and fell head first into the crater.

She was vaguely aware of the others shouting her name and a strange tugging sensation behind her navel but then she hit the ground with a sickening thud and then the only thing she was aware of was the face that was lying next to hers.

Victoria Sparkle's face.

As Vylett fought to stay conscious and Helico's face peering down at her blurred in and out of focus, the only thing that remained clear to her was her earlier vision which suddenly hit her with enormous clarity as she stared at Victoria Sparkle's face.

"This was what I saw in my vision," she thought numbly. "It wasn't Abigail that was in danger. It was me." and then everything went black.

Chapter 13

Life or Death

The blackness suddenly gave way to a white mist and Vylett wondered vaguely if she had entered another portal.

She felt disorientated as the mist began to clear. One moment she had been staring into the face of Abigail's 'oh so not a good luck doll,' and now she was finding herself being confronted with something even more scary.

Nothingness

She was not lying on the floor of the crater anymore. She was standing upright, seemingly unhurt, and in a place far more desolate than Orlost.

There was literally nothing around her except for acres and acres of flat land in all directions as far as the eye could see. It was endless and there was not a single living person or creature or even building around her.

She was completely alone.

She knew she should probably feel frightened but she didn't. Instead she felt strangely devoid of all emotion.

Then quite suddenly she felt the urge to run.

Why? She had no idea.

She only knew that she should and that if felt right.

As she began to run, she felt her heart lifting and her emotions came flooding back to her all at once. But the emotions were all good.

A good kind of scared and a good kind of confusion.

As she ran, a small patch of mist appeared before her. Hovering in the middle of it she could make out the ghostly outline of a figure and she knew that was where she needed to go.

The figure's outline grew stronger as she got nearer to it but before the figure could fully materialise a familiar voice coming from somewhere behind her, stopped her.

"Don't go through that. Not yet."

Vylett turned towards the voice and gasped. "Mother?"

Vylett stepped with uncertainty towards her.

Alanya Roze did not quite look like she had in Audrina's ballroom. She looked at least twenty years older. Her face was lined and she was much thinner. Gaunt even.

Her hair was still blonde and reached her waist but where as before it had been shiny and smooth it was now dull and coarse with flecks of grey in it.

In truth she looked drained and like she hadn't slept in weeks. But to Vylett she was still beautiful.

"Is that really you?" Vylett reached out a hand towards her, afraid to touch her in case she turned to dust.

Alanya smiled at her. "Don't be afraid Vylett."

Her voice was as soft as luck leaves. She held out her arms and Vylett ran into them, drinking in the sweet smell of her as her mother stroked her hair just like she had when she was little.

Eventually Alanya pulled back so she could look at her daughter. "I'm sorry you had to find me this way." A tear rolled down her face and Vylett quickly wiped it away.

"Why are you sorry Mother? It was the only way. You sent me visions remember? Only..." she paused, glancing around. "I never found the elevator. I seem to have come a different way. I fell you see and now..."

Vylett stopped speaking. How exactly had she managed to find a different route? Had Peaches's crater been another portal?

Alanya gently took hold of her shoulders. "Vylett, my dear daughter, do you understand where you are?"

Alanya placed her hands on her daughter's head and turned it so that Vylett was facing the small patch of mist that was still hovering a few feet away with the ghostly figure still waiting for her.

And the figure was waiting for her.

She understood that now. She'd understood the moment she'd started running towards it and felt its luring pull, inviting her in. But she had been distracted when she saw her mother.

She turned back to face her. "Yes," she said. "I'm dead aren't I?"

***

When Alanya had resolutely told Vylett that she hadn't survived her fall inside Peaches's cave, Vylett didn't feel upset, or scared, or anything really. She just understood.

But one thought did occur to her. "But if I'm dead.." she said to her mother. "Then you…." She couldn't finish the sentence. It was too hard.

Alanya smiled sadly. "Yes I'm dead too. I have been for a long time Vylett." She ran a finger down Vylett's cheek. "You've grown into a beautiful young woman. Your father must have been proud."

A tear rolled down Alanya's cheek and Vylett's body started to tremble. In her mind she still felt strangely calm but her body seemed to think otherwise. Her mother had been dead all along?

"Abigail was right," she mumbled. But then some of the fog in her brain seemed to clear a bit.

"No," she said firmly. "That can't be true. I never inherited your gifts. And also, if you're dead then how did you manage to give me all those visions?"

Alanya sighed. "Ah the visions. It's complex Vylett. If I had entered that mist over there then I wouldn't have been able to send you a vision. But you see, where we are now, well we're not quite where we should be."

Alanya paused to see if Vylett was comprehending her. "We need to enter that mist to complete the final part of our journey. This place we are in now is called the Otherworld. It's an in between place between the living and the dead and it's not good to stay here. But I am dead. Do you understand?"

Vylett glanced around her at the endless planes and felt relief that this place wasn't where she was supposed to be in death.

She nodded. "I think so. But why haven't you entered the mist already?" Vylett looked again at the figure hovering in the mist and had to resist the urge to go to it. She felt a great heaviness in her heart as though she was being kept away from someone she was supposed to be with and it was leaving her with a deep sadness.

Alanya gave a little laugh and gently pushed Vylett's hair behind her ears. "Silly girl. I wanted to wait for you of course. I don't want to cross into that mist without my only daughter. I've been waiting a long time for you Vylett."

She sighed. "In truth, I didn't think you would be joining me so soon but I would wait an eternity for you. I want you to know that."

Then she gave Vylett a disapproving look. "And then one day I sensed you were trying to find me." Another tear rolled down her cheek. "I didn't want you to come. Only the dead should come here. But I knew something was troubling you. Forgive me for helping you to come to this place." Her face turned up in distaste as she gestured to the vast planes.

Vylett glanced at the mist again, unable to draw her eyes away from it but her mother gently turned her head back to face her again, looking for her daughter's assurance.

"I forgive you," Vylett told her. "You were only trying to help me." Distracted she looked to the mist again.

"We'll go there soon," promised Alanya. "But now I want to talk to you here for a minute because we don't know what will happen when we enter that mist. Right now I want you to understand."

"Understand what?"

"That I sent you those visions to help you. That I fully expected you to find me through the elevator, still alive and well."

Vylett gave her a small smile. "I guess no one can predict what life has in store for us."

"Why were you trying to find me Vylett?"

Vylett forced herself to look at her mother and not the mist. "The Water Quarter is in trouble," she said. "The Terramangs have been stealing the magic and now there is a massive imbalance. But my friend Milo thinks that you can help save it."

Alanya raised her eyebrows. "Oh?"

"He has a water charm to bring to you," Vylett explained. "He thought that if you made a circle back on the Quarters with the other multi-gifted using the charm then you could restore the balance." Vylett shrugged. "But that's when we thought you were alive. So it's not possible now is it?"

She spoke casually. Not because she didn't care anymore but because suddenly it just didn't seem like anything to be worried about.

Alanya's tired face seemed to light up though. "If he has a water charm then anything is possible Vylett. Your friend can still find me if he enters the elevator. I can still help him. I may even be able to use it to return him home."

She smiled warmly at Vylett. "I have learnt many things since being exiled. And in this place, although you may not believe it, I have learnt even more."

Vylett felt a flicker of excitement. "So we can wait for him?"

"No! You have to go back." Another voice sounded in the desolate surroundings. "This is the Otherworld and I do not want my brother to come here. Go back Vylett and tell him not to come here."

Vylett whirled around, confused as to where the voice was coming from. Then from behind Alanya, a girl appeared, or rather materialised to stand beside her.

She was attractive with long dark hair and Vylett recognised her immediately.

It was Penelope Merren. Milo's sister.

Was Penelope dead too? But Vylett never had a chance to ask her because her body began to tremble violently and then frighteningly, her mother's face started to dim before her as though she were a lamp that was slowly losing its energy. It took a lot of effort to turn her focus to Penelope.

"Milo can give my mother the water charm," she told her between shaky breaths. "He can help to save the Quarters."

The figure in the mist was also starting to lose its outline and Vylett felt less strongly drawn to it.

"What's happening to me?" she looked down at herself and gasped as her own body began to fade before her eyes.

"I didn't know that Alanya was dead when I had that vision," Penelope said sounding strained and when Vylett looked back up, the other girl's hand was on her mother's shoulder.

"Milo shouldn't come here," she said again. She shuddered and glanced around her. "This place is rotten."

Vylett's body trembled again and she was having trouble focusing. Just before their faces faded away completely, Alanya met Vylett's eyes and smiled. "It's not your time. You've been saved."

And then she was gone and the next thing Vylett was aware of was coughing up all over Abigail.

She was no longer at the bottom of the crater with Victoria Sparkle but back in Peaches's cave with the others.

The cracks were gone. There was no division any more and Milo, Helico and Abigail were crowded around her with worried expressions.

Helico's eyes were wide and Milo's face looked a hundred times paler than normal.

Abigail's hand was shaky as she wiped Vylett's spue off her face. "Glad to see you back with us Vylett."

"Abs saved you," Helico explained to her proudly. "She levitated you out of the hole and then resuscitated you. She used to be a lifekeeper or something."

"A lifeguard." Abigail corrected him as she rolled her eyes. Vylett thought Abigail looked ready to collapse with exhaustion.

"But I wasn't quick enough to stop you hitting the ground Vylett so don't go putting a halo on my head just yet," Abigail said. "I managed to slow your fall a little but it wasn't much. I really thought you'd died at one point."

Vylett pushed herself up to a sitting position. Then she took a deep breath and said, "I did."

She looked at each of them in turn, finally letting her eyes rest on Milo who so far had been unnaturally silent. She wondered how on earth she was supposed to tell him that she thought his sister was dead.

***

Milo thought he was taking Vylett's news remarkably well.

Initially he felt as though his head had been put in one of the machines that his mother used to chop up herbs.

How could Penelope be dead? He had only seen her yesterday! Or had it been the day before? Well it was something like that.

But then when Vylett had explained Penelope was in this in-between place - the Otherworld - he realised that didn't necessarily mean she was dead. There could be other explanations.

Although how she had gotten there was a mystery and something he would have to find out when he saw her.

And then he had begun to rationalise things further. If Alanya told Vylett she could still help him get back to the Water Quarter then surely she could help Penelope too. So eventually after his initial shock, he had taken his head out of the chopping machine and began to feel optimistic. Because even though Alanya was dead, she could still be reached. She could still save the Quarters.

He wasn't going to give up yet!

Vylett was slumped down onto the ledge with her back resting against the sponge walls and her legs tucked underneath her. Her lovely new dress was stained with dirt from the crater.

"I'm sorry about your mother," Milo said awkwardly. He felt like he should put an arm around her or something but he had never been good at this sort of thing. Bond or no bond. "At least you know that when your time is eventually up, you've got someone waiting for you."

Vylett gave him a small smile. "I guess. But hey you'll have someone too. You'll have Penelope."

Milo felt a flash of irritation. "Did Penelope actually say she was dead?"

Vylett looked at him startled. "Well no but..."

"Then she might not be."

When Vylett started to protest Milo cut her off. "For now let's just assume that somehow she's just got herself stuck there and when we find your mother and give her the water charm then she can help her."

"But how would she have got stuck in the Otherworld Milo? It's a place between life and death. I really think you have to die to go there."

"Not necessarily," Milo told her shortly. "I'm not dead and you're not dead but apparently we can get there by an elevator. So let's go and look for it shall we." He turned brusquely away from her.

He knew that she wanted to talk more about Penelope but he didn't. He didn't want to think about the 'what ifs'. He just wanted to find her.

"Penelope said she didn't want you to go there," Vylett said quietly.

Milo turned back round and gave her an exasperated look. "But that makes no sense because she was the one who had a vision of me taking the charm to Alanya."

"Yes but that was before she knew my mother was dead."

"But you said your mother can still help save the Water Quarter and probably help us to get back there so long as she had the water charm. So what's the problem?"

"I just don't see how my mother can be right," Vylett put her hand wearily on her forehead. "I know she's talented, but if she's dead then she can't make a circle with the other multi-gifted can she? So I don't understand what else she's planning to do."

"Who cares! She's multi-gifted. There's probably not a lot that she can't do." Milo raised his voice and Abigail quickly cut in.

"Look.. your arguing is getting us no where," she said. "Are we still looking for this elevator or not?"

"I suppose so," said Vylett pushing herself slowly to her feet. "I don't want to argue Milo."

Milo felt a heaviness in his heart as he took in Vylett's delicate state. She was bruised from her fall, she was grieving for her mother, she had just nearly died and here he was, berating her over Penelope of all people.

"Me neither," he smiled a truce. "I guess we'll find out the truth when we see her."

There followed a few moments of awkward silence until Helico broke it with his light hearted attempt at humour.

"Vylett.. if your mother is waiting for you in this Otherworld place until it's your time to die, then does that mean you'll never inherit all her gifts? Because if so that's a real bummer!"

Vylett gave him a small smile. "I guess it does Helico. But I'm not bothered. One gift is enough for me most of the time."

Milo didn't comment. He could sort of understand why a mother would want to wait for her daughter before entering the World of the Dead, but secretly he was thinking Helico had a point.

He thought it was selfish of Alanya to deny Vylett what was rightly hers.

The next hour was pretty uneventful as they wandered Peaches's cave, looking for an elevator, all the while on tenterhooks as they anticipated Peaches to return.

They had to walk slowly because Abigail was exhausted from levitating, Helico's ankle was painful from when Peaches had dropped him from the ceiling and Vylett was bruised from her fall.

Milo did not have any physical bruises but they were there, hidden inside him where no one else could see.

All in all they were a sorry sight.

***

An hour later, Abigail who was leading the way suddenly stopped walking and pointed to a patch of mist which was hovering about thirty feet away from them. "Do you think that's another portal?"

"I don't know and I'm not sure I want to find out," said Milo. "Not if it means we have to meet another cross-patcher."

"And what's wrong with cross-patchers?" Peaches's gravelly voice sounded all around them, making them jump.

They whirled around, expecting to see her but they were still alone in the darkness. Their eyes had gotten used to the dark but it was still unnerving to know that Peaches was somewhere lurking in the shadows watching them.

"Where's the elevator Peaches?" Milo shouted into the darkness. He was feeling more and more frustrated and angry. It felt like they were never going to find the damn elevator.

No answer.

Milo wanted to unleash his magic on something, but there was nothing to move. "Peaches! You can stop your games now," he cried. "You can have me. I'll stay with you. Let the others go."

"Milo what are you doing?" Vylett gripped his arm frantically.

He shrugged. "Bluffing.." At this stage anything was worth a try.

Peaches still didn't re-appear.

"Where is she?" mumbled Helico. In his agitation he kept flitting in and out of invisibility until Abigail gave him a light slap to make him stop.

"She's playing with us," said Milo as he stared warily around him, wondering what the hair eating creature was going to do next.

For the next few seconds, no one dare move. They rooted themselves to the spot for fear of the ledge they were standing on would suddenly collapse or in case the spongy walls they were leaning against might suddenly dissolve into nothing.

It felt like they were sitting on a time bomb just waiting for Peaches to press the switch.

Finally Milo could stand it no longer. "This is ridiculous," he shouted and took a step forward towards the patch of mist in the distance.

And that's when Peaches pressed the switch.

There was a huge roaring noise which escalated to an excruciating level.

Milo put his hands over his ears at the same time burning hot embers - just like the ones he had seen in his school books of the volcano erupting in the Fire Quarter - flew at them.

At any other time, in any other location, Milo would have loved to stand back and watch as a spectator. Even now, even though he knew he was in mortal danger for his life, there was something fascinating about the way the embers took flight into the air glowing the brightest orange he had ever seen.

Only when they landed inches from his skin and sizzled on the stone cave floor did he realise they had to move.

And fast.

They ran towards the mist, trying frantically to dodge the burning hot embers. The heat from them was hot and already intensifying and if they didn't escape soon then the heat alone would scorch them.

Milo cried out as a searing hot pain shot through his arm and he looked down to see a nasty red welt where some of the skin had been burnt off.

He felt a wave of nausea but there was no time to think about it. It hurt like hell but the adrenaline pumping in his body right now was helping to keep him focused.

They reached the thin whispery mist but as Milo had feared, they couldn't enter it. When they touched it, it was solid.

"Damn!" Abigail pounded on it with her fists which did absolutely no good.

"Stand back Abigail," Milo pulled her aside as got ready to use his magic. He wasn't quite sure what he was going to do. He didn't even know if he could move a portal, but it was worth a try.

He drew on all the magic he could muster until he was buzzing with it. Whether it was due to the extra adrenaline in his body or the fact that he was getting more and more used to using magic, he wasn't sure, but he felt more powerful than ever before.

He got ready to aim and stopped as a face appeared in the mist.

"Don't do that! Come inside!"

From somewhere behind them they heard a wailing noise from Peaches.

They didn't need asking twice. The four of them rushed into the mist which now felt like mist, closing the way on Peaches.

Chapter 14

Sharrowlandi

Their saviour in the mist was a middle aged man in a tweed jacket with greying hair and light stubble on his chin. As soon as they were through the mist the man rounded on them and launched into a lecture about the safe use of magic.

"What did you think you were doing boy?" the man glared at Milo. "What were you hoping to achieve by directing your magic at a portal?"

Milo swallowed nervously, "I don't know. We were in danger of getting burnt to death. We needed to escape but the mist felt solid and we couldn't get through."

He swallowed again, feeling intimidated by this man in the tweed jacket who was staring intently at him. "I guess I thought that if I could try and move it then we might be able to enter it. I can move things with my mind," he explained.

"Hmmph" the man grumbled and then shook his head. "Kids! all novices!"

Then he sighed. "I guess you must have done something right back there though," he said as he stared at the top of their heads. "You've all still got your hair. I've not met anyone yet who's crossed Peaches's path and come out with a full head of hair."

Abigail stepped forward. "Who are you?"

The man gave her a lopsided smile. "My name is Sharrowlandi. But you can call me Sharrow." He scrutinised them. "You all look beaten up. Are you hungry?"

They nodded as they realised they were.

"Then come on, follow me."

They relaxed, glad to be out of Peaches's cave and in the company of a man who so far, aside from being a little hacked off at them, seemed blissfully normal.

As they followed Sharrow, they took in their surroundings for the first time. Milo gasped and looked at the others in amazement who were just as equally transfixed by the magnificent sight around them. Although he had never been here before, it was somehow so familiar.

So familiar.

And then Milo realised where they were.

His jaw literally dropped open.

"I don't believe it!" he said feeling somewhat in a daze.

All around them were masses of well dressed people roaming elegant streets flanked by huge skyscrapers made of glass. Milo heard a high pitch screeching above his head and looked up in awe to see a dragon flying above them, profiled against the purple sky.

It was enormous, with large scales and actual fire coming from its mouth.

And there in the distance standing higher than any of the skyscrapers and ten times as wide was a volcano that Milo had envisualised virtually every day since he had first seen a picture of it in his text books.

"It's the Fire Quarter!" Vylett who was stood next to him sounded breathless as she looked around her in wonder. "We're in the capital."

Abigail made a whooping noise and grabbed Helico in excitement. "Look at those pyramids. They're one of the Seven Wonders of the World you know. Well my World," she amended.

Milo looked at her in confusion. "What?" What pyramids?"

Sharrow made another 'hmmphing' noise. "Novices! all of you."

Milo looked to him in confusion. "What do you mean?"

Sharrow sighed and rubbed at the stubble on his chin. "This is the World of Illusion kids. Look at what you are actually seeing and not what you want to see. You really don't have much experience in magic do you."

"Are you saying that what we're seeing is not real?" Milo watched a dragon fly between the skyscrapers, feeling unease in the pit of his stomach. "Because it looks very real to me."

"Yes Milo, that's exactly what I'm saying.," said Sharrow. "You and Vylett are seeing the Fire Quarter because to you that is the most fantastic place you have heard about. Abigail is seeing a place called Egypt because to her that is the most fantastic place she has heard about. Understand what I'm saying?"

Sharrow paused and put a hand on Helico's shoulder. "Helico here did not grow up being aware of any place other than his own World of the Towerlands, and therefore is perfectly content at seeing the real here and now for what it is.

What do you think of this World Helico? More pleasant than Peaches's place isn't it?"

Milo and the others turned to see Helico looking at them with a mildly amused expression.

"You lot were starting to worry me there for a second talking about fire and pyramids. I thought you'd gone insane." He shook his head. "Although now I feel utterly lame that I don't have anywhere other than the Towerlands to fantasise about.

But this place seems cool." he told Sharrow.

Milo looked around him in dismay. He couldn't believe that none of this was real. He couldn't believe that he wasn't actually in the capital of the Quarters.

He walked over to a nearby shop selling posh top hats on the sidewalk and tentatively touched its glass window. The window dissolved at his touch and then as though someone had poured water onto a painting, everything else around him began to dissolve.

The buildings became molten liquid, the dragon melted into a green blob and began dripping down from the sky, and the volcano became a mass of orange blending in with the purple skies.

The colours blended and ran until they transformed into something else.

A different World entirely.

Milo was filled with contrasting feelings of disappointment and fascination. He exchanged wide eyes with Vylett and Abigail as they too finally saw this strange World. The World of Illusion.

They appeared to be in the middle of a village. They were stood in a large square area surrounded by quaint wooden houses and in the middle of the square was a large fountain with food stalls around its perimeter. People were browsing the goods and chatting to each other.

There were a group of men next to the fountain playing music of some kind and a small crowd had gathered round to watch. It all seemed bizarrely ordinary.

Sharrow clapped his hands together and said briskly. "Lovely! Now you all appear to be seeing the real thing. Let's move on shall we. I'm hungry even if you lot aren't. Then once we've eaten you can explain to me how you come to be here."

***

Milo's initial disappointment at literally seeing his dreams of the Fire Quarter dissolve into tiny pieces was quickly replaced by curiosity.

The village was lively and friendly and after a few disconcerting instances where he kept seeing a dragon lurking behind a food stall and Abigail kept pointing out pyramid shaped fruit, they eventually saw the village for what it was.

Normal.

And it was so refreshing from Audrina's cave and Peaches's manic behaviour that they relaxed and began to enjoy the fresh air and delicious smells that were wafting from the many food stalls.

As they passed two elderly women sat on a bench laughing and sewing, Vylett nudged Milo in the ribs. A frown was etched across her face. "I can't sense Sharrow's thoughts," she whispered. "But he looks human doesn't he?"

There was something that was niggling at Milo too and by the time he worked up the courage to voice his concern, the unease in the pit of his stomach was back.

"Sharrow? How did you know our names? Because I'm pretty sure we didn't tell you them."

Sharrow had stopped at one of the quaint wooden houses with a slanting roof and a large wooden veranda surrounding it.

"You didn't need to tell me," Sharrow opened the front door and beckoned for them to enter. "I'm a cross-patcher. It's my job to know. Now please come in and make yourselves at home."

No one moved.

"You're a cross-patcher!" Abigail changed her stance as though she were preparing to perform a combat move whilst Helico moved in front of her, ready to protect her against any evil that was about to occur.

"The cross-patchers we've met have not been human," Helico said accusingly.

"Who said I was human?" said Sharrow, giving Helico a slanting smile.

Helico pushed Abigail further behind him. Irritated, she pushed him aside and took a long stride up to Sharrow. "And none of them we have met so far have been very pleasant," she said. "What do you want with us?"

Sharrow laughed, looking amused. "Relax Abigail. I do not intend to do you any harm. Indeed I should be offended that you think cross-patchers are unpleasant. Although in Peaches's case, I agree with you."

When none of them laughed, Sharrow sighed. "Like I said before, this is the World of Illusion. I have created an illusion for you to see me differently. Believe me, if I wanted to scare you I would show you my true self." He gave them all another slanting smile. "Then you would know I wasn't human."

He gave a little chuckle as though sharing a joke with himself. "I didn't think if fair for you to see the real me initially." He paused to smile at them. "You might not have wanted to taste my cooking."

Again no one laughed and Abigail took another step closer to him, hands on hips, looking him up and down.

"Well what do you really look like then?"

Sharrow rolled his eyes and sighed. "Apparently I can look a little...unnerving... so I gave your brains a much nicer version of me for you to deal with."

"We can take it," Abigail said coldly.

Sharrow shrugged. "Fine." And then he moved quick as lightening to lightly touch each of them in turn.

A strangled cry stuck in Milo's throat. The real Sharrow was...

...Droges? It couldn't be!

But then Droges's face turned into Walt...and then into Walt's sidekick Peg. And then Milo blanched as Peg's face turned into Vylett's.

But a dead Vylett.

Her eyes were unseeing and her face had that pale sickly pallor that comes with death.

Sharrow retracted his hand and Milo was staring once again at the man in the tweed jacket with grey hair and stubble.

Helico let out a nervous laugh. "Clever trick."

"It's not a trick, its magical illusion. Magic is all about balance and where there's good there has to be bad."

At their blank faces, Sharrow waved his hands a little impatiently. "You obviously do not yet have experience of seeing magic for what it is. That was apparent when you came into this World and could not see past the illusions. You saw your surroundings as you wanted to see them right? You saw the good things."

He narrowed his eyes at them. "But when you see me, you see the bad things. The things that your brain doesn't really want to see. Do you understand?" his voice had taken on a lecturing tone.

"I think so," said Vylett. "When I saw the true you, I saw the things that I'm afraid of," she admitted. Her voice was quiet and strained and Milo was almost afraid to look at her for fear of seeing those lifeless blue eyes.

"Exactly," said Sharrow. "You saw the things that scare you. The bad things."

"So you are bad then," Abigail scowled at him and resumed her defensive stance.

"No. You misunderstand Abigail. I represent what is bad. That does not mean I am bad."

Abigail screwed up her brow in confusion. Milo felt much of the same. "Kind of like something may look bad on the outside but on the inside it's actually good?" he said in what was more of a quiet observation than a question for clarity.

"Kind of," said Sharrow and then he stamped his foot impatiently and stepped further inside his house. "Now, are you coming inside or not?"

"Yes we are." said Vylett and Milo watched her in surprise as she crossed the threshold.

"What do you have to eat?" she asked Sharrow.

***

Sharrow's house was warm and cosy.

They sat around his large kitchen table drinking mugs of thick hot chocolate. Outside it hadn't seemed too cold but now they were inside it felt like winter. Through the windows the wind was blowing hard and frost was seeping up the glass.

Milo wondered if it was another illusion.

He glanced at the fire crackling in the grate and at the stacks of crockery lined up on some wooden shelves on the walls and wondered how much of it was real.

"Sharrow? Am I seeing your kitchen for how it really is?" he asked.

Sharrow was busy chopping vegetables by the stove. "Well that depends. What exactly do you see?"

Milo shrugged. "The usual kitchen stuff I guess. Wooden table, wooden shelves, an oven..."

"And that is exactly how it looks." The frying pan sizzled as Sharrow scraped the vegetables into them. "I'll give you a tip Milo. If something is an illusion then you should be able to see a slight blurring from the corner of your eye. It's only very subtle and extremely hard to make out. It's easier to see if the illusion is a person because movement makes it easier to see."

Milo and the others stared at Sharrow, studying him intently to try and see the blurriness. But try as they might, none of them could see it. They worked at it for five minutes and gave up.

Sharrow laughed. "It takes practice. What kind of school did you lot go to?"

"A school where we weren't allowed to practice magic," said Vylett with undisguised bitterness. "Well for me and Milo anyway," she specified. "Our gifts were forbidden."

"Ah yes, you and Milo are from the Water Quarter. I believe you have the pleasure of serving the Terramangs. I have met a couple of them." Sharrow's face turned sour. "They are the most vile and obstinate creatures I have ever had the misfortune to meet."

"Yeah that's them," said Milo drily.

"And what's more, they think that because they have the ability to teleport, they can just enter Worlds at their choosing," Sharrow continued, clearly on a mission to point out all the Terramangs' negative qualities.

Milo was beginning to like Sharrow.

"They don't think it polite to knock first. They aggravate all the cross-patchers. You have my sympathy." Sharrow gave Milo and Vylett a slanting smile and then turned to Helico.

"And you Helico? Did you learn magic at school?"

"I never went to school much." Helico grinned sheepishly. He was slouched back in his chair looking as though he was ready to take an afternoon nap. "I knew all I needed to know," and then he flitted in and out of invisibility to prove the point.

"Why did you not go to school?" Abigail gave him a disapproving frown.

Helico shrugged. "Better things to do." His tone was slightly 'offish' which was unusual for Helico and he kept his eyes down but a moment later he grinned and nudged Abigail lightly. "I bet you were a real swat at school though Abs."

"Not in magic, if that's what you mean," Abigail said coolly. "There is no magic in my World. Well none that I know of. If I'd suddenly started levitating I would have been committed to a psychiatric unit."

"Ah yes," Sharrow chuckled. "But despite a World with no natural magic, your World is the most talked about amongst the cross-patchers Abigail. It sounds a most fascinating world."

Abigail looked non-plussed. "Not really,"

"But yes really," Sharrow argued, and his voice rose with excitement. "You have technology and machines that can think for themselves. That is more fascinating than any type of magic."

Milo sipped at his hot chocolate as Abigail and Sharrow began a detailed debate about the equipment in her World. None of it made any sense to Milo and he was starting to feel sleepy from the heat of the fire when Sharrow said,

"I'm low on ingredients. Would one of you mind going into the village to buy some more for me. I need to keep an eye on this cooking."

"Sure I'll go," Milo offered immediately. He needed some fresh air before he fell asleep. It felt like forever since he had last slept.

Abigail also decided to go with him and together they braved the blustery weather, making the short walk back into the village to find the food stalls.

"I had to get out of there," said Abigail, wrapping her arms around herself against the cold.

They turned a corner and a large gust of wind nearly knocked them over. Milo really wished he had asked Sharrow for a sweatshirt.

He glanced at Abigail. "Why? what's wrong? Do you not like Sharrow? Cos he seems ok."

"It's not that," said Abigail. "I just couldn't stand to talk any more about my World."

"Why not?"

Abigail gave him a sideways glance. "Don't laugh ok but it was making me homesick."

"I'm not laughing," said Milo seriously. How could he laugh when he knew exactly how she felt?

"I know it has no magic," said Abigail, "but its home to me and I'll probably never see it again."

"You don't know that. Perhaps Alanya can help you or maybe Sharrow knows the cross-patcher who controls your World."

Abigail shrugged. "I doubt it. But when all this is over I'll keep looking for it. Thanks to you and Vylett, I'm now free of Orlost and can go wherever I want." Then she added. "Well so long as I can get past the cross-patchers and keep the Terramangs from finding me."

She grimaced against the cold and swore as another gust of wind threatened to knock them down. "Who knows, maybe I'll settle somewhere that could eventually feel like home."

Milo glanced around him at the pretty pathways that weaved between the quaint houses and the little bridges that crossed them now and again. In the far off distance there were mountains with an ominous mist hovering above them and sometimes Milo thought he could see specks of gold poking through that mist.

Always mist, thought Milo.

And then there was the sound of the music coming from the village square, which instead of being muffled by the wind, seemed to be carried by it. As though the music was a physical thing that could attach itself to the wind molecules.

"I reckon if you could get used to illusions then this place wouldn't be so bad to live in," Milo told Abigail. Although perhaps not the weather," he grumbled as a drop of water fell from the sky to land on his shoulder and immediately turn into a small icicle. "Come on let's get moving," he said breaking the icicle off. "I'm freezing out here. Literally."

Milo's teeth started to chatter. "It's weird how the weather has suddenly changed."

"Maybe Sharrow's done an illusion thing to coax us into his warm house, hoping we'll never want to leave. You know like some sick fairytale." Abigail suggested with exaggerated relish.

Milo gave her an odd look, "I hope not."

When they reached the village, despite the horrible weather, it was still bustling and Milo was fascinated by the strange assortment of clothes the villagers were wearing.

The men wore tailored suits with tall hats and gloves, whilst most of the women wore long thick skirts and elegant hats. Abigail thought they looked old fashioned whilst Milo thought they just looked weird.

Apparently that's what the villagers thought of Milo and Abigail too because most of them just stared at them, gawping with a listless curiosity.

Ignoring them, Milo and Abigail picked a stall that had lots of different food stuff and gave the list that Sharrow had given them to the vendor. Milo did not know what half the stuff on the list was.

"I don't believe I've ever seen you two before," the vendor commented. "You're not from around here that's for sure," he eyed their clothes warily. "What is it you want?"

His tone was accusing and his expression was stony. His mouth fixed in a tight thin line.

The man's posture was so rigid he looked paralysed and his skin so ashen that Milo wondered if he was staring into the face of death itself.

Milo immediately went on the defensive. "Sharrow sent us," he said. And to his relief, the man visibly relaxed. He even gave them a smile.

"Well if Sharrow sent you then you must be ok. Oswald Crackenpepper's the name." The man extended his arm to shake their hands.

He really was very strange looking. He was small and shrunken, with hair was so pale it was colourless. And there was something about his voice...

...it was somehow familiar.

Even more chilling was that he was wearing a black suit like the ones people on the Water Quarter wore when they disposed of their dead loved ones to the water's depths.

He gave Milo the creeps.

Oswald gave them the stuff that they needed and they paid using a token that Sharrow had given them and then they headed back to Sharrow's house.

Oswald Crackenpepper waved them goodbye and from the corner of his eyes, just for a second, Milo thought he saw a blurriness.

***

"What have you done to your arm Milo? That looks nasty."

They were nearly back at the house when Abigail noticed the burnt area on Milo's skin where a huge blister had formed. He had forgotten all about it.

"Oh, that was Peaches' s leaving present. One of the embers got me."

"Ouch. Maybe Sharrow has something for it."

"Its ok," Milo insisted as a huge gust of wind made his eyes water and the music from the village rang louder in his ears.

"What?" shouted Abigail as huge water droplets began to fall again.

"I said it's ok," Milo shouted back, his voice sounding loud as the wind ebbed again.

Truthfully, now that he had been reminded of the burn, it was starting to make him feel fuzzy and slightly queasy. Trying to take his mind off it, he said.

"How about you Abigail? How are you doing? You don't look so great yourself." Abigail's wild red hair was matted and looking a little lank, which Milo knew wasn't from the rain. She had dirt smudges on her face and dark circles under her eyes.

Abigail frowned. "Thanks Milo, that's what a girl always want to hear."

"No I didn't mean that, I just meant.."

"Relax. I know what you meant Milo. And you're right I do look yucky. I would love a shower or a bath. And right now an umbrella," she said as the rain began to fall harder. "Although if Sharrow has one it'll probably be an illusion." Abigail rolled her eyes but she looked amused.

Milo smiled. Abigail was growing on him. He admired her strong will and the way she could keep Helico in check.

"You did a great job in Peaches's cave, saving Vylett," he said to her.

"You really care about Vylett don't you?" Abigail said giving him a sideways glance.

Milo suddenly felt flustered. "Well sure. We were exiled together. She's my friend and I thought she was going to die."

"Yes I know that Milo," Abigail said a little impatiently. "The point I'm trying to make is that you would have been more upset if she'd died than if me or Helico had died."

"That's not true. You and Helico are my friends too."

"Yes but you and Vylett are.."

"Just friends." Milo said sounding more defensive than he intended to. "And that's the end of this conversation Abigail!"

Abigail chewed her bottom lip thoughtfully. "Ok, but let me ask you this Milo...would you die for her?"

Milo stared at her. "What?"

"Hey it's a simple question Milo. Would you die for Vylett?"

The question took Milo by surprise but Abigail was right, in the end it was simple.

"Yes," he said.

The corners of Abigail's mouth turned up into a slow satisfied smile. "Then she's more than just a friend."

Milo felt taken a back and began to stutter some argument but he was saved from any further embarrassment because they had reached Sharrow's house and the cross-patcher was waiting for them on the threshold.

***

When Sharrow saw Milo and Abigail, he had immediately been full of apologies. Taking one look at their frozen fingers and red noses, he had promptly made them sit by an enormous warm log fire in a large but comfortable room next to the kitchen.

"I forget how susceptible humans are to the elements," he had said. And then he had left them by the fire whilst he finished preparing their meal.

Sometime later when Milo and Abigail were sufficiently thawed out again, Sharrow served them all a delicious meal of soup and crusty bread, followed by stir fried vegetables, followed by a chocolate and cream dessert. After his third cup of hot chocolate Milo felt more than satisfied and completely maxed out on chocolate.

But once the meal was over, Sharrow wanted to know why they had been in Peaches's cave. As a cross-patcher, Sharrow already knew who they were and where they were from but he did not know the circumstances surrounding their journey.

He listened with interest as the children enlightened him. Milo felt it was only fair to tell Sharrow the whole truth given the fact he had saved them from Peaches.

So Milo and Vylett shared the storytelling of the circumstances surrounding the Water Quarter. They explained about Milo's exile and how the Terramangs had been stealing magic from the Quarters and thus creating an imbalance which was putting everyone's lives at risk.

Milo explained about Penelope's water charm and how they believed that the charm could save the Quarters. When he reached the part about Orlost, Abigail and Helico chipped in with their own version of events.

Only when Vylett mentioned that they needed to find an elevator that Alanya had presented to her in a vision did Sharrow look about to interrupt. But he didn't. He waved them to carry on and so they explained with some emotion how they had lost Eli and Iza and finally how they had found Peaches's cave.

When they had finished, Sharrow nodded gravely. "Well that now gives me more of an understanding. And I can fully appreciate why you had to leave Orlost but it does present me with a bit of a problem."

"What's that?" Abigail narrowed her eyes at him.

"If the Terramangs should come looking here for you then I can not lie. I would have to say that you have been here. As a cross-patcher I can not lie about who crosses my portal. It is a vow I have taken."

Milo nodded. "That's fair enough."

Helico glanced nervously around him. "I'd almost forgotten about those scum," he said. "I'm surprised they haven't found us already."

"They may be able to teleport anywhere they want but they have to know where you are first to be able to find you," said Sharrow. "There are hundreds of portals. They could search for years and still not find you. You should congratulate yourselves on outwitting them."

"They'll find us," said Vylett, again convinced that they could never outrun a Terramang. "I just hope we find my mother first."

"There is one more thing we need your help with," Milo paused and swallowed. His request was a big one and there was a fairly large chance that Sharrow would reject it. He took a deep breath.

"We really need to find this elevator, but as you know Peaches was not very accommodating. Is there any chance that you could talk some sense into her so that she will let us enter?"

To Milo's surprise Sharrow laughed. It was a deep rumbling laugh that made his entire body shake.

"You want me, a cross-patcher to make some kind of deal with another cross-patcher?" Sharrow laughed even harder and Milo glanced at the others who were just as bewildered as him.

"I don't understand what's so funny," he said.

Sharrow composed himself and wiped away a tear that had rolled down his cheek. "Forgive me, I forget you do not know the rules of cross-patchers. Come on, let's go and sit in the other room. It's more comfortable."

After plonking themselves in comfortable armchairs around the huge log fire in the next room, Sharrow explained why he had found Milo's request so amusing.

"A cross-patcher can never intrude on another cross-patchers turf," he said. "It is highly insulting and intrusive. To me, the idea of doing such a thing is absurd. And it was that absurdity my friends that gave me my laughing fit. Please forgive me. I do not mean to laugh at your ignorance."

Milo felt slightly offended that Sharrow had called them ignorant but he sensed Sharrow meant no malice.

"I've just had a thought," said Vylett. "Is Audrina a cross-patcher too?"

Sharrow nodded. "Ah yes the beautiful Audrina. She is indeed. Now she is one cross-patcher who doesn't mind people entering her portal, as you found out. She loves company."

Milo thought that was a slight understatement.

"But Audrina has Eli. And maybe Iza too. Does that mean that you can't help them?" Vylett asked and her question resulted in a moment's intense silence.

"I'm afraid so my dear." Sharrow looked sympathetic and there was another awkward silence.

Right now it was looking less and less likely that they would ever again find the twins.

"What would happen if you did attempt to do that?" said Helico. "You know, just out of interest. I mean what would happen if you ever tried to interfere in another portal? Would Audrina try and kill you? Would Peaches kill you?"

Sharrow gave a short dry laugh. "Cross-patchers are not mortal. We can't die. We will never see the World of the Dead." Although Milo felt sure this should have been a good thing, he thought he detected a sadness in Sharrow's voice.

"But to answer your question Helico, if I intruded on another cross-patcher's territory, although they couldn't kill me they would have the right to try to destroy me in other ways. And that is far worse." Sharrow's expression was suddenly sombre. He didn't volunteer as to what ways he could be destroyed.

Then he suddenly brightened. "But as for the elevator. Peaches is not the only one who has access to it. I do too."

Sharrow looked at them and raised his eyebrow. "Care for me to explain?"

Chapter 15

The Book of Thoughts

Milo felt a nervous excitement growing in the pit of his stomach as he listened to Sharrow.

"The elevator is a portal of course," Sharrow said and waving his hands in a way that suggested he barely needed to tell them that because it should have been so obvious. "But it's a portal within a portal if you like. There is one in every World if you know where to look for it."

Sharrow's face became grave. "But admittance to the Otherworld is not one that is taken lightly. I have only ever known two people who have stumbled across the elevator and tried to get admittance. Both of them wanted to see loved ones again and both of them were refused."

"Refused by who?" asked Milo.

"Well by the elevator itself of course."

"Of course." Milo muttered, wondering why this was a surprise. It wasn't as though everything else they had encountered recently had been exactly normal.

"But you can admit us right?" Vylett looked at Sharrow hopefully. Her huge blue eyes looked glassy in the glow of the fire.

Sharrow nodded slowly. "I can partially admit you. I can show you to the elevator, which means as far as I'm concerned you have my permission. And as I am a cross-patcher, the elevator will then take this strongly into account and hopefully grant you admission too. But.." Sharrow leaned back in his chair and rubbed his stubbled chin thoughtfully.

"Have you thought about this very carefully because I don't believe there is a way back from the Otherworld. It is part of the World of the Dead and from there, there is no return."

"Vylett believes her mother can help us to return with the water charm." Milo said with more confidence than he felt. "And besides," he added. "Before Alanya knew about the water charm, she was sending Vylett visions to help her find her. Why would Alanya have sent Vylett visions to find her if she thought there was no way back?"

Sharrow shrugged. "Perhaps she didn't know. The Otherworld is a strange and chaotic place I believe. And I don't imagine the dead think about such things."

"Perhaps she thought the Otherworld would be a better place for me than Orlost," suggested Vylett. "She knew I was in trouble. She knew I needed help," she said as she remembered her conversation with her mother in the Otherworld.

"Perhaps," said Sharrow. "But the fact remains. Are you willing to take the risk of never being able to return."

"We have to," said Milo. "We need to help the Quarters. And I need to find out what's happened to my sister. I need to know why she's there too."

Sharrow sighed and studied Vylett carefully. "Do you really believe your mother is that gifted? Gifted enough to return you from the dead?" he looked sceptical and Vylett looked uncertain for a second.

Then she glanced at Milo and nodded. "Yes. I know she is. I can feel it."

"Then I will permit you to go there," said Sharrow. "But only because it's for a noble cause. And how about you two?" Sharrow gave Abigail and Helico an inquisitive look. "This situation doesn't really concern you. Do you really want to risk your lives just for the sake of helping your friends?"

"Well when you put it like that....er.." Helico began hesitantly but Abigail cut him off by nudging him hard in the ribs.

"Yes. We're going too," she said. "This does concern us. Milo and Vylett helped us to escape Orlost so we're going to help them. Aren't we Helico?" She gave Helico a pointed look.

Milo opened his mouth to say that actually it had been Abigail herself who had helped them to escape Orlost but he shut it again.

"Of course," Helico said quickly. "That's what I was going to say." He grinned sheepishly and poured himself another hot chocolate.

"Of course." Sharrow gave Helico a slanting smile and threw a log onto the fire. It crackled and began spitting out embers and Milo instinctively drew his arms closer to his body, not wanting to get any more burns. His arm was still painful, and even more so now that it was near heat.

Sharrow noticed and dragged a fireguard in front of the spitting embers. "I really must remember how vulnerable humans are," he said by way of apology. Then he turned to them, looking at each of them in turn.

"Of course if should you enter the Otherworld then there is also another advantage besides finding Vylett's mother that you might or might not be aware of..."

Milo raised his eyebrows. "What's that?"

"You will be safe from the Terramangs there," said Sharrow. "Like cross-patchers, they can't enter the Otherworld because they are immortal. It's the one place they can't teleport too."

"Awesome!" Helico punched the air enthusiastically and Milo felt a part of him relax. That was something at least.

They sat in silence for a while then, content to watch the flames from the fire and listen to the soft cracking sounds of the logs splitting.

Helico picked up a log from a stash near his feet and absently began tapping it rhythmically against the fireguard.

"I've been thinking," he said.

"Woah don't over do it Helico," Abigail said in a droll voice.

Helico gave her a look and then turned to Sharrow. "I've been thinking," he continued. "I know that immortals can't die. But what if someone were to chop their heads off. What then?" Surely even an immortal can't put their own head back on and still survive."

"Uurgh do you have to be so gross Helico," Abigail gave him a disapproving frown and took the log from him. She tapped him lightly on the arm with it.

Helico shrugged. "I'm just saying."

Sharrow laughed. "If an immortal were unfortunate enough to have their head removed from their body then they would be destroyed, not dead. It's not the same thing. The immortal wouldn't be able to function anymore but their soul would not enter the Otherworld which is a far worse thing. The soul would die within them and they would just be nothing. Nothing at all."

Milo shuddered. "That's horrible."

"Yes it is," agreed Sharrow. "But destroying an immortal is a very difficult thing. I think the power it would take for a human to destroy an immortal would be virtually impossible. It would be easier however for one immortal to destroy another immortal because their powers of magic are relatively matched and if their desire to destroy was strong enough then it could be done."

Helico looked thoughtful as he gazed at Sharrow. "Then you're not really immortal.."

"Helico!" Abigail looked aghast. "I think Sharrow might think that's insulting."

Helico instantly looked embarrassed. "No. I didn't mean that. I was just thinking that it's reassuring to know that an immortal can be destroyed. That's something at least."

Sharrow gave him a bemused look. "Are you considering decapitating me Helico?"

Helico looked startled. "No, no! I was thinking of a last resort if we come face to face with a Terramang."

Abigail gave him a look that suggested he had lost the plot. "Oh well that's ok then," she said. "Because of course we'll be able to do that no problem Helico. We chop off peoples' heads every day!" Her sarcasm was not lost on Helico and he frowned before turning invisible and then popping up behind her and making her squeal.

Milo and Vylett laughed and for a minute the mood was lightened - until Sharrow lowered it again.

"I do have one condition though before I allow you to enter the portal to the Otherworld." The cross-patcher looked at each of them seriously and Helico stopped messing around.

"I knew it," he groaned. "I knew it was too good to be true."

"You don't know what I'm going to say yet," said Sharrow.

"Well it's not going to be anything good."

"Do you not think sleep is good?"

"What?" Helico was yawning even as he answered.

Sharrow smiled. "I want you all to stay here overnight and have a good night's rest. Believe me when I say you will need your energy to visit the Otherworld. And that is my only condition."

No one argued. They were all shattered and Sharrow was right - they were going to need some energy to face the Otherworld. It made Milo's stomach feel funny just thinking about entering a place where the dead resided, and if made him feel even more strange to think his sister was there.

"Oh and Milo," said Sharrow. "I believe I have something that will heal that burn of yours. You should have told me. You humans are too self-heroic."

***

Sharrow let them all take a shower before bed, much to Abigail's delight, and even produced some fresh clothing for each of them, so that finally both Milo and Helico could rid themselves of their horrible Orlost uniforms.

When they were all changed into comfortable clothes which consisted of comfy pants and t-shirts (thankfully not stiff suits like the villages wore), Sharrow showed them where they could sleep.

He put them all in one room with a pile of bedding and told them to make themselves comfortable.

Milo had gone on a school trip once to another town on the Water Quarter and they had camped in some woodland. He was reminded of that trip now as the four of them made up their beds on the floor. Only this time he was in the company of much more pleasant people.

This time he was with friends.

Milo placed his blankets next to Vylett and glanced at her as she fell asleep. He thought he saw a tear roll down her face and wondered if she was thinking about her mother. Life could be so unfair. Vylett was a good and kind person and Milo couldn't think of a crueller thing to have happened to her.

He sighed. He wanted to help her, to comfort her.

He just didn't know how.

***

Sometime later Milo was still awake.

He was so tired his body ached but he couldn't switch his brain off. He couldn't stop thinking about Penelope.

What if Vylett was right? What if Penelope really had died?

And what if Sharrow was right? What if Alanya really couldn't help them return from the Otherworld?

After more twisting and turning in silent torment, Milo crept silently out of his mound of bedding and wandered out onto the landing. He paced up and down a few times, with the intent of trying to blank his mind and make himself sleepy.

He noticed there were four doors in total on the landing. One of them was the room he had just been in, one was the bathroom and he assumed the one with a light underneath was Sharrow's bedroom. Curious as to what the fourth room was, he tiptoed quietly and pushed open the door.

At first he couldn't see much. He had no flame with which to light the candles that he could see outlined on the walls.

But no sooner had he stepped foot inside the room, the candles alighted. Immediately he realised he wasn't in a room at all. He was in a narrow passageway with steps leading down to....where?

Never been one to just 'let things go', curiosity got the better of him and he descended the dust clad stone steps.

He glanced back up the stairs once to check that Sharrow had not heard him and on hearing nothing but his own quickened heartbeat he continued descending until he was in a large square room.

For a second Milo didn't comprehend where he was. And then as he took in the four walls that were lined with tall shelves - one of them filled with books and the other three with hundreds of potion bottles of varying shapes and sizes - he sucked in a sharp breath.

He was in his own house back on Syanna. He was in his father's basement.

Milo had only been in his father's basement a few times because his father was a very private person and did not like people, even his own family, intruding in his work area. But this was definitely his work area.

There in the centre of the room was his father's comfy red sofa and next to it his workbench that was covered in vials of herbs, powders, ceramic mixing dishes and a whole lot of other potion paraphernalia that Milo didn't recognise. Milo had never had much interest in that sort of thing.

"I don't understand," he muttered as he sat down onto the red sofa with shaky legs.

"You really must learn to try harder in seeing past an illusion." Sharrow's voice sounded behind him. Startled, Milo whirled around to see the cross-patcher watching him with a bemused expression on his face.

Milo coloured, embarrassed to be caught snooping around. If he could have sat further into the couch he would have.

Of course it was an illusion. And the moment Milo realised this, the room began to blend into a whirl of colours. It was becoming a water painting before his very eyes but then as though someone had reversed time, the colours solidified again and he was still looking at his father's basement.

Milo blinked and looked at Sharrow in confusion.

"I held on to the illusion," Sharrow explained. "As a cross-patcher I can see exactly what you see and I'm curious. What is this place?"

"My father's basement." Milo looked around at all the potion bottles and felt a pang of homesickness. He had not thought about his father's basement though in a long time and wondered why he was seeing it now.

"This is not a place I dream about," Milo said to Sharrow. "Why am I seeing this?"

Sharrow shrugged. "People who are susceptible to illusions often see what they would rather see. For example their brains see something that reminds them of something familiar and their brain converts reality into that image."

Milo thought about this. He supposed that the steps he had just walked down into the room had perhaps subconsciously reminded him of his father's basement. It made his head hurt trying to work it out.

"Uurgh, I'm glad I don't live in this world permanently. I would be totally messed up."

Sharrow chuckled. "Now explain to me what these are." He pointed to a prism shaped device with multiple small pipes protruding from it.

"I think that separates the magical herbs from the non-magical ones but don't ask me how because I don't know. Potions are not really my thing."

"And this?" Sharrow pointed to a thin flat metal gadget with notches on it.

"Er..not sure." Feeling useless Milo scanned the labels of the hundreds of potion bottles looking for potions that he recognised.

Each bottle was made of either blue or red glass and had a little stopper at its neck that was coated in solid silver. His father nurtured these bottles.

"That's secret sand," Milo said eyeing one of the labelled bottles. "You sprinkle that around to find things that might have been hidden by magic. A lot of kids are given it as birthday presents. It can be good fun."

Then he was struck by something on his father's workbench. There was a thick red book which was lying open and beside it was a pyramid shaped bottle. Unlike the other bottles, this one was clear glass and had a gold stopper. There was a gold coloured substance inside the bottle and Milo immediately felt compelled by it.

He walked slowly to the work bench and read the label of the bottle. It said, "Infinity Dust."

Tentatively he reached out to touch it.

"If you touch it the illusion will break," Sharrow warned.

Milo pulled his hand back and glanced at the open page of the red book. He recognised the book at once by its old leather spine.

It was his fathers 'book of thoughts.'

His father had shown it to him once on one of his rare visits to the basement.

"Everything my father thinks of related to potions goes in this book," Milo explained to Sharrow who was leaning over him with curiosity.

"Ah a potion journal. How interesting. So what is this particular potion? Infinity Dust sounds incredibly powerful." Sharrow's brow furrowed in concentration while he pondered the potion's name.

"Infinite...means something unlimited...something never ending...a never ending stream of possibilities."

"I don't know what it is." Milo studied the open page of the book, frowning at the notes written in his father's scrawly handwriting. The few odd words that he could make out did not give him much more information. Powerful, slow, absolute precision, secret..he paused on the 'secret' part. Why would the potion be a secret?

He kept reading. "Says something here about a potion designed for infinite tasks. Looks like you were right about the never ending possibilities," Milo said to Sharrow. "I can't imagine why my father would be making something like this. It has to be illegal."

Then further down the page, heavily underlined were the words - Terramangs. Not yet finished.

Milo sucked in a breath as the realisation hit him. His father was making a potion for the Terramangs.

His mind whirled back to the day of his exile and the piece of paper that Droges had so aggressively asked him to deliver to his father. He remembered his father's pale face as he had opened that piece of paper. Milo had forgotten all about it until now.

"What is it Milo?" Sharrow was gazing at him with concern.

"I don't think it matters if I find Alanya any more." Milo shut the big red book with a sigh and jumped back in surprise as his touch caused the illusion to break.

He found himself sat on a perfectly ordinary leather sofa in a perfectly ordinary basement. In place of the shelves of potions and herb paraphernalia were piles of garments and shelves full of trinkets and souvenir type objects.

He stared around in surprise.

"Ah, you seem to have found my junk room." Sharrow chuckled without embarrassment. "And I promise you this is no illusion. This is just my mess which I like to keep hidden away here - to create the simple illusion of being tidy." He chuckled again to himself and then his eyes turned serious as Milo failed to pick up on his little joke.

"Now never mind my junk room. What did you discover about that potion that would make you want to abandon your quest for Alanya?"

Milo leaned back heavily into the squashy leather sofa. "The potion is for the Terramangs. Droges asked my father to make it for him. So if the Terramangs are planning on using a potion which can do anything you want it to then what is the point of Alanya restoring the balance to the Quarters. The Terramangs are clearly just going to destroy us all anyway."

"You don't know that."

"I know that they're not going to use the potion for anything good."

"Be that may, but you can't know for sure that they intend to destroy human life. They don't need a potion to do that. They can kill someone from just a flick of their finger I believe."

Milo wasn't to be deterred. "Ok then, they will definitely use the potion to make themselves more powerful. Stealing magic from the Quarters obviously hasn't been enough. They will make peoples' lives a misery."

"That may well be," said Sharrow. "But from what you told me earlier, the imbalance will make peoples' lives a misery anyway." Sharrow put a hand on Milo's shoulder. "You need to help your people Milo. Let someone else worry about the potion. You can't know for sure what the Terramangs plan to use it for."

Milo had a sudden thought. "Maybe they want the potion to fix the imbalance. Now they've stolen the magic, I guess it would make sense they would want to fix the damage. They love to rule people after all, and they can't very well do that if the Water Quarter is destroyed. Perhaps they've already fixed it."

"No they haven't." Sharrow shook his head.

"How do you know?" Milo gave him a frustrated look which Sharrow instantly returned.

"You really do need to have a lesson on illusions Milo my boy." Sharrow wiped a hand across his brow. "Illusions do not show you the past."

He sighed and then plonked himself on the sofa next to Milo. "The illusion you saw of your father's potion was present time and I believe he stated in his book that the potion was not yet finished."

Milo sighed. "OK you win. I'll carry on looking for Alanya. Maybe she can do something about this potion too."

"You seem to be counting on Alanya Roze to do a lot of things when you find her. I hope for your sake that she is capable of such demands."

"So do I," said Milo heavily.

"Well I am going to bed." Sharrow announced suddenly, getting up off the sofa and stretching his arms above his head. "I think you should do the same Milo once you've had some time alone with your thoughts."

With that, Sharrow retreated back up the stone steps leaving Milo alone on the worn leather sofa.

The trouble was when Milo had too much time to think, his emotions took over and subsequently the urge to release magic. The more he thought about what the Terramangs might do with the Infinity Dust potion, the more worked up he got.

He felt the tingling sensations up his arms but it wasn't out of control like it had been on the Water Quarter. He could easily stop himself releasing magic.

But he didn't want to.

He wanted to unleash his anger on something. He had to remind himself that magic wasn't illegal here in the World of Illusions. Sharrow wasn't going to punish him for using it as long as he didn't hurt anybody.

He scanned Sharrow's junk room for something to target and his eyes fell upon a rusty looking bucket balanced precariously on top of an old dresser. There was another dresser on the opposite side of the room and Milo wondered if he could move the bucket from one dresser to the other.

He had never been able to use his magic so precisely as that before but lately he had had some practice. He had moved the brick wall to enter the black river. He had moved Helico and Vylett across Audrina's ballroom - albeit with some clumsiness - so maybe he could do this too.

He thought about the Terramangs using Infinity Dust for bad things and felt the magic surge strongly within him, then he focused it on the bucket and the dresser.

Instantly the bucket flew across the room but instead of landing on the opposite dresser, it flew into a mirror adjacent to it, smashing it into pieces.

Milo cursed loudly. "I am so rubbish."

He thought about cleaning up the broken pieces but he really didn't have the energy. He doubted Sharrow would even notice. Feeling deflated and incompetent, he replaced the bucket on the dresser and tried again.

Chapter 16

Lessons in Magic

Vylett was woken up by Helico gently shaking her.

"What's up? Has something happened?" She sat up. Too quickly - and felt the room spin.

"Easy. No nothing's happened," Helico reassured her. "You were mumbling in your sleep. Sounded like you were having a nightmare."

Vylett rubbed sleep from her eyes. "I don't remember" she muttered.

Actually she did remember. She just didn't want to talk about it. She had been dreaming about her mother.

She had dreamed that she had finally found her mother in the Otherworld but every time she had reached out for her she had been wrenched from her grasp. Her mother's pretty face had turned monster like and she had started wailing like a banshee, telling her that she was selfish for making her wait. Now it would be Vylett's turn to wait until her mother was ready to forgive her.

Vylett shuddered from the memory and Helico mistook her chills for feeling cold. He gathered up his blanket and gallantly put it around her shoulders.

"Where's Milo?" Vylett looked at the pile of empty blankets next to her and wondered what he was up to.

"I don't know, probably gone to the toilet or something. Don't worry, he'll be back. He won't leave us." Helico was whispering and Vylett realised Abigail was still fast asleep. A few red curls were all that could be seen of her amongst the huge pile of blankets she was cocooned under.

"I'm not worried," Vylett lowered her voice to match Helico's. "I know he'll be back." And she knew without a doubt that he would be. Milo was a solid part of her life now, and she of his, and whatever the future was to bring, she felt sure that they would never be far from each other.

Helico shifted his position and on seeing a flash of pain on his face Vylett remembered his ankle.

"Is it bad?" she asked, feeling guilty that she hadn't realised before that her friend was in so much pain.

Helico shrugged. "Not bad." But when he grimaced again, Vylett pulled up his trouser leg and gasped to see that the poor boy's ankle had swelled up to twice its size.

"Ok maybe it is a bit sore," Helico admitted. "But hey it's nothing compared to what you've been through. How are you doing?" What he really meant to say but didn't, was "how are you coping now that you've found out your long lost mother is dead?"

"I'll be ok. Thanks for asking." She gave him a light smile and then nodded towards Abigail.

"It must have been hard for her, seeing her parents again. I'm sure her gran did her best bringing her up, but still...must have been hard without a Mum and Dad. I guess now it makes sense why she felt so close to my mother on Orlost."

"Don't worry about Abs Vylett. She's a fighter. Like you." Helico was looking at Abigail with such fondness that Vylett almost felt like she was intruding on their privacy, even though Abigail was asleep.

'Helico?...can I ask you something?"

"Sure,"

"I know that was your little sister at Audrina's ball. Were you very close?"

Helico nodded. He turned his head away from her and Vylett felt a rush of tense fraught emotion emanate from him. Why didn't she keep her mouth shut?

"She's dead," Helico turned back to her and his eyes were red rimmed.

"Oh..I'm sorry Helico." There was a moment's awkward silence. "Do you mind if I ask how?"

"My parents killed her." Helico said flatly. "My only real family was my little sister Neira and my parents killed her."

Vylett was horrified. "That's terrible. How could they do that to their own daughter?"

"Ok maybe they didn't kill her with their bare hands," admitted Helico. "But nearly as good as because they killed her with neglect and selfishness."

Again Vylett could feel a catapult of strong emotions coming from Helico. Anger, sadness, guilt. But she pushed them away. This was Helico's story to tell and she absolutely did not want to intrude.

Helico breathed a weary sigh and began to explain.

"My parents are very wealthy and where I come from if you have money and you have children then some of the money should be used to marry off your child at an early age. This way you can buy into another rich household to strengthen relationships and the family name for future generations. Blah blah blah," Helico waved his hand dismissively. "All very false and pretentious really. Anyway, a few months ago I turned fifteen and my parents found me a girl to marry."

"You were to be married at fifteen?!" Vylett was stunned.

"Yes that was my reaction exactly," said Helico drily. "And what's more, my parents wanted me to lead the same lifestyles that they led. You know, go to the posh parties where everyone looks as though they've got their posh napkins stuck up their backsides."

Vylett allowed herself a small smile. It was so like Helico to try and make light of the situation.

"Anyway I refused to marry her," said Helico. "Said I didn't want to live the rich life anymore. I wanted to break away and make my own way in life."

He allowed himself a small grin. "I don't think anyone had ever rebelled like that before. I caused quite the scandal I can tell you," he said putting on a posh voice and grinning to himself as he remembered.

"Then what happened?" Vylett prompted.

"Well just to spite me my parents planned the wedding for the very next day. There was a mad rush of organising things." Helico shook his head bitterly. "Oh they really wanted to make sure that there was no time for me to plan anything stupid. But.." said Helico pointing his finger at Vylett. "Twenty four hours is still plenty of time to do something stupid." He ran a hand through his blonde curls and Vylett felt another wave of emotion from him.

This time guilt.

"I did feel bad for my intended wife though," Helico admitted. "She was attractive…" Helico raised his eyes at Vylett but she just nudged him and told him to carry on. She had felt his true emotion, he couldn't cover it up that easily.

"Well the day of the wedding came and I told my parents outright that I was leaving and they couldn't stop me. They were horrified of course and told me they would never forgive me for bringing shame on the family and of course my inheritance would be written off." Helico waved his hand. "Like I gave a damn about my inheritance anyway."

"But the hardest part was saying goodbye to Neira. She cried and cried and wanted to come with me. It broke my heart, I wanted to take her too, I really did but what life would she have had on the roads with me? Instead I promised her I would come and get her when it was her time to be married. And So I left."

"Where did you go?" asked Vylett.

"Well at first I stayed hidden in our village for a while because I wanted to hear about how my intended bride took the news. Despite everything I felt guilty for ruining her big day. Anyway a few hours later I was sitting in a bar hidden away in a corner but there were guests there from my wedding that never happened and I heard them talking."

Another fresh wave of pain hit Vylett.

"They gossiped about how after I ran out my parents fretted so much over the abandoned nuptials, they tried to make amends with the bride's family by planning a wedding for my sister and their son." Helico shook his head angrily. "Neira overheard all this but she didn't understand it, she was only eight. She thought she was going to be taken away right then and there to be married."

Helico's eyes teared up and Vylett felt like she was holding her breath, sharing in his pain that she could feel so clearly it was like her own.

"And so, apparently in her fear, Neira ran out of the house," Helico continued, "and straight into the path of some horses."

Helico licked his lips and swallowed. "Some idiots had been racing them down the streets. They were out of control. Neira was crushed to death."

When he spoke next his breath sounded shallow. "The only consolation is that she was killed instantly and didn't suffer."

Vylett didn't know what to say. "I'm so sorry Helico. That's such a tragic story."

Helico nodded. "But hey it's not all bad. For the next year I tried to live a happy life, doing exactly what I wanted because I knew that my Neira would have wanted that. But that's why I never went to school much," he said. "I wanted to tell Abigail the truth but I didn't want to tell her with everyone listening."

Vylett nodded. "I can understand that. So will Abigail too when you tell her."

Helico looked across at Abigail who was still sleeping. "Yeah," he said. "I know."

"So how did you end up on Orlost?" Vylett asked him.

Helico screwed up his face as he recalled the memory. "Not much to tell really. One day I was mucking about with some friends and playing the idiot as I usually do and showing off, using my invisibility, and then the next thing I know I'm on Orlost. And well... you know the rest."

"And now you're having the time of your life!" Vylett smiled and gave him another little nudge.

Helico laughed. "Do you know what? I actually am. I know that sounds crazy cos the Terramangs are probably out for our guts right now, but honestly, there's no where else I'd rather be." He gave a short laugh. "Sad isn't it?"

"Maybe a little," Vylett smiled. They sat in comfortable silence for a while.

"You know we all seem to have parent issues," Vylett mused. "There's you. And Eli said he and Iza had a tough upbringing, that their parents were barely around. My mother was exiled when I was young and then there's Abigail. She lost her parents too at a young age." Vylett glanced at Abigail's bundled form. They could hear her soft breathing in the silence.

Helico's eyes seem to cloud over as he stared at Abigail and again Vylett felt like she was intruding on them. She glanced away, feeling embarrassed.

"Milo's the only one who was brought up by two parents who gave him a normal life," she said. "Well as normal as they could given the fact he had to hide his magic," she amended.

Helico managed to tear his eyes away from Abigail and gave her a sad smile that tugged at Vylett's heart. "Guess we've all got some story to tell."

Then the door opened.

A thin stream of light filtered in, followed by a weary looking Milo. He looked surprised to see Vylett and Helico awake but he was silent as he climbed back under his mound of blankets.

"Is everything ok?" Vylett whispered to him.

"Yes everything's fine. I'll tell you in the morning when everyone's awake." He glanced at Abigail's still sleeping form. "I don't think I've got the energy to tell you twice."

***

The next morning Milo felt decidedly better after tucking into a hearty breakfast and discussing his findings of the Infinity Dust with the others.

Vylett had initially been particularly agitated at the news but after lengthy discussions with Sharrow, Abigail and Helico, she had agreed that it was probably best not to worry about something they couldn't prevent or predict, so instead they had pushed it from their minds and devoured Sharrow's delicious breakfast of eggs, meat and potatoes.

After a few more disastrous attempts at practicing his gift in Sharrow's junk room last night, Milo had admitted defeat and made another mental note to ask Alanya Roze for tips.

Sharrow was right. The list of problems for Alanya to sort through was getting bigger by the day. What was it now? Milo reviewed the list in his head. Correcting the imbalance, helping Penelope, stopping the Infinity Dust and now helping him use magic.

Milo sighed, wondering if Alanya would be annoyed at all his demands.

Still he was not perturbed and after his breakfast Milo was feeling re-energised and satisfied. That is until he remembered that today they would be entering the Otherworld - and then he could have quite easily brought his breakfast back up again.

Before they left the house to embark on the next stage of their journey, Vylett had another vision. Sharrow caught her as she slumped forward but the vision was brief.

"My mother just showed me some numbers but I don't know what they mean." Vylett said as leaned heavily against Sharrow.

"Well what were they?" Sharrow directed Vylett to a chair and passed her a glass of water. She took a few sips until her cheeks regained some of their colour and tried to explain.

"There were four number ones. Or else it could have been one thousand, one hundred and eleven. The numbers disappeared so quickly it was hard to make out."

Sharrow surprised them all by laughing out loud.

"This just proves that my decision to admit you to the Otherworld was correct," he said. "Those numbers represent the level of the elevator you should take." he explained. "The level of the Otherworld is different for every individual and sometimes an individual may search for a long time before finding the correct level. And if the elevator does not think that person is deserving then they may never find it."

He smiled his slanting smile at Vylett. "You however have been given a sign. If your cause wasn't a worthy one then the vision never would have reached you. The Otherworld would have filtered it."

"Like some kind of spam or computer junk mail?" Abigail said and Sharrow laughed with delight. "Yes Abigail Bookman, like those amazing computers you have in your World. Like spam."

Milo pondered the numbers. "One thousand one hundred and eleven. That's a lot of floors."

"Actually its eleven point eleven," said Sharrow. "Vylett must have missed the decimal point. But before I admit you into the elevator, I want to teach Milo something. Now come on follow me."

Sharrow led them back through the village and the food stalls - where the creepy looking vendor Oswald Crackenpepper bade them good luck for their journey - and then they followed Sharrow down a path that led away from the village centre.

The path wound around some pretty woodland and got narrower and narrower until they came to a clearing which was completely derelict except for a small pond. There was nothing remarkable about the pond but Milo thought that he could see a slight blurriness at its edges that was not from the rippling of the water.

"Yes this spot will do nicely. No one will disturb us here," Sharrow quickly assessed their surroundings. "Now Milo, before you enter the Otherworld I think you should have a quick lesson in magical aim."

"Excuse me?"

"I wasn't bothered about my mirror breaking last night but some of that other stuff was quite valuable you know, even if it didn't look it." Sharrow gave him a pointed look and Milo blushed a deep shade of red.

Of course Sharrow would have known what he had been doing. He was a cross-patcher. He knew everything.

"I'm sorry," he muttered. "I was just practicing. You're right, I do need practice with my aim. I'm rubbish."

Sharrow's eyes twinkled with mild amusement. "You're not rubbish. On the contrary I think you have a remarkable gift and given a little more practice you could be even more remarkable. You just need to be more aware of the magic in you that's all."

"What about the rest of us. Do we need to practice?" The eagerness to do something fun with magic was apparent in Helico's voice.

"No, you seem to have grasped the basics," Sharrow told him with a bemused expression. "Although what I teach Milo will also be useful to Abigail because her gift also involves being aware of her magic."

"How do you mean? I think we're all aware we have magic." Abigail looked at Sharrow as though he had lost his mind.

"Yes of course Abigail. What I meant is that you and Milo are often unaware of how much you are using. You need to use judgement. If you overuse your magic, then you become tired right?"

"Oh yes." Abigail nodded aggressively.

"Then you need to learn to know how much to use and how much to save," Sharrow explained patiently. "You don't have to use every bit of your magical energy to levitate something. You can save a bit back and still do the job."

Then Sharrow pointed to Milo. "And Milo here...he doesn't have to use all of his magical energy either to move an object because as he has found out that can be dangerous and cause a certain amount of destruction."

Milo visualised the healing tree and Sharrow's junk room and nodded in firm agreement.

"So take note kids because after I send you off to the Otherworld you are on your own. I don't know what awaits you there but being alive in a World that is meant for the dead will most definitely mean that you will need to keep your wits about you."

Sharrow looked at each of them in turn. "The least I can do is prepare you for any difficulties you may encounter."

Milo felt a knot tightening in his stomach as he wondered what difficulties they might encounter. But he was grateful at least that now Sharrow was about to give him some tips, he wouldn't have to ask the dead Alanya Roze to teach him magic.

He could now cross that from his list.

"Basically kids, when magic becomes dangerous, you need to remember one thing." said Sharrow. "It will either define you or kill you."

No one said anything as they stared back into Sharrow's now very serious eyes.

"So which will it be," he said more persistently. "Will it define you or kill you?"

"Define, define," they choroused.

"Good. Then let's get started." Sharrow brusquely smoothed down his tweed jacket.

Milo noticed it was a different jacket to the one he had worn yesterday and wondered absently how many tweed suits Sharrow had.

"We are going to re-enact what you tried to do in my basement last night Milo," Sharrow began. "Abigail please come and stand over here beside me and Helico go and stand a few paces over there away from us."

Abigail and Helico did as they were told and then Sharrow gave Abigail an orange to hold in the outstretched palm of her hand.

"Now Milo I want you to concentrate purely on the orange and move it from Abigail's palm to Helico's palm."

Abigail pulled her hand back quickly. "Are you kidding! Milo's just admitted he's a rubbish aim. He's going to blast me to the other side of that pond. No way, you're not using me as target practice, use Vylett instead."

"Hey!" Vylett protested and then looked apologetically at Milo. "Sorry," she muttered.

"Glad you all have confidence in me," Milo grumped. But Sharrow told them all to be quiet and instructed Abigail to outstretch her palm again and for Milo to concentrate.

"Now let your magic build until you feel comfortably in control and no more," he instructed. "Do not try to summon everything you've got. Now try."

Abigail flinched.

"Abigail keep still," Sharrow ordered. "Helico, hold your palm out ready."

Abigail made a face that said she was far from happy but she kept still, although she kept her eyes closed.

Milo let the tingling sensations come and thought about what Sharrow had said. He barely let the magic flow through him and then immediately released it at the orange.

To his surprise he managed to move it without hitting Abigail. Unfortunately though the orange only moved half the distance to Helico before falling to the ground.

Abigail opened her eyes in relief.

"Well done Milo," said Sharrow. "That's a good start. You were worried about hurting your friends and so you automatically kept your magic at a minimum. Now try again, draw on a bit more." he encouraged.

Feeling more confident, Milo tried again. This time Abigail kept her eyes open and grinned widely as the orange flew smoothly from her palm to Helico's.

"Perfect shot!" Helico flung the orange back at Milo who tried not to look as proud as he felt.

"See - all it takes is a little control," Sharrow patted him on the shoulder whilst Vylett gave him an appraising 'thumbs up.'

"I think I'm ready to try something bigger now." Milo was already mentally conjuring up images of moving Abigail to the other side of the pond as she had originally joked - but gently of course.

"I wish there was time Milo," said Sharrow. "But you don't have a lot of that now. You must find Alanya Roze and give her the water charm."

Oh yeah. Must find Alanya Roze. For a moment, Milo's elatedness deflated as he remembered he had an appointment with the dead.

"Right, well thanks Sharrow. And I really mean that. Thanks."

Sharrow nodded and smiled. "No problem. But remember Milo you need to be aware of more than just your magic. You need to always have your wits about you."

"Yes yes, I will....I do.." he promised.

"Do you?" Sharrow raised his eyebrows and then pulled out Penelope's water charm from his jacket pocket.

Milo's shocked expression was mirrored on the others. "Why do you have that?"

Instinctively he patted his trouser pocket even though the charm was right there in Sharrow's possession.

"I have it because you carelessly left it in your uniform when you changed clothes last night. Like I said Milo, keep your wits."

***

Abigail ranted on at Milo for being careless and stupid for at least two minutes before Helico and Milo both told her to 'shut up.' After which she refused to speak to Helico and was hell-bent on giving Milo stone faced glares.

"So where is this elevator?" she snapped at Sharrow.

Sharrow turned towards her and she gasped. "Ok, I'm sorry for being rude," she said quickly. "What I meant to say was, please can you show us where the elevator is."

Abigail was so pale she looked transparent.

"What just happened?" asked Milo.

"Just reminding Abigail of my true self," Sharrow explained and then resuming his cheery self he announced. "The elevator is right here, right where we have been practicing."

They looked around the clearing.

"The pond?" Vylett asked sceptically. She walked over to it and the others followed. Sharrow stood patiently waiting for their reaction.

"What are we supposed to be looking at?" Abigail still sounded irritated. "Is this an illusion?"

"Sort of," said Sharrow. "It is a pond. But the illusion is beneath it."

The four of them stared intently at the pond seeing nothing but their own squinting expressions. Then the blurriness that Milo had seen before became more evident until his reflection was wiped out completely.

"That's right Milo. It's working for you. You are discovering the illusion." There was excitement in Sharrow's voice. "But this is an illusion that will show you what you need to see and not what you want to see. Understand?"

"I think so." said Milo. "The thing he always wanted to see was the Fire Quarter. The thing he knew that he needed to see was the elevator.

No sooner had he realised this the blurriness disappeared to the sight of shimmering gold double doors rippling beneath the pond's surface.

The elevator to the Otherworld.

Chapter 17

The Otherworld

The doors to the elevator shimmered so brightly it hurt to look directly at it. Milo felt completely drawn to it.

It was a gravitational pull on all his senses and he had a strong desire to jump into the pond.

"Not yet," Sharrow warned. "The others have yet to see it."

Abigail, who had still not relaxed after their feud, gave Milo a frustrated glance and then like the others continued to squint intently at the pond. Their expressions were almost comical and Milo would have laughed had he not been so distracted by the beautiful golden doors beneath the water.

A few seconds later Vylett gasped as she saw it too. Her smile was filled with longing. She looked away from it just long enough to urge the other two to look harder, before returning her gaze back to the elevator.

"I don't see anything but my own stupid self," Helico shrugged apologetically at Sharrow.

"Yeah well that makes two of us," Abigail's face was red from exertion and stray red curls were stuck to her forehead.

"Perhaps you're not really concentrating on what you need to see," Milo tried to suggest helpfully.

"Milo will you shut up!" Abigail looked ready to combust.

"They are," Sharrow assured Milo. "But unfortunately the elevator does not want to admit them. It has decided that their purpose is not as strong as yours and Vylett's."

Abigail's hands flew straight to her hips. "Yes it is," she argued. "It's just as strong. We want to help too."

"The elevator understands that Abigail," said Sharrow calmly, "and it has considered your request but unfortunately as you are not directly related to the circumstances surrounding the Water Quarter, the elevator has decided to reject your request."

Sharrow's voice was soothing. "I was afraid this might happen. Quite possibly your desire to enter the Otherworld is not as strong as your friends, which is through no fault of your own. You may think you want to enter, but subconsciously you don't have the same inner desire as your friends."

"But..." Abigail tried to interject but Sharrow interrupted her to continue.

"It does not mean you do not care. It just means that the consequences of the actions in the Otherworld will affect Milo and Vylett more than yourselves."

Helico nodded in a defeated kind of way whilst Abigail stuck out her lower lip like she had just been given a terrible birthday present.

Milo and Vylett didn't know what to say. They hadn't imagined that the elevator would not admit some of them. It had been a given that they would all enter together.

And now there was an awkward tension between them all - the type that Milo hated and never knew how to fix.

Fortunately Helico did.

He sidled up closer to Abigail and put his arm protectively around her.

"That's the way it is Abs. We stay here whilst they go to find Vylett's mother. It means that we get to stay here in the land of the living and eat more of Sharrow's food. If that's ok Sharrow?" he added as an after thought shooting a quick glance in Sharrow's direction.

"Of course," Sharrow rubbed his stubbled chin with a bemused expression.

Helico nodded. "So that's that then." He turned back to Milo and Vylett.

"You two are the ones who really need to be in the Otherworld. It's your family that are there and your World that you're trying to save. Go and do what you need to do. We'll be fine, right Abs?"

Abigail's lower lip was still protruding but she attempted a smile. "Right."

Saying goodbye was awkward.

No one mentioned the very real possibility that this could be their final goodbye.

Milo was desperately trying not to think that his visit to the Otherworld might be a one way trip. The only reference made to this fact was when Helico said earnestly, "come back to us soon."

"Go ahead, enter the elevator," Sharrow prompted them.

He gave them both an encouraging nod and Milo realised if he was never able to return here, he was going to miss this man in the tweed suit almost as much as Helico and Abigail.

Trying their best to look bright and upbeat, Milo and Vylett joined hands and stared down into the pond and into the golden doors of the elevator. They didn't need Sharrow to tell them what to do next.

They knew all they had to do was step into the pond.

"Wait!" Vylett said suddenly, breaking free of Milo's grasp and turning to Abigail. "I'm sorry I lost Victoria Sparkle," she told her.

Abigail looked surprised but she just shrugged off Vylett's apology.

"Don't be. My grandmother lied. There was nothing good about her. Besides.. you can buy me another one when you return." Then she grinned and the old Abigail was back.

Vylett looked as though a great weight had been lifted.

"I'm ready now," she told Milo.

Abigail's mood free persona was like a ticket for them to enter the pond guilty free and wasting no more time, Milo and Vylett grasped hands again and stepped into it.

They could feel no water as they stepped into the ripples but immediately they were enveloped by white mist and the air around them felt heavy with the weight of its magic.

The mist cleared to reveal the magnificent golden doors - and alarmingly a whole other World under water.

Milo's vision was only slightly blurry as the water rippled over and around him and the cool temperature of the water felt only like a cool breeze on his senses but the water was heavy like that of the black river and its gravitational pull kept Milo and Vylett's feet firmly on the ground.

The water shimmered around them and when Milo took a deep breath in surprise he fully expected his lungs to fill with water but it still felt like breathing air, only heavier maybe.

In his peripheral vision he could see other buildings, other golden doors. It was an amazing thing to discover that there was a whole city beneath this water, only when he glanced around to have a look, the buildings disappeared, leaving only the double golden elevator doors in his vision and he understood that the other buildings were off limits to them.

They had only been granted access to the elevator.

The doors silently opened and with nervous trepidation, Milo and Vylett entered the elevator which would finally take them to the Otherworld.

***

The elevator to the Otherworld appeared to have walls made out of mist with the occasional glimmer of silver spiking through.

The area they stood in was about fifteen square feet and the aura of power around them so intense that Milo's emotions seemed to be in instant turmoil. He felt excited, scared, sad and guilty all at once.

"Do you feel weird?" he asked Vylett as he struggled to keep himself from both crying and laughing at the same time.

She nodded. "This is what it feels like in the Otherworld. You'll get used to it."

Then they both jumped as a soft sounding voice filled the elevator.

"Which level do you require?"

"Er, the level to the Otherworld." Vylett answered uncertainly.

There was the sound of smothered laughing and then the voice said. "Which level? You need to pick a number."

Vylett slapped a hand to her head. "Of course! the numbers from my vision. We need eleven eleven. Er eleven point eleven," she clarified to be more precise.

It wouldn't do to be getting off at the wrong level.

"As you wish," the soft voice purred, and then the elevator shot up so fast, Milo and Vylett's feet were lifted off the floor.

But instead of landing back on the misty floor, they continued to hover in the mid-space between the silvery mists, floating like airborne creatures.

"Woah this is not what I was expecting," Milo laughed nervously but his face was flooded with colour from the adrenaline rush.

"Your journey will last exactly eleven hours and eleven minutes," the silky voice informed them.

Vylett and Milo looked at each other in amazement.

"So we just stay like this for eleven hours?" Milo looked at them both floating helplessly like bobbing lily pads. "Well this is going to be fun - not!"

But then he realised that the air around them was so heavy that he could move his body so that he was lying completely horizontal and even though he was floating mid-air, the air molecules still supported his head like a pillow.

"Try this," he told Vylett as he shifted himself into a comfortable position. "I think we could get some sleep like this. It would pass the time."

Despite the fact only a morning had passed since he had last slept he still felt exhausted.

Practicing magic had drained him.

Vylett nodded and sleepily rested her head on her arms.

Neither of them spoke, each trying to wrestle with their own emotions to enable them to sleep.

Then Vylett said, "Milo. Can I ask you something?"

"Ur huh?"

"When Sharrow showed us his true form, what did you see?"

Milo was unprepared for the question and he turned his head away from her and made a great fuss of trying to get comfortable.

To tell her that he saw Walt would make him look like a coward, and to tell her that he saw her, Vylett - dead, would make him what - weird? pathetic?

Instead he told her a half truth. "Droges. I saw Droges."

"Huh...me too," Vylett sounded surprised. "I guess that creature really is everyone's worst nightmare."

They lapsed into silence as their loathing for Droges momentarily preceded anything else and then Milo asked Vylett the thing that had been worrying him.

"What if we can't get back from the Otherworld Vylett? What if your mother is wrong."

"She's never wrong Milo." Vylett gently touched his arm and then re-positioned her hands under her head. "Come on let's get some sleep. I feel so tired now."

Lying on a bed of mist had made Milo's eyes heavy too and forcing away any other further thoughts, he closed his eyes and gave himself up to much needed sleep.

In eleven hours and about six minutes he was going to see Penelope and for that he would need his energy.

***

Milo awoke from a deep and surprisingly comfortable sleep to the sound of the soft voice announcing that they had arrived at their destination.

He felt groggy and his eyelids still felt heavy from sleep but he was soon wide awake because the elevator suddenly gave a jolt and he and Vylett were flung unceremoniously onto the misty floor again.

As they jumped up, Milo still felt on tenterhooks as his emotions continued to hold a fierce battle inside his body. He was inwardly willing the good ones to win when the silvery mist cleared to reveal a wide corridor.

"And they didn't win," he mumbled as he took in the strange white figures that were hovering, rather than walking, down the corridor.

The bad emotions had definitely won the battle because all he was feeling now was trepidation.

"What?.." Vylett murmured, but she wasn't looking at him. She was looking at the scary white things.

"Ghosts," said Milo blankly. "Is it me, or do they look a whole lot scarier than the ones on our Quarter?" he asked as casually as he could.

"Yes they look scarier."

Vylett moved closer to inspect one of the ghost type things as one came to hover near her.

Milo was creeped out to see that up close it had no face. No features whatsoever. It was just a white blob, but from a distance it had the unmistakable face and body of a man.

"Look how white and misty they are," Vylett sounded almost dreamy as she gingerly reached out to touch the faceless ghost that had hovered close to her.

"Vylett don't......"

Vylett wrenched her hand away with a startled expression.

"These are no ordinary ghosts Milo. These are portal ghosts." Her eyes flashed with excitement. "These lead straight to the Otherworld."

Well that makes sense, thought Milo. To enter a World of the Dead through the dead itself.

"Come on," said Vylett and grabbing Milo by the hand she pulled them both straight into the faceless ghost.

There was the same strange spinning sensation that they had experienced when they had been exiled to Orlost, that was horribly disorientating, and then it quickly gave way to a peaceful sense of calm and yet more white mist.

Milo and Vylett stared in wonder as the mist got thinner and thinner until it was just a thin layer and looked like a delicate piece of lace curtain, or a veil.

It would have been completely transparent had it not been for the silver streaks shimmering through it.

It looked to Milo that there was nothing on the other side of the veil except miles and miles of empty land. And then out of nowhere he saw them.

Penelope and Alanya.

They were standing side by side, gleaming with silver, just at the other side of the shimmering curtain, so close that if Milo reached out he would touch them.

He felt a gut wrenching ache as he locked eyes with his sister.

"Penelope!" he murmured.

So it was true. She really was in the Otherworld.

Milo's heart beat madly with anticipation.

"What if she really is dead?" he looked to Vylett who grabbed his hand earnestly.

"Only one way to find out." Her huge blue eyes were shiny. "Whatever happens it'll be fine. Come on they're waiting."

And then she stepped first into the veiled curtain.

Milo stepped forward to follow her but before he touched the veil, his hand was wrenched from Vylett's and he had the breath knocked out of him as he was slammed to the floor.

At first Milo thought that the Otherworld had rejected him after all. Then there was a horribly familiar clinking noise and staring down at him, breathing his rancid, burning stench onto him, was the very unwelcome sight of...

...Wylaffaton.

Milo stared up at the Terramang in horror.

He felt as though the 'W' that was engraved on Wylaffaton' s armour was burning into him.

What was he doing here? How did he know?

"I thought you couldn't enter the Otherworld," were the first words that popped out of Milo's mouth.

Then he winced, clutching his side where Wylaffaton's armour had dug into him. He thought he might have broken a rib.

"I can't," said Wylaffaton and he stuck his fist into the veiled curtain to demonstrate that it was as solid as brick for him. "And neither will you. You're coming back with me."

ZOË TYSON

As Wylaffaton dragged Milo up from the floor, Sharrow's words floated back to him.

"Keep your wits."

Milo's hand flew to his pocket and he pulled out the water charm. Then he flung it as hard as he could at the shimmering curtain where it sailed straight through.

He could see Vylett staring back at him on the other side, wide eyed. "Save the Quarters," he shouted.

And then Wylaffaton grabbed him roughly by the arm and teleported him in a flash of bright white light.

***

The second Vylett had tried to get back through the veil to help Milo, it had turned solid.

It wasn't allowing her to exit and no amount of pushing or pleading with it did any good.

She couldn't get back out.

She could only look on in horror as Wylaffaton had teleported Milo, then the veiled curtain has lost its transparency and she could no longer see through it.

She stood still for a second in stunned silence and then whirled around at the sound of Penelope's harsh voice.

"I told you, you shouldn't have come. Now Wylaffaton has my brother."

The bitterness coming from Penelope was so strong that Vylett almost choked on it. She swallowed hard and then ignoring Penelope, ran into her mother's open arms.

Feeing her mother's arms around her again was the most wonderful thing that Vylett had ever experienced.

"I'm afraid," she said as she buried her head in her mother's shoulder. But Penelope yanked it back again.

"You should be afraid. Wylaffaton is taking my brother to Droges." Penelope ran a hand manically through her long silky dark hair giving Vylett a hateful look.

Vylett felt icy fear running through her veins as her mind conjured up a hundred horrible things that Droges might be doing to Milo.

Penelope was the psychic one and probably knew what was happening to him but for some reason Vylett wasn't getting a read on the other girl's emotions properly. All she could detect was the bitterness, and so she did something she'd never done before.

She probed Penelope's mind for more information.

She knew it was intrusive but she was desperate.

She sent feelers out with her mind and then her eyes widened in surprise as she felt a block on Penelope's emotions.

"Don't do that," Penelope said icily. "That hurts you know. How would you like someone poking around in your head?"

Feeling stunned and embarrassed, Vylett stuttered an apology. "I...I'm sorry...I...how did you..?"

"How did I know that you were invading my privacy?" Penelope retorted and then gave a snort.

"It's amazing the things you find you can do in this place. Although that doesn't last forever," she added and shot a strange look at Alanya that Vylett couldn't interpret.

"Can you help him mother? Can you help Milo?" Vylett gave her mother a pleading look but Penelope scoffed loudly.

"Her? She's dead Vylett. How on earth do you think she can help him. If my brother dies it will be all your fault."

Vylett looked at Milo's sister in confusion. The girl had so much bitterness and she looked extremely tired.

"Are you dead Penelope? Or did you find this place like me and Milo did?" she asked her.

Penelope gave her an odd look. "Of course I'm dead. This is not the kind of place you just stumble across."

Vylett nodded sadly. Milo would be devastated.

Then Penelope shot Alanya another odd look. "Unless of course your dead mother is sending you visions to help you."

Something was wrong.

Vylett could feel it as easily as she could feel her mother's bones protruding through her thin frame. She just didn't know what it was.

Her mother cast a disapproving look at Penelope and folded Vylett into her arms again.

In this place - the Otherworld - every single emotion Vylett had was heightened and the tension all around her seemed to be magnified ten times over.

It hung in the elements and oozed out of her mother's arms, pouring into her so that her every nerve ending felt like it was being stretched until it might snap at any moment. But where as with Penelope she could detect some kind of emotion from her, with her mother she couldn't detect any.

"What's happened mother? Are we too late to save the Quarters?" her questions tumbled out in a rush as she pulled back from her mother to study her face.

Then Vylett's fear increased as Penelope who was standing next to her went rigid and put her hands to her head.

"You shouldn't have come Vylett. For your own sake you shouldn't have come." Penelope's bitterness had turned to sadness. But again, Vylett could not tell why.

"I have the water charm," she told them holding out Penelope's own water charm that Milo had flung at her through the veil. "Your charm Penelope. The one that you saw Milo giving my mother in your vision. Only now it's me who's giving it to her I guess."

Vylett didn't have the energy to try and understand why Penelope's vision hadn't been accurate.

"Oh for goodness sake," Penelope snapped. "Like I told you when you almost died, that was before I knew Alanya was dead."

"But my mother said that she can still...."

"Your mother lied," Penelope cut her off to glare at Alanya and Vylett felt her nerve endings tighten again.

"Oh be quiet Penelope, you're worrying her." said Alanya. Then she smiled warmly at Vylett and held out her hand.

"Vylett, please don't be scared and just give me the water charm." Alanya spoke with a quiet persuasion but as she spoke Vylett's eyes widened in horror.

Her mother's facial features began to change.

It was only subtle, but her skin seemed to lose some of its tautness and her young eyes seemed to age.

Vylett automatically took a step back.

Penelope's shoulders sagged with a weary sigh. "Do you see it now Vylett? Do you see the truth? It's not Milo you should be worried about. It's yourself."

"Why?" Vylett's voice was barely a whisper. She was afraid to hear the answer even though she already knew it.

Penelope gave her another sad look and pointed to Alanya.

"Because of her."

Vylett's skin prickled and instinctively she tensed as though someone had poured cold water down her back.

Immediately Alanya's face transformed from someone with a fading beauty to someone who had no beauty whatsoever. It was as though every soft and delicate feature of Alanya's face had been erased and replaced with harsh ugly ones.

And there was something in those eyes...something unspeakable...

Vylett was reminded of her nightmare at Sharrow's house and felt her knees buckle as she took in her mother's horrendous form.

"So you're finally looking with your eyes," Penelope said to her. "Sometimes it takes a while to see things properly in this place. I should know."

She took a step closer to her, those tired brown eyes boring into hers. "Now run Vylett."

Vylett didn't need telling twice.

She ran.

Chapter 18

An Unlikely Ally

When the spinning sensation had stopped, before Milo had the chance to see where he was, Wylaffaton had for some reason, decided to whack him hard across the head and render him unconscious.

Now, as Milo came to again, he felt a dull throbbing pain in his head, followed by sharp stabbing pains in his wrist.

He winced and then panicked as he realised his wrists had been chained. As he tried to move his legs, a similarly sharp pain shot through his ankles.

He was lying flat on a table and couldn't move any of his extremities. His head at least wasn't restrained but when he swivelled around to get a look at his surroundings his vision blurred.

Wylaffaton must have hit him hard.

Turning his head more slowly, Milo saw that he was surrounded by machines.

Directly above him was a strange looking device with a sucker and leads attached to it. Four of the leads had needles projecting from them and were sticking into his wrists and ankles.

Milo's heart sank with the sickening realisation that he was in the activity room. He was strapped to a table that Vylett had probably been lying on when Droges had been trying to suck the magic out of her.

He yanked on his arm, trying to get them free of the chains and needles and cried out as something sharp pierced his skin. Blood poured down his wrist and when Milo looked more closely he could see that the chains holding his arms and legs were covered with tiny sharp points like teeth.

Unless he wanted to be a human pin cushion he would have to stay still. Obviously that was the intention.

"Yes it's wise if you don't try and move."

Milo flinched as Droges appeared in his line of vision, a very unwelcome sight, staring down at him, his foul breath threatening to kill him before the chains did.

The pink hazy glow of Orlost streaming in through the window shone on Droges's silver armour, tainting it a soft pink.

If Milo had been expecting to see a smug smile on the C.L's face for his re-capture, he was wrong. There was no smile or joy on Droges's face.

Just pure fury.

"Do you know how long it has taken to find you?" Droges growled. "Three weeks," he continued before giving Milo the chance to answer.

Milo was quietly stunned. Despite the seriousness of his situation right now, he had the inappropriate urge to laugh.

Three weeks! Hadn't it only been about three days?

The time zone must be different here, he thought. That must have driven Droges and Coldridge crazy.

As if Miss Coldridge had heard his thoughts, the door to the activity room opened and the warden marched in, looking red faced and harassed.

"So…one of the wanderers has returned," she said in a steely voice. Her red cheeks lost some of their colour when she eyed Milo's chains but her voice didn't soften any less.

"Where were you?" she demanded. "What were you thinking? And do you have to use those particular chains on him?" She directed this last question to Droges and then quickly averted her eyes back to Milo as Droges snarled at her.

A dark expression crossed the C.L's face and the intensity of the burning odour in the room moved up a notch.

Milo found that he was holding his breath. Partly to shut out the smell and partly in anticipation. Droges wouldn't like Miss Coldridge telling him what to do, even if he had made her warden.

Milo expected him to brand her but instead he spoke to her quietly and calm in a voice – which had Milo not known better – would have almost been described at civil.

Had he not known better.

"Wylaffaton found Milo at the portal to the Otherworld," Droges told her in his thick gruff voice. "That's the border to the World of the Dead," he added in a patronising tone.

"Yes. I know," Miss Coldridge said tightly, her cheeks colouring.

"Wylaffaton was unfortunately too late to stop Vylett Roze from entering the Otherworld and the others have yet to be found. But for now...at least we have this one..."

Droges's black eyes were gleaming with malice and Milo was thankful that for now the others were safe. It took him a moment to realise that Miss Coldridge was staring at Droges and her expression was one of disbelief.

"Why on earth would Miss Roze want to enter the Otherworld?" she asked Droges. "Did she realise that she can't return? What did she hope to achieve?" Miss Coldridge was speaking as though Milo wasn't in the room.

"I'm the one who knows why," he said angrily. "Ask me, not him."

Miss Coldridge stared at him in surprise. "So talk."

"She hoped to find her mother. You know...Alanya Roze," said Milo. "The woman you pretended not to know," he added for effect. "The woman who is dead. The woman who he killed!" Milo glared at Droges, no longer feeling scared but angry. In fact he didn't think he had ever felt so angry.

OK he had no proof that Droges had killed Alanya, but that's what Abigail had been told by Coldridge and now Milo believed it without a doubt.

He felt a huge rush of tingling down his arms but he remembered Sharrow's advice about saving his energy.

He had to wait until the time was right.

Besides, his head was throbbing so much that every tiny movement he made resulted in another sharp hole in his wrist.

"And why would Miss Roze want to find her mother?" Coldridge studied him curiously.

"So that she could fix a magical imbalance in my World that he caused" Milo shot a look of loathing in Droges's direction who was regarding him with a mild sort of interest. The Terramang's eyebrows lifted slightly in what could have been surprise or appreciation.

Coldridge narrowed her eyes at Droges but she was wise enough not to say anything.

"Why did you lie to Vylett about Alanya?" Milo asked her. "Why not just tell her the truth? She could have taken it."

"Could she?" Coldridge raised an eyebrow and then glanced briefly in Droges's direction before turning back to Milo again.

"I didn't tell her for her own protection. I know she can practically read minds, but I didn't want her reading mine."

When Milo just looked at her in confusion, Miss Coldridge made a noise of exasperation.

"This may come as a surprise to you," she said. "But I do care about the children here. I wouldn't want them to come to any harm. It would have done Miss Roze no good whatsoever to learn the truth."

She glanced at Droges again and back to Milo, her eyes lingering on him, and this time Milo caught the warning look in her eyes.

She was warning him to shut up.

Coldridge was trying to tell him that if Vylett had guessed that Droges murdered her mother then Vylett may have sought her own revenge on Droges. And then of course she would have probably got herself killed.

Maybe Coldridge had just been trying to protect Vylett. She had just gone about it the wrong way.

Milo remembered how she had let him find a snack that first night on Orlost, despite the strict rules. Back then he had realised she wasn't completely made of stone.

But he still felt angry with her and he turned his head, not wanting to look at her.

"Leave us," Droges said to Miss Coldridge and the deadly quiet of his voice was not something to disobey. But Miss Coldridge didn't move.

"I said leave us." Rancid burning filled the room.

"I really think that...."

There was a flash of orange as Droges branded Coldridge and in a movement as quick as lightening had her pinned against a wall in the corner of the room.

The warden visibly paled, delicately touching her face where a nasty brand covered her cheek. She looked to be in shock and in other circumstances Milo might have felt sorry for her had he not been feeling so sorry for himself at that moment.

"That is the second time you have answered back to me in the last five minutes," Droges growled at her and jabbed a bony finger hard under her chin.

"But that is not why I'm going to kill you," he said. "I'm going to kill you for not doing your job properly. You are supposed to keep this place in order and you failed. You let the children escape."

"But I didn't let them.." Coldridge protested.

Whilst Droges ranted on at Miss Coldridge, Milo looked around him, desperately trying to find something with which he might be able to use to free himself of the chains, although he didn't see how this was remotely possible, given the fact he would have to use his teeth.

He began to summon on his magic, letting it build up.

He wondered if it would be enough to break the chains apart when Miss Coldridge's wails of protest diverted his attention back to the corner of the room. It was like looking at an accident.

He didn't want to see it, but he found he couldn't look away.

"Those children escaped because of you," Droges grabbed her roughly by her hair and dragged her out from the corner.

Miss Coldridge raised her chin in what looked like a gesture of forced pride and said unsteadily, "I'm a good warden. I do take care of the children."

"Not good enough," growled Droges and then he pointed his long boney finger at her face.

She made a strangled cry that made Milo's blood run cold, and then she collapsed onto the floor.

Besides the brand on her face, there was not a mark on her that suggested Droges had killed her, but her eyes were open and lifeless and most definitely dead.

In the space of one second, Droges had removed Miss Coldridge from the World of the living.

Milo's stomach lurched, which caused an involuntary spasm of movement, causing the chains to dig in further.

He grimaced in pain and felt a mixture of saliva and blood pool down his chin as he bit down hard on his lower lip.

"You didn't have to kill her. That wasn't necessary," he managed to cry out through the pain.

"Yes it was. It was very necessary. She messed up."

"And is that why you killed Alanya too. Because she messed up?" Milo forced himself to look away from Miss Coldridge's lifeless form.

Droges narrowed his eyes at him. "She was beginning to irritate me. Not that it's any of your business."

He made a grunting noise. "Alanya had many gifts of which I wanted to siphon from her. Given time I believe I could have had them all. But she pushed me too far, always thinking she was better than me. But enough of Alanya Roze..." Droges waved his hand dismissively, clearly bored of the subject.

"What I really want to talk about is this bizarre notion you have that I stole the Quarter's magic. Why would I do something so stupid and destroy a Quarter that I am so successfully ruling?"

"But my Aunt Dor....she said..."

"She said what Miloney?" Droges eyed him suspiciously and Milo clamped his lips together.

He needed to stop speaking, or else his stupidity could land his Aunt Dor in exile.

"Nothing," he backtracked. "She just heard a rumour that the Terramangs had caused the imbalance, that's all."

"Well we didn't," Droges's gaze was unwavering. "But I should very much like to know who did."

Milo was wondering the same thing. Aunt Dor's intuition was very rarely wrong but for some reason he believed Droges. And it made sense - why would the creatures destroy their own territory? Aunt Dor had obviously got it wrong. She herself admitted that the imbalance had been messing with her gift.

"Perhaps it was just nature," he suggested whilst trying to buy for time.

Droges made a noise that sounded like a grunt and a scoff combined into one. "Don't be ignorant Miloney. That used to happen in the olden days, not today. No, the imbalance is a consequence of foul play and believe me when I say that no potion is good enough for the punishment I intend to inflict on the culprit."

At this Droges treated Milo to a particularly nasty smile. "But mark my words, I am working on it. And when I find out who it is, they will discover that death would have been a preferable punishment. No one destroys my Quarter and gets off lightly."

'No potion is good enough', 'I am working on it.' Droges's words bounced off the walls of Milo's bruised brain. He knew that Droges was referring to his father's work in progress - the Infinity Dust.

He bit down on his lip to refrain from shouting out obscurities and ending up like Coldridge.

As long as he was still alive, he still had his magic and that meant he had a chance of fighting back. What he intended to do if he ever escaped from this table however, he had no idea.

In the far corner of his mind, Milo fervently hoped that Alanya Roze was currently fixing the Quarters.

"Now Miloney, any more useless questions you want to ask me before I steal your magic and then kill you?"

Droges tapped his chin thoughtfully and paced back and forth next to Milo's head so that he could see his own scared face reflected back in the rosy coloured armour. "Perhaps you would be interested to know how Wylaffaton found you?"

Milo turned his head away from Droges's penetrating gaze, not wanting to look in those black soulless eyes.

"Maybe" he mumbled lamely.

Droges made a huffing noise and to Milo's relief, removed his face from his. He clicked his fingers. "Bring her in!" he barked.

Her? The door opened and Wylaffaton entered the room dragging behind him the last person Milo expected to have grassed on him.

It was Bea, the cook.

The woman who Abigail had entrusted to help cover up their escape by replacing the grate on the hole in the cellar for them.

"There has to be some mistake," Milo mumbled as he stared at the cook's terrified looking face.

"You see Miloney, anything's easy when you have a reliable source. You don't always need magic to find out what you want to know." Droges smirked as he revelled in the disbelief on Milo's shocked face.

"I'm sorry Milo. They made me," Bea's chest heaved with her sobs as she choked out her apology. Her podgy face was red and blotchy and Milo now noticed that her neck and arms were covered in nasty red burns – trademark brands of the Terramangs.

Bea's entire body was shaking and Milo felt sick with revulsion. They had tortured her into giving them information.

"It's not your fault Bea," Milo told her and tried his best to sound sincere through the pain that was shooting down his arms and ankles. "And besides, it's not so bad, we achieved what we set out to do. Vylett found Alanya."

A small smile of pride lit Bea's tear streaked face and she lowered her eyes and nodded.

Then Droges suddenly applied pressure on Milo's wrist.

It was not hard. But hard enough for those tiny metal teeth to dig further into his already punctured skin.

He cried out but Droges grabbed him by the head and forced him to concentrate.

"I want you to witness the consequences of your selfish actions before you die."

Then before Milo even had time to blink, Bea's body slumped to the ground. Droges had killed her with the same silent cold hearted method he had used on Coldridge.

Milo closed his eyes, squeezing them hard to stop the tears that were threatening to come.

When he opened them again, Wylaffaton was dragging the bodies of Bea and Coldridge out of the room.

One in each hand.

Milo turned away in disgust and tried to turn his ears off to the horrible rhythmic dragging noise their bodies made as they slid along the wooden slats.

Droges sighed. "Look what you have caused us to do with your selfishness. Now we have to dispose of them. Always such a chore."

He leaned down to whisper into Milo's ear. "Now, if you hold still whilst I suck your remaining magic, it will hurt less."

Before Milo had a chance to react, Droges pressed a red button above him. The Terramang smiled crookedly and a burst of rancid stench gushed past Milo's nostrils.

"Go ahead," Milo's voice was surprisingly steady. "Do what you need to do."

And so will I, he added silently.

He started to summon his magic, realising numbly that he was a few seconds too late.

The machine was quicker than he was.

It was making a whirring noise that he barely heard against the humming of his own magic and he felt the skin on his wrist tighten so that the needles stood rigid and upright.

For a moment Milo felt a rising panic-because although he couldn't ever have explained it to anyone who hadn't had their magic sucked out – it was as though a part of his soul was about to be taken.

He was starting to experience a terrifying sense of detachment from his own body when Sharrow's advice came back to him.

"Let your magic build until you are comfortably in control."

Milo tried to concentrate purely on the sensation his magic was giving him. He could feel it dwindling but Sharrow said he didn't need much to move an object. He just had to be in control. And right now he had to be quick.

It was now or never.

Fighting against the emptiness that was threatening to engulf him, Milo stared at one of the needles in his wrist, hoping that Sharrow's lesson had taught him something and that he wouldn't overuse his magic.

The needle in his wrist shot out of his skin like a catapult and amazingly it swung smoothly from the equipment above him.

Milo was vaguely aware that he had done well. Had he used much more magic then the leads from the needle could have pulled the machine down on top of him.

Immediately the whirring noise of the machine stopped and Milo felt his magic begin to stabilise again as the weird empty feeling inside of him subsided.

Droges glared at him furiously. "Did you do that?"

"How could I when it was taking my magic?" Milo snarled at him in what he thought was a good impression of a 'cover up'.

Droges banged the machine furiously and began yanking on the wires. Had the Terramang's odour been visible, Milo's vision would have been clouded by it.

But the C.L quickly recovered his composure. Smiling one of his cruellest smiles, he said.

"Then we'll just have to try again."

Droges grabbed the swinging needle and calmly began to re-connect it to Milo's bleeding wrist. Milo's heart sank as he realised he could never have enough magic to defeat Droges. What chance did he possibly have against an immortal creature that could kill with just a point of its finger?

But he wasn't about to die without a fight.

Realising he had nothing to lose, he ignored all of Sharrow's advice and summoned on everything he had. He relished in the rush the power of the magic gave him and aimed all of it at Droges.

Droges flew across the room with such intensity that he smashed through the wooden slats on the opposing wall so that Milo could glimpse the unstaring faces of the vacants in the common room. Never before had he released all of his magic in one go and the result was phenomenal.

Milo felt as though the wind had truly been knocked out of him. He felt weakened and dizzy.

But despite this, the look of shock and surprise on Droges's face was gratification enough and Milo felt a small amount of pride that he had given it his all and he could die with the knowledge that he had at least tried to defeat the C.L.

Milo still had a weary smile on his face as Droges scrambled up from the wooden debris and charged to his side.

Milo couldn't help but flinch. But with a collected calm, Droges grabbed the needle and re-connected it to Milo's wrist.

"Now that is magic worth having," he said in a breathless growl. He reached up to press the red button again when the door opened.

Milo's eyes widened in surprise as Lowish marched in, taking only a moment to glance in Milo's direction before addressing an angry looking Droges.

"Sir, we need your assistance. We have found the twins and Wylaffaton would like to know what you intend to do with them."

Milo's tired mind began to race. They had found Iza and Eli?

"The twins?" Droges's anger turned to a satisfied smirk. "Keep them detained and I will see to them when I finish up here."

He turned back to Milo but Lowish was persistent. "Sir, the girl is being very troublesome and she doesn't seem to bother how many times we brand her. I fear Wylaffaton will kill her before we have had chance to take her magic."

"Damn!" Droges thumped the side of the table and headed for the door. "I'll be back shortly. Make sure he doesn't move." Droges shot a loathing glance in Milo's direction.

As soon as Droges was gone, Milo opened his mouth to speak but Lowish cut him off.

"Be quiet Miloney. We don't have much time," and then to Milo's astonishment, Lowish reached over him and began to undo his chains.

"You're letting me go!" said Milo, ignoring Lowish's warning as one of the wrist restraints burst open with a satisfying click. Wriggling his wrist about to increase his blood circulation, Milo's mind spun with hope and questions.

"Why?" he asked incredulously. There was another click and his other wrist was freed.

"I said be quiet Miloney," Lowish snarled and Milo did as he was told as the Terramang quickly finished freeing him of the chains.

Milo barely had time to relish in the freedom of his limbs again when Lowish stepped back in a sudden movement that made his armour clink loudly. His black eyes were wide and alert.

"Droges is coming back," he growled. "Quick! Take my arm."

Milo grabbed his arm and then they were spinning a flash of white light.

Chapter 19

A Dead Experience

Milo found himself back at the curtained veil to the Otherworld. Only unlike last time he could see no one beyond it.

He hoped that was a good sign.

Still feeling incredibly weak, he turned to Lowish in confusion. "I don't understand. Why have you brought me back here?"

"The Quarters are being destroyed and neither Droges nor anyone else alive has the power to stop it," Lowish told him brusquely. "But apparently Alanya Roze can help save it. Is that right?"

"Er yes,"

"And I believe she needs a water charm to do that. I know you have the water charm so I'm giving you that chance to give it to her."

Lowish spoke so matter of fact that Milo had to blink several times to make sure he wasn't dreaming. He rubbed at his sore wrists, trying to make sense of everything.

"Go on what are you waiting for Miloney. Get in there," Lowish said impatiently, giving Milo a little shove towards the veil when Milo just stared at him.

"Wait! How did you know?" Milo asked Lowish. "About Alanya and the water charm I mean? How could you possibly know that?"

Lowish shrugged. "As soon as I heard that Wylaffaton had found you at the entrance to the Otherworld I was intrigued. I followed your trail to Audrina's cave and then to Peaches's cave. It didn't take much persuasion for Peaches to tell me you'd gone to the World of Illusion."

Lowish shrugged again. "And then it took even less persuasion for a cross-patcher named Sharrow to tell me what you were planning."

"Sharrow told you all that?" Milo couldn't quite believe it. Sharrow hated the Terramangs. He had told them that himself. Why would he tell Lowish their secrets?

"Don't worry," Lowish said with a sigh as he saw Milo's expression. "Your new friend's intentions were completely honourable. He wouldn't tell me what you were up to until I told him you'd been captured."

Lowish shook his head as though trying to solve a puzzle. "For a cross-patcher he seemed particularly concerned. Most unusual," he added quietly. He shifted his feet impatiently. "I hope you're grateful," he grunted. "If I hadn't followed your trail you would be dead by now."

"Or shell," Milo mumbled, using Vylett's term for the vacants on Orlost.

"What?"

"Nothing. Look Lowish, I am grateful. But Vylett's already given Alanya the charm."

Milo sighed, wondering why the hell he had said that. Lowish would probably teleport him straight back to Droges now. Automatically his hand went to his trouser pocket where he had kept the water charm...

And pulled his hand back in shock.

Slowly he put his hand back to his pocket. There it was. He could feel the charm's coolness through the warmth of his jeans. "I don't understand," he mumbled "I gave it to Vylett."

Lowish made a noise of frustration. "Do you have the charm or not Miloney?"

"Apparently I do," Milo was getting the increasing urge to lie down and go to sleep. His head hurt.

"Then go and give it to Alanya Roze. Now Miloney. I can't enter the Otherworld but I will wait here for you, presuming you can come back out again that is."

"And then what?"

"Then you can go where ever you want. I don't care. I have myself to worry about now. I can't go back to Orlost or the Quarters. Droges will be looking to destroy me." Lowish shifted his feet uncomfortably, then grunted out a small stream of burning scent.

"I will give you one hour in which to return," he said. "I don't think Droges will look for us here for a while. He doesn't know that I know this is where Wylaffaton found you. But if you haven't returned in one hour I will leave without you. Understand?"

Milo nodded.

He should have been extremely suspicious that a Terramang was helping him but he could see no ulterior motive. Lowish was perhaps proving to Milo what he had been beginning to suspect since Lowish had stuck up for him at the Drome.

That not all Terramangs were evil to the core.

He wished he had the time to work out the logic behind it but time was definitely something he didn't have a lot of right now.

"Thanks Lowish. But before I go, I just need to ask about Eli and Iza. Will Droges kill them?"

Truthfully Milo was scared to know the answer. It seemed obvious. But Lowish shrugged him off.

"They haven't really been found Miloney. That was just a decoy to get Droges to leave the room."

Milo smiled with relief. Whatever was happening to the twins right now, it couldn't be as bad as being with Droges.

"See you in an hour," Milo said to Lowish and then he stepped into the shimmering veiled curtain. He felt a change in the air's density, like a soft pleasant breeze, and then finally he was in the Otherworld.

***

Milo's first assessment of the Otherworld was one of confusion. From the other side of the shimmering veil, all he had seen were planes and planes of flat bare land. Now though he seemed to be in a city of ruins. He was surrounded by buildings that were derelict and falling apart.

If it was possible the place was even more silent than Orlost and a hundred times more creepy. If this was where you spent your life after death then Milo hoped he wouldn't die for a long time.

Some of the buildings were huge and looked as though at some time or other they may have been grand and impressive.

Majestic even.

It could have been a magnificent kingdom of white marble that glistened like diamonds had the sun been shining on it.

Except there was no sun. The sun didn't exist here.

All that existed was a world of crumbling white buildings that looked dull in the dim light of this sunless city.

"Penelope! Vylett!" Milo cried out into the emptiness and despite the space between the buildings, his voice did not echo.

Where were they? He was wondering where to start looking for them when from behind a pillar of crumbling marble, Penelope appeared.

Milo let out a relieved breath but this was quickly followed by a string of emotions at seeing his sister again. She looked...different.

She looked...dead.

Milo's relief quickly turned to shock as he took in Penelope's disturbing appearance.

Her usually glistening hair was dull and lifeless and she seemed to have aged at least ten years. She was thin and fragile looking and her eyes had a weird haunted look in them. One thing that was still the same however was the way that one side of her mouth was turned up in a familiar smirk.

"I'm not sure what surprises me most," she said as she started towards him.

Milo noticed she was wearing the same green satin dress that she had been wearing the day of his exile and how just days ago it had fitted her curves so perfectly, it now hung off her boney shoulders.

"The fact that a Terramang just saved your life or the fact that you and your little friend Vylett think Alanya can actually save the Quarters as well as 'bring you both back from the dead,'" she air quoted these last few words with her fingers.

"Where is Vylett?" Milo looked around him but Penelope grabbed his hand and began to lead him through the marble ruins.

"She's this way and you need to help her," said Penelope quickening her pace.

Something in Penelope's tight voice made Milo's hair stand on edge. He wanted to know what had happened to Vylett but first he needed to know what was happening with his sister.

He pulled on Penelope's arm, and spun her around to face him. He swallowed loudly.

"Pen, what's happened to you?..you look...kind of different." That was putting it mildly. "Are you.." It was taking great effort to get his words out. "Are you dead?"

Penelope's eyes filled with sadness and Milo's stomach twisted painfully. He of course knew what she was going to say.

"Yes Milesey, I am. But I think you already knew that."

He nodded feeling dazed and lightheaded. Yes, he had known deep down. He just hadn't wanted to admit it. To believe it.

"How?" he asked numbly.

Penelope shrugged. "Droges. But that doesn't matter right now. What matters is that.."

"But why do you look the way you do?" Milo said before she could finish speaking. "You look...horrible." He supposed he could have been more subtle but that was the only word that came to mind.

"Always the charmer," Penelope smirked. "Look we haven't got time for compliments. Besides.." she said frowning, "looks like you need a few improvements yourself. You've looked better Milesey." She stared down at his mangled feet and scarred wrists.

"I'm fine."

"You really shouldn't have come here little brother," Penelope said as she dragged him quickly inside a building that still had most of its walls intact.

It was darker inside the building but the light coming in through the many cracks made it relatively easy to see.

"But you know I needed to do this Pen." Milo suddenly felt very small as he stood in the darkened building with his old looking sister staring at him in a way that he couldn't decipher.

"I don't have time to explain everything Milesey. Right now Vylett needs your help." Penelope shot him a backwards glance as she led him through a narrow gap in the building. "Alanya can't save the Quarters. But maybe now that you're here you can help to save Vylett."

Milo's blood ran cold. "Save her from who?"

"From her mother," said Penelope and Milo was shocked at the bitterness in his sister's voice.

Then she led him down some steps to the sound of Vylett's anguished scream.

***

When Penelope had shouted for her to run, Vylett had stuffed the water charm into the pocket of her dress and ran blindly across the deserted planes.

As images of her mother's grotesque face flittered through her mind, the bare landscape around her transformed into a city of beautiful ruins.

Vylett's eyes widened as she found herself running between the crumbling white pillars. In her surprise she had made the mistake of slowing down and Alanya had roughly grabbed her from behind.

Stifling a scream, Vylett had let her mother take her into some derelict building. She was vaguely aware of Penelope bringing up the rear but she was more aware of the things that surrounded her. She ran a finger along the crumbling marble walls, wondering if she was strong enough to break off a piece and use it to protect herself.

At this moment in time, she would have given anything to have Iza's belt.

As Vylett had descended a steep stairwell in some kind of shock, she passed a few people along the way. Well she thought they were people, they were so withered and skeletal it was hard to tell.

They all had the same haunted eyes which seemed to stare right into her soul as they reached out their arms to her, crying out for help. Vylett wanted to stop and help them but Alanya kept pushing her forward down the steps.

"Why do they look like that?" Vylett whispered to Penelope who was right behind her.

"Because they shouldn't be here. They should have entered the mist by now. That's what happens to people who stay here. It's what's happened to me, and to her…" Penelope gestured to Alanya.

Vylett met Penelope's dark eyes, which were so unlike her brother's, in the dim light of the stairwell and swallowed. "Why don't they all enter the mist then?"

"They can't," said Penelope. "They've been here too long. They're lost souls now. It's too late for them."

"And what about?.." Vylett nodded towards her mother, not wanting to say her name out loud. "Is it too late for her. For you?"

"Not yet," Penelope answered. "We can both enter the mist now if we want. But your mother doesn't want us too." Penelope's last few words came out as a grimace. And this time Vylett didn't have to probe Penelope's mind to see what she was feeling.

Where Alanya was concerned, Penelope felt nothing but true hatred.

When they had reached the bottom of the stairs, Alanya had shoved Vylett into a small room, completely bare except for an old fire grate in the corner. Then she had used magic to lock the door. When Penelope had started to protest, Alanya had slammed her against the wall.

Penelope put her hands on her head and moaned softly.

"Penelope!" Vylett rushed to help her but Alanya put a restraining arm on her. "Leave her Vylett," she said coldly. "She's having a vision."

Alanya went over to Penelope and put a hand on her shoulder. It looked like a gesture of comfort but Vylett now knew better.

Alanya was trying to see what Penelope could see.

Alanya smiled with satisfaction and said, "good. Go get him." And then Penelope had disappeared, leaving Vylett wondering who Penelope had gone to get and wondering what kind of demon had taken over her mother.

She was starting to feel dizzy and shaky and she leaned back against the cold brick wall.

Alanya moved closer to her and tried to stroke her hair but Vylett pushed her hand away.

"What happened to you mother?" she murmured. She couldn't stop her body from shaking. She was shivering, yet she could feel beads of sweat on her forehead.

Alanya's fingers felt icy cold on her skin as she stroked her cheek. This time Vylett didn't have the energy to shake her off. She wondered if she was in shock or whether her body was actually dying now that she was in the Otherworld.

"Don't be sad Vylett. I don't want to hurt you. You're my daughter." Alanya smiled and pushed back the hair from Vylett's clammy forehead. "And don't worry about your friend. He's here now."

"Milo? Milo's here?"

Alanya cocked her head to the side as though she were listening for something and then her eyes narrowed dangerously.

"Get back Vylett!" she warned and then casually Alanya shoved her into the metal fire grate.

Vylett screamed as she banged her elbow on the grate and then cowered further into its opening as the door and its surrounding wall suddenly collapsed in.

***

Milo had severely underestimated the strength of his magic as he blasted the door down. His state of weakness after fighting Droges in the activity room had suddenly rectified itself the moment he had stepped into the Otherworld but all of Sharrow's advice had gone from his mind.

He had not been thinking about his magic when he blasted down the door, he had only been thinking about Vylett who was on the other side of it.

"Easy Milesey," Penelope said from behind him. "Everything's magnified in this World."

Clouds of dust from the rubble entered Milo's lungs and he was coughing and spluttering as he ploughed through the huge gap in the wall.

"Is this the boy who has been impressing you so much of late Vylett?" Alanya Roze's voice was mocking as she looked at her daughter who was squashed into some kind of fire grate and rubbing her elbow.

Milo was relieved to see that apart from looking a little pale in the face, Vylett seemed otherwise unharmed.

As Alanya turned to face him, Milo couldn't quite masque his surprise as he took in her withered state.

Truthfully, she was grotesque.

"Let her go," Milo demanded and hoped that he sounded more confident than he felt.

Alanya didn't seem at all phased however that he had just blasted half the room away but merely strode towards him and held out her palm.

"Give me the water charm Miloney."

Vylett climbed awkwardly out of the fire grate. "I'm the one who has the charm mother," she said. "I showed it to you remember. Right before you turned into a monster and kidnapped me." Vylett rubbed her elbow and moved quickly to Milo's side.

"Actually Vylett for some reason I have the charm again," Milo held it out to show her. "Although I have no idea why."

Vylett patted her empty pocket and glanced at her mother in astonishment. "Why would that happen?"

Alanya shrugged. "I don't know and I don't care. Just give it to me Miloney." Her withered looking eyes were hard as stone but Milo kept his fist tight around the charm.

"She does know why that happened," said Penelope angrily, pushing Alanya aside and turning to Milo.

"The reason the charm went back to you Milesey is because a water charm is all about balance and protection."

She took a moment to glare at Alanya before turning back to Milo. "If a water charm senses danger, it will go back to its previous owner in order to keep things balanced and protected. When Vylett tried to give Alanya the water charm it sensed it wasn't being used for good. Therefore it went back to you little bro."

Milo felt a growing anger as he stared at Alanya's withered form. He took a step closer to her.

"I don't understand," he said to her. "When Vylett nearly died in Peaches's cave she said that you promised you'd try to help save the Water Quarter. She said as long as you had the water charm you could re-balance the magic."

Alanya gave a careless shrug and Milo tried hard not to wipe the smug grin off her face.

"If you didn't plan to use it for that. What do you want it for?"

"She wants it to become more powerful," Penelope's voice was flat.

Alanya laughed, a high pitched mocking sound that grated on Milo's nerves. "Don't be so dramatic Penelope. That's not the only reason. I want it to destroy Droges."

Alanya laughed again. A manic, twisted laugh. "Droges exiled me. Me, a multi-gifted!" Alanya's eyes were so crazed in that moment that it was impossible not to feel a little scared.

"And then he killed me! No one does that to me and gets away with it. Be sure I will have my revenge."

"And so how do you propose to do that?" Milo didn't want to look into those eyes but he had to hear the truth.

"That's really none of your business," Alanya said tartly. "But if you really want to know then I guess I can enlighten you of my great abilities." She raised her chin arrogantly and Milo had to force himself not to blast her through the brick wall she was leaning against.

She took a step closer to him but Milo didn't move. He wasn't going to be intimidated by her. Multi-gifted or not.

"When Droges exiled me, I knew that I couldn't kill him," said Alanya. "So I thought that ruining the Quarter he rules would be the next best thing." Alanya paused to make sure she had their full attention before continuing.

"And it worked. I have caused an imbalance so great that Droges will never be able to rule the Water Quarter again because soon there will be no Quarter left to rule."

Vylett made a gasping sound and exchanged a shocked look with Milo before rounding on her mother.

"It was you! You were the one who stole magic from the other Quarters? You were the one who caused the imbalance?"

"Of course! Who else could manage to do such a task?" Alanya's arrogance was suffocating.

Penelope glared at her and shook her head at Milo.

"Aunt Dor was partially right Milesey. But not in the way she thought. The imbalance messed up her instinct. It was Alanya who messed up the Quarters. She's telling you the truth. It wasn't Droges." Penelope looked at Alanya as though she was something nasty she had trodden in.

Alanya scoffed loudly and ran a hand manically through her wild untamed hair. "Why would Droges destroy his own Quarter? Really children, you need to use your brains more. Droges wants power yes, but he's not stupid enough to take it from the other Quarters."

Milo was taken aback with shock. Droges had told him the exact same thing just hours ago but never for a single moment had he expected the great Alanya Roze to be the one who had caused the imbalance.

Never.

She was the one who was supposed to be helping them.

"How did you cause the imbalance if you were on Orlost?" he said narrowing his eyes at her. Not that it really mattered anymore but he wanted to know out of curiosity if nothing else.

He felt Vylett shivering next to him and unconsciously put an arm around her. She was deathly pale and was swaying slightly. He held her more tightly.

"I am multi-gifted Miloney, it was easy." Alanya's smile chilled Milo to his core and he felt shivery himself in that moment.

"As soon as I arrived on Orlost all those years ago, I was able to tell immediately which people still had a little magic left in them and then it was just a case of hunting out someone who had a gift for controlling energy and balance and then siphoning that magic out of them and combining it with my own."

"Siphoning? You mean stealing," Penelope corrected with a disdainful look on her face.

"I prefer to call it siphoning," said Alanya un-phased, then she paused to make sure she had their full attention again.

"After I acquired my new gift it was easy. There was always a Terramang or two lurking around on Orlost and I knew they were always going back and forth to Syanna. So…unbeknown to them, stupid creatures that they are, I transferred my new gift into them so that every time they went back to the Water Quarter they unconsciously upset the balance of it. Simple!"

She laughed a cruel harsh laugh. "They had no idea! Every time they touched something on the Water Quarter, its balance would be disrupted. Their new magic was trying to balance out something that was already balanced. The magic from the other Quarters was drawn to it, like a magnet."

She held out her hands, palm up. "See! Brilliant! Thanks to me, Syanna was slowly sinking under its own water. The greatest come-uppance that could ever have happened to the Terramangs."

"You're insane," Milo said with disgust. "What about all those innocent people on the Quarters? What did they ever do to you? People are dead," he cried. My teacher is dead.

Alanya gave a careless shrug. "I admit that's unfortunate. I really didn't think much beyond destroying the Terramangs, but that's life Miloney. Sometimes sad things happen and that's the way it goes." For all the remorse she was showing, anyone would think Alanya had just accidentally killed a couple of bugs, not hundreds of innocent people.

It made Milo sick.

Vylett began to pace the room. "But you must have made the Terramangs more powerful," she said to Alanya. "Why would you want that?"

"I didn't leave my magic in them sill girl," Alanya said harshly and Vylett blushed red.

"I took it straight back from them every time they returned to Orlost," said Alanya. "They were barely aware anything had happened. They probably thought they'd eaten one too many energy potions that day."

"So well done you've successfully destroyed the Quarters," Milo said. "You've made Droges mad. So why do you want the water charm to make him even more mad?"

Alanya looked at him as though he were senile. "Droges killed me," she said slowly. "He killed me and now I'm stuck here in this vile place."

Her eyes flitted wildly from side to side as though she were expecting something or someone to jump out at any minute. It made Milo feel edgy. He was starting to feel shivery and sweaty and wondered if this was how Vylett felt.

"I want to make him more than mad. I want to destroy him. That water charm will give me the power to do that." Alanya grabbed hold of Vylett's hands looking like an excited child.

"When you told me you had a water charm, I thought 'this is it! This is how I can finish Droges forever'. You see, this World has taken my youth and the best of my magic. But with that charm I could reach Droges through his dreams, his nightmares." She gazed off into the distance looking wistful, lost in her own crazy world of revenge.

"With a little practice I could destroy his mind completely," she said dreamily. "He would become like the people he takes magic from on Orlost. He would be nothing."

Alanya's cold eyes came back to focus on Milo. "That would be my final revenge. So give me the charm Miloney?"

Milo had to admit that it was tempting.

There was nothing he would like better than to see Droges destroyed. But his instinct, as well as Penelope's warning look, was telling him not to give the charm to her. If the charm was going to make Alanya more powerful, then there was no telling what else she planned to do with it.

"Will you help save the Quarter's first?" he asked her.

Alanya laughed that horrible sharp laugh. "Don't be ridiculous Miloney. I'm dead. I can not suddenly return to the Quarters to make a stupid circle," She turned to Vylett. "Does this ignorant boy really make you happy?"

Milo was beginning to feel a dread rising in him that was similar to claustrophobia. "If I give you the charm so you can destroy Droges, will you then use it to let me and Vylett get out of here?"

Alanya studied him carefully, like he was a laboratory specimen that she couldn't quite figure out. "No. Why would I?"

Vylett began to cry then, softly at first and then her body shook with great heaving sobs.

When they had subsided a little, she said. "Because I'm your daughter mother." Vylett's voice was pleading as she fought against the shivers that wracked her body.

Alanya's eyes softened. "Vylett my dear. I do not intend for us to be separated ever again. First I will destroy Droges and then you and I shall cross into the mist together." She shot a look of loathing at Milo. "Your friend Miloney can stay here and do what he wishes. But you are coming with me. I told you I would wait for you. At last we can be together."

Chapter 20

Touched by Death

Milo stared at Alanya wondering how it was possible for someone to be so twisted. "Vylett's not dead you twisted monster. You can't take her with you."

"That doesn't matter," Alanya said casually. "She's here now."

"I get why you want revenge on Droges. I really do," said Milo. "But what I don't get is why you sent Vylett those visions to find you here before you even knew we had the water charm. Why did you do that if you had no intention of helping us save the Quarters?"

In a sudden movement that took Milo by surprise, Alanya grabbed him by the wrist, so hard that he couldn't feel his fingers.

"Vylett is my daughter and a daughter should always be with her mother. I've done what any mother would do. I protected her from pain. I saved her the trauma of the imbalance."

Her eyes softened as she looked at Vylett. "I guided her here painlessly through the portals."

"Oh very considerate," Milo tried to yank her arm off him but she wasn't letting him go yet. "And believe me it hasn't been painless."

"You should be thanking me you ungrateful little fool," Alanya snarled at him, her fingers digging painfully into his already bruised skin. "I didn't ask for you to come here but now you are you're free from the Water Quarter."

"Yeah thanks for that. You have led me to a World of the Dead with the belief that you could help me escape and help Syanna. Thanks a lot."

He finally succeeded in prising her fingers off his wrist and he rubbed the tender skin. "Well I'm not giving you the water charm."

Vylett took a step closer to her mother. "You caused an imbalance that could have killed me. Your own daughter! You made me go through exile. Do you realise how terrifying that was?"

Alanya nodded. "Yes. I do. I went through it too remember. But Vylett, isn't it better that you're here with me rather than on Syanna right now, or Orlost?"

"I would have been fine on Syanna if you hadn't caused that imbalance," Vylett argued.

Alanya ran her fingers through Vylett's hair, looking for all the world like a caring mother. "You have a gift that is too powerful to hide Vylett. I knew you'd be exiled before the imbalance killed you. I always thought of you first you know." Vylett turned her head away but Alanya forced it back again.

"Once you were on Orlost it was easy to send a vision to you because you were most vulnerable to magic there. I knew you'd find me. I knew you'd be safe. We can be together now just like it should be."

Vylett pulled away from her in disgust. She looked like she was fighting back tears.

Milo turned to Penelope. "There must be a way for me and Vylett to leave this place. We're not dead. There must be a way out of here."

Penelope shook her head. "No. There isn't."

"But we have to," Milo persisted, feeling his palms grow sweaty in his agitation. "Lowish can take us somewhere safe. He's waiting for us at the other side of the veil."

"Lowish?" Vylett looked at him in disbelief.

"Yeah, long story," Milo told her. "But he said he'd only wait an hour. We should go now and see if we can just get through the veil."

Penelope hung her head with a sigh. When she lifted her head she looked even older.

"You can't get through the veil Milesey. There really is no escape."

"So what are you saying? That me and Vylett are stuck here for good. No! I don't believe that"

"Not Vylett," Alanya chided. "Just you. Vylett's coming into the mist with me."

"No!" Penelope shook her head from side to side manically. "No, you can't take her. We won't let you."

Penelope looked at Milo wide eyed. "If Alanya drags Vylett through that mist then her body is still going to be whole. It should just be her soul that enters."

"And?" Milo was confused.

"And her soul won't be able to leave her. It'll be trapped inside a dead shell. She would be forever trapped inside her body."

Milo felt cold as he contemplated that horrible thought. To be forever paralysed.

Vylett shivered, looking like she might faint. Milo squeezed her hand tightly. "I won't let that happen."

Alanya laughed her shrill laugh. "You really can't stop me boy. You're stupid if you think you can."

"Vylett's staying here with me. We'll be ok."

"Will you?" Alanya raised her eyebrows and gestured to their miserable surroundings. "Yes you're probably right because me and your sister have positively bloomed whilst staying here."

Milo took in his sister's withered looks and the skeletal people that caught his view through the gaps in the cracked walls of the ruined building they were in and wanted to scream. He had no idea what the hell he was supposed to do.

Alanya held out her palm. "The charm Miloney. Don't make me take it from you." She spoke with a collective calm but Milo was certain that despite her withered state he didn't stand much of a chance against Alanya Roze. She may have lost some of her magic. But she was still multi-gifted.

She was still more powerful.

"Go into the mist Alanya," Penelope snarled at her, holding her hands up to keep her at arm's length. Then she pressed Milo's fingers together, pressing the charm into his palm.

"Do not give it to her Milesey," she said urgently. "Do what you have to do to keep it. If you have that water charm then it will protect you in this place. You and Vylett could stay here comfortably enough. You might even be able to restore this place," she gestured to the ruins with a half hearted wave of her hand. "Just do not give it to her."

Alanya gave an exaggerated sigh. "Oh Penelope. You really are an expert in creating drama. I would protect Vylett if she entered the mist with me. I could make sure that her soul separates, I would see to that. The charm would see to that."

She grabbed Vylett by the shoulders and pulled her away from Milo's grasp. "Don't listen to Penelope Vylett. She doesn't know what she's talking about. If you give me that charm I can cross you over safely. You have to realise that I wouldn't let any harm come to you."

"But you have mother," said Vylett. Her eyes were filled with tears but her mouth was set with determination.

"You led me to this place believing you could help people. You told me that Milo could escape from here. It was all lies." Vylett's voice was full of disappointment. "Sharrow was right, there is no escape from here. But I'm not coming with you either."

She moved back to Milo's side and took his hand. "I'm staying here with Milo."

Alanya stepped back from her. "That's not an option I'm afraid. I'm not leaving you."

Then she turned her attention from her daughter back to Milo. "Now Miloney give me that charm or I promise you'll see the darker side of me."

"I'm already looking at it aren't I!" Milo exclaimed. "How much darker can it get?"

He felt Penelope give him a sharp kick in his shin – a warning to shut up – but he was too angry to shut up.

"And after you've destroyed Droges, will you give me the charm back so I can live happily in this place?"

One of Alanya's eyebrows curled up in cruel amusement. "Maybe."

"Liar!"

Alanya's eyes flashed with anger and she made a sudden grab for Milo. He tried to push her away as she grasped hold of his clenched fingers.

"Give me the charm!"

"There's no point Alanya. It won't go to you. It'll come back to me again remember?"

"No it won't" Alanya's smile was cruel satisfaction. "Not this time. This time I will be more clever. This time I will convince the charm I want it for good," She gave a short laugh. "You know that it will believe me."

Milo stared at her in disgust. Unfortunately he did.

"No mother!" Vylett pounced on Alanya's back - which must have taken all of her courage - and tried desperately to grip Alanya's arms but despite her withered state Alanya was still far stronger and she shrugged Vylett off her easily.

Milo wasn't quite sure whether his next move was intentional but as he watched Alanya fling Vylett like a rag doll, the magic that had begun to regenerate inside him surged up and he blasted Alanya to the other side of the room.

Wow that felt good! His magic really was intensified here.

Alanya hit the opposite wall so hard that it's already crumbling bricks caved in altogether, leaving a clear window back into the dull, faded ruins of the Otherworld.

Alanya screamed in rage and that skeletal body of hers flew several feet into the air to land directly next to him.

It was hard to imagine that this gruesome crazed woman had ever been beautiful.

Milo tried to use his magic to blast her again but he felt depleted already.

Alanya laughed as she struck him hard across the cheek. "You should really learn how to use that magic of yours."

Then suddenly he was staggering backwards as Alanya performed the same magic that he had used on her. He slammed to the ground feeling as though he had been hit in the chest by a missile. He was struggling to breathe from the impact and wanted to sit up but he felt paralysed.

He realised that Alanya was using magic to pin him down.

"Oh Miloney. Did you really think you could outwit me? Even in this place I am still more powerful than you." She prized his fingers open to grab the charm, and then stopped as Penelope made a familiar wailing noise.

She was having a vision.

Alanya's head whipped around to where Penelope stood clutching her head near the fire grate.

"What? What is it? Answer me!" Alanya rushed to Penelope's side and put her hand on her shoulder.

In that instant Milo felt the magic hold on him released.

His lungs filled with much needed air, but the relief was short lived as his body began to shake again.

He felt like he had the flu.

He willed his body to quit being pathetic. Now was not the time to get ill!

"You lied! Alanya suddenly screeched and grabbed Penelope by the throat. She flung her through the open gap in the wall, before flying out to grab her again.

"Penelope!" Milo made to climb through the gap after them but Vylett grabbed him by the arm and began pulling him towards the door he had blasted apart.

"Come on quick! Penelope's trying to help us. She'll be ok."

Vylett pushed him with surprising strength through the door and reluctantly he ran up the crumbling stone steps.

Once outside, they ran as fast as they could.

Soon they could hear Alanya's wail of despair following them and they dodged between the marble pillars as they caved in every time Alanya blasted one.

"Maybe it's a good thing if she kills us," Milo gasped as another pillar crumbled beside him. "Maybe then our souls can go into that mist."

"I'm not sure it's possible to die in the Otherworld," said Vylett as she led them through a narrow crumbling archway whose bricks wobbled precariously as they scraped the walls.

"I don't feel right," Milo told her, unable to ignore the feverish pains that were plaguing his body.

"It's your magic trying to leave your body, you must fight it Milo," Vylett urged as they moved into the dark shadows of the archway. "Fight against it and you'll start to feel better."

Milo chanced a glimpse behind him but Alanya was no where in sight. "I think we lost her," he said as he stopped to lean against the archway wall and catch his breath.

"She's not as powerful as she thinks she is," said Vylett. "Not anymore. If we can make it to the veil then maybe Lowish can help us somehow. Come on."

"You really think a Terramang's going to help you!" Alanya's mocking voice sounded above them, stopping them in their tracks.

Vylett cried out in surprise as Alanya jumped down through a hole in the roof. She stared at her mother open mouthed.

Alanya's appearance in the last few minutes had changed dramatically. She no longer looked crazy and wild. Her eyes had taken on a red tinge but she was calm and composed and somehow that was far more frightening.

She held out her palm to Milo. "For the last time, give me the charm Miloney." As she spoke, at the other end of the archway, a patch of mist appeared.

Milo ignored her, staring at the mist. His emotions seemed to tumble in a mad frenzy around his ears. Part of him had the irresistible urge to run towards that mist. Yet the other part of him knew that he wasn't able to.

The mist was for Alanya.

He turned his attention back to her and then Penelope appeared at the end of the archway. Her outline against the narrow exit was black and eery and Milo couldn't see her face but the cocky stance of her outline was a dead giveaway.

"Give her the charm Milesey," Penelope had a huge gash across her face where Alanya had obviously inflicted her wrath. "Trust me on this. Just give it to her."

Milo looked at her open mouthed. She couldn't be serious! "You've just been telling me not to give it to her," he said angrily. "What's going on?"

"Just do it Milesey."

"No Pen, I'm not giving it to her."

"Yes you are." Penelope glared at him. Then she moved away from the archway, disappearing from view. A triumphant looking Alanya quickly followed, dragging Vylett with her.

***

As Milo hurried after them a dark shadow fell across the exit of the archway. The shadow elongated and the body of whom it belonged to dashed into the archway blocking his way.

Milo couldn't see the person's face because of the contrasting light outside and his heartbeat increased as the figure zoomed in on him.

"Who are you?" he asked and then the figure moved impossibly fast and clamped its hand over his mouth.

"Be quiet," it hissed.

It was a man's voice. And Milo's mind was a blur of confusion because the voice was familiar.

He knew that voice.

He twisted around until he was staring into the very unexpected face of..

Oswald Crackenpepper.

The street vendor from the World of Illusion.

Milo started in surprise. "What are you?.." he began to ask, but Oswald silenced him with a look. The old man's eyes told him to ask no questions. He put a finger to his lips and pushed Milo up close against the archway wall where they were still out of sight of the others.

"Give her the charm. The charm restores balance," Oswald's papery thin voice seemed to sound inside Milo's head and he suddenly realised why his voice had been familiar that first time he had seen him behind the fruit stall.

It was Oswald's voice that he had heard in Audrina's ballroom.

It was the voice that had persuaded him to fight against her.

"It was you!" Milo said to him but Oswald's voice projected more strongly in his mind.

"The charm restores what has been ruined." Then he dissolved into a shadow and disappeared into the walls of the crumbling marble.

Milo rubbed his eyes almost wondering if he had just imagined the whole thing. Then Alanya's voice filtering clearly into the archway cleared his head.

"Miloney!"

When Milo exited the archway, Alanya's jaw dropped at least an inch as she stared at him.

"You have been touched by death." She continued to stare him with what was obvious disbelief.

"What?" Milo narrowed his eyes feeling weirdly nervous. Oswald had touched him. Was she saying Oswald was death?

Vylett looked pale as she studied him also and then said calmly. "Give her the charm Milo,"

He looked back at her confused. Why did everyone keep telling him to give crazy Alanya Roze the charm.

"Remember what the charm is for," Vylett gave him a long pointed look.

Milo stared back at her and Oswald's words came back to him. 'The charm restores what has been ruined'.

He glanced again at Alanya's withered state and suddenly he understood. Alanya had been ruined. She had not always been this crazy selfish woman.

"You lot had better be right about this," he mumbled as he fished the charm out of his pocket and reluctantly handed it to an eagerly waiting Alanya. Her greedy eyes were huge as she reached for it. But Milo felt it pulling back to him like a magnet.

It didn't want to go to her.

Alanya's eyes were focused hard on the charm. She was trying to sway it because Milo could feel its magnetic pull lessen.

Against what felt logical, he willed it to go to her, trusting the voice of the creepy stall vendor.

A second later, Alanya gave a happy cry as the charm relented and she was finally able to grasp it. She cradled it in her palm, gazing at it adoringly, much like a mother holding her newborn baby for the first time.

Milo held his breath as her eyes took on that glazed red fiery look again. They were full of greed and malice.

And then ever so slowly they began to soften.

A look of fear and confusion crossed Alanya's face and then she crumpled to the ground.

***

Vylett had felt Milo's mixed emotions the moment he had exited the archway. It had taken her only seconds to put his chaotic feelings together and discover that someone had told him to give her mother the water charm, hoping it would restore her to her former self.

It was so simple really, Vylett comprehended. Why hadn't she thought of that too!

Now though, as she crouched down next to her mother who was lying completely still, she wondered if it had been the right thing to do after all. Her mother was still grasping tightly to the water charm but her eyes were closed and she was translucent pale.

"Mother?" Vylett shook her by the shoulder but she didn't move.

Vylett stared at her face. Her features were suddenly so much softer. So much younger.

"Do you see that?" she glanced quickly at Milo who nodded, looking just as fascinated.

She turned back to stare at her mother and felt a nervous apprehension as colour started to seep back into those pale hollow cheeks. It wasn't as though Alanya was coming back to life exactly. Vylett knew that wasn't what was happening, but the charm was fixing something that had been broken. With every passing second, her mother was transforming into the beautiful woman that Vylett had seen in Audrina's ballroom.

This was who her mother really was. Not the monster who had pushed her into the fire grate.

"Mother?" Vylett repeated. And Alanya opened her eyes. Eyes that had lost that ugly redness. Eyes that Vylett saw herself everyday in the mirror.

"Vylett?" Alanya glanced around her as though waking from a dream. She looked disorientated.

"What have I done?" her voice shook but she didn't look ashamed so much as bewildered.

"I think the question you should be asking is what haven't you done?" Penelope scoffed.

Alanya grasped her daughter's hands and Vylett was surprised at their warmth and softness.

"I was wrong. I don't know what happened," she said shakily, grabbing Vylett's hand so tight her knuckles turned white.

"You weren't yourself," Vylett told her, unable to think of anything to make her feel better.

Alanya gave her a weak smile. "You're a better person than I was Vylett. You are your father's child." She twisted herself into a sitting position. "I'm sorry that I led you here. I never meant to put your life in danger." Her voice cracked with emotion and she cupped Vylett's face with both hands, urging her to understand. "I just wanted revenge on Droges," she explained. "He robbed me of my chance to see you grow up."

Alanya glanced around her, at the crumbling marble pillars as though suddenly seeing them clearly for the first time. "When I died and came to this place I guess it became difficult to see things clearly," she said with a frown.

Vylett squeezed her hand gently. "But you were on Orlost Mother when you caused the imbalance. That was before you came here."

Alanya glanced sharply at her and then her face softened again. "I know. And I have nothing to say that can justify why I did that."

She shrugged sadly. "I wanted revenge so badly and I knew I had the power to do it."

"But people are dying," Vylett said.

Alanya lowered her eyes and this time she looked ashamed. "Sometimes having too much magic is not always a good thing Vylett." Then she cupped Vylett's chin in her hand again and stared at her intently.

"Always remember that Vylett. Never let your magic rule you. You are the one who rules it."

Vylett nodded, not really understanding and then Alanya got to her feet.

She turned and looked longingly at the patch of mist that was still hovering near her. When she turned back to Vylett, her eyes were misty.

"I'm sorry you had to see me that way Vylett. It must have been hard and unpleasant."

There was nothing much Vylett could say to that. It had been hard and it had been unpleasant.

"I have to go now," Alanya walked dreamily to the mist and then glanced first at Milo and then Penelope.

"I'm sorry," she said to them. She moved closer to the mist and Vylett felt Milo take her hand.

Before Alanya stepped into the mist and from Vylett's life forever, she threw the water charm to her.

"Use this to do what you need to do."

"How will I know what to do?" Vylett felt a surge of panic.

Alanya smiled at her warmly. "You'll know."

She turned briefly to Milo. "Look after my daughter."

Then a dark figure appeared in the mist that Vylett recognised from her previous visit to the Otherworld. She heard Milo gasp beside her and then her mother was gone, swallowed up into the mist.

Vylett didn't have time to grieve because the second the mist disappeared an incredible feeling started to take over her body. It was both terrifying and exhilarating at the same time.

She knew it was magic.

She could feel it, sense it.

More magic than she had ever felt before seemed to be flooding through her whole body and into her every nerve.

"Something's happening to me," she said. She started to pace around, unable to keep still because she felt completely wired.

One moment it was a wonderful feeling, a feeling of tremendous power and in the next she desperately wanted it to stop because deep down she knew what was happening to her and it was frightening her.

"Don't fight it. It's yours?" She felt Penelope take her by the shoulders, forcing her to keep still and look at her. "It's yours," she repeated and for once Penelope's smile was missing its smirk.

Vylett nodded, her eyes were wide and scared.

"Well I don't know what's happening. What's wrong with her?" Milo's anxious voice floated across to her but it sounded distant and far away because the magic flooding through her seemed to be making a loud rushing noise in her ears.

Or was it just fear that was making itself heard?

"Is she in pain?" she heard Milo say and then from somewhere nearby she heard Penelope's mocking voice.

"No she's not in pain you idiot. She's the luckiest girl in the world." There was both excitement and envy in the other girl's voice and Vylett knew that she was right. There was no getting away from what was happening to her.

As soon as her mind began to process this, the rushing sound began to subside and she felt more in control again.

She laughed out loud revelling in a rare moment of complete happiness.

Milo threw his hands up in frustration. "Will someone please tell me what's going on. Vylett what just happened to you?"

"Oh come on Milesey, even you're not that stupid," Penelope scoffed. "Well actually maybe you are," She gave him a tap on the forehead. "Come on bro, what happens to the first born of a gifted parent when they die?" Penelope sounded like a school teacher reprimanding him for not doing his homework properly.

Milo's eyebrows rose as he finally understood. He stared at Vylett in astonishment.

"You've inherited Alanya's gifts! All of them?" he was looking at her as though she had suddenly sprouted two heads.

Vylett laughed at the horror on his face and nodded.

"Vylett is now multi-gifted." Penelope's smirk was back but in truth she looked just as awed as Milo.

Vylett didn't think however that their awe matched hers right now.

Milo just stared at her in astonished silence. She wanted to say something but she couldn't stop her legs from shaking and her heart from pounding.

And that was when she fainted.

Chapter 21

A Final Goodbye

Some time later, Vylett had regained consciousness and was looking calmer and a lot less anxious.

Milo wished he could feel the same himself. He wasn't quite sure how he felt about a multi-gifted Vylett yet. 'Intimidation,' didn't seem to quite cover it.

"Are you ok?" he asked her tentatively.

"Yes. Yes I am." Vylett's eyes sparkled with renewed energy and seemed to convey that she was telling the truth.

"And my mother was right. I do know what I need to do," she looked down at the water charm that she was still clutching. It seemed to Milo that it was glowing ever so slightly, as though Vylett had transmitted some of her radiance into it.

"But first things first. We need to get out of here."

"Well that's the first sensible thing you've said since you got here," said Penelope and for an awful moment Milo realised he had forgotten that she was still there. The thing with Vylett had overshadowed everything else.

Feeling more than guilty he turned his attention back to Vylett. "I agree with you. But how?"

He gestured to his sister. "Penelope said there's no way out of here."

"There is with this," Vylett held out the charm.

Milo was sceptical. "Are you sure? Aren't water charms all about balance and protection and whatever. Why could that work for us?"

"Trust me Milo. I can just feel it. I can't really explain."

Yes, Milo decided. 'Intimidation' didn't cover it.

Vylett seemed oblivious to his awkwardness. "But Milo I'm going to need you to help me."

"Me! How?"

"Just stay with me ok and remember Sharrow's advice. Remember how to control your magic."

Milo frowned as Vylett clutched the water charm tightly and closed her eyes. This new Vylett was definitely going to take a little getting used to.

He ignored his sister's amused smirk and concentrated on what Vylett was doing.

At first nothing unusual happened but then he caught a silver shimmer in his peripheral vision and turned to see that the veiled curtain had materialised next to them. He tried to see if Lowish was still waiting for him on the other side but the veil didn't look like it had when he had entered it.

It was no longer transparent. It had more of a frosted glass appearance.

Vylett put her hands to the veil and began feeling it, closing her eyes as if she wanted to block out every other sense apart from the touch of the veil.

Milo looked to Penelope. "What is she doing?" he spoke in a whisper, not wanting to disturb Vylett's concentration.

Penelope shrugged. "Only she knows. But listen Milesey, I do know that there isn't much time. I need to tell you something before you go." Her eyes turned serious and as she spoke, a patch of white mist appeared behind her. Milo instinctively stepped closer to her.

"You have to find a way to stop Droges from using father's potion," said Penelope. "You know what potion I'm talking about?"

Milo nodded gravely. The Infinity Dust.

"Yeah well that's the potion that helped to kill me," Penelope said bitterly.

"What? How?"

Penelope shrugged. "I discovered it not long after you were exiled. I went down to father's basement to get some peace and quiet." Her eyes became distant as she got lost in her memories.

"I saw father's book of potions and I saw what it was going to be used for. There was no way I wanted to let Droges get hold of it," Penelope began to speak quickly.

"I went to see Droges and...well I tried to blackmail him." She spoke matter of fact as though blackmailing the C.L was something that she did all the time. But there was a note of pride in her voice and her lips curled up into a smirk.

Milo raised his eyebrows questioningly. "Blackmail? You tried to blackmail the leader of the Terramangs? How stupid Pen!"

"I know I know...stupid." Penelope waved her hands dismissively. "But I had to try. I told him that if he let you come back then I would keep quiet about the Dust."

Milo felt a flash of irritation at his sister's rash behaviour.

"Pen.." Milo shook his head. He had always thought that her self-assurance would land her in trouble one day. But at the same time he was secretly pleased that his sister had wanted him back that badly.

"And?" his voice broke, betraying his gratitude.

Penelope gave a bitter laugh. "And he killed me. He didn't confront father about his poor security of the potion or torture me or drag out the process. He just raised his finger to me and killed me."

"It didn't hurt," Penelope said when Milo didn't say anything.

She turned to look at the white mist that was still hovering behind her like a second shadow and Milo used this brief distraction to wipe the tears from his eyes. When Penelope turned back to him, her own eyes were glassy but determined.

"You have to stop that potion Milo. I had a vision. If Droges gets hold of it there's no question that he will take over all of the Quarters. You have to find a way to stop it."

Then Milo was distracted by a flash of white light.

He turned and saw that the bright white light was coming from the water charm. Vylett was touching it to the veil and very slowly as Milo watched, the veil began to thin until eventually a small opening slowly appeared.

Milo gawped in astonishment.

Vylett's hand was shaking as though touching the veil was an enormous struggle.

"Help me Milo," she said between deep breaths. "I need your help to keep it open. If I remove my hand it will close before we've had chance to go through it. You need to use your magic. But not all of it..." she warned. "You can't shatter the veil. It has to remain intact."

Milo nodded weakly. He understood. To break the divide to the Otherworld would be disastrous. It would become an open theme park to immortals and the living. The veil was there for a reason. To break it would be to break the process of death as the Worlds knew it.

"You have to be quick Milo," Penelope's voice was urgent and sharp. "Vylett's using the charm as a conductor for her magic. She's channelling her thoughts into it and its protecting her by providing an exit. But she can't hold it for long. Once it closes it won't re-open for her. That would upset the balance of the veil."

Milo swallowed hard and stared at his sister. "But what about you?"

Penelope shrugged him off with a wave of her hand. "Don't worry about me Milesey. I've got a whole new World waiting for me." She stared longingly at the patch of white mist behind her.

"I have to go now," she said and a dark figure appeared in the mist.

Milo sucked in a loud breath because just like when Alanya had entered the mist, Milo recognised the figure.

It was quite clearly Oswald Crackenpepper.

Alanya had been right. Oswald was death itself. Only Penelope didn't seem afraid of him. Her face looked brighter than it had done in years.

"Well I guess this is goodbye Milesey. Guess I'll see you again when it's your turn to come here. Now go. Help Vylett."

"No wait!" Milo didn't know what he wanted to say to her but he didn't feel ready to let her go yet. This wasn't a normal goodbye and he knew he would never get another chance. He wiped a hand across his face, trying and failing to stop the tears that kept coming.

"Oh for heaven sake, come here," Penelope stepped out of the mist and grabbed him in a tight hug. "Loser" she said hoarsely. She gave him a bright smile, which in true Penelope fashion, was bordering on a smirk, and stepped back into the mist. She reached for Oswald's hand and then she was gone.

Milo didn't think anything had ever hurt so bad. That is until he felt a hard thump on his arm.

"Will..you..help..me!" Vylett looked ready to rip his head off. Her face was red and blotchy with the effort of holding the veil.

Milo gasped, rubbing at his arm, wondering where she had got the strength to hurt him like that.

Then ignoring the empty feeling in his stomach from Penelope's departure he summoned on just a little of his magic and concentrated exactly the way Sharrow had taught him to. The second he felt the magic surge through him, and not a moment more, he aimed it at the veil.

The opening widened a fraction and gasping with relief Vylett pulled her hand from the veil and rushed through the gap. "Come on Milo!"

Milo rushed after her, glancing back only for a second in the hope that Penelope may have reappeared.

She hadn't.

The second they exited the veil, it closed up and once again it was transparent. Except this time Milo could clearly see the marble ruins on the other side instead of just bare landscape.

Vylett slumped to the ground in exhaustion. Beads of sweat trickled down her forehead.

"Are you ok?" she said with a shaky breath. "I'm sorry there wasn't much time for you to say goodbye to Penelope. I didn't think. I was just trying to get us out of there whilst I knew how. It just came to me and..."

"It's ok," Milo reassured her. "I'm ok."

Vylett wiped away a tear looking ashamed. "Really?"

Milo could have lied and pretended that he was absolutely fine after saying goodbye to his dead sister but he didn't have the energy to put on a brave face for Vylett. Besides..she would know he was lying. Gifted or not, she would have known.

Instead he gave her a small shrug. "Not really, but right now I have to be. We have to decide what we're going to do next, now that we know Alanya can't save the Quarters."

"Well maybe she can't, but I can," Vylett's eyebrows rose and she held out the charm. "I know exactly what I need to do."

"I have to tell you Vylett that you are starting to freak me out," Milo admitted. "I mean...you're multi-gifted now. Just how many gifts do you have?" He rubbed his arm which felt bruised and sore.

Vylett noticed and blushed. "I don't know. I guess I'm still finding out." She giggled nervously and rubbed his arm. "Sorry."

"Well you're obviously an expert on water charms now. Penelope said you knew exactly what you were doing with it. She said that once that veil closed it wouldn't open up again because of upsetting the balance and whatever. How did you know what to do?"

"I really can't explain it," Vylett's brow was furrowed as she thought about it. "I just sensed what I needed to do." Her eyes flicked suddenly to the veil. "I also had to send someone into the Otherworld in replace of us."

"What do you mean?" Milo looked at her warily. He didn't like the sound of where this was going and he didn't think he could take any more bad news right now.

"Right well don't ask me how I know this but I just do," said Vylett. "But it's like this. The elevator at Sharrow's place had granted us proper access to the Otherworld right?"

Milo nodded.

"Well to just leave it without a replacement would have upset the whole balance."

"So you sacrificed someone to rot in there in order to save us?"

"Not just someone. Her." Vylett pointed to the veil. Milo turned and then felt his jaw drop open in surprise.

It was Audrina.

"She wanted to die..remember?" Vylett explained. "But she's immortal and so normally she can never enter the Otherworld. But the charm agreed the exchange and because of her immortality, she won't rot in there. Her soul is different to ours."

Vylett looked at Milo like she needed his approval at what she had done. "I don't think she's a bad person Milo. I think she was just lonely, and now she's free of the caves."

Milo could tell that Vylett was trying to justify what she had done but he was too distracted by Audrina to give his approval.

He stared at the shimmering orange princess and watched in amazement as she picked up a piece of rubble which turned to crystal marble in her hand. Various people who had not crossed into the mist rather disturbingly began emerging from derelict buildings and making their way towards Audrina like bees to a honey pot. But as they got close to her, their skeletal frames became less skeletal and their haunted faces became less haunted.

"She's giving them her magic," said Vylett quietly.

"Can she enter the mist?" Milo asked her, wondering what Penelope would think of the immortal princess.

"I think so, but only when she's ready."

Milo smiled as the crumbling marble pillars transformed into beautiful marble structures as Audrina glided by and touched them.

He shook his head. "Why do I get the feeling that Audrina's not going to go into that mist until she's spent the next several centuries creating another ballroom," he said.

Vylett laughed. "So I did the right thing?"

"Yeah you did the right thing."

Vylett sighed with relief. "So where is Lowish? I can't believe he wants to help us. Do you really trust him?"

"Yeah I think I do. It's a long story but basically he saved me from Droges and brought me here to help you. Only...now he doesn't seem to be here," Milo glanced around him, seeing nothing but white haze.

"Lowish where are you?" He shouted loudly into the desolate misty realm of the portal.

In answer, there was a clinking noise and an angry looking Lowish appeared a few feet away from them in the haze.

"There you are!" He said with his usual gruffness. "I expected you to exit the veil the same way you entered it. Do you realise how big this place is?"

Lowish looked very strange standing there in the middle of the white misty surroundings of the portal. He looked out of place. Kind of like being in a house that was completely empty except for one piece of lonely furniture.

"I'm sorry but there really wasn't time to be that specific," Milo said a little shortly. "We were kind of in trouble in there."

"Where's Alanya?" Lowish's eyes skitted about a little fearfully. Obviously her powerful status had made quite an impact in the past with even the immortals.

"My mother's left the Otherworld." Vylett's voice was steady but Milo could tell by her eyes that she was struggling to hold it together. "She's in the World of the Dead. I have her gifts now so I'm the one who has to go back to the Water Quarter and re-balance the magic."

Lowish stared at her in a way that was almost comical. "You?"

"Yes. Me. Why is that so difficult to believe?" Vylett raised her chin defiantly. "I have to make a circle with the multi-gifted from the other Quarters. I have to go and find them."

"I've saved you the trouble," said Lowish gruffly. "I've already found them. Whilst you two were messing around through that veil I brought them to the Drome. They're waiting for Alanya." He shifted his feet awkwardly. "Well now they're waiting for you I guess."

Vylett's face lit up with relief. "Thanks Lowish. That's a big help. So can you take me back there now?"

Lowish shifted nervously from one foot to the other, his armour clinking in rhythmic time to his feet. "I guess. But I can't stay. I take you and then I have to leave. If Droges catches me he'll destroy me. And you too." He paused to give Vylett a strange look. "Once you go back there you do realise you won't be able to escape? He'll find you."

"I know. I'm willing to take that risk." The muscles in Vylett's jaw tightened and Milo's response was immediate.

"No. He won't find you," he told her firmly. "I won't let that happen."

"I don't want you to come with me Milo," Vylett told him quietly. "I'm not putting you in danger too." Her huge blue eyes bore into his with such intensity that he wanted to look away because it was painful to see how desperately she wanted him to stay.

But he stared right back at her. "Well that's tough because I'm coming. I'm willing to take the risk too and you're not talking me out of it Vylett." She smiled then and nodded. Her eyes glassy with appreciation.

"Besides..." said Milo, "I need to find a way to stop my father making that potion." Milo stopped speaking and looked warily at Lowish. He wasn't sure how much Lowish knew, if anything, about the Infinity Dust.

But Lowish merely shrugged. "I know about the potion, and I agree with you..it should be stopped. Droges already has enough power."

"So..are you ready?" Lowish held out his arm to them.

"Actually Lowish can you take us back to the World of Illusion first. I want to say goodbye to Abigail and Helico." Milo tried to sound apologetic but Lowish puffed out a stream of rancid breath his way.

"They're fine," he grunted impatiently. "And there's really no time. The Water Quarter is getting worse by the minute. Trust me on that."

"He's right," said Vylett. "We should go there now."

"I just think they'll want to know we're ok. It won't take long."

Vylett met his eyes, understanding that he needed to do this to be able to settle his mind.

"Ok," she relented. "But we have to be quick." She turned to Lowish and shrugged. "To the World of Illusion then please Lowish."

"Hmmph. Since when did I become a transport service," The Terramang grumbled. But with another grunt and unnecessary roughness Lowish grabbed hold of Milo and Vylett and quickly transported them in a swirl of white mist.

***

They landed smoothly back in the busy village of the World of Illusion. Milo felt dizzier this time than he had the last few times they had teleported.

"I'm not sure I'll ever get used to that," he grumbled as he shook his head a few times to clear the ringing sensation that filled his far too sensitive ears.

"It's not good for a human to teleport frequently," Lowish said absently. "Unbalances your molecular system. Or something like that," he grunted.

Lowish looked around the village with distaste whilst Vylett told Milo that next time they teleported Milo should take the water charm to help the dizziness.

"Let's hurry this up," Lowish growled impatiently whilst all the time glancing cautiously around him. "I don't like this place. Always seeing things you don't want to see."

Milo chuckled to himself. Lowish really was the oddest Terramang that he had ever known. He thought Lowish had missed the boat when the Gods were handing out ruthlessness to those particular immortals.

Milo smiled. "This way," he said after spotting a shock of wild red hair at a food stall.

Helico and Abigail were stood with their backs to them, and were clearly having some kind of quarrel. They seemed to be locked in a tug of war with a fruit hamper.

Vylett made a little coughing noise to get their attention. "Hey guys we've got more important stuff to do than eat you know."

Abigail and Helico turned around and huge grins spread across their faces.

Then there was a lot of hugging and laughing - much to Lowish's agitation. On seeing Lowish, Abigail looked ready to attack, but Milo quickly assured them that Lowish was an ally now and not an enemy. Abigail looked more dubious than Helico but both of them were too happy to see their friends again to question it further.

"I knew you'd be ok. Didn't I tell you they'd be ok Helico," Abigail flung her arm around Helico's neck and unabashedly gave him a big kiss on the lips.

Milo felt a little embarrassed and made a discreet coughing noise to break them apart.

Abigail pulled away from Helico with a little giggle and turned her attention back to Milo and Vylett again. "I knew you'd be ok," she repeated, but she looked like she'd just let out a huge breath that she'd been holding all this time.

"Me too. I knew that too," Helico pretended to sound dejected. Then he grinned and said, "so...tell us what happened? Did Vylett's mother save your World?"

"Er, no not exactly," said Vylett. "I have to go and save it myself." At Helico and Abigail's shocked looks, Milo and Vylett quickly explained, giving them the basics.

"Sounds like you have had quite a journey," Sharrow's voice sounded behind them and Milo turned around quickly, surprised to realise how much he had missed the old man.

But he didn't see Sharrow. He saw Droges.. and then Vylett's dead eyes. He sucked in a sharp breath.

Milo shook his head a few times as though trying to clear his vision and then thankfully he saw Sharrow as he really knew him.

The aging man in the tweed jacket.

Sharrow's eyes widened and he smiled appreciatively. "It seems like you learnt much in the Otherworld Milo. I do believe you just saw through my illusion."

"But there were no illusions in the Otherworld," Milo said confused. Well none that he had noticed anyway.

"Weren't there? Are you sure about that? Was everything really as it seemed?"

"No it wasn't," Vylett answered before Milo had a chance to think. "At first it looked like there were just acres and acres of empty land but then after a while there was this whole city of marble and bricks and ruins."

"Sounds weird," said Helico. "So which was real? The buildings or the land?"

"The buildings, according to Milo's sister anyway," said Vylett. "When I noticed them she said I was finally seeing with my eyes."

"Good. That's what I like to hear," said Sharrow. "And now I am even more intrigued to hear more about your adventure." Then he sniffed the air slightly and looked over Milo's shoulder. "And I should thank this immortal for bringing you back safely."

Milo frowned in confusion and then suddenly remembered that Lowish was standing awkwardly nearby looking extremely uncomfortable.

Lowish accepted the praise modestly but looked very much like he wanted to bolt. His eyes never stopped darting around.

"Do not worry Terramang. I will not keep the children here longer than necessary," Sharrow assured him. "But first why don't you all come back to my house. I have something I want to show you."

"We can't," Milo exchanged a glance with Vylett. "We have to go home. Vylett knows how to save the Water Quarter."

"Can you spare an hour? I don't imagine that will make much difference to the state of things on the Water Quarter and I think you will definitely want to see what I have to show you," said Sharrow. "It could prove useful to you back on the Water Quarter."

"And besides..." Sharrow gave them a slanting smile. "I imagine you won't say no to a small bite to eat before you go and save your World. Every hero needs energy you know."

At the mention of food, Milo and Vylett suddenly realised that they were starving.

Lowish was going crazy with impatience but as he didn't really have anything else to do he agreed to wait for them. They agreed to meet him by the food stall -where Abigail and Helico had been quarrelling- in one hour's time.

As Milo made to follow Sharrow back to his house, he caught a blurriness in the corner of his eye and felt as though someone were watching him. Heart beating a little faster he didn't have to turn around to know who it was. But he turned anyway.

Oswald Crackenpepper stood behind his food stall staring at him.

His face was as pale and sunken as ever and his mouth was still set in a grim line but his dark eyes seemed to twinkle. He gave Milo a wink and then disappeared. To who knew where was anyone's guess.

Milo wondered how many jobs Oswald actually had.

As he followed the others back to Sharrow's, Milo remembered Alanya's words. "He's been touched by death."

He shivered. He hoped that didn't have a double meaning.

Chapter 22

Something Good, Something Bad

As soon as they entered Sharrow's house, the cross-patcher led them straight up stairs in the direction of the room where Milo had slept yesterday. Was it only yesterday? It felt like forever ago.

"What are we doing?" he asked, all the while aware that time was ticking away. He didn't understand why Sharrow was delaying them. Did he not truly understand how catastrophic the imbalance was? Other multi-gifted were waiting for Vylett to complete their circle right now.

His thoughts were interrupted by Abigail's excited voice. "You'll see," she said brightly.

When Sharrow opened the door to the bedroom, Milo forgot all his worries. After his initial surprise in which his jaw dropped open, his face broke into a huge grin.

Lying amongst the bundle of blankets were Iza and Eli.

***

After another happy reunion in which Milo felt giddy with relief, he came to realise that not all was quite right with Iza. It was not immediately obvious what with all the hugging and questions and then more questions. Everyone was speaking over each other, trying to find out what had happened to the twins, whilst Eli wanted to find out what had happened to everyone else. But in normal circumstances, Iza's voice would be heard more loudly above the rest.

She would have made sure that she was heard.

But she was unusually quiet and subdued. Jittery even. When Milo gave her an awkward hug she almost blanched as though frightened he was about to attack her.

On noticing Milo's confused reaction, Sharrow pulled him aside. "She has been through much. She needs time to adjust again."

"What happened to her?" Milo could hardly hear himself speak over the noise of the happy reunion.

"She will tell you in her own time. For now, just be content to know that I found her and that she will be fine. Time is a great healer. Or so I have heard. For an immortal time is of no real importance, it..."

"Sharrow why did you go and look for them?" Milo interrupted him before he got lost on a different tangent.

Sharrow raised his eyebrows in surprise. "Isn't that obvious? I wanted to help you," he said. "I do not agree with the way the Terramang's rule your World. And I certainly do not agree with them taking people from their own Worlds and trying to steal the magic within them."

Sharrow was speaking quietly but his repressed anger was evident in the tightness of his mouth and for a second Milo caught another glimpse of his true self.

As Vylett's lifeless eyes stared back at him, he sucked in a sharp breath and then relaxed when they quickly reverted back to Sharrow's eyes.

"Sorry," Sharrow apologised. He rubbed his stubble chin and said, "and I do not agree with other cross-patchers holding people captive against their will. As you know I do not have any control over another cross-patchers' turf but as soon as I heard that Audrina of the caves was admitted to the Otherworld I was able to enter her patch and save your friend Eli."

Sharrow shrugged then. "Where ever Eli chooses to go next will be his decision. I shall not make it for him."

"And Iza, was she in the caves too?"

Sharrow chuckled and guided Milo out of the room. "You ask too many questions. That is a common human trait I believe. Always curious. Now come, let me get you that bite to eat."

"A small bite to eat" transpired to another feast of warm crusty bread, roasted vegetables and thick hot chocolate.

Throughout the meal, Eli sat closely to Iza coaxing her to eat. Thankfully Abigail was considerate enough not to goad Iza over her odd behaviour or make any smart comments. To her credit she looked just as concerned as the others.

Conversation was brief as they ate. There wasn't time to tell the twins everything that had happened in the Otherworld and Milo didn't particularly feel up to telling them about Penelope yet and so they ate quietly, content for now that everyone was alive and safe.

"Eli has something he wants to tell you?" Sharrow announced as they scraped the last of the roasted vegetables into their mouths.

Everyone looked expectantly to Eli who smiled and put a protective arm around Iza. "We want to come with you to the Water Quarter. Both of us."

"And us too!" Abigail announced quickly as she wrapped her arm through Helico's.

"No! No way!" Vylett stood up and pushed her chair away so that it made a loud scraping noise on the floor. "I really appreciate what you are all trying to do but I can't promise that I can protect you all."

She began pacing the kitchen in her distress. "If Droges catches you he will kill you and I know I have all these gifts now but I don't know how to use them all properly yet." Her words were pouring out in a rush and eventually she stopped pacing to take a breath.

"Look," she said, regarding them all seriously. "My mother couldn't defeat Droges so I won't be able to either." She lowered her eyes, avoiding their gaze. "I'm sure that Lowish will take you home again," she said quietly.

Helico uncharacteristically gave her a frustrated look. "Vylett. When will you understand that we're a team now," he said. "We don't want to go home. We've been in this together since Orlost and we're not leaving you to face this alone."

He looked at the others around the table. "While you and Milo have been away we've had plenty of time to discuss this and we're certain about it. We're not going to change our mind on this Vylett. If we die, then we die. And that's our decision to make."

Apart from Milo, the others nodded enthusiastically.

It was quite an impressive speech from Helico. Heartfelt. But Vylett didn't soften.

"You shouldn't think like that Helico," she said. "Life is too precious to risk it all away in a moment of friendship. If you die then I would never forgive myself."

"And if you die then we would never forgive ourselves for not at least trying to help you," Helico stared her down defiantly and there was a moment's awkward silence in which no one knew what to say.

Eventually Eli said, "please let us help you Vylett. We started this journey together and we know the risks of entering your World but that's our problem, not yours."

Vylett looked to Milo who really didn't know what to say. He felt the same as Vylett. He didn't think the others should come and risk their lives for the sake of a World they didn't even belong to.

In the end Sharrow was the go-between. "Take the help your friends are offering Vylett. If Droges finds you then you may need the help of your friends and of their magic," he advised.

"Although I'm not saying I agree with what they are doing," Sharrow frowned. "And I especially do not think Iza should go but I will not stop them. It is their free will. However I do think it's very commendable," he said giving them all a nod of approval.

"Well if Iza is coming then I think we ought to know what happened to her," Milo announced loudly. "I think that's only fair. If we can understand what happened to her then we might be able to protect her. Otherwise how do we know what we say or do will make things worse."

Iza's eyes were wide and nervous as everyone looked at her, waiting for her response.

She swallowed hard. "Ok. I..I was looking for the cave from Vylett's vision," she began in a shaky voice. She stopped and began swallowing repeatedly, clearing her throat and looking at Eli for reassurance. Large tears rolled down her face and she shook her head. "I can't," she said.

"Will you allow me to show them?" Sharrow asked her in a gentle voice.

Iza nodded and then before Milo had a chance to ask how Sharrow could show them, the cross-patcher touched each of their shoulders in turn and Milo suddenly found himself staring at the masses of rocks near Audrina's caves.

He knew he wasn't really there but he knew it wasn't an illusion either. Sharrow was about to show them what had happened to Iza. Milo could not see the others, but he knew they were seeing the same thing as he was.

With nervous anticipation, Milo spotted Iza leaping wildly across the caves from afar and then her image zoomed in so that he was following her more closely. It was like he was floating behind her.

It felt strange to know that you weren't really in a place but to feel as though you were whilst simultaneously feeling detached from it.

Iza bounded over rocks close to the ravine for a while and then the image fast forwarded until Iza found a part of the ravine which was narrow enough for her to leap across. She headed towards the woodland at the edge of the black river and even through the images that Sharrow were showing him, Milo could again feel the eeriness of those woods.

The hairs on the back of his neck seemed to stand on end and the creepy feelings only intensified as Iza ..and now himself... entered the woods.

The sky above them darkened as Iza headed deeper into the dense foliage and the atmosphere noticeably dropped a few degrees. It was just the perfect setting for a creepy woodland stroll.

Iza seemed to be drawn to something because she moved with a definite purpose. "Why did she wander away from the caves?" Milo wondered. "Why would she go back towards the black river?"

"She was being drawn there." Milo jumped slightly as Sharrow's voice sounded in his head.

He felt nervous as he watched Iza walk through the woods and he wondered if it was his fear or hers that he was feeling. He knew she was ok. She was sat here with them now alive and well but something bad had obviously happened to her.

Fallen twigs and debris crunched underneath Iza's feet as she walked purposefully deeper and deeper into the thick woodland which was so dense there was no footpath to guide her.

Then weirdly Iza began sniffing the air like a wild animal, or perhaps a Terramang, in a way that sent Milo's heart beating faster.

She entered a clearing and Milo's skin prickled again as he saw several figures gathered there, as though waiting for her. Milo knew instantly that the many identical looking figures clad in black were cross-patchers. He could feel their cold prickling aura as clearly as he could feel Sharrow's grip on his shoulder.

There were probably about twenty of them. All of them in black suits and all of them with short black hair that was styled into a small point on the top of their too largely proportioned heads.

Milo instinctively tried to shout to Iza to stop as she edged fearlessly closer to the cloned black people but nothing came out of his mouth. The people in black – and Milo couldn't help but call them people because despite their large heads they looked as human as he did – were gathered around a deep hole in the ground, into which two of them were lowering a long wooden box.

A coffin, Milo realised with a racing heart.

One of the people in black slowly walked up to Iza and cupped her chin gently in his hand. He appeared to smile warmly into her eyes as he lifted her chin and mumbled some words that did not make any sense.

Iza gazed at him transfixed and nodded. Then moving very slowly but with certainty, she climbed into the coffin and lay down. The people in black began lowering the coffin again further into the hole with long thick ropes, carelessly tipping it at an angle so that Iza's head banged loudly against the pale wood.

Milo felt sick and he was vaguely aware of Sharrow's hand gently squeezing his shoulder.

Iza lifted her head up and looked groggily at the men in black. "What are doing to me?" As if coming out of a trance, she kicked out at one of the black clad men and then winced as though her foot had kicked something hard as steel. Milo knew that those men's bodies were more solid than Lowish's armour and his head started to feel fuzzy as they lowered Iza further into the ground.

Iza looked like she tried to spring out the coffin but she fell limply back into the wooden box and one of the men in black laughed. "Don't fight us. Let us take care of you. Do you want us to take care of you?" Iza looked trance like again and nodded as the coffin hit the bottom of the hole with a thud.

She didn't look scared anymore. She actually smiled back at the men as though she really thought they were looking after her.

"The soil is just a blanket," they told her in silky smooth voices as they sprinkled gravelly dirt on top of her.

Then one of the men in black made a vicious snarling voice and Milo's eyes widened to see Sharrow step into the clearing.

"Sharrowlandi. How dare you enter our territory without permission." One of the men in black released his hold on the rope and in one long stride had pressed his face up close to Sharrow's.

"How dare you drug a human with your magic," Sharrow counteracted.

"She entered our territory," the man snarled. "We can do what we like with her. Leave us now Sharrowlandi and we will not destroy you too." The man's tone was deadly but Sharrow did not waver.

In a movement quick as lightening, Sharrow lifted Iza out of the coffin and vanished with her.

The men in black were left standing alone in the clearing, stunned and furious.

As their image began to fade and Sharrow's kitchen came back into focus, Milo heard one of the men in black say, "find him."

The kitchen came completely back into focus and Iza leaned heavily into Eli as everyone stared at her in shock.

Eli's face was whiter than Milo had ever seen it and the anger and hurt that he felt over the obscene treatment of his sister was evident in his dark eyes. "You're safe now, you're safe," he kept repeating to her.

Vylett began pacing back and forth in the kitchen again and for a moment it looked like her skin was glowing. Power seemed to emanate from her.

Again Milo felt intimidated which he knew was stupid and irrational but he didn't know this Vylett, this powerful, unpredictable Vylett.

"Will they find you?" she asked Sharrow. "Can they find you?"

"Always so many questions," Sharrow replied in response. He smiled warmly at her and began clearing away their plates. "Do not worry about me Vylett, you have enough to worry about. I can take care of myself."

How could they not worry? Sharrow had already told them that it was illegal to cross another cross-patchers turf and interfere. He had just committed a crime in helping Iza and now the men in black were out to destroy him. "Do not worry about me," Sharrow repeated more sternly as he looked at their worried faces.

"I have to come with you Vylett," Iza said in a more steady voice. "I can not stay here with him. He's one of them," she looked nervously at Sharrow and fidgeted in her chair.

"Sharrow won't hurt you. He's not like them," Milo reassured her but Iza was adamant. "I know that deep down but I can't stay here. I want to come with you."

"Sharrow, she needs pills. Iza takes pills but she lost them all." Abigail said quickly as though suddenly realising that this was the answer to her problems. "Isn't that right Eli, Iza needs her pills."

Eli smiled at Abigail, and it was a silent thank you for understanding.

"She doesn't need pills. She just needs time," said Sharrow. "Time to recover and heal."

"I can not blame her," Sharrow continued. "She needs to do what she needs to do."

"And you?" Milo asked him.

Sharrow gave him a slanting smile. "And I will do what I need to do. Do not worry, I have many protectors in the World of Illusion."

Milo immediately wondered if Oswald Crackenpepper was one of those protectors. Weirdly it made him feel slightly better to think that the 'face of death' might be watching over Sharrow.

***

Lowish was still waiting for them in the same spot they had left him. It did not look like he had moved an inch. His eyes were still darting nervously around the village and Milo actually felt a little sorry for him. His sympathy quickly turned to anger however when Lowish refused to teleport all six of them. "I am not a transport service," he growled angrily.

"Lowish please..." Vylett turned her big blue eyes on him but Lowish was not to be easily swayed.

"You'll all be killed," he grunted. "I realise why you have to go back" he growled at Vylett, "but as for the rest of you, you don't need to be there. You have no idea what it's like on the Water Quarter at the moment. If Droges doesn't kill you then the intensity of the magic will. Trust me it is not pleasant."

Everyone was suddenly quiet as the seriousness of the situation began to kick in. "It's what we want Lowish," Milo said quietly.

In answer, Lowish turned his back on them like a child in a huge grump and refused to speak to them. The only noise he made was the occasional grunting as he heavy breathed a load of rancid stench their way.

"Lowish, how about I propose a deal with you." Sharrow put a hand on Lowish's shoulder and Milo had to stifle a laugh as Lowish jumped about two feet into the air.

"Don't do that!" he growled but curiosity got the better of him and he snapped, "what deal?" as his coal black eyes narrowed to slits.

Sharrow smiled. "You transport these children back to the Water Quarter and I will make sure that no Terramang enters this World without my permission. You can stay here for as long as you wish. You will have protection."

Lowish seemed to consider this for about one second and then began shaking his head madly.

"No. I'm not staying here where everything's messed up. I'll take my chances. Besides...a Terramang can go where they like. If Droges want to come here, then he will."

"That's true," agreed Sharrow. "But I also have the ability to create the sort of illusions that would make him want to leave again as soon as he entered." Again Lowish seemed to consider the offer for all of another two seconds.

"No," he shook his head again. "I will take my chances."

"As you wish," Sharrow did not seem offended. "But I think you should still take the children to the Water Quarter. Let them do what they feel they have to do."

"Fine!" Lowish branded the ground next to him in frustration, creating a large scorch mark on the smooth pavement. He stomped grumpily over to the children, armour rattling loudly and held out his arms. "Then let's make this quick."

Everyone hurriedly thanked Sharrow heartily for his hospitality - except Iza who was still a jittery mess - but before Milo took hold of Lowish's arm, he pulled the cross-patcher aside.

"Will they find you...the other cross-patchers?" As he spoke there was a loud rumbling noise which echoed deeply all around them. Sharrow cocked his head to the side listening, and Milo didn't fail to see the deep lines of worry etched onto his face.

"That's them isn't it? They're trying to get in." Milo could imagine a huge invisible wall covering the perimeter of the World of Illusion that the other cross-patchers were trying to breach through.

Sharrow smiled a little sadly. "They can try Milo but I have my cavalry protecting me."

"But for how long?"

"Promise me you won't worry about this. You have bigger things than me to worry about right now. I am more powerful than you could imagine Milo. I will be fine. Now go...the Water Quarter needs you."

"Actually they need Vylett," Milo mumbled as he glanced at his multi-gifted friend who was urging him to join them.

"She's still the same Vylett Milo. Her new magic doesn't change that," Sharrow said quietly, predictably reading Milo's mind. "And she needs your help. Now go."

Milo nodded, feeling a little ashamed. "Thanks for everything Sharrow." Milo hated goodbyes and this one particularly was one of the hardest.

He took hold of Lowish's arm and disappeared in a swirl of mist, with Sharrow's slanting smile still printed on his eyelids and the loud echoing noises that sounded in the World of Illusion still ringing in his ears.

Chapter 23

Safety in Magic

Rather awkwardly, Milo touched Vylett's arm once they were back on solid ground. "They were coming for Sharrow. Did you realise that?"

"Yes I know," she said a little shortly. "But there was nothing I could do about it Milo."

Milo wanted to ask her if she was sure about that, to know exactly what magic she had now but she jumped in first.

"I couldn't have helped him," she repeated and her eyes registered the hurt she felt. Milo felt utterly crappy. What was wrong with him. Was he jealous?

"And before you ask, no I can't read your mind Milo. That isn't one of my gifts. And I didn't even have to sense your thoughts. Your tone of voice said it all."

Milo blushed, preparing some kind of apology but Abigail distracted him by asking, "is this your World?"

Milo didn't recognise the large rocky ledge which Lowish had brought them to, but he did recognise its sorry looking surroundings which held the grimmest scene that Milo had ever seen.

"Yes," he said bleakly. "This is home."

***

They were stood on firm ground and when Vylett looked around her, she couldn't believe what she was seeing.

Utter chaos resided.

The houses in the bottom of the valley were completely submerged in water and so were most of the houses further up the hillside. She couldn't see her own house high up on the mountain from this distance but the water was quickly gushing up towards it.

She watched in horror as people floated past them, some alive, some dead. Those that were alive were either crying out for help or else fighting with each other, using both physical and magical strength.

It was hard to watch.

She gasped as one unfortunate sailed clean out of the water, soaring upwards like a bird, his arms spread wide like wings.

The man looked exuberant and graceful but there was a manic look in his eyes and seconds later the group watched in horror as he exploded into flames, his charred remains floating back down into the water in a giant ash cloud.

Vylett tore her eyes away, trying to keep control of her body as she felt the imbalance of the water's magic start to affect her.

Flashes of orange from the valley side were evidence of the Terramangs' attempts to keep control of the gifted ones. Vylett doubted their brands would do any good.

Syanna was out of control.

Water splashed onto the rocky ledge, lapping at Vylett's feet and she looked down at the platform, seeing it properly for the first time. It was a black shiny marble, huge and with pointed turrets sticking out of the water at the far end of it.

"Lowish...is this...?"

"The Drome, yes," Lowish said. "Well what's left of it anyway."

"Come on," she said, realising she needed to pull herself together. "We need to get inside, that's where the other multi-gifted are."

"If they are still there," said Lowish.

"They are. I can feel their energies. Is there a window we can break into Lowish?"

Lowish quickly glanced nervously around him and then seeing that they were alone, he broke into a nearby window - the old fashioned way - using his elbow.

"I can't come inside," he told them. "Droges might be there." Lowish stood awkwardly as the group prepared to crawl through the window.

Vylett thought he looked lost and had to resist the strange urge she suddenly had to give him a hug. She knew he wouldn't appreciate that. Not for a second.

"Thank you for everything Lowish," She really meant that and as the others enthusiastically chorused their thanks too, Lowish actually looked a little embarrassed.

"Good luck and try not to get yourselves killed," he grunted.

As they climbed through the window Lowish called back to them. "By the way how did you manage to get out of the Otherworld? I'm curious."

Vylett turned and held out the water charm smiling. "With this." Then she looked him straight in the eye, "and good luck to you too Lowish."

Then there was a bright white light and Lowish was gone.

After Lowish disappeared everyone felt a strange sense of abandonment - and suddenly very vulnerable.

"Well I'd best go and find this circle," said Vylett after several moments had passed in which no one had said anything.

She immediately began tuning into her senses to try and get a feel where the other multi-gifted might be. She had to concentrate hard because even though the magic was more balanced inside the Drome, it was still heightened and like in the Otherworld, all of her senses felt magnified, so that it felt hard to focus on one thing at once.

She urged the others to be silent who were regarding her with a mild interest and then wiping their chaotic emotions aside she pushed outwards with her mind until she touched upon a strong sense of magic that did not belong to her little group of friends and that she could tell straight away belonged to that of a multi-gifted.

If someone's depth of magic could be measured and made visible, then it would have been like looking at a mirror image of her own magic.

"Come on this way," she told the five sets of eyes that were still studying her intently.

***

Five minutes later they were walking down unfamiliar darkened corridors that had the lingering stale scent of Terramangs.

"Where are we?" asked Eli.

"I think we're in hell," said Iza as she stared unabashedly at the dim candelabras and the crumbling stone walls.

Vylett was concerned about Iza. She still seemed extremely unstable and her emotions were hard to ignore. The girl was in silent torment and was afraid of anything and everyone at the moment.

Vylett really hadn't wanted to bring her along. In all honesty she didn't see how Iza could help. The poor girl didn't even appear to have the energy to use her magic at the moment and Vylett was afraid that Iza wouldn't survive.

Vylett had no idea what was going to happen in the next hour but the one thing that kept her going was knowing that her friends around her were strong and capable. But Iza....

"Where is everyone?" said Milo interrupting her thoughts.

The Drome seemed completely empty. There were no prisoners wandering around or Terramangs antagonising each other with their 'playtime' antics that usually involved branding each other for fun and destroying half the interior furnishings in the process.

"The Terramangs must all be outside trying to stop people killing each other," Vylett said tersely. "I thought people would have eventually come inside the Drome. The magic is so much calmer here."

She looked warily down the silent corridors. "I don't like the fact that we can't mingle in the crowds. If a Terramang comes down this corridor now we won't have a chance."

"But you must have some type of gift that could..." Milo started to say and then stopped speaking as she turned to him in frustration.

"Just how gifted do you think I am Milo? I'm not even sure what I'm capable of yet. I could have a hundred gifts but so long as Terramangs can kill me with just a point of their finger I will never be powerful enough to defeat them. Why can't you understand that?"

She realised she might have gone too far when an obvious awkward silence followed but Milo was beginning to get on her nerves with his assumptions that she was now invincible. She didn't like the pressure, and she didn't have to read his emotions to know that he was uncomfortable around her.

It hurt.

She could understand how she might seem all powerful and different now, but she was still her. If Milo was struggling to understand it, then he should think how she felt right now!

She was still coming to terms with having so many gifts. She was still finding out what she could do. She knew she could detect how much magic someone else had, she had sensed what she needed to do with the water charm.

And somehow she knew that she was capable of using her magic to heal.

She knew it in the same logical way she knew that two plus two made four or in the same genetic way she knew that she had two arms and two legs. She had sensed it the moment she had touched Milo's bruised arm when they had exited the Otherworld and she could sense it whenever she looked at Helico's swollen ankle, but she hadn't yet had the time to find out for definite.

In truth it scared her to know. Healing was the gift she was most excited about using but also which frightened her the most.

As if reading her thoughts, Helico turned to her now. "I don't want to slow you down. If you guys need to run, then run. I'll be ok."

"We're not going to leave you Helico," she said. "Besides...out of all of us you have the least chance of getting caught. You can just go invisible."

"I guess," said Helico. "But if the Terramangs catch us now Vylett, surely they would let you still perform the circle to save the Quarter. It's in their interest as well."

"Maybe," Vylett admitted. "But that's assuming they give me the chance to explain why I'm back here. I was supposed to be exiled remember." She sighed. "But even if they let me perform the circle, they'll probably kill the rest of you. You're not supposed to be here at all. You don't even live here."

There was another subdued silence as they wandered down the desolate corridors and then Iza made a little screeching noise that made everyone else jump. "What is that?!" she cowered against Eli as a small creature scuttled about in front of her.

"Its ok Iza, it's just an Hourdite," Milo told her as he made little kicking motions at the creature to send it on its way.

The Hourdite neatly avoided his foot and stared at him defiantly. Vylett clutched the water charm in her pocket more tightly.

"And just what exactly is an Hourdite?" Eli pushed Iza behind him protectively where she peeked at the creature warily over his shoulder, her eyes were wide with terror.

Considering Iza didn't know what they were, Vylett was surprised at her reaction. Hourdites actually looked quite cute. They were tiny white furry creatures with hugely bushy tails and heads that were slightly too big for their bodies. Their long eyelashes made them look endearing but in fact they were using them to eye up loot.

They were definitely not as cute as they looked.

They were nasty little thieves and if you didn't want your skin to be mauled to the bone it was best to give them what they wanted. But there was no way that Vylett was letting this little wretch have the water charm.

It's nose twitched with excitement as it sniffed around her.

"They're thieves," Vylett told a trembling Iza. "But they'll tear you to shreds trying to get what they want. Just kick it and it'll go away."

"Go away!" Iza screeched at it. But she didn't kick it. She backed further away from it, pressing herself against the wall. She was shaking with fear and looked a little crazy.

"Iza!" Abigail marched up to her and slapped her hard across the face. Iza blanched and stared at Abigail in shock.

"I'm sorry for doing that but you need to get it together," Abigail said harshly, looking a little flushed. "It's just a tiny creature. Are you telling me you can't defeat that? Come on Iza, you need to get your toughness back or else you're not going to stand a chance."

"She's right," Vylett told Iza but with more softness than Abigail. "Come on Iza send it away."

The others murmured similar encouragement and after a moment Iza wiped her eyes and let Eli pull her away from the wall.

She moved tentatively towards the Hourdite who turned its long eyelashes on her and moved swiftly towards her, surprisingly fast for such little legs.

Iza's eyes turned wide with fear. And then suddenly they turned hard. In a movement far faster than the Hourdite, she leapt neatly over it and gave it a hard kick.

It squealed and scurried quickly into the shadows.

Iza rubbed her hands together. "That felt good," she smiled, looking a little more like herself.

"Although you didn't have to slap me quite so hard Abigail." She frowned at Abigail, rubbing her cheek which had turned a little red and then her frown deepened as the Hourdite began to crawl back to her.

Iza got ready to give it another kick but she didn't have to. The creature's little feet suddenly lifted from the floor.

In surprise Iza turned to see Abigail grinning. "Stupid creature," Abigail laughed as she levitated the wide eyed Hourdite further and further down the corridor.

But her laugh stopped short as a hand emerged from the shadows, grabbed the Hourdite and threw it aside. There was a small clinking noise and the rest of the body belonging to the hand emerged from the shadows...

In the form of a Terramang.

The group froze. All thoughts of a stupid Hourdite forgotten.

"I believe this is the part we're supposed to chop its head off Helico?" Abigail gave Helico a pointed look.

Helico actually glanced around as if looking for a weapon and then gave up. "I don't know why I ever thought that was a good idea."

They stared at the Terramang who was staring back at them sizing them up. "We have two options," whispered Vylett. "We run or we fight."

They ran.

The Terramang followed them, hot on their trail. "Droges will be very happy you're back," it growled after them. Then in one swift movement, the Terramang whose name Vylett did not know, made a beeline for her and grabbed her by the throat. Roughly he began pulling her away from her friends.

"Come with me. All of you." The Terramang spoke gruffly into her ear whilst looking at the others.

Vylett felt cold chills down her spine. She drew on her magic to fight him off but she didn't know where to begin. A lot of the magic she was aware of so far wasn't very physical. That was Milo's thing.

"No!" she said defiantly. "I'm not going anywhere with you. I'm here to help restore the imbalance." She was surprised at the confidence and power that emanated from her voice but the Terramang narrowed its eyes at her in suspicion and squeezed her throat harder.

"Liar!" It tried to drag her away but her friends circled protectively around her, ready to fight.

"Move out of my way!" it demanded. Then it's mouth opened in surprise as it found itself being lifted up and away from Vylett.

Abigail

The corridor filled with a smell of burning. The smell of the Terramang's fury, as its feet dangled off the floor.

Abigail's pale face was red with the exertion but she didn't have enough energy to move him far. She had used too much magic already to move the Hourdite.

She gasped and the Terramang fell back to the floor, looking even more furious.

In one quick movement, it grabbed Vylett again and wrapped its strong arm around her neck.

"I'm sorry," Abigail looked mortified.

Vylett wanted to tell her that it was ok but the Terramang's finger at her neck silenced her.

"Try anything like that again and I'll cut her throat." It's boney finger at her neck was positioned like a knife and Vylett swallowed loudly, feeling the pressure of his finger beginning to choke her.

She frantically searched within herself trying to gage what powers she could use.

She could probably push it away easily enough but then it could just as easily kill them all.

The Terramang pressed its finger harder into her neck.

"Let her go. She can save the Water Quarter!" Milo demanded.

Vylett looked desperately at Milo, willing him to blast the Terramang away from her. She knew he could do it. But what happened next was a bit of a blur to her.

What she felt was an invisible force yanking her away from the Terramang and knew vaguely that it was an invisible Helico.

She wordlessly let him pull her away as Iza pounced on the stunned Terramang knocking him clean off his feet.

"Go on Iza!" Eli cried encouragingly.

The Terramang rose unsteadily to his feet and pointed its finger at Eli.

Vylett knew he intended to kill, rather than brand, and she held her breath. But Eli did something that shocked everyone except Milo. Because Vylett could feel that Milo already knew.

Eli branded the Terramang. He branded him in the exact way the Terramangs liked to brand stuff.

Vylett stifled a laugh as the Terramang staggered back in complete surprise making a horrible throaty noise.

"See how you like it," Eli spat at it.

"How dare you..." the Terramang began but Milo blasted him so hard, the rest of its words were cut off as it hit the wall with a sickening thud.

It's armour clanked loudly as it slumped to the wall.

"Quick lets go," Vylett said as the Terramang started to lift its head.

"Just a second," said Iza. She marched up to the Terramang and landed a hard kick in its face. The Terramang slumped forward unconscious.

"No one tries to kill my friends," she said angrily. Then she turned to the others with a smile of satisfaction. "Now we can go."

***

They felt exhilarated as they raced down the corridor. They passed no one as they ran down stairwells, further and further into the belly of the Drome.

Vylett could feel the magic of the other multi-gifted getting closer and closer, guiding her to them.

When Helico started to lag behind because of his ankle the others automatically slowed down for him.

"No," he said sharply. "Don't stop. There's no time. That Terramang will be waking up soon. And you know it won't take him long to follow our scent."

"Don't try and be heroic Helico, we're not leaving you." Abigail paused to catch her breath and turn her fierce determined gaze on him. "We're in this together."

"I'm not being heroic Abs, I'm being practical. Go on, I need a moment to rest and then I'll catch you up."

"But.."

Helico silenced Abigail's protests with a quick kiss on the lips and then disappeared.

Abigail knew as well as the rest of them that it was no good trying to persuade him to change his mind so reluctantly she began to run ahead with the rest of them.

She turned back once in the hope that Helico would reappear and when he didn't she put her fear and frustration into her running.

As Abigail speeded ahead of all them, Vylett knew instinctively that she could easily overtake her if she wanted to. She could feel it in her inherited magic and she had to deliberately restrain herself not to do so.

She was so busy focusing on this that she forgot to tell Abigail which way to go and they found themselves at a dead end. But Vylett recognised where they were.

"Droges's office is just a few corridors away," she said to Milo quietly.

"Then we need to be careful," was all he said.

"But the multi-gifted are also just a few corridors away," she said absently.

Then from somewhere close by they heard a man screaming. The man's scream turned into a frenzy of frantic shouts. "No! I'm telling you I don't have it!" the man's words echoed down the corridor and filled Vylett's heart with dread. Blood pounded in her ears.

"That's my father," she said, feeling as though her voice belonged to someone else. "He must be in Droges's office. Droges has got my father!"

She made to run towards Droges's corridor but Eli put a firm hand on her arm. "If Droges sees you, he'll kill you. If that's your father then we need to think this through for a moment and not do anything hasty."

"Droges doesn't worry me." Vylett felt something inside her harden and she blinked back the tears that were threatening to come. "I have to do something."

"And we will do something," said Milo. "But Eli's right, we can't just go barging in."

"But my father Milo..?" Vylett felt an uncharacteristic surge of anger and accidentally released a small amount of magic with her mind which caused several of the candelabras behind Abigail to smash and plunge them all in semi-darkness. Thankfully there were more candelabras lighting the way further up ahead.

Abigail winced and shouted, "damn it Vylett!"

"I'm sorry!"

Feeling mortified, Vylett put her head into her hands, feeling completely torn. The multi-gifted were waiting for her. But how could she leave her father?

Milo's determined gaze was unwavering as he forced her to look at him. "Ok here's what we're going to do Vylett. You are going to find the other multi-gifted and do whatever it is you need to do to save this place. And...." Milo stressed this last part as he saw her about to protest,

"and I will go and check out what's happening in Droges's office. If your father's in trouble I'll do what I can to help."

"But how?"

"I have a plan. Don't worry. Just go to the others Vylett."

"Ok" she said reluctantly. "You win Miloney Merren. Just be careful though."

Vylett quickly hugged each of them in turn and then they started to head back down the corridor.

They smelled the Terramang before they saw him. As soon as that horrid stench reached their nostrils they made a run for it. But they were too late. The Terramang turned into their corner before they'd had chance to escape.

They were trapped in a dead end.

It looked like the same Terramang they had just battled with because its face was bleeding where Iza had kicked it. It smiled a horrible smile and pointed its finger at them. "You are not getting away this time."

"Oh yes they are." Helico's familiar voice sounded around them and then the Terramang bizarrely lurched forwards, falling flat out on the ground before them. Helico reappeared and stared at the Terramang with disdain before addressing the others. "Come on let's go!"

Vylett led the way as she leapt over the sprawled Terramang and in the direction of corridors that led to Droges's office.

***

Milo's calm was quickly starting to dissolve.

The fallen Terramang who hadn't taken long to recover, was now definitely out to kill them. The stone walls around them crumbled away as the Terramang's brands and killing attempts rebounded off them.

When a brand hit the wall or the ceiling, orange sparks flew off them, but it was the damage that came without any sparks that worried Milo.

Those were the killing attempts.

Somehow though he managed to avoid both types. Judging by the colourful orange fireworks around them, the number of brands that the Terramang was hurling at them was phenomenal.

They did their best to dodge them by ducking and running from side to side and occasionally Eli sent a few of his own brands back at the Terramang. But from his cries of pain, Helico sounded like he was unable to avoid them all, most likely because he was the slowest and stubbornly refused to stay invisible.

Milo knew it was because he didn't want to appear to be a coward.

For Iza and Abigail, avoiding the brands was easy. They were both incredibly fast.

But apparently Vylett was faster. After another scream from her father sounded down the corridor, it was like someone had pressed a button inside her. Suddenly she was running at lightning speed towards the scream.

Milo cursed. "No Vylett! Go to the circle." At the speed she was going there was no chance he could ever catch her up.

He had no idea what they were going to do. Sooner or later one of those killing attempts was going to work.

He glanced back as he realised Iza and Abigail had fallen behind him. They had deliberately slowed down to wait for the Terramang. When it approached them, they pounced on it.

It worked for all of two seconds before the creature was up again and was now hard on Milo's heels, leaving the two girls desperately trying to catch them up.

Great! So this is what he had become, Milo thought bleakly. He was the filling of a sandwich between an immortal and a multi-gifted.

He made the mistake of glancing back to see how far the Terramang was. And tripped.

The Terramang looked exuberant as it closed in on him. Milo drew on his magic to blast it but the Terramang was quicker. It was prepared this time and disappeared in a cloud of mist.

When it reappeared it's ugly face was just two inches from Milo's.

Milo held his breath against the smell, trying to still his pounding heart. The Terramang placed its cold hands around Milo's neck and Milo thought the creature meant to strangle him but then he felt a searing pain on his flesh.

The creature was branding him.

He felt a wave of dizziness from the pain and wanted to throw up but suddenly the Terramang released him and the nausea subsided.

Milo barely had chance to think of what to do next when the Terramang pointed his finger at him in what Milo had now come to think of as the 'kill shot'.

Milo felt frozen in time as he willed his stupid magic to do something. But he had lost all concentration.

Then he recoiled as the Terramang's eyes began to roll eerily into the back of its head before it collapsed heavily onto the ground.

Shakily Milo stood up wondering what the hell had just happened.

"I think I've stunned it," said Vylett who was standing where the Terramang had been stood just moments before. "I think he'll be out of it for a while."

Milo looked at her in awe. "What did you do?"

Vylett looked a little embarrassed. "I'm not sure exactly. When I saw he was trying to kill you I just kind of grabbed onto the water charm and told it to protect you." She shrugged and nudged the unconscious Terramang. "At least I hope he'll be out of it for a while. He doesn't seem to want to give up this one."

By now, the others had caught them up and were looking from the Terramang to Vylett with obvious appreciation.

"Nice one Vylett," Helico looked suitably impressed.

Milo felt a flash of irritation. "She doesn't even know what she did," he mumbled.

Helico gave him an odd look and Milo quickly looked away. What the hell was wrong with him?

Abigail was looking at Vylett like she had never seen her before. "You are amazing."

Vylett looked flustered. "Like Milo said, I don't even know what I did Abigail. It's no big deal. And anyway it was the water charm really, not me."

"Yeah but still..." Abigail started to say but on catching Milo's eye, Vylett awkwardly brushed her off.

"Look I'd better go and find the circle. Milo can you really help my father?"

"Yes," he told her. He shivered then, whether from cold or shock he wasn't quite sure and wished he had an extra layer of clothing on.

No sooner had he thought this, he felt a warmth flood through every part of him, as though he had just drank a soothing warm drink by the fire in the middle of a freezing cold winter. His eyes widened as he caught Vylett smiling sort of shyly at him.

"Better?" she asked.

"Yes..er thanks," he said not able to meet her eyes. His inferiority complex had just hit an all time low. His one gift seemed completely menial now.

"I guess you can add that one to your list," he said and his words came out sounding more petulant than he intended them to.

And then Vylett hugged them all once more. When it was Milo's turn she whispered into his ear. "Don't hate me."

"Vylett I don't..." Milo started to stutter but Vylett was already heading back down the corridor. Without turning back she rounded the corner and disappeared from sight.

***

It took every ounce of Vylett's strength to pass Droges's corridor and not go down it. Instead she headed towards the direction in which she could feel the magic of the multi-gifted.

It didn't take very long to find them. A few twist and turns later, Vylett found herself in a large room which looked like it was used for storage purposes.

Except it had seven people stood anxiously waiting for her.

Honestly she was stunned. She hadn't expected there to be so many other multi-gifted.

"I'm sorry I'm late. There were a few...incidents.." she apologised lamely as she fumbled her way towards them through the assortment of old junk and heavily branded furniture that cluttered the room.

The furniture was so badly damaged by the Terramangs' magic that Vylett couldn't understand why the Terramangs didn't just destroy it completely. What was the point in keeping it?

But as she found a way to the centre of the room where the others were arranging themselves in a circle, she realised why. She could feel the Terramangs' magic emanating from the junk and knew that the creatures would never destroy something that held their own magic, even if it was something as menial as old furniture.

"Is this why you decided on this room.." she asked, gesturing at the hordes of stuff around her. "Because of its magic?"

"Yes," said a petite lady with kind eyes and short stylish hair that was even redder than Abigail's. "The Terramangs' magic is a primary magic and although it is not the same as the magic that runs through the Quarters, it is magic none-the-less and it will help to strengthen our own magic that we are going to be combining shortly."

"Combining?" Vylett swallowed nervously as the group smiled at her and began joining hands.

"Yes we must combine our magic into one for the re-balance to work," the lady's voice was soft and Vylett felt a little soothed in her presence. "Do you have the water charm?"

Vylett nodded and produced the diamond shaped charm from her pocket. She felt, rather than heard, a collective sigh around the group.

"Then if you'll please join us Vylett," The lady beckoned her forward.

Vylett stepped uncertainly towards a man wearing a strange silky garment who offered his hand out to her. The man smiled and it was a genuine smile. No one seemed annoyed that she had keeping them waiting for hours.

Maybe days.

Vylett smiled back but before she took the man's hand, she said. "What do I need to do?" She was suddenly more nervous that she'd ever felt in her life.

"We'll guide you," said the man and then silently, just for her mind only, he projected, 'believe in yourself. You can do this.'

She took a deep breath to try and centre herself. "Ok I'm ready."

The lady with the red hair seemed satisfied. "Good. Then place the charm in the middle of the circle and then join hands Vylett."

Vylett did as she was told, placing the charm, which was slippery with her sweat, in the middle of the circle and then taking a steady breath she clasped hands with the red haired lady and the man in silk and completed the circle.

Chapter 24
The Circle

"Ok so what's the plan?" said Helico as soon as Vylett had gone.

"What?" Milo was still distracted by Vylett's last words to him. Did she really think he hated her? What if something went wrong and he never got the chance to tell her that he really didn't.

He really really didn't.

"The plan to help Vylett's father?" Helico prompted. "You said you had a plan."

"Yeah you did say that," Abigail volunteered unhelpfully.

"Well I lied," Milo said flatly. "I just said that so Vylett would go and make the circle."

"So what do we do now?" Iza sounded a little hysterical. Her eyes were back to being jittery and she looked wired up to attack anyone who tried to mess with her.

Milo sighed. He felt tired. Really tired.

He could feel the Quarter's imbalance messing with his magic and he had to concentrate to keep it under control. His body was craving just a few hours of normality. And right now he really didn't want the responsibility of helping Vylett's father.

He looked at his friends feeling slightly annoyed that they seemed to be relying on him to fix the situation when he didn't have a clue what to do about it.

Eli broke into the silence and as usual took charge. "Well first things first. If Vylett's father is in Droges's office then we need to know what we're up against. We need to know exactly who is in that office and what they're doing to him. Then we can try and lure

Droges away somehow, race in and rescue Vylett's father." He made it sound so simple.

Milo gave him a grateful look.

"Is there a window in Droges's office Milo?"

"Actually there is," said Milo as he forced his brain to try and think on Eli's wavelength.

Another loud shout from Vylett's father brought Milo out of his slump. He needed to get it together for Vylett's sake. He was not going to think about the 'what if's'.

Vylett was multi-gifted. She would be fine.

"Here's what we'll do," he said, painfully aware that another Terramang could come charging down the corridor to kill them again at any moment.

"I'll go and see what's happening whilst you lot stay here and watch my back. Better still, go back to that dead end around the corner where Vylett blew the lights," he said as an afterthought. "You'll be less likely to be seen in the darkness and can attack the Terramangs if they come by."

"I think we were just lucky with that other one," said Abigail sounding unsure. "I don't know if we could defeat another one. Not without Vylett."

"Where's your confidence Abigail!" Iza rounded on her and Abigail took a step back warily.

Iza looked a little crazed. Her lips were curled back over her teeth. "Of course we can defeat them," Iza shouted loudly at her. "They won't be expecting us to fight them Abigail."

Abigail held up her hands in a show of defeat. "Ok ok Iza calm down."

"But she's right," said Helico. "I bet no human has ever fought back with a Terramang before. We've got the element of surprise on our side."

"Exactly," Milo said.

"But what if Droges attacks you?" Abigail looked at Milo. "We won't be there to help you."

"Droges won't see me. I'll just scout out what's going on and come straight back," Milo promised.

"Don't worry Milo. We'll get any of those stinking creatures that come this way," Iza snarled in a way that was ironically reminiscent of a Terramang. Then she sprang against the wall causing Milo to jump back out of her way.

"Er..great Iza. I believe you." And looking like she did right now, Milo wasn't lying. She looked manic. "Look after her," he mouthed silently to Eli.

Then after wishing him luck, his friends headed back to the dead end whilst Milo crept quickly to Droges's office.

When he neared it and heard several raised voices inside he started to have second thoughts but he plucked up his courage and crept into the office adjacent to Droges's, which luckily was unlocked.

This other office was very similar to Droges' office. There was still a large glass panelled window at the far end of the room which looked into the powerful still depths of the water, only today that powerful water was not still. It was frothy and turbulent and the intensity of its magic so strong that Milo was afraid the glass might crack.

Eyeing a small glass window to his left, he crept up to it. The bottom of the window just reached his forehead and he had to stand on tiptoes to see. Praying he wouldn't be seen, he snuck a peek.

Milo sucked in a breath as he surveyed the scene in Droges's office. He felt strangely detached, as though he were stood in the sidelines watching a stage production, a little like the ones his school put on once a year in the school's tiny auditorium.

Droges was pacing back and forth across his office shouting angrily at three people sat in chairs before him. All three people were tightly bound to their chairs with ropes. Milo ducked down beneath the window again, shock coursing through him.

He knew those three people.

One was Aubreus Roze, Vylett's father. This much he had already figured. But the other two...

One was Larrus Merren, his own father and the other one, looking as strong and dignified as ever, with her silver bun swaying slightly, was his beloved Aunt Dor.

What could Droges possibly want with them?

Was Droges punishing them for his and Vylett's escape on Orlost?

And more to the point, why where they back on the Water Quarter? When Oswald Crackenpepper had shown Milo images in Audrina's ballroom of the Quarter's destruction, his father and Aunt Dor had clearly been on the Fire Quarter.

Had Droges brought them back here just to torment them? With everything else that was going on right now, Milo thought that hardly seemed likely.

He peeked another look at them. Apart from a few cuts and small brands on their bodies, they otherwise appeared relatively unharmed.

Their voices were muffled and Milo pressed his ear as close to the window as he dared.

"I'm giving you three last chances," Droges was saying to Aubreus. "Three chances and then I'll kill you and then your daughter when I find her. And I will find her. So first chance. Where is it?"

"I've told you, it's all been destroyed," said Aubreus. "Larrus's basement was flooded yesterday, all his potions have been digested by the water." Aubreus's face was bright red and he kicked angrily against his chair, struggling uselessly with the restraints.

"And I've told you that Wylaffaton's already seen you and your two chums here in possession of the Dust in the Fire Quarter."

Dust? Droges was talking about the Infinity Dust?

Milo's mind was working overtime. Was the Dust finished? And if so, had his father defied Droges and told Aubreus Roze and his Aunt Dor about it?

Milo's heart began to pound. He had to get them out of there. He looked about the office wondering what he could use to distract Droges.

"So second chance," Droges said more loudly and Milo's attention was diverted back to the window. "Where is it Roze?" Droges took a threatening step towards Aubreus.

"He's already told you. We don't have any. Wylaffaton was mistaken. I have not yet completed the potion." Milo's father sounded weary and looked twenty years older.

"Liar!" Droges snarled at him and struck him hard across the face.

Milo flinched feeling his magic building up in anger. He could not imagine the pressure his father must have been under recently, what with Penelope's death and his own exile, not to mention that his lifetime's work had been destroyed by the water.

Milo felt a fresh wave of hatred for Alanya Roze for causing the imbalance.

"I don't believe I directed my question at you," Droges growled at Milo's father and then Milo's heart nearly stopped beating as Droges looked over to the window, right in his direction.

Milo quickly ducked his head down not hearing anything for a few seconds except for the blood pounding through his hears and then after re-gathering his confidence he risked a peek again.

Droges did not appear to have seen him and was stood in front of his father who's chin was raised in defiance. Aunt Dor had lost some of her composure and she looked close to tears as she pleaded with the C.L.

"Please don't harm him."

Droges laughed cruelly, raised his arm to hit her and then at the last minute turned his attention back to Aubreus. "Last chance Roze. Where's the Dust?"

Aubreus didn't answer.

The corners of Droges's mouth turned up into a sardonic smile. "Fine. If that's how you want to play it. Walt get over here!"

Walt! Milo's stomach did a double flip.

Walter Pymus? His arch enemy Walt? Had he just heard right?

Then he saw a movement from the corner of his eye which proved that unfortunately he had.

Milo's eyes widened in shock as Walt appeared to emerge from the huge glass panelled window and strut his pudgy self across the room towards Droges.

Milo's mind raced, not quite able to believe what he was seeing. Walt had unfolded from the glass as though he had been moulded from it. Had Walt possessed a gift all along or had it suddenly happened since the imbalance had started?

Really it didn't matter. What mattered was that Walt had somehow become Droges's new sidekick.

Was Walt the new Wylaffaton? It had suddenly occurred to Milo that Wylaffaton was no where to be seen which was unusual because he was rarely away from Droges's side.

Milo shook his head to clear it again. Walter Pymus? He felt as if the Water Quarter had just turned 360 degrees on its axis.

Milo clenched his fists as Walt stood dutifully by Droges's side and then raised his eyes ever so slowly in Milo's direction.

***

Everyone knew that Walt was a bully and everyone knew that Droges was a bully but since when had it become acceptable for humans and Terramangs to form such an alliance? But no sooner had Milo formed this thought, his own unlikely alliance with Lowish came to mind and he realised that it was possible.

He also realised with a sinking heart that an alliance between Walt and Droges could only be an alliance of the worst possible kind.

Although Milo was certain that Walt had seen him, Walt didn't admonish this fact and turned his attention back to Droges.

"Search the potion maker" Droges ordered Walt.

Peeking as much as he dared from his vantage point, Milo expected Walt to roughly manhandle his father but Milo was hit with a further nasty surprise when Walt's eyes appeared to glaze over and become strangely unfocused as they penetrated Milo's father.

"He has nothing except a used handkerchief in his pocket," reported Walt once his eyes had returned to their normal piggy self.

Milo fell back against the wall, tearing his eyes away from the window.

So not only could Walt camouflage himself as glass but he also had some weird internal vision? Uurrgh the thought that Walt might be able to see inside someone, possibly into their very soul made Milo feel cold and shaky.

Gritting his teeth he reached up to the window again. Just in time to see Walt step away from Aunt Dor and turn to Droges to tell him, "she's got nothing but a lipstick and some old sweets. Just old lady stuff."

Cheek!

"Now for Mr Roze. Let's see how truthful he was being," Droges smiled nastily and stood back to let his new second in command do his weird eye trick again.

After a few unnerving seconds, Walt's eyes re-focused and he turned to Droges with a satisfied smile. "It's in the left pocket."

Milo's heart beat faster. A look of such pleasure crossed Droges's face that Milo knew the rancid odour in that room must be at suffocating levels right now.

Droges silently held his palm out to Aubreus and silently Aubreus reached into his pocket and very reluctantly handed over a small clear bag filled with a pale gold substance that Milo recognised as Infinity Dust.

His heart sank as Droges greedily grabbed the bag. "So you were lying Mr Roze. Well there's a surprise. And I do believe you've had your three chances. Well I don't lie Mr Roze. I keep to my word. And I don't need this Dust to kill you and your daughter. I've got my own magic for that."

"No!" Aunt Dor cried out as Droges pointed his finger at a pale faced Aubreus.

"Kill me but not my daughter," Aubreus said holding his head high.

Milo felt utterly helpless.

Then there was huge shuddering motion beneath him that shook the entire room and sent him stumbling against the wall where he smacked his head hard against the window frame.

Momentarily stunned, he slouched against the shaking wall. The room was still shuddering but it had subsided to more of a gentle vibration. It took Milo a few moments to realise that the Drome was relocating itself

Milo's bruised head filled with images of giant legs beneath the Drome's structure sloshing their way through the water carrying the heavy burden of the Drome.

He shuddered, and it had nothing to do with the vibrating room.

His head automatically turned to the giant glass window at the end of the room but there were no giant legs to be seen. But it turned out that giant legs where the least of his problems right now. The room had stopped shaking and Droges was ranting and raving that he had heard someone close by and was yelling for Walt to go and check things out.

Milo heard Walt leave Droges's office but he didn't come into the room where Milo was. Relieved, Milo kept huddled down on the floor, trying to keep calm.

He must have been sat there about five minute, wondering what to do, when the door opened.

Two seconds later, Droges stood before him.

***

Before Milo had a chance to say or do anything Droges had grasped him hard by the wrist and was dragging him out of the door and into his office.

His father and Aunt Dor gave startled gasps when they saw him. Aunt Dor's eyes shone with tears. "Milo! What are you doing here?"

"He's been spying on us through the window," Walt grassed him up to Droges.

Droges looked sickeningly happy. "So Lowish abandoned you did he? Brought you back to me. Perhaps that idiot is not so stupid after all."

"Tie him to the desk," Droges ordered Walt but Milo rounded on Walt. There was no way Milo was going to let Walt bully him again.

Not this time.

Milo glared at the fat boy, warning him with his eyes not to even think about it but Walt only glared back challenging him.

Well if that's the way he wanted it.

"Get out Walt this doesn't concern you," Milo said in the laziest voice he could muster and then summoning on his already heightened magic, he blasted an unprepared Walt across the room.

Walt's eyes were wide as he flew several feet into the air and out the open door where he hit the stone wall in the corridor with such force that he fell to the ground in an unconscious heap.

Droges eyed Walt's slumped form with distaste and pushed Milo further into the room.

"Don't even try to use your magic on me or I'll kill your family."

"Don't you dare hurt my son," Larrus Merren rasped. "You've already killed my only daughter. Do not take my only son from me too."

Droges ignored him and pushed Milo towards his desk. As he did so Milo's hand brushed past Aubreus Roze and Milo felt Vylett's father push something soft and cool into his hand.

Milo knew by its powerful energy that it was Infinity Dust. Aubreus had obviously not handed all of it over to Droges.

Milo kept his eyes straight ahead and clenched his fingers tightly around the Dust.

Droges ordered him to lie on the table and then leaned over him so that Milo got a full whiff of his stench.

"Where's Vylett Roze?" asked Droges. "Is she in the Drome too?" The C.L glanced around as if Vylett might come marching through the door any second.

Milo met Aubreus's eyes for a split second and they were wide and afraid, silently willing him to stay silent.

Aubreus needn't have worried. Milo wasn't going to tell Droges where Vylett was.

He stared back at Droges unfazed. "No, she's not here" he said and then he turned his head away from his stinking breath.

Droges gripped his head and spun it around so that Milo was forced to look at his ugly face.

"I'll find her," he said and then Milo's body began to feel strange. He frantically tried to form some kind of spell with the Dust but he was not quite sure what he wanted it to do.

His head was starting to feel fuzzy and it was a horribly familiar fuzzy, like the one he had experienced on Orlost in the Activity Room when Droges had tried to steal his magic.

Only this time, the effect was more evident. Milo couldn't understand how Droges was doing it without the use of his machines until he saw Droges clutching the Infinity Dust that Aubreus had been forced to hand over to him.

Oh God! Droges was using the Dust to suck the magic...and the life.. out of him.

Milo's fingers went limp and he felt some of the Dust slip through his fingers. He was just lucid enough to manage to turn his hand palm down to hide the Dust before the entire room began to spin.

Aunt Dor's cries washed over him like a small breeze as he succumbed to Droges's wish and surrendered his soul.

He could feel the magic being syphoned out of his blood, feeling himself becoming shell, and then the strangest thing happened. His thoughts became clearer again and his senses came flooding back.

But he wasn't attached to his body anymore. He was floating very slowly up above it, looking down at himself, lying still and lifeless on Droges's desk.

He was dying.

Everything looked like it was happening in slow motion as Milo watched Droges lean over his body whilst Aunt Dor and his father shouted and cried and desperately tried to free themselves of their restraints.

Then it was as though someone had pressed the 'turbo' speed as Milo suddenly started to float insanely fast, into a white mist and towards a familiar shimmery veil with silver streaks in it.

***

The lady with the red hair, who Vylett had discovered was called Intha, was demanding the circles' full attention before they began combining their magic. Or rather she was demanding Vylett's full attention because she was newly multi-gifted and the others apparently already knew the stuff she was telling them.

Still clasping hands with Intha and the man in silk, Vylett tried to concentrate on what Intha was telling her.

"There is no doubt that the water charm will help speed up this process," Intha said, tearing her eyes away from Vylett's for just a second to look at the water charm in the middle of their circle. "The charm is a most remarkable source of balance and we are very fortunate to have it." She gave Vylett a grateful smile. "But what is unfortunate," she continued. "Is that it comes at a price."

She paused then and Vylett felt a wave of apprehension. A quick assessment of the emotions around her told her that she was the only one who felt this. Feeling young and inexperienced, Vylett pushed their emotions aside and turned her attention back to Intha who was regarding her with a serious expression.

"The charm will demand much of you Vylett and I need to know that you are up to this. We need to know that you are up to this."

Vylett felt horribly uncomfortable as all the members of the circle turned to stare at her.

"I'm listening," she told Intha.

"It's very simple really," said Intha. "You mustn't break the circle during the re-balancing. It is vital that no one breaks the circle," she stressed, looking around the group who were quick to reassure her.

"By placing the charm between our combined magic, it will aid the re-balance," Intha explained. "But if we break the circle as our magic is flowing between us then the charm's balance will be disrupted."

"And what would that mean?" asked Vylett.

Intha paused a moment and then said, "most likely the eight of us will die. Do you understand?"

Vylett nodded and this time when Intha addressed the group, her eyes lingered longer on Vylett. "This is complex and serious magic we are about to involve ourselves in. Do you understand?" she repeated.

"Yes," Vylett answered feeling slightly annoyed. She knew she was capable of this. "I won't break the circle," she told Intha, "I can do this."

"No matter what happens?" Intha persisted.

"No matter what happens," Vylett assured her, brushing off her inner anxieties. She knew what she had to do and she knew there was no way she would break the circle. She wished they had more faith in her. But the man in silk squeezed her hand and projected, 'I have faith in you' into her mind. She smiled at him gratefully.

Intha's face relaxed. "Good," she said. "Then let's begin." Her eyes sparkled with excitement and it was obvious she was looking forward to this.

Vylett knew she should be feeling honoured to be a part of this group of talented multi-gifted who were about to save all four Quarters but if she was being honest, she just wanted to hurry it up and get back to her father and to Milo.

"And I must stress that where ever possible we try to keep verbal communication to a minimum," said Intha. "Our circle must be peaceful. If you must communicate, do it by using your mind only."

Then Intha closed her eyes.

As the others followed suit and Vylett closed her own eyes, Intha's voice protected into her mind.

"We must release some of our magic and send it around the circle until our magic is combined and flowing freely between every member of our circle."

Vylett wanted to ask how she would know when it was safe to finally break the circle but Intha read her mind.

"When the re-balance is complete you'll feel it. Only then we may break the circle. But only then."

Ok ok she got it! She must not break the circle!

"Let's begin," said Intha in her ever soothing voice and then slowly Vylett felt a different kind of magic enter her body. First from Intha's side and then from the man in silk.

Right there and then she nearly broke the circle with the sheer shock of it. There was something horribly intrusive about having someone's magic forced into you. She felt out of control and she wanted to break apart from them.

Forcing herself to try and relax she tried to send them her magic too but she had no idea how to do this. She tried to physically push it with her mind and then Intha's voice projected into her mind.

"You're not relaxing Vylett, you're trying too hard. You must relax and you must do it now or else our magic can't get past you without breaking the circle. And like I said, if that happens then we all die."

No pressure then!

Vylett forced herself to try and relax, which was no easy task under the circumstances. Especially after seeing first hand on Orlost what happens when your magic leaves you.

She didn't want to become shell.

But deep down she knew this was different and that it was just a temporary abandonment of only some of her magic and she would still have magic flowing through her from the other multi-gifted. But it was still hard.

Vylett forced herself to think of happier times, of holidays with her father, of her love for animals and then her thoughts took a different track and wandered to Milo and of her time on Orlost, which bizarrely had become one of her happy thoughts.

And then, when she felt more relaxed, she willed her magic to leave her body.

She hadn't realised before now that it was even possible to transfer your magic into someone else and she could feel her magic's reluctance to leave her. Or perhaps it was her own.

She felt Intha telling her to speak to her magic and coax it like a small child. Somehow Vylett understood what Intha meant and after giving her magic silent permission to leave her, she felt if flow out of her body.

It was a strange feeling to have some of your magic disappear and be replaced with someone else's, only for that to disappear and be replaced by the next person's magic in the circle. But the magic started to pass through the circle so fast that soon it became too difficult to differentiate one person's magic from another, even her own.

Vylett began to relax as a feeling of calm and steady control started to flood though her, as the magic in the circle combined into one continuous flow.

Although her eyes were closed, Vylett knew that the water charm in the middle of the circle was glowing brightly. She could see its brightness through the darkened lids of her eyes. More importantly she could feel it working. The heightened feeling was disappearing and she could feel balance restoring itself.

In was an immensely powerful feeling and Vylett was just starting to enjoy the experience when the room seemed to jolt beneath their feet. She stumbled and automatically opened her eyes.

As did the others, all of them looking around the room wide eyed.

Vylett was relieved to see that she was still holding hands with Intha and silk man but she thought that this was mainly their doing and not hers, because her hands felt limp in their tight sweaty grasps. Indeed she thought that silk man might break her knuckle if he squeezed any harder.

"I'm ok," she projected and she felt his hold relax slightly. But as the ground continued to vibrate she was the one who held on a little tighter.

"It's just the Drome moving. It'll stop soon," Intha's voice reverberated in Vylett's head and she must have sent this message to all of them because everyone nodded in understanding, relief passing over their flushed faces.

"Still, I think it will be safer if we sit down," projected Intha. "Keep the magic flowing everyone and keep your eyes shut."

As Vylett slowly sat down onto the vibrating ground, careful not to break the circle, she could feel chinks in the smooth flow of magic that had been flowing through the circle.

Just before she closed her eyes she was disturbed to see that the water charm was vibrating in a way which definitely was not due to the vibrating ground. But she concentrated on closing her eyes and closing the chinks in the flow of magic.

Now the group were on the floor they were closer to the charm and Vylett felt its power like a comforting caress on her senses. The man in silk gave her hand an unexpected but reassuring squeeze and then she was lost in the exchange of magic once again, revelling in its power and control.

That is until the magic seemed to take a different course.

Its track changed suddenly and Vylett was suddenly aware of every single gift that she had.

And there were so many!

She wouldn't have thought it was possible had the magic not been reassuring her that it was.

She realised that the circle had nearly completed its process and the magic she was now feeling was the re-balancing of her own gifts.

She could feel in great detail, the intensity of all of her new gifts. Some more powerful than others, but surprisingly, out of all of her gifts, the one that was the most powerful of all, was that of her original one.

Her gift of reading emotions.

That was the one that came most natural to her. That was the one that determined who she really was. The other ones were just extra traits really.

She was finding it increasingly hard to relax as the circles' emotions began to flood into her. Excitement, nervousness, confidence...the list went on. But there was not one negative emotion among them. None except her own, which were now multiplying by the second because not only was she feeling the circles' emotions but now those further away were penetrating her.

She wavered in her control as she felt a glimmer of Abigail's determination somewhere close by. Then a sharper emotion invaded her which was undoubtedly from Iza and made Vylett's breath catch. Iza was clearly distressed.

"Don't break the circle!" Intha's soft voice sounded sharply in her head and Vylett tried to block her friends' emotions and concentrate.

Her eyes peeked open for just a second and she shut them quickly as she saw the water charm jumping up and down madly on the ground and glowing so brightly that Vylett could hardly look at it.

She clung tightly to silk man's hands and then felt her hands shake as she felt the strongest emotion of all invade her.

Milo's emotions.

Oh god! She was struggling to breathe. Milo was dying. She could feel it as clearly as she could feel Intha's firm pressure on her knuckle.

"Concentrate Vylett," Intha was shouting at her now and Vylett no longer knew whether verbally or silently.

"He's dying!" she shouted back and likewise her mind was so fogged up that she didn't know whether she had just spoken out loud. But she didn't care about the peace and calm in the circle right now. She only cared about Milo.

"You'll die too if you let go Vylett. Come on, you're stronger than this," Intha's voice was a scream in Vylett's head.

But Milo was dying. How could she keep going? She had to help him.

"I...can't....leave...him," she felt like she was being pulled apart in all directions and felt the fear from the members of her circle envelope her.

Silk man's voice was gentle but persistent. "You have Alanya's magic Vylett. You probably don't realise this, but besides Intha, you are the most powerful person in this circle. We can not do this without you. Don't let us down now. Vylett look at me."

Vylett opened her eyes to stare into silk man's concerned eyes.

"Vylett. If you break the circle you won't be able to help your friend because you'll be dead."

"But..."

"The re-balance is nearly complete," silk man said more urgently. "You must hold out for a little longer. Then you can help your friend."

But it will be too late by then, thought Vylett.

An insane thought was already crossing Vylett's mind. What if Intha had been wrong? How could the woman really know they would die if they broke the circle. Right now Milo was all that mattered to her and it was a risk she was willing to take in order to save him.

Then as Vylett felt Milo's soul separate from his body, without even thinking what she was doing, she broke free from silk man's hand.

She broke the circle.

***

"Why aren't you fighting Milesey?"

"Penelope?" Milo felt a lightness that boarded on euphoric as Penelope's face appeared in a misty form through the veil.

He reached out eagerly to touch the silvery streaks, wanting to join her, but Penelope's harsh voice made him hesitate and his body slowed before it touched the silver shimmers.

"No! don't you dare cross the veil Milesey. You have to fight it."

"But..."

"No buts..you're not thinking straight. I'm your annoying spiteful sister remember. Do you really want to spend the rest of eternity with me?"

"I don't think it's my choice anymore," he told her thinking of his lifeless body on Droges's table.

"As long as you stay on the other side of that veil you still have a choice. Don't you dare let Droges beat you. You have to go back Milesey. You can't chicken out of a bad situation now. I thought you had more guts than that."

"But.." Milo looked at her helplessly. His floating self was still trying to move into the veil and he didn't think he could stop it. Didn't know if he wanted to stop it.

"Do you really want our parents to be left completely childless," Penelope was saying. "And besides," she sighed. "That little friend of yours needs you. She's in trouble. Again." Penelope rolled her eyes.

"Vylett?" Milo's floating self twitched in agitation and he found himself wanting to pull away from the veil. "Is she dying too?"

"Not exactly...but trust me...she's going to need you."

Then Penelope's misty form glanced quickly behind her to something Milo couldn't see and when she turned back to him she looked agitated. Almost afraid. "I have to go now Milesey. It's...busy here at the moment."

"In the Otherworld?"

"No. I can't enter the Otherworld now. You're seeing me in the true World of the Dead right now. Just don't join me ok. Go back."

"Are you afraid of something Pen. I won't go back until I know you're ok."

"I'm dead Milesey. That means there's nothing to be afraid of anymore," her tone was typical sarcastic Penelope. "There's been a few changes happening here lately, that's all. Now go back."

As Penelope said this Milo had a flash of the scene taking place in Droges's office. For a second he saw his body again, lifeless on the table, only it wasn't completely lifeless. His fingers were moving ever so slightly, grasping onto something in his hand.

The Infinity Dust!

Milo desperately tried to think of the words that would make the Infinity Dust obey him but the words wouldn't come.

He felt a flicker of hope as he felt a loss of pull on his body as though Droges had given up. But he didn't return to his body, instead he began to float back up towards the veil.

Milo realised with a sinking feeling that Droges had won. He looked at the shimmering veil with the silver streaks. It was so enticing.

He reached out towards it.

Chapter 25

Do or Die

Vylett was having a horrible dream. As far as nightmares went this had to be one of her worst.

It had started out pleasant enough. She had finally spotted Milo.

She had been searching for him and now she had seen him.

She had broken into a run, barely able to contain her excitement. She waved to him, her heart lifting, signalling to him that she was coming to him, because somehow she felt it was important to tell him that she was coming. Then just like that, everything went horribly wrong.

What happened next seemed to happen in slow motion, as it always did in dreams.

Droges appeared out of nowhere. One minute, Milo was stood alone and the next Droges was standing between them, facing towards Milo.

Vylett could smell Droges's rancid odour even at this distance. She barely had time to think about what he was doing when she saw him raise his finger towards Milo as though he was raising a sword.

Droges was going to kill him and Vylett was filled with a fear so intense that she could hardly breathe. Her legs were still moving but they were surely someone else's because hers were not normally so heavy.

Her eyes made contact with Milo and that's when she knew she couldn't make it. His eyes were already saying goodbye.

"Nooo!" from somewhere within she found her voice, willing her stupid lead filled legs to move faster. Had to move faster. Why didn't she use her 'superpowers?'

"Don't harm him. Please don't harm him," she heard herself shout.

From somewhere behind her she thought she heard someone calling her name. The voice was familiar but it was muffled and sounded very far away.

And she couldn't stop now. She had to get to Milo.

Why couldn't she make her lungs work properly? Her breath was too short in her chest.

She had nearly reached him when time seemed to stand still. She was only vaguely aware of herself screaming as Droges brought his arm down in a great sweeping action and lunged that invisible sword right into Milo.

Vylett watched in dream like horror as Milo crumpled like a piece of paper and fell to the floor. The ground seemed to shudder beneath her tired feet as he lolled lifelessly onto his side.

That's when Vylett felt her world end and a new one begin and it did not include forgiveness.

Droges turned his cold dark eyes to Vylett and laughed. "Even Alanya's daughter couldn't save him."

He laughed again and his evil face blurred and swayed as Vylett felt everything began to spin.

Too fast, she was spinning too fast.

And then she couldn't see Milo's body anymore. He had blurred in with all the other moving objects.

And then just as she thought she couldn't bear it any longer she felt a sense of relief as she felt Milo's still form as she collapsed onto the ground beside him.

When she woke, it wasn't Milo's body next to her. It was silk man.

Vylett stared at him feeling sick, as events slowly came back to her.

She had broken the circle.

Then his body started shaking and Vylett let out a relieved breath.

He was alive.

And small movements from the other members of the circle told her that they were alive too.

Vylett let out a shaky breath. Then she remembered Milo.

"Milo," she murmured as she willed the room to stop spinning. She remembered it all now. She may have been dreaming after she broke the circle, but she knew the crux of it had been real.

Droges had killed Milo.

She slowly sat up and silk man put a hand on her arm. "Vylett?"

"I'm sorry.. I.. I wasn't strong enough." Memories of Milo's emotions flooded back to her as members of the circle slowly began to move to sitting positions. Their faces were pale and all of them were looking at her with something like sympathy, or was it disappointment?

Vylett's finger brushed against something cool and shiny and she saw the water charm lying beside her, which was now still and no longer glowing.

She could feel that despite breaking the circle the re-balance had worked. Her body felt back to normal and so did the atmosphere. No one seemed to have died so why was everyone looking at her so strangely.

"What is it?" she said, wanting to run from the room to find Milo but knowing that something was also very wrong here.

Silk man squeezed her shoulder. "She wouldn't blame you. She always knew."

"Who?" Vylett's throat felt dry and she refused to zone into silk man's emotions.

"Intha," said silk man and his gaze fell somewhere behind her.

As Vylett slowly turned around, wishing more than anything else in the world that she had a gift of stopping time so she wouldn't have to look at Intha, she noticed that the room looked like it had been hit by a hurricane.

The Terramangs' already battered furniture was in bits. Sharp wooden splinters scattered the room, lying precariously between the subdued circle members. And that's when she saw that not everyone in the circle was moving.

Intha wasn't moving.

Vylett spotted her stylish bright red hair poking out from behind a lady who was leaning over her, tearing off pieces of her own clothes to cover Intha's lifeless body like a shroud. When the lady had used the last piece to cover her face, Vylett found her voice.

"No.. she can't be dead. The rest of us aren't dead..."

"The rest of us didn't initiate the circle," silk man told her gently.

"What do you mean?" Vylett asked, wondering vaguely how she still had the ability to speak.

"Intha chose to initiate the circle because not only was she the most powerful one among us, but the most experienced," silk man explained. "It only made sense that she be the one to do it."

He paused and sighed. "But she lied to you when she said that all of us would die if you broke the circle. She knew that she would be the only one. But she thought that if you believed it was all of us then you would be less likely to break it."

"Well it didn't make any difference did it?" Vylett said flatly. "I still broke it." She found she couldn't stop looking at Intha's covered body.

"And I promised I wouldn't," she said, her voice cracking. "Intha put her trust in me and now she's dead." She moved closer to Intha, needing to see if she really was dead.

Silk man pulled her back. "Don't torture yourself." He spoke in his gentle manner and the other members of the circle closed in on her as though they were re-forming the circle.

A woman who Vylett thought might be from the Earth Quarter because of her creamy complexion began stroking her arm in a soothing rhythmic motion. "You are so inexperienced to all this Vylett and Intha knew you would most likely break the circle. And your genetic gift of emotions makes you particularly vulnerable. These things take time." The others nodded in strong agreement.

"Then why did she let me in the circle?" Vylett said feeling angry.

"Because like I said, aside from Intha, you are the most powerful among us," said silk man. "We needed you. And even though you broke the circle, it still worked. The re-balance is complete."

Vylett clutched her stomach, wondering how it could hurt so much when it felt so empty.

"I've killed her," she shook her head over and over in disbelief and felt short of breath as the circle moved closer to her, smothering her in their need to comfort her.

"Listen to me Vylett," silk man turned her head, forcing her to look at him. "We couldn't have done this without you. If you hadn't joined us then not only would she have died anyway, we all would have. You have just saved our World Vylett."

But Vylett just shook her head over and over again, the consequences of what she had done not able to sink in.

"I believe this is yours," silk man took her hand and placed the water charm in her palm. She clutched it tightly, hoping to find some relief from it.

The other members of the circle were still gawping at her with their concerned faces and she thought she might suffocate from their kindness which she did not deserve.

Unable to bear it she broke free from silk man's grasp and pushed her way out of the huddle.

"I have to find Milo," she said as she blindly stumbled through the debris.

"Vylett?" Something in silk man's tone made Vylett stop and turn to him as she reached the doorway.

"Your gift of emotions is who you are. That gift is a part of you, not Alanya, but you. You are a kind person. Never believe you did the wrong thing. You didn't. Ignoring your gift would have been wrong."

"But.."

"Some day you'll realise this and I hope you'll forgive yourself. Intha would want that."

Vylett nodded numbly. "Maybe," she said, and then she ran out of the door before any of them could say another word that might further shatter her already broken heart.

***

For now, Vylett couldn't even think about forgiving herself for Intha's death because right now she had to find Milo. Even though in her heart she knew he was dead. She had to see for herself.

She could no longer feel his emotions and she wasn't sure if that was because the magic on the Quarter was no longer heightened or because Milo was no longer alive.

As Vylett reached the bend that would take her to Droges's corridor she stopped short. Whatever she had expected to see after the re-balance it wasn't this.

During the time she had been part of the circle, utter chaos had resided in the Drome.

There were bodies strewn all over the place. Some people were wounded, some were attending to the wounded and some people were crying. Some with grief and some with joy at being reunited with loved ones.

Even some of the prisoners had returned and were wandering about the place with confused expressions.

Vylett spotted Abigail hunched over one of the wounded and caught a glimpse of Helico stood beside her. Then she saw Iza and Eli and Vylett felt a tug in her stomach that was becoming painfully familiar.

She couldn't stand what she was seeing.

She wanted to go to them...but she had to find Milo first.

Feeling completely wretched she ran by them and to Droges's corridor.

She stopped when she saw the slumped form of Walter Pymus in the distance outside the office door.

She swallowed loudly. Then gathering her courage she burst forward again, managing only a few steps before rough hands grabbed her from behind. She was pulled into the shadowy recess of the corridor and a hand clamped over her mouth.

"Be quiet," hissed the voice. Then the hands released her.

Vylett turned to see Lowish gazing down at her. "Now listen.." he growled.

***

As Milo reached towards the veil, he brought his hand back again. He wanted to enter that veil. So much. But he still felt a tug, pulling him back.

He could no longer see Penelope who seemed to have disappeared, and he reached for the veil again when a most welcome voice sounded in his head.

"Don't you dare leave me Miloney Merren."

Vylett's voice floated up to Milo like a wonderful caress and he wondered if he were dreaming.

With all the energy he could muster he looked downwards and then the scene in Droges's office came into view.

Lowish seemed to be there - which made no sense to Milo - and he was locked in some kind of struggle with Droges. This meant that Droges was no longer leaning over Milo's body.

Instead Vylett was. And Milo saw something glitter in her palm.

She was holding the Infinity Dust.

Milo observed in a dream like trance as Vylett grasped hold of his hand.

He flinched in surprise as his spirit self felt the cool grains of the Dust sandwich itself between their palms. He felt a jolt of magic enter his fingers and suddenly he knew what he needed to say.

'Take me back to my body.'

It was all the precision the Dust needed. Two disorientating seconds later Milo opened his eyes to see Vylett staring down at him.

"Welcome back," she smiled.

He sat up quickly and then wished he hadn't when the room spun in a way that made him feel sick. He lay back down again and when it came back into focus, Vylett was still smiling down at him like a wonderful vision.

For a second Milo thought that he might be dreaming, or worse, hallucinating, but Vylett's warm, slightly sweaty palms on his pounding forehead told him that she was one hundred percent real.

But he sobered as he looked into those huge blue eyes and saw the tortured expression there. He felt a knot in his stomach that came with the realisation that although Vylett had saved him, it must have come at a price.

Then Milo's attention was diverted back to Droges and Lowish, who were still locked in some kind of horrific struggle.

The smell from them was overwhelming.

"Quick!" said Vylett leaving his side to go and untie the prisoners. Milo quickly hurried to help her.

Whilst untying their ropes, Milo glanced at the warring Terramangs.

Surprisingly Lowish seemed to be winning the fight. He had the C.L's arms pinned behind his back so that Droges couldn't fire any brands or kill shots.

But then Droges caught sight of Milo. Alive and well. And his face contorted in fury.

Milo worked faster at untying Aunt Dor's ropes.

He had just finished when Droges ripped free of Lowish's grip and charged for him.

Milo had no time to think of a strategy. He could only watch numbly as Droges raised his finger to him.

Droges was too mad to even siphon his magic. Now he just wanted to kill him.

But at the last second, Droges changed his mind. He dropped his finger.

Milo let out a breath and said. "Good. Let's talk about this."

Droges ignored him and slowly, in what seemed like slow-motion, he re-directed his 'kill shot' to Vylett with a sideways sardonic smile at Milo.

Milo wasn't sure if Vylett still had the water charm on her but he knew by the startled look on her face that she wasn't prepared enough to use it properly.

Abigail's words flitted back to him. "Would you die for her?"

He hadn't hesitated then and he didn't now.

"No!" Milo heard himself cry and without a second thought he leapt in front of Vylett. He felt something hard hit him in the chest and he felt a little short of breath.

But that was all.

The pain disappeared and his eyes widened. He was still alive.

There was no veil to the Otherworld floating in front of him. No Penelope shouting at him to go back. Just Droges and everyone else in Droges's office staring at him.

Every single person in the room was looking at him in stunned silence.

It took Droges a full five seconds to recover from his shock. "Impossible." His voice was almost a whisper but his armour began to rattle gently, exposing his rage.

Droges aimed his finger again at Milo and again Milo felt as though someone had thumped him in the chest. But that was all.

"Impossible!" Droges roared this time and the smell in the room was unbearable.

Milo swallowed nervously, not understanding why he was still alive. Lowish was looking at him curiously, but from his peripheral vision, Milo could see Aunt Dor. And she had just a hint of a smile on her face.

She knew something.

"Let's see if you are both immune," Droges recovered his composure and knocked Milo roughly out of the way. He pointed his finger at Vylett again and Milo saw Aunt Dor's smile disappear.

Vylett however seemed composed. "The Dust Milo," she said quietly and flicked her eyes to his hands.

"What?" said Droges distracted.

But Milo had understood and was already pressing together the cool grains of Infinity Dust that still lingered on his fingers.

"Destroy the Terramang!" he shouted and pointed in Droges's direction.

Droges and Lowish both recoiled and fell backwards.

Milo glanced at Vylett and then rushed over to the Terramangs. They were both completely still.

Milo remembered what Helico had said about cutting off the heads of immortals to destroy them and so was relieved to see that both Droges and Lowish still had their heads intact.

But he hadn't wanted to destroy Lowish. Why was Lowish not moving?

"Lowish?" Milo swallowed nervously as he leaned over his too still body. There was no smell coming from his nostrils and Milo felt sick at its tell tale absence.

"I didn't ask it to destroy Lowish," he said, not looking at any of the others. His voice didn't sound like his own. "I only meant for Droges..."

He felt a gentle hand on his shoulder and looked up to see his father's reassuring face.

"Unfortunately the potion has to have very precise instructions," he explained. "You only stated for a Terramang to be destroyed. The potion did not know you specifically meant Droges."

"But I was thinking Droges," Milo began. "I meant Droges. Surely it.."

His father cut him off with a sad smile. "That doesn't matter Milo. The potion wouldn't know that. It's one of the flaws of the potion I could never manage to correct. It's one of the reasons it is so dangerous."

Then his father gave him a curious look. "I get the feeling you knew exactly what that potion was Milo. How did you know? And how did you know what to do with it? Did you guess?"

"No. Sort of. Long story. I can't believe this," Milo began pacing back and forth. "Does that mean I have just destroyed all of the Terramangs?" he asked incredulously and his stomach flipped as he contemplated what he may have just done.

"Hopefully," Aubreus Roze said as he stared bitterly at the unmoving Terramangs. Then he nodded at Milo with something like respect. "Well done son."

Milo glanced at Vylett. "I can't have killed them all. Can I? I didn't want to kill them all," he protested.

Vylett stared back at him, her big blue eyes sympathetic and understanding as always.

"It wasn't your fault Milo," Aunt Dor put her gentle arms around him and turned him around to face her. "The Quarters will be a better place without them now."

"But you don't understand Aunt Dor. They weren't all bad." Milo looked at Lowish again, guilt and sadness washing over him.

Vylett was the only person in the room who understood how he felt and not just because she could read his emotions. Lowish had proven to them that not all Terramangs were evil. Most of them were undoubtedly just under Droges and Wylaffaton's evil influence.

He truly believed that under different leadership they could change.

"Come on," said Vylett coaxing him away from the bodies. "Don't blame yourself. Lowish knew what was at stake coming back here."

"Why was he here anyway?" Milo felt anger begin to override his grief. "He said he wasn't coming back."

Vylett shrugged looking drained. "I guess he cared more than we thought." She turned away from Lowish's lifeless form and went to wrap her arms around her father who hugged her back tightly.

"I stopped the imbalance," she told him quietly. "I have mother's gifts. That means.."

"It's ok," Aubreus pressed his face against Vylett's. "It's ok," he soothed.

"Maybe the Dust can bring Lowish back?" Milo said distractedly as he realised he still had some Infinity Dust on his fingers. He felt a small flicker of hope.

"No Milo," Mr Merren shook his head. "That's one thing the Dust can't do. It will do almost anything you ask of it if you do it in the right way, but it will not bring something back that has lost its life. I do not have the ability to invent a potion that has that type of power. Besides which,.." he added sombrely, "imagine if their bodies and not their souls returned? It would be like something from a horror story. You can not mess with death Milo."

"Well if you can't mess with death then how come I'm still alive?" Milo finally asked the question that was on everyone's lips. "Why couldn't Droges kill me? Am I some kind of freak?"

Aunt Dor gently rubbed the sore brand on his neck. "Now don't quote me on this because I've been wrong before, but I believe you've been touched by death somehow."

Milo exchanged a glance with Vylett. "Oswald Crackenpepper," he murmured, remembering how the strange man had touched him in the Otherworld. "Alanya said the exact same thing," he mumbled.

So Oswald really was death.

"Vyett, Oswald touched me. And he was the one in the mist that took your mother and Penelope. I think death really has touched me."

"And you knew that too didn't you?" he added.

"I'd forgotten," Vylett admitted. "I wonder if his touch has protected you somehow," Vylett looked thoughtful. Then her eyes widened. "I wonder if that means that nothing can kill you now."

"Vylett don't say that you're scaring me."

"But wouldn't that be a good thing?"

Milo thought of Penelope in the World of Dead, and how he had wanted to reach her through that veil so much when Droges was killing him. But somehow just couldn't quite make it.

Now he was beginning to think that it wasn't just Vylett who helped to bring him back. What if he just wasn't capable of dying?

Milo thought again of Penelope. If he never died he would never see her again. "No," he said, in answer to Vylett's question. "I don't think it would."

"Milo, don't worry about that now. Just be glad that you are safe and that Droges is gone," Aunt Dor tried to wave away his worries in her usual reassuring way.

"And do not be worrying about those Terramangs either," Aubreus Roze added. "If you hadn't destroyed them, then we would have anyway," Aubreus Roze spoke casually, as though destroying Terramangs was something you did every day.

"What do you mean?" Milo narrowed his eyes at him.

"The three of us were on the Fire Quarter when Wylaffaton brought us back here," his own father explained. "I think Droges has had him spying on me ever since he asked me to make the potion. And I suppose Wylaffaton must have discovered I told your Aunt Dor and Aubreus about it."

Mr Merren's face was lined with worry and he looked tired as he ran a hand through his hair.

"I had to tell them," he said to Milo. "I didn't know what else to do. How could I hand over a potion that could do almost anything to the Terramangs? I might as well be giving everyone on the Water Quarter a death sentence. We had to think of something," he said, glancing at Aubreus and Aunt Dor.

"Anyway.." he continued. "The potion was finished and I'd been delaying telling Droges. But time was running out. Droges had given me a time limit. So the three of us went to the Fire Quarter to think of a plan."

"And your plan was to use the Dust to destroy all the Terramangs" Milo said flatly. It wasn't a question.

His father pulled him close to him. "It was either them or us Milo. Droges had already killed..." Mr Merren stopped speaking suddenly as though realising he had said something he shouldn't have. He quickly lowered his eyes but not before Milo saw the torment in them.

Mr Merren blinked several times and swallowed loudly.

"Its ok, I know about Penelope," Milo told him, feeling some of his anger ebb at seeing his father's grief.

To Milo's surprise, his father turned to him and chuckled. He ruffled his hair and then cleared his throat a few times.

"I get the feeling you have a lot to tell me," he said gruffly. "And I for one would love to know how you managed to get back here without Alanya. But I'm suspecting that Vylett here might have had something to do with it. Now she has Alanya's gifts."

Mr Merren looked over his shoulder at a blushing Vylett, who in return looked to Milo awkwardly.

Milo knew she was thinking the same as him. Actually it had been Lowish who had helped them to return. But for some reason, neither of them admonished this.

"This has been a hard time for all of us," Aubreus said. "But you're both safe and that's all that matters. There will be time for questions later."

Milo nodded and then said. "I need to see." No one needed to ask him what he meant. They knew he was talking about all the other Terramangs.

He needed to see if they were all destroyed.

As they filed out of Droges's office, Milo's numb brain silently processed that Walt had disappeared.

***

"How did you do that?" Milo asked Vylett as they wandered through the corridors of the Drome. "How did you bring me back? I was dying."

Vylett glanced away suddenly looking embarrassed.

"Ok you did something else amazing didn't you," he sighed. But he was smiling.

"Actually it sort of is amazing," Vylett's face lit up. "I think I can heal people. Well I know I can. Isn't that unbelievable?"

She was trying not to sound too excited but it didn't pull off. She was practically bursting with excitement.

"Unbelievable," Milo agreed, unable to reach the same level of enthusiasm. Every time Vylett mentioned a new gift, he felt further and further intimidated. "So you healed me?" he asked.

"Well no," Vylett admitted. "I tried to but you were too far gone. You were dying. But the magic I was trying to heal you with must have boosted you because then you did the rest yourself."

"How do you mean?"

"You used the Dust," Vylett told him and then she shrugged. "So really I didn't do that much."

"Whatever you say," Milo gave her a wry smile. But secretly he was still wondering what would have happened if he hadn't used the Dust. Would he have died? Or was he now suddenly immortal now that he had been 'touched by death'.

It seemed ludicrous. Trying to change the subject, he said. "So..what was the circle like? Obviously everything all went to plan."

Vylett glanced away. "Sort of," she said and then seemed to clam up.

Milo wondered whether it was because he had made her feel that way, by feeling jealous of her gifts.

"Vylett I..." and then he stopped speaking because right up ahead there were crowds of people crying and running about. They looked distraught but also some were laughing and hugging which seemed a bizarre contradiction.

Milo's first observation was that he could see no Terramangs and his heart fluttered. But then he didn't see any of them lying on the ground destroyed either.

He caught a glimpse of curly red hair peeking through the crowd and then a mop of dark blonde beside it.

Abigail and Helico.

He automatically began to head over to them but Vylett but a restraining arm on his.

"Before you go over there, there's something you should know," she said. "After I completed the circle, I passed Abigail and the others here in the corridor. But I didn't have time to stop. But I did see that.." she paused, her big blue eyes wide and strangely empty.

"That what?"

"That Eli's dead."

Chapter 26

The Memorial Dance

Milo easily spotted Eli's pale chiselled face among the masses of still bodies that scattered the corridor.

There was not a mark on him but his body was contorted at a funny angle and even though his eyes were closed there was a hint of a grimace on his face.

For a horrible moment Milo thought Iza was dead too as she lay limp next to her brother's lifeless body but then he noticed small convulsing motions that were intermittently wracking her petite frame as her grief consumed her.

Abigail enveloped Milo in a huge hug as he slowly went to them. Her pale face was stained with tears and she had a hard time talking. Most of her words were incoherent.

"Was it the Terramangs?" Milo looked past her to Helico. He knew that the emptiness he had seen in Vylett's eyes was now mirrored in his own. He couldn't bear to look at Eli.

Helico shook his head. "No mate. This whole building started moving and people came pouring in. God you should have seen them man, it was like they were all possessed. Then it all seemed to go crazy after that. And one of them..."

"It was him!" Abigail screeched suddenly and pointed her finger. Milo followed its direction and felt all his emotions return at once.

It was Walt.

Vylett instantly put a restraining arm on Milo's but he shook her off. "You! You killed Eli!"

Physical anger resided over the magic in Milo's body and he lunged towards his arch enemy in a fit of rage, hating him more than he ever knew was possible.

Walt was pale and didn't move as Milo went for him.

He pounded his fist into the pudgy boy's chest but Helico pulled him off. And it was only because he didn't want to use magic to overpower his friend, that he let Helico pull him away.

"Now's not the time mate," Helico's voice was calm but he was looking at Walt with an equal amount of hatred.

Walt was mumbling a stream of pathetic excuses, "I didn't mean to alright. I thought I could just see inside people... I didn't know I could harm people.."

"Liar!" Milo shouted. "You're a worthless waste of space. You're not even worth spitting on."

"I don't know about that," Abigail said and she spat at his feet. Walt just stared at her with loathing and then turned to leave.

"And if you're looking for Droges, don't bother. He's dead," Milo called to him.

At this, Walt turned back around, his mean eyes full of suspicion. "Dead? Terramangs can't die idiot."

"Oh sorry, yeah I am an idiot," Milo dramatically slapped a hand to his forehead. "What I meant to say was that he has been destroyed. Because immortals can be destroyed..obviously. Didn't you know that? Idiot?"

Walt clenched his fists but Helico took a threatening step towards him and Walt backed off. He shot Milo a sceptical look and then ran off.

"Coward," Vylett mumbled and then she kneeled down next to Iza. She put an arm around her but Iza flinched and moved herself into the foetal position where she slowly rocked back and forth, staring at nothing but Eli.

"I feel useless," Vylett said. "How will she get past this?"

No one answered because truthfully no one thought she could. Iza was even more broken now than she had been in the World of Illusion.

"She's grieving," Aubreus Roze appeared through the crowd and wandered over to Iza. He whispered a few words that no one else could hear and amazingly managed to gently coax her away from Eli's body.

"I believe there is a potion cupboard somewhere here in the Drome?" Aubreus asked Mr Merren who had appeared by his side.

Mr Merren nodded. "Yes. And I'm sure we could find something there that will help ease her pain for a while."

Iza didn't object as Aubreus lifted her gently into his arms and then he and Mr Merren quickly made their way to another part of the Drome.

After they had left, no one knew what to say as they looked at Eli's body just lying there still and lifeless before them. They just knew that his death had left a great big hole in all of their hearts.

"We'll give him a cremation," Milo said. "We'll give them all a cremation," he glanced at all the other lifeless bodies and was determined to give them all the send offs they deserved after this terrible injustice.

"Eli was one of the most decent people I've ever met," he said as he found an abandoned jacket on the floor and placed it over Eli.

Vylett gently touched his arm as he began looking for other pieces of clothing to cover the other dead with. "Maybe Penelope is looking after Eli right now," she said.

Milo nodded and wiped his face. Then he allowed himself a small smile as he thought of his sister's manipulative ways and the many boyfriends she had had.

"Poor Eli," he said wryly.

Vylett laughed and then she grew quiet as she looked at the bodies. "I can't believe my mother caused all this," she said quietly.

Milo squeezed her arm, not having anything to say that could make it better. She squeezed it back and together they surveyed the rest of the chaos around them.

It was going to take a while to clean up the mass destruction that had hit Syanna.

It did not take long for Milo's fear to be confirmed. After spotting body after body of motionless Terramangs that were sprawled around the Drome and outside of it, it was apparent that he had destroyed all of them.

It made him feel weak to think that he had eliminated a whole species of creature without even trying. And he felt only slightly better when his father told him that the Infinity Dust was going to be destroyed as soon as Syanna had been restored. No one else, besides himself and Vylett would ever know that it had been made in the first place.

The news that the Terramangs were destroyed spread faster than wildfire and soon rumours were circulating as to how it had happened.

Most people logically blamed the imbalance, reckoning that because the Terramangs had a different type of magic to humans, they just couldn't take it. Most people latched on to this and stuck with it, wanting to find a plausible explanation that they could accept.

Most people feared the unknown after all.

The news did help to lift the mood of the grieving however, some were joyous in fact and this did make Milo feel a little better.

Some time later when all the dead had been respectfully moved to a designated part of the Drome and the majority of the injured were being healed by the help of potions, Milo saw Vylett's new healing techniques first hand. Now that no Terramangs were hovering around, people no longer felt like they had to hide their gifts and Vylett's use of healing was an extremely useful one.

She moved around the injured, placing her hands on their wounds whilst onlookers watched in admiration as their wounds just disappeared.

Milo felt that tug of envy in his stomach rear up again like an ugly monster and forced himself to shove it away. What Vylett was doing was a fantastic thing.

When most people were feeling better and some order had been restored, Aubreus Roze made an announcement.

He had gathered as many people as he could in such a short space of time, to congregate outside the Drome where with the help of a potion, he magnified his voice so that every single person could hear him.

Milo was stood with Vylett, Abigail and Helico amongst the crowds, watching Aubreus make his speech as he stood on an elevated podium.

"The events that have taken place over the last few days have been terrible for all of the Quarters," Aubreus began. "Many loved ones have passed away, but be assured they will always stay with us in our hearts." There was a moment of respectful silence and then Aubreus cleared his throat and continued.

"But some good did come of the imbalance. In the end it destroyed the very creatures that caused it in the first place."

There was a united applause and Milo bit his lip. It had been decided that Aubreus would stick to the rumour that the imbalance had caused the Terramangs' elimination but also that it was best to let everyone still believe that the Terramangs had caused the imbalance too. Aubreus didn't think it would do any good to tell people that Alanya Roze had actually caused the imbalance.

Vylett was obviously in agreement with this. She didn't want people to know her mother had caused so much destruction, which was understandable. But even so, Milo thought it was wrong. All Terramangs hadn't been evil. Lowish had been proof of that.

Why should Alanya's reputation be kept untainted?

Vylett's head was lowered as if she knew that what Aubreus was doing was wrong but she raised her head when her father mentioned her name.

"It is thanks to my daughter Vylett and seven other multi-gifted that balance has been restored to the Quarters," Aubreus said. The crowd burst into applause, cheering and shouting Vylett's name.

Vylett blushed, looking like she wanted the ground to swallow her up.

"And now this brings me to a more delicate subject," Aubreus projected into the crowd. "The leadership of our Quarter." The applauses died to a subdued silence.

"The elders of our towns have decided that an election should be held to determine the next Council Leader," said Aubreus. "Votes will be cast during the course of the week. I myself will be putting myself forward for the position and anyone else who wishes to do so will be most welcome."

Milo exchanged a small knowing smile with Vylett. Aubreus Roze was one of the most influential people on the whole of the Water Quarter. There was no doubt he would make an excellent C.L.

Most people were going to vote for him.

Aubreus rambled on then for a while about voting systems and ballot boxes and Milo went into a daydream.

Just for a second he thought he smelt the whiff of a Terramang and instantly became alert, glancing hopefully through the crowds.

But there was nothing.

He laughed to himself silently. He never would have imagined that he would one day hope to smell that smell again.

"As for the Drome," Aubreus was saying. "I am not yet sure what it shall be used for. For now the elders have decided that it shall be used for the C.L headquarters like before, but also a place to pay our respects to our lost love ones." There was another loud applause.

"Then in time, depending how the Council sees fit, we may convert it to a school," Aubreus shouted above the noise. "And it shall be a school in which magic shall be taught and not hidden."

Aubreus laughed as the crowd went wild with excitement and flashes of multi-coloured lights shot up in the air as some of the gifted exulted in their new found freedom.

"And now I wish to conclude this announcement with another announcement."

The crowd quietened and Aubreus moved aside to let Aunt Dor join him on the podium.

She cleared her throat a little nervously. Stray strands of silver hair were still unravelled from her bun but she was as composed as ever.

"I believe that several days ago, Droges had agreed to hold an end of year dance for the school students," she said to the crowd. "And that dance was going to be held tonight."

This prompted a lot of incessant chatter amongst the school children, Milo and Vylett included. They had completely forgotten about the dance.

"Now, I don't know the exact reason for the dance. But my intuition tells me.." she paused and smiled, taking a moment to make sure that everyone knew she meant, 'gifted intuition'.

"My intuition tells me that Droges had begun to realise that the imbalance was bringing out peoples' gifts, especially when the person was in a highly emotional state. And so what better ploy than to put a whole lot of teenagers who are already hormonally challenged.."

This got a few laughs.

"..altogether in the same room and see what happens."

There were a few angry murmurs and lots of angry swear words being thrown around directed at the Terramangs. Aunt Dor shushed them and Aubreus waved his hands to silence them.

"But tonight we have decided to still hold that dance," Aubreus told them, making eye contact with the kids in the crowd. "Tonight will be a memorial dance in memory of those who have died today and in celebration of the restoration of the Quarters."

The crowds burst into the loudest applause yet.

Even Milo's spirits felt lifted.

***

There were only several hours to go until the memorial dance but already the main hall of the Drome was beginning to look like a memorial/festive area.

Whilst volunteers were busy setting up a corner that would be filled with candles that would be lit later in the evening and hanging streamers from the ceilings, Mr Merren took the opportunity to pull Milo, Vylett, Helico and Abigail aside and ordered them to get some much needed sleep before the dance.

None of them complained, they were exhausted. Milo honestly believed he could sleep for eternity. However he persuaded his father to wake them after two hours so they wouldn't miss the start of the memorial service.

Mr Merren gave them his word and then he found them a small unused room in the Drome where they could lay their heads for a while.

Milo's mother was with Iza, currently holed up in a room which had quickly become a place for the more serious cases of bereavement.

On discovering Milo's return, Mrs Merren had embraced him in a hug so hard she had nearly broken his ribs. Then she had taken Iza under her wing, understanding the girl's grief because her own grief was still so raw.

The last time Milo had checked, both she and Iza were lying side by side, heads slightly touching, locked in a potion induced sleep. Milo hoped their sleep was dreamless.

Camping down for the night in the Drome reminded Milo of staying the night at Sharrow's and he hoped the old cross-patcher was ok. The sounds of those other angry cross-patchers trying to enter Sharrow's World were still fresh in his mind. He made a big effort to push his fears aside. There was nothing he could do.

Just before they went to sleep, Helico asked Vylett to heal his ankle.

"Oh of course, sorry Helico I forgot." Vylett was very apologetic which Milo thought was unnecessary because she couldn't be expected to heal every single wounded person.

He ruffled his pillows feeling grumpy again as Vylett put her hands on Helico's ankle.

"Ah you're a genius Vylett," Helico's face lit up with obvious relief at being pain free and Milo's grumpiness melted a little. He really was being completely crappy.

As he settled down to sleep, Vylett leaned over to him and kissed his cheek. Milo looked at her in surprise but she just smiled and turned over to go to sleep, leaving Milo feeling flushed but feeling a little better and a little warmer inside.

As he pulled the thick soft blankets over him, not even the thought of Vylett's kiss or Helico's snores could rob him of sleep.

And thankfully his sleep was dreamless.

The next thing Milo knew, his father was gently shaking him awake and telling him the memorial service was about to begin.

It looked like nearly all of Syanna had turned up for the memorial as Milo stepped into line with the crowds of people queuing up to light a candle for those who had died. When it was his turn, he lit two.

One for Penelope and one for Eli. Then after a moment's hesitation he lit one for Lowish.

"I know Sharrow said that an immortal's soul can't travel to the Otherworld," he said silently as the flame burst forth. "But I hope you're at peace anyway." Then he was sure he imagined it but for just a second it looked like the flame burned a brighter orange.

He turned to Vylett who was stood behind him. "Do you think we should light one for all those on Orlost?" he asked her.

Orlost was something they had discussed very briefly since the imbalance had been fixed but was something neither of them wanted to think about at the moment.

They had no idea what would happen to the people on Orlost now that no Terramangs were around. Most were barely functional to wash themselves, never mind feed themselves.

Vylett nodded and they lit a candle for them and then Vylett tapped Milo on the arm.

"Look," she said smiling and pointing. "Look!"

Milo turned and felt a lump in his throat. Stood at the very end of the line of queuing people, holding hands and ready to light their candles, were his mother and Iza.

He smiled and moved aside to let Vylett light her candle.

She lit just one.

She didn't say anything but Milo knew that it was for Alanya.

***

The rest of the evening was actually quite pleasant. Even Iza managed to keep awake long enough to try and enjoy the festivities, in memory of her brother.

"Wow! Audrina would be proud of this place," Helico remarked as he took in the indulgent decor of the hall where no expense had been spared.

Milo had to admit the room was a little reminiscent of Audrina's ballroom, except the cake that stood between the candles was half the size that Audrina's had been and the ceiling was filled with silver streamers rather than silver balls. But the food was just as spectacular and the tables just as lavishly decorated.

There were even people walking round re-filling drinks and offering countless helpings of tiny chocolate truffles. Even the dozens of lit candles were flickering in time to the music.

They were small gestures, but enough to lift grieving hearts just a little bit for one night.

"I wonder how she's doing? Audrina I mean," Milo said absently as he popped a fifth truffle into his mouth.

"Ah Audrina, the lovely orange goddess," Helico sighed in mock admiration and Abigail punched him lightly in the ribs. "Ah Audrina the horrible ugly psycho," Helico amended with a rakish grin at Abigail who rolled her eyes at him.

In the hours that followed, the residents of Syanna indulged in the delicious spread of food and danced until their feet hurt. When the slow slushy songs began, Abigail and Helico got up to dance.

Milo smiled as Helico dragged a laughing Abigail onto the dance floor and expertly began waltzing her in time to the music. Every so often Abigail's feet would levitate slightly off the ground just to deliberately put Helico off his track. They both looked very happy, laughing and being silly with the silver streamers dangling down on them.

Aubreus Roze had agreed that Helico and Abigail could stay on the Water Quarter for as long as they wished, given that there was no Terramang anymore to teleport them home and he didn't want to risk using the Infinity Dust when it was so unreliable.

Neither of them seemed to mind. In fact they both looked extremely content.

Milo looked at Iza sleeping soundly in a corner surrounded by cushions and turned shyly to Vylett. "Do you want to dance?"

"I never thought you'd ask," she smiled.

Chapter 27

Revelations in the Woods

Milo had never really danced before and never with a girl so at first it was awkward. But he figured out you didn't really have to do any fancy footwork for a slow dance and as he and Vylett swayed gently to the music, he began to relax.

The floaty fabrics of girls' dresses made soft swishing noises and after a while, Vylett rested her head in the crook of Milo's shoulder.

"We're not exactly dressed for a party are we?" she said as she took in their dirty and torn clothes. They had not had chance to return to their houses yet and see what possessions had been salvaged.

Milo laughed. "What? I think we look great. We should dress like this always."

"Idiot!" she giggled and then she turned serious. She lifted her head to look at him. "Milo, I'm still me," she said and Milo was alarmed to see tears in her eyes.

He swallowed hard. "I know, I do know," he said feeling awkward. Their feet had stopped moving so they were just stood still looking all serious in the middle of the dance floor. "It's just weird that's all," he tried to explain and realised he was doing a rubbish job of it.

He pulled away from her slightly. "First I thought I knew you and then I didn't and..."

"And you still know me," Vylett persisted.

"I know," said Milo. And he did know. "It's just taking me a while to get used to."

"Ok," Vylett wiped her tears and seeming satisfied pulled him back towards her and nestled her head again in the crook of his shoulder.

"Well time is something we'll hopefully have a lot of," she said pulling him back into a dance. "You really do have the easiest emotions to read you know." Her voice was muffled in his shoulder and Milo was sure she was laughing.

He frowned, getting ready to say something back and then felt Vylett's body shake as she laughed silently into his shoulder. "See," she said.

Milo couldn't help but laugh back. Then he felt her stiffen. "What is it?"

"Walt's here," Vylett murmured without lifting her head from his shoulder.

Milo glanced around and spotted Walt and Peg on the dance floor.

He held onto Vylett more tightly, but more to stop his fists clenching than anything else.

So far Walt had very wisely been keeping his distance since word had gotten around that he had killed someone. Now it looked like Peg wanted him to keep his distance too. They were both exchanging angry words and after giving him a loathing look, Peg marched off leaving Walt to look pathetic and foolish on the middle of the dance floor.

"Looks like Peg didn't mind Walt when he was a bully," Vylett commented as she pulled them into a dance again. "But now he's a murderer she doesn't want to know him. I wonder what she'd think of me if she knew about Intha," she said quietly.

Vylett had finally told Milo all about breaking the circle and how Intha, the circle's leader, had died as a result.

"It wasn't your fault Vylett. I know it's terrible that she died, but you also saved the Quarters. And me," he added. "Which, by the way, I am very grateful for."

Vylett smiled, "I know and I will forgive myself. It's just going to take time."

They didn't say anything then for a few minutes, content to sway along to the music. Then feeling a little nervous, Milo said, "Vylett?"

"Yeah?" She looked up at him, her face curious. "What is it?"

"Do you have to ask. Can't you read my emotions?" he gave her a questioning look.

Vylett frowned. "I'm trying not to Milo. That would be an invasion of your privacy. But now you've mentioned it...." she pretended to concentrate. "Mmm, you've been lying about something right?"

"Right," Milo paused nearly changing his mind and then he thought what the hell. "You know when Sharrow showed us his true form and I said I saw Droges?"

Vylett nodded, telling him to continue.

"Well I did see Droges," he said. "I wasn't lying about that. But I also saw someone else."

"Oh?" Vylett raised her eyebrows and Milo glanced away feeling embarrassed. When he plucked up the courage to meet her eyes again he could tell that she already knew what he was going to say.

"I saw you."

She nodded slowly. And then he added "I saw you dead."

Vylett's jaw dropped slightly and Milo felt some satisfaction that she hadn't known that part.

"And that's what frightens me the most," he finished and let out a huge breath for finally admitting it.

Vylett didn't say anything and for an awful second Milo thought that he'd scared her off. Then silently she placed her arms around his neck.

At first Milo thought she meant to kiss him again, but then he felt a warm soothing sensation spread around his neck.

"I'm healing your brands, keep still," Vylett told him.

Milo felt both relief and disappointment. Then Vylett smiled and kissed him lightly on the lips. After a few moments she pulled away and Milo looked back at her surprised.

"Well you weren't going to do it," she smiled.

"I wanted to," he admitted.

"I know."

***

After dancing to two more tracks, Milo felt more content than he'd ever thought possible.

So he was disappointed when Vylett suddenly glanced towards a huge time dial that was hung on one of the walls and said, "we have to go outside, I need to show you something."

Milo followed her off the dance floor where she grabbed Helico and Abigail who were talking to some other kids.

They looked drunk with giddiness.

"Where are you taking us?" Abigail only half complained as they exited the Drome and into the darkness of the night. It was muggy and warm and lots of little black flies were swarming around them.

"We were just getting to know people. We were pretending we were from the Air Quarter," Abigail gushed. "Thought that would be more plausible than saying a Terramang actually brought us here."

Abigail continued to ramble on until Vylett shushed her.

"We have to be quiet," Vylett warned them as she led them across the drawbridge and down the road and into the woodland where Penelope had taken Milo all those days ago. The Drome had relocated itself back to its original position, for which they were all thankful for.

Once they were well into the woodland and out of sight of the Drome, Vylett ran ahead leading the way, obviously forgetting how fast she could run now.

Sometimes Milo thought he'd lost sight of her as she disappeared between the trees but then he would catch glimpses of her blonde hair flashing between the branches.

"Why are you bringing us into creepy woods Vylett?" Abigail rasped when they caught her up. "You do realise there's no party in here?"

"Shush," Vylett said and then they heard movement in the trees.

It was just a small rustling of leaves and a few twigs breaking and could easily have been an animal but the familiar clinking noise made them all stand stock still. Even Abigail stopped giggling. Milo's heart began to race with anticipation.

He hardly dared to hope.

There was a waft of rancid burning. And then there he was, creeping out of the trees, as silently as was possible whilst wearing a coat of armour.

It was Lowish.

Abigail did a bad job of suppressing a screeching noise and Helico had his hand clamped over his mouth in shock.

Milo just stood and stared, hardly able to believe it. "It's impossible," he whispered. "I destroyed you. I lit a candle for you," and then wondered why he felt the need to tell him that.

Lowish grunted and shook his head slightly like Milo was causing him a headache.

"I never meant to.." Milo added quickly and then tensed when Lowish rattled his way towards him, taking long strides.

But there was no tell tale fury coming from Lowish. The Terramang just held out his hand to him.

At first Milo thought Lowish meant for him to shake it, a truce for destroying him, and then he saw something glinting in the Terramang's palm.

The water charm.

"I gave it to him just before I came into Droges's office to try and save you," Vylett explained. "He was waiting outside the door. He came back to help us," she shot Lowish a grateful look.

Lowish shifted his feet and smoothed down his armour.

Sometimes it was hard to distinguish the emotion of a Terramang because their faces always looked aggressive, but Milo thought Lowish may have been embarrassed. Milo had definitely come to realise at least that when Lowish shifted from one foot to another, this was a sign that he was uncomfortable.

"Our plan was for Lowish to get Droges away from you whilst I tried to save you with my magic," Vylett continued to explain. "It wasn't much of a plan," she admitted. "But we didn't have much time. Lowish was then going to try and teleport Droges to Sharrow's place and try and trap him there but then you took us all by surprise and destroyed the Terramangs."

Milo looked from Vylett to Lowish aghast. They had had this all planned?

"So how did the water charm come into all of this?" Abigail stepped closer to Lowish, hands on hips. Then much to Lowish's surprise and irritation she gave his armour a quick prod.

"Just checking you are definitely real," she told him and then quickly took a step back before she riled him further.

Vylett took the charm back from Lowish and put it safely back in her pocket. "I gave Lowish the water charm in case Droges tried to destroy him," she said. "I hoped it would protect him." She smiled at Lowish. "Luckily I was right."

Milo shook his head in disbelief. "This is crazy."

He still could not believe that Lowish was stood right in front of him.

"Well why didn't you tell me he was still alive?" he said to Vylett. "You know how horrible I felt after I thought Lowish was destroyed. I can't believe you didn't tell me this."

Milo gave her an accusing look, feeling hurt and betrayed.

"Don't start getting angry Milo," Vylett berated him. "For one thing I didn't know for certain the charm had definitely saved him. I didn't know until he came through those trees just now."

She sat down on a wooden stump looking tired. "The two of us agreed that if all of us managed to get out of Droges's office alive then we would meet here at this time and this place. Where no one would see him. He had to keep hidden remember, because at that point Wylaffaton was looking for him."

She sighed. "I was going to tell you Milo, but when I realised that you had destroyed every single Terramang I thought it was best to keep quiet."

"Why," said Milo. "What did it matter?"

"Well you saw how the adults reacted when they realised all the Terramangs had been destroyed," said Vylett. "If they'd discovered Lowish was still here...well I didn't know what would happen. He wouldn't be welcome here."

Vylett looked apologetically at Milo. "I thought that if you knew there might be a chance Lowish was alive then the adults might have picked up on it. Who knows what kinds of gifts people have now since the imbalance. I didn't want to take the risk. I'm sorry."

Milo nodded in agreement, still trying to get his head around things. "No, it's ok. I understand all that I think. But..." he stared at Lowish.. "We put your body with all the other Terramangs," he told him. "You were definitely destroyed."

Lowish made a huffing noise and the woods filled with the familiar rancid stench. "Well obviously I wasn't Miloney." He shifted his feet uncomfortably and raised his eyes upwards as though trying to remember.

"One minute I was in Droges's office and the next I woke up buried beneath lots of other Terramangs." Lowish's face was screwed up in disgust.

"I'm sorry about...well the rest of them," Milo tried to apologise but Lowish brushed him off.

"Droges is gone. That's all I care about."

Vylett jumped from the stump and linked her arm through Lowish's, much to everyone's amusement. "The charm protected you until you were safe." she said to him happily.

Lowish scowled and unhooked her arm from his. Then clearing his throat he said something that shocked all of them. "They're not all destroyed," he said.

"What?" Milo exchanged worried glances with the others.

"Wylaffaton is still alive." said Lowish.

Milo's legs felt unsteady as he whipped his head from side to side, looking fearfully around the woods.

"Not here," Lowish told him. "Wylaffaton is in the World of Illusion."

Helico groaned and ran a hand through his messy blonde hair. "Great," he mumbled and kicked at the wooden stump so that shards of bark broke off.

Water immediately began to bubble up from the ground to digest them and Helico jumped back in surprise.

Milo would have laughed had he not been so deep in thought about Wylaffaton. "Why him?" he said to Lowish. "Why did he survive and not the others? That doesn't make sense."

Lowish shrugged like he didn't care to try and analyse such things but Vylett's mind was ticking away, already figuring out the logic.

"It must have been the inaccuracy of the potion," she said slowly. "Milo, you told the potion to destroy the Terramang but you didn't say where. Maybe it just destroyed those on the Quarter you were in."

"Maybe," Milo muttered. But he wasn't really bothered why Wylaffaton had not been destroyed. He was just bothered by the fact that he hadn't been.

"So why is the great Wylaffaton in the World of Illusion?" Helico asked Lowish. He put his foot out to kick more bark off the stump and then thought better of it.

"Because that's where he thinks you lot are," Lowish grunted. "It didn't take him long to figure out your trail. Wylaffaton is still hunting me for betraying Droges but at the minute you lot are number one on his list."

"Well that's just great," said Abigail, hands back on hips. "So what now?"

"Hang on a minute," said Milo. "What does Sharrow think of Wylaffaton being in his place? He can't like it?" Milo said to Lowish.

Lowish grunted. "Sharrow is using those tricks he likes to do to keep him there. But it won't last long," he said. "Sharrow's got his own problems right now and sooner or later Wylaffaton will realise Droges is destroyed and then he'll do anything he can to make you pay."

Abigail looked agitated. "What do we do now? Hide again? I'm sick of running."

Helico put an arm around her but Lowish gripped her elbow taking her by surprise. "Yes you hide," he growled, putting his face so close to hers and looking so angry that even Milo and the others could smell his breath. But it was the intenseness of his gaze and not his smell that made Abigail lean back from him.

"You hide, unless you want to die." Lowish growled. He released a shocked looking Abigail and began to pace back and forth and then stopped when his armour began to clink loudly.

"Me and Sharrow will try to destroy Wylaffaton," Lowish told them slowly and then he looked seriously at each of them in turn. "No we won't try. We will destroy him." Lowish's black eyes were fierce with determination and Milo thought that every one of them was looking back at the Terramang with a new found respect.

"But in the meantime I suggest you all go to one of the other Quarters for a while. Lie low. Take a holiday or whatever."

Automatically images of the Fire Quarter rolled around Milo's head.

Well that didn't seem such a bad idea.

"And what will you do Lowish? Will you go straight to Wylaffaton?" Vylett asked.

The Terramang shifted his feet again. "I have two jobs to do first," he said gruffly.

Milo exchanged confused glances with the others. "What jobs?" he asked him.

"Well first of all I'm going back to Orlost. I can't do much about those who have lost their magic. I can't return it to them, but for those who haven't I can return them to their homes."

"Lowish that's wonderful," said Vylett, "I really think.."

"Then I am going to go and help Sharrow," Lowish rapidly continued. "There is now a full scale war going on between the cross-patchers. The portals are being exposed and if it's not sorted out soon then there will be no order any more, people will be able to come and go through portals as they wish."

Milo felt a fresh wave of fear for Sharrow. "Let us help" he said to Lowish. "Let us help you and Sharrow."

"No Miloney. It's not a fight for humans. Concentrate on lying low for a while. Sharrow has enough help."

Then Lowish put a hand on Milo's shoulder and bent his head close to his. "But just remember that Sharrow can't always be keeping a hold of Wylaffaton. Sooner or later Wylaffaton will figure out that you've come back here. And he might figure it out before I've had a chance to destroy him. So keep hidden."

"I just want to help Sharrow," Milo protested.

Lowish branded the ground next to Milo's feet in frustration, and making everyone jump in the process. "Do you want to be killed?" Lowish growled at him.

"But.." Milo almost got ready to say that actually he seemed to be immune to death now but after a quick glance at Vylett he kept his mouth shut. Abigail and Helico didn't even know about that yet.

"Miloney, I'm not going to take you to Sharrow's so don't keep asking me." Lowish raised his voice and then after a quick cautionary glance around him lowered it to a whisper. "I'm not going to change my mind."

"Ok ok but stop calling me Miloney Lowish. Only my mother calls me that when I've done something wrong. Just call me Milo."

Lowish gave him an odd look and then shrugged. "Ok. But I can't make any promises. Some things are hard to change." He made a grunting noise and Milo got a face full of rancid smelling stench.

Milo blinked and discreetly turned his head away. "Fair enough."

"I want to come with you to Orlost," Vylett said to Lowish suddenly.

Milo turned to her. "Are you serious?"

"Yes. I want to help those who have lost their magic. When I was forming the circle with the multi-gifted, I learnt how to transfer some of my magic into someone. If I could do that to the vacants on Orlost then maybe they can be helped." She gave a little shrug. "Maybe they can lead a normal life again."

She stroked Milo's arm. "I've thought about this Milo."

"For all of two seconds," he said sullenly.

Vylett sighed, her blue eyes begging him to understand. She turned to Lowish. "Please let me try," she pleaded.

To Milo's surprise Lowish reluctantly agreed and then Milo felt he could hardly talk her out of it. Once again Vylett was doing something amazing and as much as it made his heart hurt to be separated from her, he knew he had to let her get on with it.

"You lot go into hiding and I'll meet you all as soon as I'm done," Vylett promised them all.

"But what about your parents?" Helico pointed out. "Are we really just going to up and run without telling them? They've just got you back."

Milo hated how Helico made it sound like they were being selfish but what choice did they have. Lowish was right. Wylaffaton was going to find out about Droges sooner or later and then he would come to the Water Quarter.

They had to leave. Or maybe Milo wanted to go the Fire Quarter so badly that he didn't want to stay.

Maybe too much had happened.

"We won't be gone long," he said. "We'll just lay low for a while until Lowish and Sharrow get rid of Wylaffaton. We'll leave our parents a note or something telling them not to worry." It sounded lame, even to him but right now they had no choice.

"Then let's go," Lowish said gruffly to Vylett. "We have to do this quickly, Sharrow needs me."

Milo was still amazed at Lowish's loyalty to Sharrow. It was a strange alliance but one that he was very thankful for.

"Now?" A brief look of panic flashed across Vylett's face as she glanced at Milo and then she straightened and said. "Ok. But first you need to take Iza home. Eli's dead and she needs to be with her family."

Lowish sighed and grunted. "Nothing but a transport service. Fine. Then bring her now."

Twenty minutes later, Helico had returned with a fragile looking Iza where Lowish was still waiting in the woods, ready to take her home. She had some colour back in her cheeks and the dark circles under her eyes were less prominent but she was a long way from being herself again.

She smiled as she approached them but it did not hide the pain in her eyes. "Stay safe," she said giving each one of them a heartfelt hug.

Milo promised her that one day he would persuade Lowish to let them visit her. He wasn't sure if this would ever happen but it felt like the right thing to say.

When Iza hugged him goodbye she said, "we've both lost siblings Milo, but at least they're together now and in a better place."

Milo nodded, feeling a lump in his throat. Something nagged at his brain. A memory. But he pushed it away.

"Iza," he said suddenly feeling awkward. "I know Eli felt embarrassed about his gift and I never got chance to tell him that it was ok...." he trailed off.

"He knew," Iza smiled at him and then she took hold of Lowish's arm. Lowish held his other arm out to Vylett.

Looking teary eyed, Vylett gave Helico and Abigail a quick hug. Both of them seemed reluctant to let her go. The four of them had become so close in such a short space of time.

Vylett turned a little awkwardly to Milo. "I wish I'd had time to pack a bag," she laughed. "Pack some stuff for me. No need to ask where you'll be," she smiled knowingly. "I'll ask Lowish to take me to the Fire Quarter as soon as I'm done on Orlost."

Milo nodded, his throat felt tight and he didn't trust himself to speak.

"And when you leave a note to your parents, please leave one for my father too." she said.

"Of course," he promised her.

Lowish hurried them along and Vylett gave Milo a quick kiss on the cheek. "I'll see you soon," she said. Then she grabbed hold of Lowish's arm.

"Vylett..." Milo wanted to say something, something heartfelt but no words would come.

Vylett met his eyes. "I know," she smiled.

And then they disappeared in a swirl of white mist.

Epilogue

Milo slung his backpack over his shoulder and took one last look around his bedroom.

It was damp with the water that had seeped in from the imbalance and was beginning to smell but it would be restored. That is, if his mother wasn't too mad to make it nice again.

He put the letter down on top of the bed. It said,

"I have to go away for a while. There are some things I need to do. It's too difficult to explain but I will be back as soon as I can."

Milo hadn't known what else to put. That was the truth.

Then he had quickly scribbled at the end. "Please understand."

His mother would find it soon enough. His room would be the first place she would look when she realised he was missing. Milo had to force himself to push away the guilt in the pit of his stomach.

As he headed back down the hall he passed Penelope's room.

It was still open.

He peeked inside and saw that it looked like it always did. Messy and girly. It was strange to think she would never be in it again. Once again, Milo realised he was glad to be leaving the Water Quarter for a while. At the minute the memories were too hard.

Oh Penelope what's going on at your end?

Milo had finally remembered what had been nagging him when he had been speaking to Iza before Lowish took her home. It was a memory from when he had been floating towards the veil of the Otherworld - when he had nearly died in Droges's office.

Penelope had said that things were changing in the World of the Dead. She had acted odd, as though she was afraid of something.

Milo felt useless knowing he couldn't help her. He knew what Abigail would say. She would tell him that Penelope was dead and so how afraid could she actually be?

But he knew better. He had experienced the dead. He knew that feeling afraid was very possible.

Still, Penelope was free of the Otherworld and easily capable of fighting her own battles.

Milo knew he had to let her go.

He sighed and then raided through some of her clothes and packed them in his bag for Abigail.

"Bye Pen," he whispered and shut her bedroom door.

***

After leaving the letter, Milo headed over to Vylett's house to deliver an identical letter, pack Vylett some of her clothes and then headed back to the Drome.

Helico and Abigail were stood waiting by the entrance as planned.

"The coast is clear," Helico said. "All set?"

"Yep let's do this."

The three of them headed quickly down the darkened corridors of the Drome.

The memorial dance was still in full swing and unfortunately they had to pass it to get to the elevator that would take them to the Fire Quarter.

Thankfully the doors were closed but just as they passed, Milo heard the distinct sound of a click. Without thinking he automatically turned back at the sound.

The door was open ajar and the cool air of the corridor rushed into the dance hall like a soft breeze that made the abundance of lit candles inside flicker out of sync with the music that was playing.

Aunt Dor's face peeked out through the gap at him. Milo stopped, his breath catching in his throat. Of course she would have known!

He opened his mouth to make up a string of excuses but she just nodded and smiled. She silently mouthed 'be careful' and then she shut the door. She was letting him go.

"What it is?" Helico called back to him.

"Nothing," Milo told him and then he caught up to them, feeling a little lighter inside.

The sounds of the dance got quieter and quieter as they headed downwards and to the elevators. When he spotted the familiar glass doors, Milo began to feel a stir of excitement.

Finally he was going to be traveling to the Fire Quarter and without any Terramangs stopping him.

They stepped into the glass box and pressed the button for the Fire Quarter.

The elevator sped downwards and underneath the clear water. The brightness of it glowed brighter as they quickly plunged deeper.

Abigail shook her head. "Do you know that in my World an elevator is just an elevator. It's not a portal or doesn't go underwater. Travel is just not this easy. This is..." Abigail struggled for an appropriate word.

"Cool?" Helico offered.

"I was going for something like 'weird' but I guess it's kind of cool," Abigail said with a half smile.

She turned to Milo with curiosity. "So why take us to the Fire Quarter? Why not the Earth or Air Quarter. What's so special about the Fire Quarter?"

"Abigail it's the Fire Quarter!" Milo feigned shock at her ignorance. "It's the capital. It's where some of the most fantastic creatures live and where Wylaffaton will have the hardest time finding us because it's also the busiest Quarter."

"Whoah just back up a bit there Milo Merren. What was the part about fantastic creatures?" Abigail gave him a wary look. "What the heck kind of creatures are we talking about?"

"Dragons," Milo tried to sound casual but couldn't quite wipe the grin off his face at Abigail's reaction. He laughed. "Relax Abigail it's going to be fun, I promise you."

"Dragons sound awesome," Helico nodded in approval and punched the air with his fist. "Oh come on Abs!" he grabbed a dubious looking Abigail into a hug.

Milo laughed again, felt himself beginning to relax. He wished Vylett were with them. The elevator seemed empty without her bubbly presence.

As if reading his mind, Helico put a hand on his shoulder. "She'll be here again soon mate. She'll come back."

Milo attempted a smile, determined not to bring the mood down. "I know. I just wish I could tell her what an idiot I've been recently. I was jealous," he admitted.

"You don't say!" Abigail pretended to sound shocked and then gave him a teasing look. "You idiot Milo." She hooked her arm through his and smiled. "She knows how you feel Milo. She can tell what you're thinking remember? Hell she probably knows what we're all thinking most of the time."

"I know, I just want her to hear it from my mouth. To explain properly."

"And you will. Soon." Abigail squeezed his arm and then became engrossed in watching the soothing rhythms of the water. The intensity of the magic at this depth was a powerful hum on all of their senses.

It was intoxicating in a way that it was hard to feel negative.

Milo found himself silently planning on what to say to Lowish when he brought Vylett back.

He had to convince him to let them help Sharrow. He had to. Sharrow needed their help. They owed the man in the tweed jacket that much.

Feeling suddenly optimistic he turned back to Abigail with a grin. "You'd best get used to the dragons Abs," he said in a teasing tone, using Helico's preferred shortened version of her name.

Abigail raised her eyebrows. "And why's that Miloney?"

"Because tomorrow we're riding them."

Helico high fived Milo as Abigail's jaw dropped open. "Dragons are mythical creatures, they're not real!" She waved her hands in exasperation. "And I'm definitely not riding one," she added defiantly with hands on hips.

He cheeks were flushed and her hair was as wild as ever.

Helico slapped Milo's hand in another high five and Abigail gave them an irritated look as they both doubled over laughing.

"Boys," she muttered and turned away to look out of the clear glass walls of the elevator. It made a slight juttering motion and then changed course so that it was traveling sideways.

"Oh my goodness," Abigail breathed. She was pointing to something in the distance.

Milo turned to see. He had been laughing so hard that he had also missed the transition from water to fire.

He pressed his face up against the glass, not wanting to miss a single thing.

Up ahead the bright white of the water was beginning to darken and the elevator began to make its ascent towards a fiery glow.

Milo felt as though a huge weight had been lifted from his shoulders as the elevator burst through the last part of the water, leaving one Quarter behind and another Quarter filled with new magic, just moments away.

* * * * *

ABOUT THE AUTHOR

Zoë Tyson is originally from Hull, East Yorkshire but wrote most of this novel whilst living in Shanghai China with her husband Simon. This is her first novel which is self-published in paperback and e-book formats.

You can like her page on Facebook and follow her on Twitter. Find out more at www.quarterofmagic.com

17750620R00221

Printed in Great Britain
by Amazon